HER
STORY
SO FAR

Jill Carlyle

HER STORY SO FAR

a novel

Published in the United States by Her Voice Publishing, an imprint of the Empowered Press, LLC, Orlando, FL.

ISBN 978-1-957430-26-3 (paperback)

ISBN: 978-1-957430-28-7 (hardcover)

ISBN 978-1-957430-27-0 (ebook)

Library of Congress Cataloging-Publication-Data is available.

Library of Congress Control Number: 2024951257

http://theempoweredpress.com

publish@theempoweredpress.com

Cover design: Onur Aksoy

http://onegraphica.com

The Empowered Press can bring authors to your live event. For more information or to book an event please email: publish@theempoweredpress.com

Owning our story can be hard, but not nearly as difficult as spending our lives running from it.

— Brené Brown

PART ONE

Nothing ever goes away until it has taught us what we need to know.
Pema Chödrön

Chapter One

September 18, 2018. Lake George, NY.

His thick, gray hair, peppered with traces of his youth, never grew back after his last round of chemo treatments. With each breath, the death rattle gurgles and hisses from his chest like a snake ready to strike. My beloved Alex will be gone soon. I knew this day was coming. Though nothing could have prepared me for the gravity of watching him slip away—how death doesn't come cleanly but rather settles into the room with a suffocating stillness, stripping away every illusion of control.

There were no symptoms, just a diagnosis. A routine health screening prompted a visit to our family doctor three years ago. Everything was normal except his elevated PSAs.

I'm not ready to say goodbye to the man lying in front of me. I barely recognize him, yet over thirty years of memories are stuck on replay as I watch him sleep. He's been like this for the last few days. His gaunt grayish-blue skin matches the cap Mary, his hospice nurse, placed over his bald head. She crochets them for all her patients, she says. They help keep body heat from escaping.

The room feels heavy with memories, a collection of a lifetime we shared that now seems suspended between this moment and the past. Thirty years of marriage flash before me in fragments: Alex walking toward me on our wedding day, his face lit with a smile so radiant it outshone the spring sun; the moment he held each of our daughters for the first time, his awe at their tiny fingers curling around his; the nights we stayed up in our cramped apartment, dreaming of the life we would one day build. And we built it.

Alex's dreams were as ambitious as his heart was big. An international lawyer, he spent years working tirelessly, eventually making partner ten years ago—just before we bought the house on Martha's Vineyard, the place where we gathered every summer as a family. His career took him all over the world, but he always found his way home. And somehow, amidst all that, he made me believe in my dreams, too.

I think of my books, the stories I've written—the romance novels that made me a bestselling author. I think of how I often wrote him into my leading men—their strength, their loyalty, their tenderness—all the pieces of him I loved. And now, the hero of my own life story is slipping away before my eyes.

I lean forward in the chair by his bed, clasping his hand in mine. It feels frail, so different from the strong, capable hands that once held mine through every milestone. My thumb gently brushes the veins that now protrude too sharply, and I close my eyes, willing myself to stay grounded in this moment, though everything inside me wants to run from it.

And yet here we are, the final chapter. A love story coming to an end, not with the grand flourish I'd always imagined, but with this quiet, agonizing unraveling. I wonder if he knows I'm here. I wonder if he can feel the words I want to say but can't seem to find.

The steady hum of the oxygen machine fills the room, punctuated by the sharpness of his breaths. I glance out the window, where the afternoon light filters in, golden and indifferent. I think about the life waiting for me outside this room—about the girls, our grandkids, my career. About what comes next. But the truth is, I can't see beyond this moment.

For now, I sit and hold his hand, letting the grief wash over me. I don't tell him it's okay to go—not yet. I'm not ready.

Instead, I press a kiss to his hand and whisper the only words I can manage. "I love you."

CHAPTER TWO

S ometimes, the story chooses you...

"Mom?" Lexi, our oldest, peeks her head into my studio. Her visit is unexpected but familiar. Out of all our grown daughters, she's the one that stops by most often—and without notice.

"Didn't we just have lunch yesterday?" I love to tease her. I lay my reading glasses down on the glass top surface and push the worn leather chair under my desk.

"Well, hello to you, too." She kisses me on the cheek and flicks a piece of lint off my sleeve. Alexandra Johanna Kincaid, Lexi for short, is a hybrid of her dad and me, right down to her name.

"I just finished up work for the day. Let's get out of here—the walls feel like they're closing in." I shut the lights off and set the AC to 78 instead of turning it off like Alex always tells me to do when I'm finished working for the day—it's been a hot summer.

"Aren't you picking Dad up from the airport?"

She doesn't forget details, especially when it comes to keeping track of her dad and me.

"He texted me from Rome and told me he would take a car."

I flip the bottom lock on my office door, closing everything up for the night.

"That's weird," she says.

I think it's weird, too, but choose not to dwell on it. Alex has been in Italy on business for the last two weeks, and I'm anxious to see him. He's traveled a lot for work this year.

Lexi and I step through the sliding glass door of the main house, and a wave of nostalgia washes over me. For a moment, it's like stepping back in time. The way she pushes her long brown hair out of her eyes and crinkles her button nose when she's getting ready to sneeze. Even at twenty-seven, her mannerisms still remind me of when she was a little girl—the power of a simple gesture to bridge years, resurrecting those long-ago moments.

"I want to be two things when I grow up," she told me when she was about ten. Those conversations happened nearly every night in the kitchen. Lexi insisted on helping with dinner. She was usually on salad duty and in charge of setting the table—although she always delegated at least one of those tasks to her younger sister, Lia.

"I want to be a teacher and a mommy," she'd say.

"But I thought you wanted to be a writer, like me and Great-Grandma Lolly?" I asked, intrigued by the ever-shifting dreams of childhood. But for Lexi, this wasn't just a fleeting ambition—it was a conviction, a calling she carried from that moment on. She didn't just dream; she did. At twenty-one, fresh out of college, she became a middle school teacher, married Wendall, her high school sweetheart, and welcomed their twin daughters, Maddi and Finnegan. Today, she's the assistant principal at Lake George Middle School.

"How's the book coming?" she asks, hands on her hips like a supervisor, making sure my work for the day is completed.

"First draft is done." My words carry a mix of anxiety and relief.

I've been working on my debut memoir for nearly two years.

Before that, I was perfectly fine riding the coattails of three back-to-back romance bestsellers.

"How was work today?" I try to keep the focus on her despite my own distractions.

"Stop trying to change the subject, Mom," she teases and steers the conversation back to my book. "I know this has been challenging for you. But you did it, right?"

"I did, but I'd rather write about my fictional characters' lives and romances instead of mine. Memoir writing was never something I thought I'd do." I throw her a half smile and sort through the mail.

Alex's delay continues to nag at me. Since his text from Italy hours earlier, there's been silence. Impatient and eager, I send him a message:

> Hi baby! What's your ETA? Can't wait to
> see you!

The moment the message bubble pops up, a familiar sound echoes through the house. A key turns the front door's deadbolt, and I hear the words, "I'm home!" The bubble on my phone vanishes as Alex appears in the archway, his presence bridging the gap between waiting and reunion.

I'm immediately struck by how worn-out he looks. Usually, he's the very definition of tall, dark, and handsome, but tonight, he seems almost unrecognizable. His salt-and-pepper curls are messy, and his striking blue eyes are dull, like they carry the weight of exhaustion. At 6'3, Alex's height and presence command attention, but something about how his broad shoulders slump tonight makes him seem smaller. The goatee that he meticulously keeps in line has a rough edge.

Even now, though, there's something undeniably magnetic about him, something that still pulls me in despite the exhaustion. I remind myself that it's just the flight—hours of travel have to wear anyone down.

"Hey, honey." He hugs Lexi and then me.

"Hi, Dad." Her voice carries the same warmth it always has, soft and familiar.

"Ladies, how are you? Lex, you've kept your mom company while I was away?" His voice fills the room, though it feels like he's already moving on to the next thing in his mind.

I can't help but jump in.

"She did." I smile, pulling him close once more. I notice the fatigue etched in his features; after three decades, our lives are as entangled as they come, and my heart yearns for him with the intensity of those early days, whether he's gone for two days or two weeks.

Tonight, there seems to be a subtle impatience, a flicker of disconnect that I choose to overlook. I willingly ignore the nuances of his responses, perhaps slightly dismissive, focusing instead on the simple joy of his return. I brush away the undercurrents and shifts in attention.

"I gotta run. You two kids need some alone time." Lexi swipes her keys off the table, taking the placemat with it.

"Sorry, Mom." She bends down to pick it up, but I beat her to it.

"Don't worry about it. Tell the kiddos Glammy and Grandpa say hi..."

Alex interrupts me, "You don't have to rush off, Lex." He pours her a glass of wine, trying to persuade her to stay, but she hands it to me instead.

"You and Mom enjoy. You haven't seen each other in two weeks. Love you both, bye!" She's out the door before Alex can say anything.

* * *

I put the last of the dry dishes away in the same cupboard they've lived in for the last fifteen years. It's funny, really—just about everything has stayed the same here, except, of course, now it's just two out of the five of us left in this house. The silence that used to be filled with the sound of laughter and footsteps is almost jarring.

Alex is asleep on the couch, his full belly protruding from under his unbuttoned shirt. I can't help but smile at the sight of him; I've always loved being his wife and taking care of him and our girls. I reveled in creating a comfortable, warm home for all five of us. Now, Lexi's married with six-year-old twin girls, both with Wendall's dark eyes and her quick wit, always racing around, arguing over dolls or making up stories, while her youngest, Brody, is a whirlwind of a five-year-old who barely sits still for more than five minutes, constantly trying to keep up with his big sisters.

Then there's Lia, just shy of a year younger than Lexi. She's busy navigating the challenges of being a newly single mom to her two boys—Simon, who's three and is the spitting image of his father, serious and observant, and Sutton, just two, with his wide smile and contagious giggle. Despite all their promises to each other since middle school, Lia and Doug didn't make it as a married couple, but they've managed to co-parent with a level of grace that sometimes surprises me.

Ari, our baby and the last to leave the house. A freshman at NYU, just like Alex and I once were. She's studying pre-law, determined to follow in her father's footsteps, though she's got that wild streak of independence that's all her own. With her fiery red hair and striking green eyes, she's always stood out—a blend of my personality and Alex's intensity.

I swear I still hear the girls playing outside or arguing about who wore whose sweater without asking. The memories reverberate off the walls most days. This house feels too big for just the two of us most of the time.

I live for family gatherings when we're all under one roof, and I'm grateful for the quickly approaching holiday season.

"Alex, honey?" I snuggle up next to him and listen to his heartbeat. He wraps his arm around my waist like a well-choreographed dance. His hazel eyes flutter open, and he looks disoriented for a moment.

"I don't want to wake you, baby, but I thought you might want to finish your slumber upstairs." I secretly hope he catches a second wind between the couch and our bed. It's been weeks since we've made love, and I feel our disconnect deeply.

He clears his throat and slides to the edge of the couch. I can see him trying to orient himself.

"Yeah, sorry, Kelsi. I guess the travel and jet lag got me." Alex staggers upstairs. I follow his lead.

I sidle up next to him in our king-sized bed, gently rubbing the tip of my finger up the inside of his forearm—a signal we've given to each other since the first time we made love.

"I missed you." I kiss the nape of his neck, expecting a response.

"Kelsi. I'm so tired..." His voice drifts off, and he's sound asleep.

Chapter Three

September 14, 2015.

Alex, it's not uncommon for these tests to yield a false positive the first time around. PSA levels can and do fluctuate in some men. You are a healthy forty-nine-year-old man; I'm not worried, and you shouldn't be either. We're going to wait six weeks, retest, and go from there," says the man who's been our family physician for twenty-seven years.

"Why are we waiting six weeks, Dr.? Why not sooner, like, in two weeks?" It's not like me to question an expert, but this is my husband's life, and he hasn't bothered to ask our opinion; he made the decision for us.

Alex interrupts before he can respond to my question. "Kelsi, Dr. Wilson knows what he's talking about." I look over at my husband sitting inches from the doctor's desk, his hands folded on his lap, calm, collected, and totally buying what the doctor is selling: time. I revert to silence.

I find Alex standing in the kitchen, staring out the window at our perfectly coifed lawn. His arms hyper-extended, steadying him on the edge of the sink. I approach him from behind and wrap my arms around his V-shaped torso, laying my head on his strong back. Every muscle is tense. Finally, he crosses his arms over mine—a familiar response; we stand in the stillness. Together.

I nestle the side of my face into his starched white work shirt; remnants of his morning cologne penetrate my senses. "Alex? Where are you?" I ask.

"I'm here, Kels. Just thinking about things."

I can usually see straight through to his soul—but not lately—something has been blocking my view.

"You want to talk about today? Wilson's office?" I say. He turns around and breaks his stoic gaze.

"No. Here, let's have some wine." He unwraps my arms from his waist, grabs the open bottle, and pours us each a glass. He hands me mine and, with his other hand, leads me into the living room, our favorite room in the house. The room that is the keepsake of all our firsts—our first sofa with the frazzled dingy brown and cream pillows from our first apartment; our first real coffee table that doubled as our dining room table the first few years we were married; the 80s-style faux bear skin rug that I always hated, but Alex loved, and was the subject of our first real argument.

My fingers find their way to his collar and loosen his necktie—I'm hoping it loosens him up, too. We quickly polish off the first bottle and open another. We haven't spent time together like this in a while; he's been traveling for work or working late, and I've been busy working on my latest manuscript. But tonight feels a little more like "us."

"Make love to me." His hands cradle my face with a tenderness that takes me back to the early days of our love. His eyes lock onto mine, burning with a depth I can't quite decipher and a longing so fierce it stirs something deep within me—a hunger I haven't felt in years but suddenly crave with every fiber of my being.

He parts my legs, and our lips meet, slow at first but with growing urgency, the weight of his body pressing me back into the cushions. The warmth of his skin seeps into me as his fingers unfasten each button with a slow, practiced ease. The fabric loosens, parting like a whispered secret, his touch leaving a trail of anticipation in its wake. For the first time in months, I sense the wall he's built starting to crumble, piece by piece. But there's something different—a desperation, almost.

My thoughts are interrupted by a sharp ding from his phone. His body stiffens for a fraction of a second before he pulls back, reaching for the device on the coffee table.

"Who is it?" My voice is light but curious.

He glances at the screen, his jaw tightening for a moment before placing it facedown without replying. "No one important. Just one of our new paralegals. She always has questions after working hours. Drives me nuts." He leans back toward me, his hands ripping off the tie I loosened, taking his shirt with it. His lips brush my forehead.

Another ding pierces the room, followed by a second and a third. His hardness pressing against me softens. His head drops with a sigh. "What the fuck?" He picks up the phone, shuts the ringer off, and slides it across the floor. "There. No more interruptions."

His hands grip the edges of my jeans, tugging them down with ease, leaving nothing but the sensation of his touch. I let myself get lost in him—the warmth of his breath, the familiar weight of his body, the way his hands trace my curves with a tenderness that feels like home. It's been so long, and the intensity of it all consumes me.

His tongue traces a slow, deliberate maze around each nipple, teasing and exploring before gliding down the valley between my breasts, leaving a trail of heat in its wake.

Kissing his way down my torso, I quiver and run my hands through his thick curls. I peak, and he enters me. His release follows a few short minutes later. His breath is short and fast. His passion borders on frantic, like he's trying to memorize every inch of me like this is the last time. I push the thought away, telling myself it's just because we haven't been like this in so long. He's been so stressed with work. This is just him finding his way back to me.

He carries me to our bed. Naked, we lie tangled together, his chest rising and falling steadily beneath my cheek. His fingers trace lazy circles on my back, and for the first time in months, the tension in his body seems to have melted away. I close my eyes and let myself breathe him in.

I'd forgotten how much I missed this—him, us. The way he held me tonight, like he couldn't get close enough, like every touch was a promise. It reminded me of when we were first together, the fire we couldn't keep from consuming us, the intensity of those early years that softened over time but never disappeared completely.

"Love you, Kels," he murmurs into my hair, his voice low and full of tenderness.

"I love you too, Alex," I whisper back, my heart swelling. I press a kiss to his chest and nestle closer, wrapping my arms around him like I never want to let go.

* * *

I lie, listening to my husband's soft snores; he doesn't move when I slide my naked body out from under the covers. I'm wide awake, as I usually am at this time, and decide to get a little work done before sunrise.

I've learned how to move quietly through these early mornings. I know how to place my feet on each step just right so the creaks in the wood don't wake anyone. I've silenced my steps for years. I round the corner of the foyer, and there sits a half-eaten charcuterie board we called dinner, along with two empty bottles of vino. A long, red drip stain runs linear from the mouth of the finished bottle to its base, leaving a ring on the already weathered table. The two brass candelabras we first lit on our wedding night twenty-seven years ago sit on either side of the bottles, covered in drips of hard wax.

My hand catches the crumbs from the table, and I make sure things are put in their proper place: bottles in the recycle bin, crusted red wine washed and dried from the rim of each glass, every last water stain wiped so not even our DNA is detectable.

Okay. Kels. You've done everything short of reorganizing the kitchen junk drawer. Go. Write.

The never-ending list of let-me-do-everything-else-before-I-write is my Achilles heel.

The fall air reminds me that summer has passed as quickly as it arrived. The season scarcely feels like a memory. I enter my studio through the unlocked door and blow a warm stream of breath into my freezing hands, tuck them under the sleeves of my sweatshirt, and press the heat mode on the thermostat. The stagnant air smells like the place is about to catch fire.

I wrap myself in the quilted throw passed down from my Lolly. Its warm memories tell ten thousand stories of my life.

My mother wasn't a fan of Grandma Lolly, short for Charlotte, but I adored her. She was everything my mother wasn't, and I wanted to be just like her.

Chapter Four

1975. Upstate New York.

Sissi, would you mind pourin' me another cup of java?" Lolly asks, an unlit cigarette bobbing from the corner of her mouth.

"It's Marissa, Charlotte. I haven't been Sissi since I was twelve, and you know where the coffee is." Mom points to the old baker's rack in the corner of the kitchen, where the coffee pot sits on a crocheted doily, surrounded by sugar, creamer, and mismatched mugs. She calls it her coffee station, an attempt to keep what she deems "clutter" off the counters.

Mom doesn't drink coffee, but Dad does, and so does Lolly—especially during her visits every summer. Sometimes, she sneaks me sips when Mom's not looking, which makes me feel special like I'm part of some secret club.

"Well, you'll always be Sissi to me," Lolly says with a wink, her fingers never stopping their rhythmic clicking on the typewriter. "You're gonna make me lose my writin' flow here if I gotta get up one more time..."

I glance over at Mom, who has her back turned, busily wiping down the already spotless counter. Lolly's typing slows, her cigarette hanging on for dear life, as she leans back in her chair. I seize the opportunity.

"I'll get you a cup of java, Lolly," I say, hopping off the stool and moving closer to her.

Lolly pauses and pulls me into a one-armed hug.

"That's my girl," she whispers, the faint scent of tobacco and lilac lotion enveloping me.

I pour her a cup, making sure to take three quick sips before handing it to her. She likes it black, and I've decided I do too.

"Well, you're about the sweetest little Cheese Weasel there ever was. Thank you, my darlin'," and kisses my cheek.

I giggle at the nickname only she calls me. It's one of our secrets, like the sips of coffee or the words she teaches me when Mom isn't around. I lean in closer, my curiosity tugging me toward the words she's typing today. Her fingers pause on the keys, and I take the chance to sneak a peek at the paper.

The page is covered in words that jump around like they're playing a game, full of Lolly's big way of talking. Some of them I know, but others look like secrets I haven't learned yet. I remember when I was six and tried reading out loud from one of her pages.

"Fah, fah, fah-uh-k you," I sounded out, proud of my first-grade reading skills.

"Kelsi Johanna! What? What did you just say?" my mother shrieked like she'd just seen a spider spinning around with a fury that made me jump.

"Fuck you, Mommy," I'd said, confused by her reaction. It was just a word on the page.

Mom's face turned redder than the beets she forced me to eat the night before.

"Charlotte, take your filth somewhere else. Franklin and I are trying to raise a decent human being," she snapped.

Lolly didn't even care. She just peeked over her glasses and said, "Relax, Sissi, she's gonna hear it one day, anyway."

Ever since then, Mom has done everything she can to keep me away from Lolly's typewriter. But I'm eight now. I can handle it.

"Whatcha writin' about today, Lolly?" I ask, sliding into the chair beside her.

Her lips curl into a smirk as she takes a sip of coffee.

"Just life, baby girl. The good, the bad, and the downright ugly. But you don't worry 'bout the ugly stuff. That's for grown folks."

Her words feel like a shield, protecting me from something I don't quite understand yet. But I also know that Lolly sees me as more than just a kid.

In the summers, Lolly stays at her cabin on Mirror Lake in Maine, where she writes for hours and teaches me how to skip stones on the water—when my mom lets us visit. In the winter, she drives south to Florida, always stopping here for a week on her way down. She and Mom argue every time, but she always comes back.

"Are you gonna stay with us for Christmas, Lolly?"

"Hmm, we'll see, darlin'." Her voice is soft, but I catch the hesitation in her tone.

Mom clears her throat loudly. "Kelsi Jo, go grab your spelling book. You've got homework."

I roll my eyes when my mom turns her back. Lolly winks at me, her fingers already flying back to the typewriter keys. I head toward the other room, but not before I hear her mutter, "Can't stifle the written word, Sissi. That girl's gonna be a writer one day, you wait."

The thought makes me smile. Maybe she's right. Maybe one day, I'll be just like Lolly.

Chapter Five

September 15, 2015.

The click of my laptop powering on is interrupted by the slow creak of my studio door. I glance up, expecting the dim glow of the morning, and see the silhouette of my husband's body framed by the leftover light filtering in from the back porch. His body, at almost fifty, can go up against any thirty-year-old—strong and resilient. It's hard to think that anything could actually be wrong with him.

A rush of cool, crisp air carries a pile of rust-colored leaves over the threshold where Alex is standing. Swiftly, he shuts the door behind him.

"Everything okay, Kels? I woke up, and you were gone."

"I couldn't sleep, so I thought I'd work. When I left, you were peacefully snoring, so I left you a sticky on the bathroom mirror," I tease him, trying to evoke the memories of last night.

Stickies are our love language.

"The wine got to me a little." He runs his hand through his graying hair.

"Well, I thought I might have worn you out last night. It's

been a while since we've made love. I've missed you." My teasing tone quickly turns to seriousness.

He half-smiles and leans against the bookshelf, taking in a deep inhale.

"Those preliminary test results just have me thinking," he says, staring at the floor.

"Listen, Wilson said everything would be fine. He said you're a healthy forty-nine-year-old man, right?" I ask and affirm simultaneously.

"Right," he replies.

"I love you, Kelsi Jo," he says almost apologetically, looking right through me.

I walk over to my husband and wrap us both into Lolly's quilt.

Six Weeks Later.

I wasn't expecting a call from him so soon after he left for work.

"Hi babe. Your morning okay?" I try to smile through my shallow breaths and rapid heartbeat. I have a feeling his call isn't to remind me of tonight's dinner plans.

"Hey, KJ," he replies, not sounding like himself.

Radio silence.

"Alex, you there?" I ask.

"Wilson's office just called. He wants to see us this afternoon." I hang on to his words for a moment.

"Okay," I pause. "Did he give you the results? Is there any indication of the results? Why do we have to go into the office?" I know the answers to all my questions, but I ask them anyway. On Monday, Dr. Wilson ordered a PSA test and a full blood panel for Alex. Today is only Thursday—it hasn't even been a week.

"He doesn't want to discuss the results over the phone." His answer is flat. "We need to be there by four this afternoon."

How could they have the results so soon?

"Alright."

I try to sound encouraged.

I try to believe that the doctor wants to tell us face-to-face that there really is nothing to worry about.

I try to tell myself that because he's been our doctor for so long, he wants to look at our faces and basically tell us *I told you so.*

But I can't convince myself.

The truth is, he wouldn't have called so early in the day and left Alex hanging if the news was good. He would have relieved him of all anxiety and told him he was fine, but he still wanted him to come in to discuss the other lab work. And that "There's no need for Kelsi Jo to tag along. It's nothing you can't tell her yourself when you get home."

"I'll pick you up at 3:30." He doesn't wait for me to say goodbye. Click. The disconnect lands like a gavel, sealing something unspoken, something inevitable.

I sit for a moment, staring into the ether, and my mind empties like the tide pulling away from the shore, leaving nothing but stillness in its wake.

* * *

The car horn blares steadily and insistently, cutting through the background noise. My body tenses at the sound, a sharp reminder that time is slipping away. I glance down at my phone, and there it is—a notification glowing on the screen.

3:15 p.m.

KJ, on my way. Wait for me outside.

My stomach drops as I catch the time in the corner of my screen: 3:34 p.m.

Shit.

The realization hits me hard, guilt and panic clawing at my chest. I was supposed to be ready, supposed to be waiting. Now, I scramble to pull myself together, my heart racing as the minutes tick louder in my head. I grab my purse and keys and run through the house as quickly as I can to get to Alex, who now has his hand on the horn, without pause. The beep sounds more like a foghorn than a car horn and fits the mood of the moment: chaotic and unrelenting. My keys fumble as I lock the frosted glass front door behind me and run to the car. I'm panting as I climb into the passenger seat.

"Alex," I say tensely, "I heard you from the first beep. Was it really necessary to lay on the horn the entire time?"

"I texted you to let you know I was on my way and to wait outside for me." Alex is edgy and snaps.

"I didn't see it. I'm sorry, babe." I grab his hand—how can I be mad? This is no time to challenge him.

He exhales like he's been holding his breath for days. "It's okay. I'm sorry, too. I shouldn't be taking it out on you," he says.

We ride in silence and hold hands like you do when you're first dating—the not-wanting-to-let-go-because-you-just-found-each-other hand-holding. Facing unwanted results reminds me how quickly the years tick off. Thirty years is not enough time. There are so many days I feel like I just found him.

The walk from the parking lot to the door feels more like a hike through rough, mountainous terrain rather than a short two hundred feet. My stomach is a compilation of butterflies and hard knots as we await our escort back to a room.

"Mr. and Mrs. Kincaid, Dr. Wilson is ready for you. Please follow me. We're headed back to his office." She leads the way down the brightly lit hallway.

A million electrodes pulsate down my spinal cord, creating a shock to my soul—a chill runs from my scalp down the center of my body as we walk into the doctor's office. Dr. Wilson stands up and tucks the lower half of his tie in between the two middle buttons on his shirt, clears his throat, and straightens his stark white lab coat. He extends a handshake to both Alex and me. It's all so formal.

"Please, have a seat." He settles into a large leather chair, the creak of the worn upholstery punctuating his authority. As he exhales, the room seems to shift around him, shaped by the weight of decisions only he is meant to make. He makes a few clicks on his computer keyboard and clears his throat again.

I know how Alex must have felt now when he laid on the horn and waited for me. If I had a horn right now...

"Alex, we received your test results, and we need to do some additional investigation." The doctor shifts from one side of his chair to the other and looks at his computer screen. He keeps clearing his throat and messing with his stupid tie.

"Cut the bullshit, John. I've been your patient for damn near three decades. What is going on?"

This is out of character for Alex, but he wants answers. And so do I.

"Alex, your PSA levels came back high—higher than six weeks ago. The CBC panel is off, and we need to figure out what's going on."

"Higher than six weeks ago," I repeat out loud. "What do you mean, higher than six weeks ago?"

"His levels are higher, Kelsi." He almost looks ashamed.

"So, you are saying that over the last six weeks, while we waited for a 'retest' like you suggested, his PSA levels elevated. What exactly is 'high'?" I'm fuming. I'm so furious I can't even cry.

"Yes, that's what I'm saying." He turns and looks at Alex. "Alex, your PSA level is above ten. Six weeks ago, it was a four."

I knew something was wrong. I can't hide the anger and sadness at the core of my being.

"What's our next move?" Alex asks calmly—too calmly—like he's trying to gather all the facts so he can make his strategic move in a high-stakes court case.

"I want you to see Dr. Mark Simonton. He's expecting you and knows you've been a patient of mine for three decades. We go all the way back to med school, and he's the best urologist in Lake George." He hands Alex a card.

I grab it before Alex has the chance to.

"I took the liberty of having my nurse make an appointment for you first thing tomorrow," Dr. Wilson says.

The appointment is for 8 a.m. I hand the card to Alex, who shoves it into his back pocket without looking at it.

Alex looks at the doctor with bewilderment painted across his face. "You just laid a heavy burden on me and my wife, Doc. I don't know what a '10' PSA level means, but I can't imagine a good outcome."

The doctor fidgets, his voice tight as he explains, "Alex, Kelsi, I understand how shocking this is, but I need you to know that your last annual exam didn't show any signs of concern. For men around fifty, it's standard to start monitoring PSA levels, Prostate-Specific Antigen, but yours didn't raise any red flags at the time. When PSA levels come back at a zero, it's often normal, but they don't stay zero forever. The jump in PSA can sometimes happen if prostate cancer starts developing rapidly. This is why we need to take care of this immediately."

His words swim in my mind, swirling with confusion and frustration. My heart is pounding, anger boiling as I glance at Alex, his face a mix of disbelief and helplessness. This isn't supposed to be happening. They should've caught it sooner; they should've tested more. We cling to the desperate hope that this is all a mistake, a misunderstanding—but the cold weight of reality is pressing down hard, and we're left feeling like someone needs to be held accountable. And right now, the doctor is standing in the crosshairs.

"I will be working closely with Dr. Simonton. There are so many treatments for prostate cancer." He tries to sound reassuring, but this time, Alex and I aren't buying it.

. . .

"Do you want me to drive us home?" I ask.

"Nope." He opens the passenger door and motions for me to get in.

I clutch my purse until my knuckles turn white and stare out the side window. Alex turns the music up and drowns out the silence.

We ride home, feeling even more confused after the jarring results yet evasive explanation delivered by the doctor. I begin to notice things looking to the side instead of straight ahead. Like where the sidewalk ends at the four-way stop just before we turn into our subdivision. Or how the old maple tree outside Ida's house slightly leans to the left. A sign advertising a lost cat, an orange tabby named Marmalade, flaps weakly from the rusted lamppost on the corner of our street. The fresh white paint on the Miller's picket fence stands out, contrasting with the faded paint on the porte-cochere as if desperately trying to claim a new beginning.

I spot the ice cream truck, a relic from another era, slowing as it passes by a group of kids, their voices a distant echo of laughter and playful bargaining. I remember a time when our girls would have run towards it, coins clinking in their pockets. Today, though, it feels like an artifact from a world I've suddenly stepped out of.

The playground adjacent to the school seems eerily quiet. The usually squeaking swings are still, the bright yellow slide untouched by the late afternoon sun. A solitary soccer ball rests near the goalpost, waiting for the next kick that might not come until tomorrow.

Alex's grip tightens on the steering wheel, his knuckles mirroring the whiteness of mine. I glance over and see his jaw set firmly, eyes forward. A single tear escapes, carving a path down his cheek. The weight of the news rests between us, an unspoken fear and sadness.

Suddenly, the world outside feels so magnified; the drive home feels both too short and agonizingly long.

When we finally pull into our garage, Alex puts his SUV in park and leaves it running. He doesn't look back—just walks inside, leaving me to handle the rest. So, I do. I shut off the engine and leave his keys in the ignition.

Alex never takes his keys out of the ignition.

Chapter Six

October 26, 2015.

I'm not sure if he's going to bed or needs some time alone to digest the diagnosis and what lies in front of him—of us. I stand at the base of the stairs and look up as he walks into our bedroom and closes the door behind him. He shuts me out, something he's never done before. I force myself to remember this isn't about me. I'm not the one who was just diagnosed with cancer, yet a part of me has been.

I drop to the living room floor, hug my knees tight, and let the tears fall, tracing wet trails down my legs like rain on glass. The weeks of waiting and knowing something wasn't right, but staying silent because that's what you're supposed to do when someone with fancy degrees tells you it will all be okay.

The big clock that hangs at the bottom of the staircase ticks louder than I remember. Hearing the passing of time and not knowing where it is taking us puts everything in perspective. I dry my tears with the last Kleenex in the box on the foyer table, hang onto the railing, and ascend the staircase. The humidity of the hot shower hits me in the face as I enter our bedroom. The bathroom door is wide open. Alex is lying on the shower floor in a fetal position, crying in a way I've never seen him cry. The water cascades over him, and I immediately jump in the shower with him—it doesn't matter that I have my clothes on.

He looks up at me. "I tried to scrub it off, Kels." The words barely cross his lips.

I wrap him in my arms, shielding him from the hot water that has turned cold. His body trembles like a leaf in the wind, vulnerable and exposed. The intensity of the moment weighs heavily in the air, making it difficult to breathe.

My heart aches watching this man, my rock, crumble before me. My clothes cling to my body, drenched, but the water isn't the reason my skin feels cold. It's the realization of the battle we have ahead.

"I should have..." His voice cracks, tears mixing with the water cascading down his face.

"You should have what?" I ask.

"Kelsi, I tried to scrub it off of me. All of it." His voice cracks, raw and broken, before dissolving into sobs that drown beneath the steady stream of water. His body shakes, each sob hitching in his chest, jagged and uncontainable, lost in a storm of emotions.

"We'll face this together. We always have, always will." I stroke his soaked hair.

His grip on me tightens as if he is holding onto life. The shower's hum provides a melancholic background to our embrace, a poignant reminder of the fragility of existence.

"Baby, it's okay." I just hold him.

"I'm so sorry, Kelsi."

"Alex, there is nothing to be sorry about. We'll get through this together. We will get you whatever treatment is out there."

I reach up and turn the shower off, the water dripping to a halt. Alex stands up, his hands braced against the tiles, his head bowed.

"Come on," I whisper, wrapping a towel around his shoulders. "Let's get you comfortable."

He lets me lead him to the bedroom, his movements slow and

heavy, like he's carrying the weight of the world. I dress him in his comfiest pair of pajama pants and pull an old, well-worn T-shirt over his head, my hands brushing against his skin as I tug it into place. His usual scent, faintly mixed with the lingering smell of soap, stirs something deep within me—comfort, longing, and fear, all tangled together.

When he finally meets my eyes, there's something in his expression I can't quite name—maybe just the weight of what we've learned this morning. His fingers reach for my face, brushing a damp strand of hair behind my ear.

"Kelsi," he whispers, his voice hoarse, thick with emotion. "I don't deserve you."

"Alex..." I begin, but he shakes his head, silencing me.

His hands trail from my cheeks to my waist as he peels my wet clothes off me. The moment feels different—more desperate, more urgent, more raw. As he draws me into our bed, his lips meet mine, tender but insistent. It's not just passion; it's need. It's as though he's trying to say everything he can't find words for, trying to eradicate whatever storm is raging inside him.

I give in, matching his intensity, letting him carry me into a world that is only ours. His hands, his touch, his whispered words —they are all so familiar yet feel brand new. We haven't made love this much in years, not with this kind of fire or longing.

I strip away the pajama bottoms I'd just helped him into moments ago, my hands lingering before I move. Slowly, I climb onto him, straddling his lap, guiding his hardness into me with a deliberate, aching need. I feel every inch of him as he fills me—stretching, claiming, sending a shiver that ripples through my entire body.

A deep, guttural groan rumbles from his chest, vibrating against my skin and igniting something primal inside me. His hands roam hungrily, one cupping my breast, kneading, teasing, while the other finds its way to my lips. I take his fingers into my mouth, sucking, swirling my tongue around them, tasting the salt of his skin.

His breath hitches, his body tensing beneath me as he moves in perfect rhythm, his fingers slipping lower, gliding through the slick heat between us. He strokes me with deliberate precision—each touch a note in a symphony only we know, building and swelling until I'm trembling, lost in the crescendo, unable to hold back any longer.

We release in unison.

He holds me like I'm the only thing tethering him to this moment, and I let him. I let him because I want him to know he's not alone and that we'll face it together, whatever comes next.

"I love you," I whisper, my voice barely a breath between us. He doesn't answer—not with words. Instead, he presses his lips to my forehead, lingering as if mapping the shape of me into memory, as if this moment is something he's afraid to lose.

The world outside fades, time slips through the cracks of our embrace. We don't speak—just exist, drawing sustenance from the heat of each other, from the unspoken things pulsing beneath our skin.

It's just after nine when he finally stirs, kissing my temple and murmuring something about getting cleaned up and grabbing something to eat. I watch as he heads to the bathroom, his movements slow, his shoulders slumped. I lie there in the quiet, my body still warm from his touch. The intimacy of the moment lingers.

His phone buzzes on the nightstand, its bright light cutting through the dimness of the room. Without thinking, I reach over and glance at the screen. The name flashing across it makes me pause.

Eve.

Confused, I pick up the phone, answering it with a laugh. "Eve? Did you *mean* to call Alex? This is his phone."

There's a brief hesitation on the other end before her familiar voice filters through. "Oh, Kelsi! I must've dialed his number by mistake. I meant to call you, actually. My phone's been acting up all day."

I laugh softly, shaking my head. "No problem. He's just in the bathroom, anyway. What's up?"

"Oh, nothing important," she says breezily. "I'll let you two get back to your evening. We'll catch up soon, okay?"

"Sure thing," I reply, still smiling as I hang up.

Alex emerges from the bathroom moments later, his hair damp and his expression unreadable. "Who was that?" he asks, toweling his face.

"Eve." I place his phone back on the nightstand. "She accidentally called you instead of me."

His movements pause for the briefest of moments before he nods. "Must've been a mistake," he says, his tone even.

I reach for him, pulling him back into bed and my arms.

Two weeks later, Alex is diagnosed with Stage 4 prostate cancer.

CHAPTER SEVEN

MAY, 1986. NYU.

Across the tree-lined sidewalk, I spot Eve, her arms flailing like she's trying to flag down a rogue New York taxi.

"Kels! Over here, Kelsi." Her fiery energy is impossible to miss, even in the sea of students and tourists scattered across the famous quad of NYU—a hub of life and chaos that only the city can provide. I shield my eyes against the setting sun and quicken my pace, weaving through the lawn dotted with picnic blankets, Frisbee players, and couples lounging on benches.

I sidestep a half-empty cup of coffee and narrowly miss a spinning saucer that zips past my ear. The faint strum of a guitar weaves through the low thrum of conversation, giving the chaos a kind of rhythm.

Eve's voice cuts through the hum of the crowd—impatient yet threaded with unmistakable warmth. When I finally reach her, slightly breathless, she catches my hand and pulls me down beside her, the two of us collapsing onto the blanket in a tangle of laughter and limbs.

She's beaming, practically vibrating with excitement. Her grip is tight, her nails painted a shocking shade of electric blue that somehow matches the wild streak of cobalt eyeliner she's wearing. Eve always has a flair for the dramatic. Today, she's rocking a pair of cutoff denim shorts, artfully frayed, and an oversized man's button-down shirt that's been splattered with paint—likely her own. The sleeves are rolled up haphazardly to her elbows, exposing stacks of mismatched bracelets jangling on her wrists. Her unruly curls spill over her shoulders; a chestnut mane streaked with hints of auburn that catch the light framing her delicate features. Even disheveled, Eve has an undeniable magnetism that draws people in and makes them linger.

"I want you to meet someone." She grins, her eyes sparkling with mischief. The guy she gestures to is sprawled across the blanket with easy confidence like he owns the space.

She hasn't mentioned anyone new, but with her, that doesn't mean much. Since our freshman year, she's had a revolving door of love interests—some fleeting, some more serious, but all of them captivated by her eccentric charm. Eve has always been a free spirit, blowing through life like a whirlwind. She's the kind of person who buys concert tickets on a whim, skips class to paint murals on abandoned buildings and takes off for weekend road trips with barely a tank of gas.

Her beauty is as unconventional as the rest of her. A smattering of freckles dusts her nose, and her wide, dark eyes seem to hold endless stories. Men flock to her, drawn by her unapologetic authenticity, but she rarely holds on to any of them for long. Relationships, for Eve, are more like artistic experiments—vivid, messy, and fleeting.

"Alex Kincaid, meet Kelsi Jo Barker."

He reaches his hand out to shake mine. "Nice to meet you, Kelsi Jo."

"Likewise," I say, taking my hand back from his and looking at Eve, waiting for her to break the awkward silence between the three of us. "Well, I've got to get to class..."

"Really? Already?" I can clearly tell she's a combination of nerves and anxiety, which makes me wonder about the connection between Eve and Mr. Blue Eyes.

"Yeah," I smile and lose my balance as I try to stand up.

"You okay?" Eve's new friend asks and helps me steady myself.

"Thanks," I say and wipe off invisible dirt on the seat of my pants. "See you tonight for study group, Eve?"

"Yeah, I meant to tell you I'm not going to make it. Alex and I are going out," she says.

Her loss, I think to myself. She's the one who's in danger of failing chemistry. I shrug it off.

"Okay, then. See you when I see you." I wave a cordial goodbye to Alex and give Eve a quick hug.

Chapter Eight

Ari appears at the double doorway of our master suite—arms crossed, her expression firm but gentle. "Mom, you need to eat. If you don't do it for yourself, do it for Dad."

We've always called her our 'ginger girl'—her hair a striking, fiery red, the kind people spend a fortune trying to replicate in salons. But she wears it effortlessly, a natural beauty with a presence as bold as her color.

"I'm not hungry." I glance up at our youngest, standing over her father and me. For a moment, I see the little girl she used to be—but that image fades, replaced by the woman she's become.

"Mom." She bends down and takes my hands in hers. The whites of her green eyes are streaked with broken blood vessels from lack of sleep and sadness.

I want to be strong for her—for all my girls—but the truth is, I don't have the strength, which makes me question the kind of mother and grandmother I am. I am unable to summon the capacity to care for and support my family at this moment.

They are losing their father. But I am losing my husband. I just can't do it. I can only be in one place—next to Alex. I sit by his side during the day and sleep next to him at night. I want my husband in our bed. I want to lie with him, touch him, breathe in his skin the last few nights of his life. And I want him to be comfortable. I refuse to lay him in the hospital bed hospice delivered. It sits in the corner of our bedroom with dirty towels, sheets, and clothes that need to be washed. I leave his side only to go to the bathroom when I absolutely can't hold it any longer. Our friends and neighbors take turns running errands and bringing in food, so the girls and I never have to leave the house. They are a silent army of angels.

I've been wearing Alex's oversized gray Yale Law sweatshirt and a black pair of leggings for the last forty-eight hours. It smells like him. He's nearly worn the sweatshirt out since Ari announced she would be attending Yale as soon as she graduates from NYU in the spring.

"I'll sit with Dad. I'd like to spend some time with him, anyway. Lia is downstairs feeding the boys. I'm sure they'd love to share a meal with their Glammy." She tilts her head, kisses my cheek, and makes everything seem okay.

Shouldn't I be doing that for her?

I look at Alex and stroke his arm—no movement. I try to lace my fingers through his, but they are like weighted noodles.

"Ariana isn't letting this one go, my love." I bend over and gently kiss him over his wool beanie, and a dozen little fuzzballs stick to my lips and nose. I pluck them out, lift the cap, and rest my lips on his balmy skin. I promise to be back shortly.

Reluctantly, I relinquish my seat to Ari; my body resists as I cross the threshold of our room into the upstairs hall. I don't want to go downstairs and eat. I stop and lean against the spindled rail at the top of the staircase; it feels like the only thing holding me up as I turn around and see the backside of my daughter sitting with her dad. Memories flood my mind of all the times they've shared together. She is his 'mini-me.' Everything her daddy did, she wanted to do, too. Everything he was, she wanted to be.

"Daddy, can I go to work with you today?" she'd ask when she was on spring or summer break. Sometimes, he'd take her and give her little tasks to do, like filing or organizing his desk. She watched him work, listened to the language, and wanted to be a lawyer, just like her dad.

I stand here mesmerized by the moment, listening to the one-sided conversation between daughter and father; I wonder if he can hear her?

Of course he can, I tell myself.

"Hi, Daddy," the tears choke her words. "I know you can hear me. You've always been a good listener. That's the thing I love about you the most. I've always been able to come to you with anything. You always had a way that no one else did. Not even Mom, but don't tell her I said that, or I'll deny it." I hear her smile through her tears and watch her wipe them from her eyes with her long sleeve-tee. Her mid-length hair cascades across her face; she anchors a few straggling strands behind her ear.

"We have the best conversations, don't we?" She pauses and grabs her father's hand, and holds it to her face. "Your hand, Daddy. I always wanted to hold your hand when I was a little girl, remember? Wanna know another secret?"

She waits for a reply she knows she's never going to get.

"I want to hold it even as a big girl."

My heart shatters into a million pieces as I watch my grown-up baby struggle to keep it together. I want to go to her, but I don't dare. Instead, I remain a voyeur and listen to my daughter's heartbreaking monologue to her father.

Ari pauses for a moment and gently kisses the back of her father's hand.

"Remember my first 'big-girl' trip to Martha's Vineyard?" She pauses again, still waiting for a reply.

Oh, how I wish he would.

My knees give way, folding beneath me as if the ground itself has been ripped out from under my feet.

"We walked along the beach and watched the waves. I was petrified of the water, and you held my hand so tight and made me feel so safe. You told me that anytime I was scared to close my eyes and think about how it feels when you hold my hand. Daddy, if you're scared right now, I'm here to return the favor. Don't be scared. I love you." She sobs into her father's limp hand. The hands that will never give her away, the hands that will never hold her children, the hands that make his daughter feel safe. As much as I don't want to leave my husband's side, they need this time together.

I barely compose myself and make my way downstairs to the very busy kitchen. I'm glad to see that it is just our immediate family. I'm not up to seeing friends right now.

"Mom!" Lexi turns and sees me as she is delegating tasks to Lia. "How's Dad? We've been trying to get all this food that's been dropped off organized between the refrigerator and freezer." She opens the door to the freezer, and a frozen casserole nearly lands on my toe.

"Shit! I'm sorry, Mom," Lexi screams. She bends over to keep the round plastic casserole dish from rolling into the next room.

"Mommy, language!"

"Maddi, I told you not to reprimand me. I am your mother, remember?" Lexi scolds the almost nine-year-old authoritarian who is eavesdropping from the TV room where the grandkids work hard to keep busy under their parents' strict orders.

"But, Mom, you told us not to..."

Lexi quickly interrupts her. "Madison, not the time, child!"

I look around, ignoring the spat between mother and daughter. God, I remember those days with my own girls. I'm not getting involved with that. Not to mention, I don't have the strength. My focus is to, as quickly as possible, get some nutrients into my body and head back upstairs.

"Your Dad is about the same. Ari is spending some time with

him," I say. "If you decide you want some alone time with Daddy, make sure you do it soon." My voice trails off at the thought of the end. But it is real and happening, and we have to face it.

Lexi is filled with dread. "I can't bring myself to say goodbye. It feels so final if I do. It's as if I'm admitting he's really going."

Handing her the casserole, I draw her close. "Think of it not as 'goodbye,' but as sharing moments. I know he hears us, your laughter, tears, and stories; they'll be his comfort. And when it's time, he'll take those memories with him and watch over us. He'll never truly leave you, Lex."

Lia stands at the counter, stirring the chicken noodle soup in silence, the aroma of warm broth mixing with the smell of our neighbor, Ida's home-cooked kindness. The ladle scrapes softly against the pot, a rhythm that normally would bring comfort, but tonight, it barely registers. She pours the steaming soup into a bowl and the clink of the spoon against the ceramic echoes in the stillness of the kitchen.

I sit at the table, watching her, my fingers tracing the grain of the wood. I can't help but notice how thoughtful everyone's been —how the casseroles, cards, and the quiet offers to help have filled the space that grief tries to hollow out. It's like a tide of kindness trying to shore up the crumbling walls of our lives.

The soup is hot, but I barely feel its warmth. I force a spoonful into my mouth, but the flavor doesn't break through the heaviness pressing down on my chest. Each swallow feels like swallowing air. All I can think about is getting back to Alex.

The minutes down here stretch like hours, and I can feel the pull of the stairs behind me, drawing me back to his side. I need to be with him—where I belong. I take a few more bites and push it away.

Ari is still in the same position she was in when I left her. Holding Alex's hand. She must feel my presence in the room because she reaches for me with her other hand. I kneel down next to the bed, holding on tight to my baby girl as she clings to both her father and me like a lost child.

"Your dad loves you, Ariana." I look into her emerald-green eyes and see her soul.

"I know, Mama. I know."

"Mom?" Lia calls my name from downstairs. Her voice cuts through the quiet, piercing the bubble of time that has all but frozen around Alex and me and Ari. I bristle at the sound, an unwelcome interruption in the fragile stillness that has settled over the moment.

"What?" I snap, trying to keep the irritation from spilling into my voice, though I can feel it bubbling beneath the surface.

"Eve's on the house phone," Lia calls back up. Her voice carries a slight edge, like she's unsure if this is the right thing to do. I see her standing at the foot of the stairs, waiting for my answer. I clench my fists, feeling the weight of frustration press into me.

"Tell her I can't talk," I say curtly. The last thing I need right now is to be pulled away, even for Eve. Not now. Not when Alex is fading with every breath, and every second with him feels like it might be the last.

Lia hesitates. "Mom, she says it's an emergency," she adds, her voice softer, as though she knows I'm seconds away from snapping.

An emergency? *It's always something with Eve lately,* I think to myself. And every time, it's nothing. I sigh, feeling the exhaustion weigh down my bones. My feet drag slightly as I descend the stairs. I head towards the den, away from the constant sound of Alex's shallow breathing. His presence lingers with me, even from afar. I want to be with him, to keep vigil, but instead, I pick up the receiver.

"Hi, Eve," I say flatly, trying not to let my weariness bleed into the words.

"Kels!" she gasps on the other end. Her voice is shaky and breathless like she's been crying. "I've been trying to reach you for hours! Your phone goes straight to voicemail, and you haven't answered any of my texts."

I sigh again, squeezing my eyes shut. "I told you," I say calmly, almost robotically. "My ringer is off. I'm not checking texts right now. Alex…"

She doesn't let me finish. "How's Alex?" she blurts out, panic edging her words.

I take a deep breath, feeling my throat tighten. "Mary doesn't think he'll make it through the night," I say quietly.

There's nothing but silence on the other end of the line. A heavy, suffocating silence that stretches too long. My grip tightens on the phone as I wait for her to say something, anything. Finally, her voice comes back, small, trembling.

"Can I come say goodbye?"

Fifteen minutes later, a sharp, insistent sound grates against the quiet stillness of the house. My heart sinks. I don't need to look to know who it is, and now I regret telling Lia to answer the phone earlier. I told Eve it wasn't a good time, that this was meant to be for family, but she insisted. Her words echo in my head: "I'm like family, Kelsi. You know that."

Lia brushes past me, her face strained as she reaches for the doorknob. And there she is—Eve, standing in the doorway with red-rimmed eyes and tear-streaked cheeks. Her clothes are slightly disheveled; her hair pulled back in a haphazard bun looking like she rushed here without a second thought. I can see the desperation in her gaze and the urgency in the way her hands shake as she clutches her purse.

"I told you it wasn't a good time," I say quietly, but there's no force behind my words. I don't have the energy for a confrontation, not today. Not now.

"Kelsi, please," she breathes out, stepping over the threshold as if the door wasn't even a barrier. "I need to say goodbye. I have to."

My chest tightens, and I glance up the stairs back toward Alex. Part of me wants to push her out, to tell her to leave and respect our final moments as a family. But another part—the part that remembers decades of friendship, of shared memories and laughter—keeps me rooted to the spot. She's right. She's been here since the beginning. Maybe she does deserve this.

"Alright," I murmur. "But don't stay long. He's...he's barely hanging on."

Eve nods frantically, wiping at her eyes as she moves past me, making her way toward mine and Alex's room like it's second nature. Everything feels different. I follow her up the stairs, my steps slow and heavy, each one weighted with the finality of what's coming.

When we reach the door, I hesitate. The soft hum of the oxygen machine fills the room, and Alex lies there, his chest barely rising and falling. His skin is pale, almost translucent, and the sight of him like this makes my heart clench. This isn't the man I married. This is...death.

Eve rushes to his side, sinking into the chair next to him, her hands immediately reaching for his. She's crying openly now, her sobs filling the small space, and I watch her, confused. Her grief seems so raw, so visceral, and I can't understand why. Yes, they've been close—hell, we've all been close—but this feels strange. It's as if she's losing more than just a friend, more than someone she's known for decades.

"Alex," she whispers through her tears, squeezing his hand. "I'm so sorry...I'm so, so sorry."

I stand there, awkwardly watching this unfold, not knowing what to do with myself. Her tears are a torrent, and she rests her forehead on the back of his hand, her body trembling with each sob. My stomach twists as I try to reconcile what I'm seeing with the Eve I know. It's almost like I'm intruding on something private.

"I'm here," Eve continues, her voice breaking. "I'm here, Alex...I'll always be here."

A lump forms in my throat, and I step closer, feeling the need to intervene. I place my hand gently on Eve's shoulder, trying to pull her back from whatever abyss she's spiraling into. "Eve," I say softly, "maybe it's time to let him rest."

She flinches at my touch but doesn't move away. Instead, she slowly raises her head, her face wet and blotchy from crying. She looks up at me, her expression pained and desperate, and for a moment, I think she's going to say something. But she doesn't. She just nods, wipes her face again, and exhales a long, shuddering breath.

"I just...I needed to say goodbye," she whispers, her voice hollow now, drained of its earlier panic. "I'll leave you all to your family now."

I nod slowly, even though something inside me still feels unsettled. "I'll call you tomorrow," I say, though I'm not sure I will. But it's enough for now. It has to be.

She stands up, giving Alex's hand one last squeeze before she turns toward the door. I walk her out, watching as she leaves the room, her shoulders slumped and her steps slow. As soon as she's gone, I close the door behind her and lean my head against the glass pane, closing my eyes.

Chapter Nine

These days, with our contrasting schedules, our apartment feels like a revolving door of hellos and hurried goodbyes. I push the door open with my shoulder, my hands filled with coffee and a stack of textbooks. The aroma of toast lingers in the air.

"Eve?" I call out, hoping she's home.

"Hey! Feels like forever since I've seen you." Eve pokes her head out of her room, her hair twisted up in a messy bun that's somehow both casual and chic. She flashes me a smile, her voice filled with playful exaggeration.

I grin, setting my textbooks down on the dining table, careful not to let my coffee slosh over the sides of the cup.

"I know, right? It's been a whirlwind few months." I sigh, sinking into the chair across from her.

Eve walks over and collapses into the chair opposite me, tucking one leg under her as she adjusts her sweater. There's a relaxed air between us, like always. I take a sip of my coffee and raise an eyebrow at her.

"So, how are things going? Are you still seeing that guy from the park? What was his name again?" I lean back in my chair, genuinely curious.

Her face relaxes, and she waves her hand dismissively. "Oh, Alex?" She shakes her head with a soft laugh. "That seems like a lifetime ago. We really haven't caught up in a long time, have we? I mean, he was nice and all—super hot, but it was just a one-time thing. We went on a date and had a decent time, but... Alex wasn't really my type."

I smile, relieved for some reason. "So, nothing stuck, huh?"

She shakes her head again, leaning forward on the table. "Nope. I've moved on. Actually, I've been seeing someone else lately—someone way more interesting than that law-school nerd."

"Oh?" I raise an eyebrow, intrigued. "Tell me more."

She grins, clearly excited now. "He's this guy I met at a gallery opening the night after Alex and I went out. He's different... thoughtful, into art and travel. I don't know. We'll see where it goes. He hasn't even tried to sleep with me."

"Sounds like you're having fun—or maybe not?" I say, nudging her foot under the table with mine.

She laughs, nudging me back. "Yeah, for now. We'll see." Her eyes sparkle as she starts telling me about their last date, the conversation flowing as easily as ever.

I glance at the clock and realize I'm running late. "Gotta run. Will you be home later?"

Eve smirks, her lips curling into a familiar grin. "Not sure. See you when I see you."

She retreats back into her room, and I rush out, mentally preparing myself for a long day of lectures.

Chapter Ten

New York in the '80s is something special—gritty and magical at once. The distant wail of a saxophone drifts from a subway entrance, adding a soulful note to the rhythm of the city. Neon lights blink above storefronts, casting pink and blue reflections on rain-slicked pavements, and the scent of street food—hot pretzels, chestnuts, and something deep-fried—fills the air. I've been living in the city for a few years now, but sometimes I still feel like that starry-eyed freshman just arriving at NYU, trying to find my place in the chaos.

It was my freshman year when I first met Eve. She was my randomly assigned roommate in the dorms, the kind of person who could turn any situation into an adventure. I remember the day we both showed up, lugging our bags up those endless stairs, our futures still undefined. Eve burst into the room with an oversized duffle slung over one shoulder, her auburn curls a wild halo around her face, her eyes alight with excitement. She turned to me with a wide, lopsided grin and said, "Well, looks like we're stuck together, huh?"

We were best friends from that very first day. Eve was a force

—bold and magnetic, always pulling me into something new. She led me to the hidden gems near campus—the tiny hole-in-the-wall coffee shops and smoky dive bars that never made it into guidebooks but quickly became our favorite haunts.

It was Eve's idea, of course, to get our own place after freshman year.

By then, we were both sick of the cramped dorms, of waiting in line for the showers, of RAs knocking on our door at midnight to tell us to keep it down. We spent months scouring the city, desperate to find something halfway decent on our shoestring budgets. And then, somehow, we landed a tiny apartment just off campus—worn floors, exposed brick, and a kitchen the size of a closet, but it had a fire escape big enough to sit on, and that was all we needed. On warm nights, we'd perch there, feet dangling over the edge, watching the city move beneath us, talking about everything and nothing until the sky began to lighten. It was perfect in the way only a first apartment can be.

Moving in felt like stepping into adulthood, even if the rent barely left us enough for groceries. We scraped together every dollar from our part-time jobs, signed the lease, and declared ourselves officially independent.

It's late when I get home, my bag heavy on my shoulder as I walk through the lobby, past the mailboxes that always smell faintly of dust and stale paper. I wiggle my key into the lock until the tiny metal door creaks open. The usual assortment of bills and junk mail spills into my hands, but one envelope catches my eye—a legal-sized, white envelope with no return address, my name and address neatly printed across the front.

I pause, my heart giving a strange little kick. Handwritten letters are rare.

Bypassing everything else, I slide my finger beneath the flap and tear it open in the dim glow of the flickering overhead light.

Dear Kelsi Jo,

I hope this letter finds you well. Though our meeting was brief (and several months ago), I haven't forgotten about you. I know this might be forward, but would you be open to dinner? The Italian place, Trattoria di Nonna, around the corner from you, has rave reviews. Meet me there on Saturday night, 7 p.m.?

Warm regards,

Alex Kincaid

Alex? My mind races. Then it clicks. Alex, as in Eve's Alex—the guy from the quad. The surprise made me forget the sticky mailbox key, the saxophone in the distance, everything.

Last summer, Eve made it very clear that he was not her type before impulsively announcing she was leaving to study abroad. One day, she was here, talking about this new guy she was seeing, and the next, she was catching a flight out of JFK. "I'll be back by the end of our senior year," she had promised.

That's Eve. Spontaneous.

Outside of our short meeting, I remember bumping into him once at a campus holiday event, and he never crossed my mind again.

I tuck the letter into my jacket pocket and head back to my apartment. The city noises fade into the background as my mind wanders. Do I want to accept Alex's invitation? I've never been asked out on a date by a letter. If not for anything, it's creative and intriguing, to say the least.

What would Eve think? But she's miles away, exploring Europe. And she told me she wasn't interested in him. Besides, she's got a new boyfriend already.

* * *

I step off the curb and onto the cracked sidewalk; the warm scent of garlic and simmering tomatoes wraps around me before I even reach the door. The tiny neon sign in the window hums softly, casting a red glow onto the pavement—Trattoria di Nonna, a place I've passed a hundred times but never stepped inside.

Pushing open the heavy wooden door, I'm immediately hit with the rich, heady aroma of fresh bread and something slow-simmering, the kind of scent that clings to your clothes and makes your stomach growl. The place is small but in a way that feels intimate rather than cramped. The lighting is low, the kind that turns everything golden, flickering of candles stuffed into wax-dripped Chianti bottles.

A few couples are scattered around the room, leaning in close over plates of pasta and glasses of deep red wine. An old jukebox hums in the corner, spinning out Sinatra's "I've Got You Under My Skin," the croon of his voice melting into the quiet murmur of conversation. The red-checkered tablecloths look worn but well-loved, and the walls are cluttered with faded black-and-white photos of smiling faces—family, I assume, generations of them, their lives stitched into this place.

A handwritten menu board by the register lists the daily special:

Nonna's Sunday Sauce

It's underlined as if it's a warning not to order anything else. The scent alone tells me it's probably a solid choice.

My eyes scan the room, and then I spot him at the bar, looking completely relaxed, with a glass of wine in front of him. He seems taller than I remember—broad-shouldered and fit, with dark curly hair that frames his face in a way that softens his strong jawline. His navy blue button-down is open at the collar, and it looks like something a guy who's trying to balance law school and being effortlessly cool would wear.

I feel a flutter of nerves but approach him anyway. He sees me just as I get close and stands up, that easy smile spreading across his face.

"Kelsi," his voice warm and inviting.

"Hey," I say, trying to play it cool. "Sorry, I'm late. I wasn't sure if I'd recognize you."

"No worries," he says with a laugh. "I'm glad you made it."

We move to a table by the window, and it doesn't take long for the awkwardness to melt away. He's surprisingly easy to talk to, and soon enough, we're trading stories about classes, professors, and random NYU stuff.

"So," I say after a lull in the conversation, "what happened with you and Eve?" Eve was so nonchalant when I asked her a few months ago. I'm curious to hear his interpretation.

He leans back in his chair, scratching the back of his head. "Yeah, we went out, but it wasn't, really...I don't know. She's great, but we didn't click. She wasn't really my type."

I raise an eyebrow. "Your type?"

He chuckles, avoiding my gaze for a second. "I mean, Eve's fun, but...I don't know. She's not...you."

That catches me off guard. "Not me? What makes you so sure I'm your type?"

Alex shrugs, his expression turning more serious. "I couldn't stop thinking about you after we met at the quad. Then, when I ran into you just before winter break, I felt something. I wanted to get to know you better. That's why I asked you to come tonight."

I feel my cheeks warm, and I don't know what to say for a second. "I wasn't sure if this was, like...a date? No one's ever asked me out in a letter before."

He laughs again, a low, easy sound. "I was hoping it would be. But, I have a thing for letter writing. Letters. Like real letters. There's something about it that feels more personal. It's kind of old-fashioned, but it is authentic to me. And since you're a writer,

I thought you might..." He leans forward his eyes locking into mine.

"How'd you know I was a writer?" I smile and trace the edge of my wine glass.

"I'm studying to be a lawyer. We know how to dig around for information."

He raises his glass, and I meet him with mine. "To letters," he says with a grin.

"To letters," I repeat, clinking my glass against his.

"And," he adds with a laugh, "to Eve for introducing us."

We both chuckle at that, and the atmosphere between us feels lighter. As the conversation flows, so does an undeniable connection. Sitting there with Alex, it's like the rest of the world fades into the background. I didn't expect this, but here we are, and for the first time in a long time, I feel like something special is just beginning.

Chapter Eleven

Y ou're dating Alex Kincaid? You're kidding, right?" Eve asks, sounding more horrified than happy for me. "Um, no...I mean, yes...we're dating."

I'm sitting across from her, feeling excited to see my best friend and hear all about her time abroad, but something is off. She's not the same Eve. She's withdrawn and quiet, and there's a sadness in her eyes I can't quite place. She casually mentions she spent a lot of her time eating her way through Europe and putting on an extra 10 pounds. I laugh, and try to lighten the mood. But the laughter doesn't reach her eyes.

"When did all this transpire?" she asks, cutting me off before I can explain. "I leave for less than a year, and now you're in love with a guy I went out with?" There's an edge to her words, one that feels like an accusation, and I'm left feeling like I need to defend myself.

I blink, unsure of how to respond. We're sitting in the same old apartment we've shared for the last two years, yet everything suddenly feels different. The tension in the room is thick, pressing in on me from all sides. This was supposed to be a happy reunion, but now it feels like a storm cloud is hanging over us.

"We've been seeing each other for a little while now. About five months after you left for Europe," I continue carefully, "I got a letter in the mail from Alex. He asked me out. It was sweet and a bit unexpected. I didn't plan for this to happen, Eve. It just did." I pause, smiling slightly at the memory, but my smile fades when I see her expression. "You went out with him one time and told me you weren't interested. What's going on?" I probe her for answers.

She's quiet for a second, her face falling as she stares at the floor.

"Why didn't you ever tell me?" Eve demands, raising her voice. "Don't you think I had the right to know?" Her eyes are wet, tears hovering on the brink, and I feel a stab of guilt. I've never seen her like this—so raw, so hurt.

I try to keep my voice calm, but my frustration creeps in. "Eve, you said you weren't into him! You said you didn't care! I didn't think it was something you needed to know. And I didn't seek him out. He came to me. It wasn't like I was trying to steal someone you cared about. Not to mention, I had no clue how to get in touch with you."

Tears begin falling down her cheeks, and I'm shocked. Eve never cries, at least not like this. Not in front of me. "Eve, I didn't know—" I start to say, reaching for her hand, but she pulls away, wiping her tears with quick, angry movements.

"It's fine," she mumbles, grabbing a tissue and blowing her nose. She tosses the tissue onto the old beat-up table we found on the street a couple of years ago, and for a moment, it feels like a lifetime ago that we were just two carefree college roommates.

"Eve, please," I say softly, trying to reach her. "I didn't mean to hurt you. I didn't know you felt so strongly about Alex. If I had known, I—"

"It's fine," she repeats, her voice hollow. She stands up abruptly, her movements stiff, and I watch her walk toward her bedroom. She doesn't even look back at me. The door slams shut behind her, and I'm left sitting there, the weight of unspoken words hanging in the air.

I sit in stunned silence, trying to make sense of what just happened. My heart twists with confusion. Why is she reacting this way? What am I not seeing? The Eve I knew wouldn't have cared about Alex—so why does it feel like she does now?

The room feels heavy, almost suffocating, and I can't shake the feeling that there's something she's not telling me.

Chapter Twelve

September 19, 2018.

A little after 2:00 a.m., I awaken to a cacophony of moans. Alex is still unconscious but clearly agitated. A wet crackle accompanies each labored breath. I jump out of bed, slide on my panties and robe, and run to find Mary. She's already at the top of the staircase.

"Mary, Alex...there's something wrong with Alex. He's..."

"Yes, I heard on the monitor. Let me check his vitals and see what's going on," she says.

She goes to Alex's bedside and pulls both lids up, and his eyes roll back in his head. I look on as she finally finds a faint pulse through the tangle of purple vessels below his paper-thin skin. He continues to moan as his body twitches. His oxygen level is low.

"Mrs. Kincaid, wake the girls," she pauses, "It's time."

I can't move. I was just lying with him. How can one minute I feel his skin on mine, and the next minute he leaves me?

Mary takes my hands in hers and gently whispers, "Go get the girls, hun."

Ari appears in the hallway. She's so connected to her father that she feels it without me waking her.

"Mom…" Ari says, still half asleep.

"Wake up Lia and Lexi."

Ari opens Lia's door to wake her. I trip over the extra oxygen tank as I make my way to Lexi's room at the end of the hallway.

"Mom, Lia's not in her bed…" she sounds panicked.

I interrupt her when I see the girls sleeping together on Lexi's bed, just like they used to do when they were little girls before Ari was born.

"They're here, Ari. In Lexi's bed." Seeing our girls lying together, sisters holding onto each other—tightly grasping onto a piece of their childhood as one of the most important people in their life involuntarily leaves them.

I kneel next to Lexi's double bed. The bed she forbade me to get rid of when she left home and started her family with Wendall.

"Girls, wake up," my voice is more than a whisper, startling them awake. "It's time to say goodbye…" The words barely cross my lips.

"Where's Ari?" Lia asks.

"She's with Daddy. Let's go," I say.

Lexi throws the white eyelet comforter off them, and they run to their father's side for the last time.

Ari lights a candle on each nightstand, the dresser, and the credenza that sits just below the middle window in our bedroom.

"Alexa, play The Beatles," Lia commands to the AI device. The Beatles are Alex's favorite band.

Although my body is quivering like I'm stranded in the middle of a New York blizzard, having Alex's favorite things fill the room calms my palpitating heart. The girls and I surround the bed, laying our hands on the man we love so much. The aroma from the candles reminds me of the many nights Alex and I intimately shared in this bed.

"Mom, I'm not ready to say goodbye," Lia whispers, laying her head on my shoulder. She weeps for the man who taught her how to ride a bike and gently pulled her first tooth when she was too afraid to do it herself (and did not want Mommy to do it).

"I know, baby," I reply and kiss the top of her head.

Ari and Lexi stand on the opposite side of the bed. Lia is the closest to him and nestles her face next to his. Each breath he takes is more labored than the last.

Mary touches my shoulder, "Mrs. Kincaid, I'm going to go downstairs and give you all time with Alex." I meet her gaze and shake my head okay.

"I'm here if you need me," she says.

I cover her hand with mine and squeeze it. I want her to know how much I need her and how grateful I am for her being here. The energy when our hands meet says everything that can't be spoken at this moment.

Alex looks so small lying in our king-sized bed. No more oxygen, feeding tubes, or IVs taking up space. He's lost so much weight in the last few weeks.

"Remember our family movie nights, girls? We'd all pile up in this bed on Friday nights when you were little?" I smile at the memory, yet the tears burn my cheeks.

"We did it for years, even when we were older. After Ari was born. I wouldn't have admitted it then, but I would turn down hanging out with my friends for our special Friday night family slumber parties."

A long hush trails, and we take it all in.

"There's room," I say, breaking the silence. I'm firmly planted in the memory. The girls look at me like I'm crazy.

CHAPTER THIRTEEN

November, 2000.

"Pile in, my sweet girls!" Alex stands at the threshold of our bedroom, arms wide open like he's welcoming royalty. His grin stretches wide, and even though he's had a long week at work, his energy is magnetic, instantly pulling the girls into our cozy little world.

They come barreling in, dressed in their matching Thanksgiving pajamas, which I know Lexi is secretly thrilled to still be part of, even at twelve and a half. She's on the brink of teenhood, but moments like these keep her grounded, and I cherish that. Lia, just eleven months younger, mirrors her sister in height but not in temperament—she's got that fiery independence, always ready to challenge her sister's lead.

"Look, Daddy! I made your favorite—truffle popcorn!" Lia's voice is full of pride as she thrusts a giant wooden bowl into Alex's hands.

Alex chuckles, catching the bowl before Lia topples over. "Whoa, careful there, sweetheart!" He ruffles her hair and takes a deep whiff of the popcorn. "Mmm, smells delicious. You're the best, Lia." His praise makes her beam, and I can't help but smile as I watch her little chest puff up with pride.

"Did you bring the drinks, Lia?" Lexi asks, already taking on that bossy, maternal tone she sometimes adopts with her younger sisters.

"No!" Lia defiantly crosses her arms over her chest. "I made the popcorn. I thought you were getting the drinks!"

Lexi rolls her eyes dramatically. "I had the baby." she retorts as if Ari is a hundred pounds of pure responsibility in her arms.

"Ari can walk, Lexi," Lia fires back, narrowing her eyes. "She has feet, you know!"

The bickering starts to escalate—typical sibling rivalry. I can already see where this is going, so I jump in before it spirals out of control.

"Girls, girls," I say gently, trying to keep the peace. "Lia, thank you for making the popcorn. Lexi, would you mind getting us the drinks before we start the movie?"

Lexi lets out an exaggerated sigh but heads for the door, her long legs taking her quickly across the room. "Fine," she mutters. "But Lia owes me one."

"Root beer for me, Lexi!" Lia calls out, already knowing what's coming.

"No soda this late," I cut in, my voice firm but playful. "Just water, please."

Lia shoots me a dramatic pout, her lower lip sticking out like she's eight instead of almost twelve. But she knows better than to push her luck.

As Lexi heads downstairs to get the drinks, Ari crawls up into my lap, her tiny hands clutching at my shirt. She's still so little, but every day, she seems to grow faster, trying to mimic her older sisters. She nestles in close, her warm body melting against mine as she gazes up at Alex with those wide, admiring eyes.

Alex climbs into the bed beside me, balancing the bowl of popcorn on his lap. He smiles down at Ari, gently brushing a stray curl from her forehead. "You ready for the movie, little one?"

She nods eagerly, though I'm pretty sure she's more interested in the popcorn than the movie itself.

A few minutes later, Lexi returns with a tray of water bottles, passing them around like we're at some grand event. "Here you go," she says, handing one to Lia with just a hint of an eye roll. Lia takes it without a word, too engrossed in the bowl of popcorn to care about their earlier spat.

The lights dim, and we all pile under the blankets, limbs tangled, hearts full. The movie starts, but more than anything, it's the comfort of these moments, these Friday nights, that matters most. Alex leans over, whispering in my ear as Ari drifts off to sleep in my arms.

"Life doesn't get better than this, baby," he says and softly kisses my ear, his voice full of love.

I look at him, at the girls nestled between us, and my heart swells with contentment. "No," I whisper back, kissing his cheek. "It really doesn't."

We clink our water bottles together in an impromptu toast to our own little tradition.

Chapter Fourteen

September 19, 2018.

I look at the girls and touch Alex's chalky gray lips. I rub lip balm over them one last time.

"Pile in."

We all climb into bed with Alex, cocooning him in the love that he's created for us. I nestle into his side, his body still warm beneath my touch. I can hear Lia slipping in behind me, wrapping her arm around both of us, her fingers trembling as they stretch across to reach her father. Lexi curls into Alex's other side, laying her head on his chest, her hand resting gently on his shoulder as if to anchor him to us just a little longer.

Ari hesitates at the foot of the bed, her red hair falling messily around her face, tears glistening in her green eyes. She finally crawls up, laying her head on his knee like she used to when she was little, as if she's just waiting for him to ruffle her hair or comment about her day.

The room feels heavy, as if we're all holding our breaths and waiting for something. I know, though, that this is the end. I press closer to Alex, my lips brushing his ear as I whisper, "You can go now, my love. We're all here, and it's time to rest. Thank you for the most incredible life. I love you." My voice cracks, and I press my forehead to his chest, feeling the slow rise and fall of his breaths growing more and more shallow.

"Let It Be" plays softly in the background, filling the space with the calm notes of Alex's favorite song. We begin to hum along, our voices uniting in a melody we've all heard countless times before, but tonight, it's different—it's a farewell.

Ari's sobs break the melody, and I feel Lexi tighten her grip around Alex's arm, her own tears mingling with the song. Lia's face is buried in my shoulder, her body trembling as she holds us all together, though I know she feels like she's breaking apart.

Slowly, the rhythm of Alex's breathing falters, then quiets. His chest stills beneath my cheek, and we know—he's gone.

But we hold him anyway, as if he's still here, as if he'll wake up and pull us all into one of his infamous group hugs. I lift my head and rest it over his heart one last time, my tears wetting his shirt. And together, all four of us, sing him to Heaven.

Chapter Fifteen

A light drizzle dampens the path leading from the street to the front door as family and friends arrive at our home to memorialize the man we all love. The girls and I stand together, wearing all black, just like we're supposed to, welcoming our guests with a hug and a "Thank you" for every "I'm so sorry," just like we're supposed to. I look around and see the memorial set for Alex—all his favorite things—memories for everyone to touch. I find myself keenly aware of things that seem out of place, off, in the space that has always been so safe. It doesn't feel like home right now, even though family, friends, and familiarity surround me.

My eyes land on our family portrait. It usually hangs above the dining room table, silently witnessing years of family meals and conversations. But now, it's been moved—propped up on an old easel that must have been dragged out from the basement. Someone went to the trouble of setting it up as if trying to make the portrait mean something at this moment. But standing there, seeing it displaced, only underscores the shift—how things that once felt permanent are suddenly rearranged and uncertain.

Everything in this house is the same, yet nothing feels like it belongs anymore.

I sneak out of the receiving line and stand in front of the nearly decade old portrait, chewing on what's left of my broken acrylic thumbnail. There's chatter in the background that's getting easier and easier to drown out with the memories of our life as I stare at the image of my husband. I've held my emotions together with strands of the thinnest thread all day, all for show— I know how to do that. I know how to pretend. I'll find time to break down when I'm alone.

Our last family photo together—just the five of us a few weeks before Lexi married Wendall. She was a few weeks pregnant with the twins. Lia had just graduated with her MBA and was living with Doug, not too far from our house. Ari, our baby, was only ten; she was adamant that she would stand by her daddy in that picture. The memories overtake the moment. I'm trying to make them come to life right now. How can I transport myself back there and steal another ten years?

My eyes burn as if they're filled with fire, each tear I refuse to shed searing against my will. I can feel myself crumbling, collapsing slowly onto the cool, unyielding floorboards beneath me. The scream I want to release is trapped inside, suffocated by the weight of memories, all of it too painful to bear. I am slipping out of control, my limbs foreign and useless, as if they've abandoned me. Just before I completely fall, arms wrap around me— tight and firm, like a net pulling me back from the brink. My legs, my ears, my senses—all detached. All I can hear are these awful sounds, guttural and raw, echoing from the hollow spaces inside me. The sobs are mine, though I've never heard anything like them before. I'm unraveling, each thread that held me together for so long coming loose, breaking apart in front of everyone. I am powerless, and the fear that I may never be whole again grips me like a vice.

"Mom," one of the girls call out to me. I hear her, but my wet and weighted eyes won't open.

"Has she eaten?" I think that's Ari. She's always so worried about me eating.

"Do we need to call 911?" A voice chimes in.

*No, no, no! I'm fine. Really, I'm fine...*I think I say it loud enough for everyone to hear, but I realize that my lips aren't moving.

Then, silence.

I wake up in bed, disoriented, with Lexi and Lia sitting beside me. As I push myself up on my elbows, nausea washes over me like the aftermath of a wild night—except I haven't touched a drop of alcohol in months. My dress feels heavy against my skin. My shoes are gone, but I notice my right big toe poking through a small hole in my pantyhose. It's such a tiny, ridiculous thing to focus on, but I can't look away. I let myself fall back onto the mattress, afraid that if I move too much, the queasiness will win, and I'll lose whatever remains of my composure.

"What's happening?" I ask the girls.

"We're not sure, Mom. You passed out downstairs when we were receiving everyone," Lexi says.

Then Lia chimes in, "We were going to call 911, but Mary checked your vitals and said you passed out from sheer exhaustion. Uncle Cory carried you up the stairs."

"You scared the hell out of us. Have you eaten?" Lexi asks.

I half smirk, half laugh under my breath, and bring my hand up to my face to discover a lukewarm wet cloth covering my forehead.

"Have you been talking to Ari?" I ask and set the washcloth on Alex's nightstand.

"When was the last time you ate, Mom?" Lexi presses me for an answer.

"I don't know. I, I..." I stutter, trying to remember.

"I didn't think so." My brother Cory responds as he walks into the bedroom. "I brought you something to eat." He sets a tray of what looks and smells like Ida's homemade chicken noodle soup, crackers, and some orange Gatorade over my lap, and Lia props up the pillows to support my back.

"Thanks, brother." I try to smile, but it feels like I've forgotten how to. I try like hell to eat the soup and muster a few slurps, but I'm thinking about all the people downstairs—the guests who are here to celebrate Alex.

I should be down there. This day isn't about me; it's about Alex, I think to myself.

"I need to get back downstairs," I insist.

"Please, Mom. Eat. You need some nutrients." Ari takes the spoon and tries to feed me.

"I appreciate the gesture, sweetheart, but I need to get down to the guests." I hand the tray to Lexi.

My body betrays me as I push myself upright, my legs trembling beneath me. The room tilts, and before I can steady myself, I collapse back onto the bed. The weight of it all—grief, exhaustion, pain—presses down on me, leaving me breathless, unable to do anything but sit in it, swallowed whole.

I'm suffocated by the thought that I'm never going to feel any better than I do right now.

"Okay, Mom, if you insist on going downstairs, at least drink your Gatorade and put on some different shoes so you don't fall." Lexi grabs my black flats out of the closet and puts them on my feet. She wins that battle. At least I can go back to pretending I'm okay.

The formal living room hums with quiet conversation, a space transformed into a living tribute. Family and friends cluster around, fingers trailing over framed photographs capturing decades of laughter and milestones. Alex's work awards gleam under the soft glow of the table lamps, neatly arranged beside his academic certificates. His golf clubs lean against the wall, trophies lined up like silent witnesses to his victories. Each relic tells a story—the weight of a life well-lived. The girls have done an incredible job curating these moments, piecing together the essence of Alex in a way that makes his presence almost tangible.

Once today is over, I can crawl back into a corner of myself and never make another appearance. Guests are everywhere, filling the rooms where our growing family spent many nights and holidays, cooking, sharing stories, and mostly laughing. Now, these memories are bullet points.

I make my way into the kitchen, where the aroma of food is far more pleasing than the act of eating it. I want so badly to engage with these people who have showered our family with love for years, especially the last few weeks of Alex's life, but I can't right now. My smiles are fake, my comments are canned, and the faces of our guests—those I've known for decades—I barely recognize. I can't see past the pain.

"Kelsi Jo, I've got this covered. This is the last thing you need to be doing," Eve says as I start drying the dishes and stacking them up next to the sink. I hold the two ends of the damp towel in both hands and glance up with a half-smile.

Eve turns off the water, breaking through my haze of numbness. She turns, and without a word, she pulls me into her arms. The embrace is tight and familiar. Her well-manicured hands, still clammy from doing the dishes, press gently against my back while her cheek rests against mine. There's dried mascara crusted underneath her left eye, a remnant of the tears she's been quietly shedding.

I know how much Alex meant to her and Charlie. I pull back slightly and look into Eve's watery eyes, knowing this is hard for her, too.

"Charlie loved Alex," she whispers, her voice cracking as she blinks away the tears and looks away. "He really did."

Charlie Hatmaker. A man who came into Eve's life long after her first marriage to Brandon ended—a marriage built on youthful dreams and adventure but short on stability. Brandon was an artist and a photographer with a spirit that was restless and untamed. They met just before Eve's senior year at NYU, and the connection was instant. She left for her study abroad trip with Brandon's photos tucked in her suitcase and a promise that they'd build a life together when she returned. And they did. A week after graduation, they married. For ten years, they roamed the globe, living hand-to-mouth, doing photography jobs wherever they could find them. No kids. Brandon never wanted children; he believed they couldn't raise a family when they barely had enough money to feed themselves. They wandered, unmoored, until eventually, Eve's heart grew tired of the constant uncertainty.

And then Charlie walked into her life—tall, confident, and older by twenty years, with the kind of presence that commanded a room. It was during one of Brandon's shoots in New York City, a job that Eve was less interested in than the charming man she met on set. Charlie was nothing like Brandon. A businessman, powerful and wealthy in the tech world, Charlie was everything Brandon wasn't—grounded, secure, and madly in love with Eve from the moment they met. She divorced Brandon and married Charlie within a year, and for the first time, Eve had a partner who could give her the world—not just emotionally but materially.

With Charlie, Eve traveled the globe again, but this time, it wasn't with a backpack on a shoestring budget. They stayed in five-star hotels, flew first-class, and dined in the finest restaurants. Despite the opulence, Charlie was kind, generous, and utterly devoted to Eve. Though Charlie had a grown son and three grand-children from his first marriage, he and Eve never had children together. Eve always said that Charlie gave her everything she never knew she wanted—a life filled with ease, deep love, and endless adventure. He was her anchor, her partner in exploring the world. Yet, beneath her words, I could always sense something unfinished, a quiet longing she never spoke aloud. It was as if, despite all the joy and stability Charlie brought her, a part of her still ached for something she couldn't quite name, a missing piece she'd never find.

"I'm glad Charlie was able to get here for the service," I say finally, my voice low. "Alex always thought the world of Charlie. You know that."

Eve smiles softly, her lips trembling. "I know he did." She steps back and wipes her eyes, trying to compose herself. "Let me make you some tea. You look like you need something warm."

As Eve moves to the kettle, her movements so familiar, I can't help but think about how deeply our lives have become intertwined. The kettle starts to hum, and my mind drifts back to that first trip to Italy—the beginning of what would be years of shared laughter, secrets, and memories. I remember how it felt back then, when everything was new. Alex and I had been married about ten years, and Charlie was this charming, worldly man who had swept Eve off her feet. I admired their bond, the way they moved through life like a whirlwind of spontaneity and joy, while Alex and I were more grounded, raising kids and working on our careers. But together, the four of us created a magical friendship.

Tuscany's rolling hills, the vineyards stretching as far as the eye could see, the small towns with their cobblestone streets, all of it became a part of us. We would sit for hours in tiny cafes, wine glasses in hand, the warm Mediterranean breeze carrying our conversations late into the night. That was the trip where we all became family, not just friends. But even then, I sensed something in Eve, a restlessness, as if she was always looking for something more.

The kettle whistles sharply, pulling me back to the present. I glance over at Eve, wondering if she ever thinks about that first trip to Italy like I do.

PART TWO

The truth will set you free, but first it will shatter you.
Glennon Doyle

Chapter One

June, 1987.

A slow, rolling wave tightens my stomach and twists my insides hitting me before I even open my eyes. Two weeks of this—of pretending it's just a lingering flu, of convincing myself it's nothing. But deep down, I know better. I shift onto my side, pressing a hand to my abdomen as if that might steady me, my gaze fixed on the thin slats of light bleeding through the blinds. It's graduation day. Of all the mornings for this to come crashing down on me, again, of course, it has to be today.

I tiptoe out of bed unsure if Eve is still sleeping, the old wooden floorboards creaking beneath my bare feet as I make my way to our shared bathroom. The pregnancy test sits there on the counter, mocking me. I bought it on a whim last night, and now it feels like the most important thing in the world.

I don't know if I'm ready for this answer.

I pick it up with trembling fingers, tearing the foil open, the sound absurdly loud in the quiet apartment. My breath comes in shallow bursts as I do what needs to be done, then set the test face down on the counter, refusing to look. I lean against the sink, gripping the cold ceramic, my heart pounding in my chest.

Ten minutes. I try to breathe, try to steady my thoughts. It's probably nothing. Stress, finals, the chaos of graduation—it has to be. I've convinced myself for weeks that everything is fine.

But my period is six weeks late.

The truth gnaws at me, and I can't ignore it any longer. I stare at the ceiling, at the crack that snakes through the plaster like a scar, trying to hold onto that last thread of denial.

Finally, I flip the test over.

Positive.

I freeze, the room suddenly too small, too quiet, too still. My pulse quickens as I stare at the result, and my breath catches in my throat. I'm pregnant. The words echo in my head like they're from someone else's life.

And yet...there's a warmth beneath the shock. A flicker of something unfamiliar, something that feels like...joy. I feel it bubble up inside me, and I can't help it—a small smile forms on my lips.

I place a hand on my stomach, feeling the weight of the future shift beneath my fingertips. I should be panicking, but instead, I feel strangely excited. Unexpected, yes. But something about it feels right, like this is the beginning of something I didn't know I needed.

I'm feeling a mixture of excitement and nerves bubbling from the pregnancy test. I step into the kitchen, Eve is awake and sitting at the small round kitchen table, cradling a cup of coffee between her hands. Her messy hair cascades down her back; she still looks half-asleep.

"Morning." She doesn't look at me when she greets me. Things have been tense since I told her I was dating Alex.

"I'm pregnant," I blurt out like I have no control over anything coming out of my mouth.

Her coffee cup freezes halfway to her lips. Her eyes widen in shock, and she stares at me as if I've just told her the most horrifying news possible. For a second, I expect her to smile, to give me some kind of congratulations, but instead, she puts the cup down with a hard clatter, her fingers trembling against the ceramic.

"You're kidding, right?" Her voice trembles.

I laugh awkwardly, trying to break the tension, hoping she'll come around. "Nope. I'm pregnant, Eve. Isn't it crazy?"

But there's no laughter from her. She frowns, her brow furrowing deeper than I've ever seen before. She's not happy. She's upset, and I can't figure out why. We've always been there for each other through everything, and yet this news seems to have hit her differently.

"Are you going to keep it?"

"Well, yeah. It never crossed my mind that there'd be another choice."

"Of course it hasn't." her voice is cold and distant. "What if Alex ditches you? What if he walks out? Are you prepared to raise this baby by yourself?"

The words hit me like a slap. My heart pounds in my chest as I stare at her, speechless. "What? Why would you say that?"

Eve looks away, her eyes focused on the window like she's somewhere else entirely. Her fingers are clenched around the windowsill, white-knuckled, and her body is tense, as if she's bracing for something. I wait for her to laugh it off, to tell me she's just messing with me, but she doesn't. The silence stretches on, heavy and awkward.

She finally speaks again, but her voice is barely a whisper. "You haven't thought this through, Kelsi. What about your dreams? Your career? This will change everything."

I take a step closer, my hands shaking slightly as I try to reach her, to get her to understand. "Eve, Alex and I love each other. He isn't like that. We'll figure it out together."

But she just shakes her head, her expression distant, unreadable. "You don't know that."

There's something in her tone that makes my stomach twist, something she's not saying. I can't understand why she's being like this—why she's not happy for me. She's always been my biggest cheerleader, my best friend. But now, it feels like there's a wall between us.

"Eve," I say softly, "what's going on?"

She doesn't answer, just stares out the window as if she's watching a scene unfold that only she can see. The air between us is thick with something unsaid, something I don't understand. I don't know what's happening, but I can feel Eve slipping further away from me with each second that passes.

In the pit of my stomach, doubt begins to form, not about Alex, but about our friendship—about what might have changed while she was gone.

Chapter Two

The front door bursts open with a gust of crisp November air, sending a swirl of golden leaves skittering across the porch.

"Ahh, Mom, your sauce!" Lexi's voice rings through the house before I even see her. She inhales deeply, her eyes fluttering shut in pure appreciation as she shrugs off her coat.

Before I can respond, a stampede of little feet barrels toward me. Maddi, Finnegan, and Brody crash into my waist, their tiny arms wrapping around me in a fierce group hug.

"Glammy!" they squeal in unison.

My heart aches and swells at the same time. *This* is what makes the house feel alive again.

"All right, all right, wild ones." Lexi's voice carries the kind of exasperation only a mother of three can master. "Pick up your coats and put them where they belong. Shoes, too. You know the rules."

The kids groan but obey, shuffling out of their sneakers with exaggerated sighs.

"Lex, it's okay. Let them be kids," I say, ruffling Brody's curls before he scampers off. "A coat or three on the floor won't hurt anything."

Lexi exhales through her nose, handing Wendall their overnight bags—luggage better suited for an international getaway than a two-night stay. "Fine. But if I break my neck tripping over a boot, it's on you."

I laugh, pulling her in for a hug. The familiar scents of her shampoo and autumn air cling to her sweater, and for a brief moment, I swear I can feel Alex here with us, in the warmth of our daughter's embrace, in the laughter echoing through the foyer.

Lia arrives next, juggling a tray of homemade pastries and a bottle of wine. "Okay, someone please take this before I drop it. And if anyone says, 'You made too much,' I will *fight you.*"

"No complaints here." I relieve her of the tray, setting it on the counter as she shrugs off her coat.

The kitchen hums with life, pots simmering, glasses clinking, the low murmur of conversation weaving between the scent of roasted garlic and tomatoes. The season always starts like this: Thanksgiving week, with food, family, and the unspoken promise that no matter what changes, we will always gather.

From the time they were old enough to read a recipe, my girls were in the kitchen with me, learning how to stir, chop, and season. Over the years, they perfected their own signature sides— some became holiday staples, and some were quickly vetoed after one unfortunate year of pumpkin mac and cheese.

It was always Lexi who took charge, self-appointing herself as my sous chef from the time she could hold a wooden spoon. Lia, of course, had other ideas.

"Why does Lexi get to be the boss?" she used to protest, arms folded tight across her chest, her seven-year-old face a mask of determination. "I'm just as good as her."

I would explain, over and over, that Lexi was the oldest, but Lia would shake her head, undeterred.

"She's not *that* much older. We're the same age for, like, *two months* every year."

"One month," Lexi would correct every single time.

Eventually, they shared the title. And maybe it was meant to be—Lia found her true calling in cooking. She went to culinary school after her MBA, and today, she runs a thriving catering business.

I hear the door swing open again, and I don't even have to look up. "Ari."

"I knew I'd find you here." She saunters into the kitchen like she's been here all day, already shrugging out of her coat.

I turn just in time to catch her bending over the stove, sneaking a taste of my sauce. She slurps from the wooden ladle with a slow, deliberate motion, then smacks her lips in satisfaction.

"Ari!" I scold, swatting at her arm.

She grins, utterly unbothered, and goes in for another taste.

I point the spoon at her like a weapon. "Put that that down! If you keep at it, there won't be any left for the others."

With a dramatic sigh, she mutters something about how she's practically *saving* the sauce by taste-testing it.

Then, just as quickly, her playful bravado fades. She hops onto the only clear spot on the kitchen counter, her legs swinging absently. "How are you, Mom? *Really?*" Her voice softens, her dark eyes searching mine. "I don't want to bring the mood down, but...I worry about you. Alone in this big house. Day after day."

I get up in the morning, try to breathe, and make it through another day, is what I want to tell her, but that's not the answer I want her to hear. I want her to think I'm okay.

I take a breath, steadying myself.

I glance at Ari, perched on the counter, and suddenly, I see her as she was at four years old—sitting there in her footie pajamas, watching her father lift her onto the counter so she could 'help' me cook.

Some things don't change.

I place a hand over hers, squeezing gently. "I miss him," I admit. "Every day. But I have you girls. And that...that makes all the difference."

Ari nods, her eyes shining just a little too much. "We miss him too."

I swallow hard and pat her knee. "Now, grab a knife and start chopping. The lasagna's not going to assemble itself."

She hops off the counter with a grin, and just like that, the moment shifts.

Outside, the last of the autumn leaves dance in the wind, swirling against the glass panes of the kitchen window. Inside, the house is warm, alive.

It's different without Alex.

But we are still here. We are still us.

And for tonight, that is enough.

"Are you back to work yet? What are you doing with your days?" She's relentless, and I'm trying to come up with an answer that will satisfy her inquiry.

"So many questions, my girl." I carefully shape my response.

"You know, I don't have to go to law school right after graduation. I can move back home and help you for a few years and then go—"

"Absolutely not. I'll be just fine." I quickly interrupt her.

Ari was accepted into her father's alma mater, Yale Law School, and there is no way I'm giving her a pass on this.

Ari wraps her arms around mine, "I love you, Mom. What can I do to help?"

"Would you mind setting the table?"

* * *

"Dinner's ready!" The sound of little feet overhead sounds more like the hooves of a thousand galloping horses running for the stairs. I'm certain the ceiling is going to cave in any minute.

From the family room, I watch my girls handle the kitchen chaos with their own children exactly the way Alex and I used to.

"More salad, less garlic bread, please," Lexi says to all the kids.

"Whoa! Let me help you ladle that sauce so you don't spill it all over the counter and all over yourself," Ari chimes in like the good aunt she is.

"Mommy! Maddi stepped on my foot, and I spilled my lasagna all over the floor," Finni screams.

I chuckle under my breath.

By design, I wait for everyone to sit down in the dining room.

"Come on, Mom," Lia says, nudging me to get my food.

I pick up one of the plates we've used for every family meal since we were married. I pull it to my chest and stand alone, waiting for Alex to say, "Go ahead, babe, get your plate," and pat my butt as I make my way to what's left of the food. He is still so alive in every moment, yet his absence is present.

Suddenly, I feel his warm breath against my ear, sending a shiver down my spine. I drop the piece of lasagne from the spoon back into the dish, set my plate down, and quickly turn around.

"Alex?" I say out loud, not caring who hears me. I don't want to move. Maybe if I stay right here, he will come back to me.

"Alex, where are you?" I ask again, "I'm not leaving until I see you."

"Mom?" Lexi walks into the kitchen. "Who are you talking to? Come sit down and eat."

She looks at me like I need rescuing. I start to tell her I need a few minutes when I hear his voice again.

"Kelsi Jo, go. I am here." Alex's voice instructs me. He is right. My family is waiting.

I look at Lexi and smile. "I'm just talking to myself. I'll be right there."

After we finish cleaning up the remnants of dinner and tuck the kids into bed, I wander into the living room. The soft glow of the

fireplace casts flickering shadows against the walls, offering
warmth in the cozy space. I find the girls already huddled together
on our beloved pillowy white pit-style couch, a tradition they've
held onto as tightly as our Thanksgiving turkey itself. They're
wrapped up in their pajamas, the weight of the day giving way to
quiet relaxation.

Usually, this is their sacred time—just the three of them—but
tonight, the pull of the couch and the comfort of their closeness
are too strong to resist. For the first time in years, I decide to join
them, sinking into the softness beside my daughters, ready for
whatever conversation the crackling fire might bring. I sit in
between Ari and Lexi, and we all snuggle together in a big bear
hug. I haven't held my girls like this since they were little. I need
them as much as they need me.

"Mommy," Lexi reaches for my hand. "I miss Daddy." She
hasn't called me Mommy in years. Tears fill her blue eyes. "I'm
sorry. I shouldn't be doing this right now. You don't need this."

Her sisters hold her tight and close as she releases all she's been
holding back.

"You don't need to apologize. You're here with those who love
you. It's okay to miss Daddy. It's okay to cry," I say and hold my
daughter tight. She buries her head in my neck just like the day
her best friend moved across the country. Lexi tried to be happy
for her. Even at seven years old, watching her friend cry because
she had to leave, Lexi was the encourager—leading with empathy
but never showing her soul to anyone if she thought it would
upset them.

As a mother, I want nothing more than to tell her it is all
going to be okay. As a wife mourning the death of her children's
father, I cry with her.

"Lex," Lia lovingly addresses her sister, "We all deal with it
differently."

Ari moves to the other side of her sisters and leans into the
hug we are sharing.

"Lexi, I love you. You're my SHEro, and even SHEros cry." Ari hands Lexi a Kleenex.

Lexi looks up at her little sister, takes the tissue, and blows her red, stuffy nose.

"Thanks, baby sister. I love you too."

We sit there for a while, silently remembering Alex. I'm buried in thought. How do I move my family forward into days and years without him?

About ten minutes later, Ari takes a sip of her cold Baileys and coffee and immediately spits it back out into the mug, splattering all over her face.

"Ugh! Warning! Don't take a sip of your coffee. It's cold!" She exclaims.

They break into a belly laugh, partially at Ari's reaction but mostly to break free from the chains of sadness.

"Hey, dork! We've been sitting here for thirty minutes. Did you really think your coffee would stay warm?" Lia and Ari are always messing with each other. They are always playing practical jokes on each other.

"Here, girls, give me your mugs. I'll make a fresh coffee pot and freshen up your drinks." I gather the coffee cups and head to the kitchen.

The aroma of fresh coffee beans infiltrates my soul with memories of the past. I can't help but watch the girls through the archway that separates the dining room from the formal living room.

They are all spread out on the couch with their respective quilts Grandma Lolly made when they were kids.

"Hey, Ri-Ri," Lexi says, still congested from crying.

Ari rolls her eyes at the mention of her nickname, "It's Ari. Didn't you get the memo?"

"Yeah, whatever," Lexi laughs, and the girls chuckle along with her. You'll always be my little Ri-Ri."

They know the inside joke. When Ari was born, Lexi heard her dad and I call her our little Ariangel, so she decided on the nickname Ri-Ri. This was fine with Ari until she was in high school and suddenly became embarrassed.

I listen in on their conversation after I stop laughing at their silliness.

"Listen, Ariana, what is going on with you? You were very busy texting last night and this afternoon, and you never do that. Your cell phone hasn't left your side, even during dinner, which is a big *no-no* around here. I saw your phone tucked under your lap. I'm surprised Mom didn't say something." Lexi has always been inquisitive and wants to know everything about her sisters' lives. We all noticed her phone connected to her hip during dinner, but I didn't bother to say anything.

"What?" Ari's conspicuous smile was a dead giveaway. "Well, maybe there's someone I might have met..." Her voice trails off.

They are like little high school girls trying to find out who the one girl in their 'group' has a crush on.

Lia screams, "Ariana Charolette Kincaid! How come I know nothing about this? You tell me everything."

"Calm down, you weirdos! There's nothing much to tell... yet," she says covertly, which has all of them demanding more information.

The beep coming from the coffee pot catches my attention. I add a shot of Baileys to each cup of java, put them on the holiday serving tray and divide them up between all of us.

"Here we go girls. Nice and hot so don't forget to drink it this time." I look at my girls, who look like they were deviously planning something.

"What is going on here?" I act like I hadn't been eavesdropping on their conversation.

"Well..." Lexi starts to tell me what they had been talking about and that their sister has been keeping a secret from them, when Ari interrupts.

"Okay! Mom, nosey sisters, yes, I'm seeing someone. But it's not serious," she glares at Lexi, "Happy now?" Lexi throws the pillow at her like it's a basketball.

A wide smile reaches across Ari's face. That is something I've never seen before. It looks like love. "That's wonderful. Tell us everything! We can't wait to meet him," I say excitedly.

We all sip on our soul-warming libations and listen as the baby of our family tells us all about her new love interest. His name? Chadwick Rutger, Chad for short. He's a year older in age but not in school. She met him at NYU a few years ago in one of her pre-law classes. They've been in the same cohort, both have the same goals and career aspirations, and both have been accepted into Yale Law School next spring. The best part, she mentions, is that they've been friends for three years.

"Our relationship has grown into more than just friendship and we are going to explore the feelings we are having," Ari says.

"Oh my Lord, two attorneys. How many attorneys does it take to..." Lexi is joking.

Well, kind of.

"I think that's just great," I put my mug down and take Ari into my arms. "Why don't you invite him to come home with you sometime?"

"I will, Mom. I didn't think this was the right time. Plus, he's spending time with his family. They live in San Diego, so he doesn't get to see them often." That is all Ari is going to say. Hopefully, we will meet him in person the next time.

We talk for hours about everything. Memories of their dad seep into the conversation here and there, but mostly they just catch up on life outside of the sadness and heartbreak.

This is the best night we've had in years. We fall asleep talking in front of the fireplace, embers still burning when we wake up the next morning.

Chapter Three

January 14, 2019.

A soft, pre-dawn glow filters through the curtains, casting the room in a muted haze. The clock reads 6:00 a.m., but time feels suspended in the hush of the house. Silence presses in, thick and absolute. In the stillness, I'm acutely aware of the empty space beside me—a hollow stretch of sheets that still holds his absence. Four months without Alex, yet in that fragile moment between sleep and waking, my mind betrays me. For a split second, I forget. And then the remembering crashes in.

Mornings were always our thing. The early hours felt like stolen moments before the world demanded our attention. Alex had this habit of leaving me small sticky notes. Simple, scribbled messages that became tiny anchors in my day. A joke from yesterday, plans for dinner, or a quick "Love you." Over time, I'd gathered these notes and placed them in a shoe box.

The notes aren't grand declarations, but they're pieces of him, reminders of our everyday life together. Picking one up, I read his words, feeling a quiet connection to the love we shared. This morning, I need one of his morning notes more than anything.

The tradition of the notes started innocently enough. Early in our relationship, when we were still finding our rhythm, Alex would leave for work before I woke. The first one was a simple "Have a great day!" on a bright yellow sticky note.

The notes became our love language. We'd find them everywhere: the bathroom mirror, the fridge door, inside my favorite book. Sometimes funny, sometimes romantic, but always honest. A small, tangible way for him to stay with me throughout the day.

I roll out of bed, my feet touching the cold floor. A deep yearning pulls me to me towards my side of the closet where the shoe box lives. Fingering the lid, memories flood in, each note representing a unique day in our life together.

I pull out a faded yellow note. The ink has smudged, and the adhesive is no longer sticky. It reads, "Remember that dance in the rain? Let's do it again." My mind drifts back to that evening, early in our relationship. We'd been caught in a downpour and had danced, soaked to the bone, in a parking lot. The spontaneity, the pure joy of the moment, encapsulated our love.

Tears prick my eyes. Holding the note close, I make my way to the bathroom. On the mirror are the remnants of countless notes he'd written. I put them there in his last days. The note in my hand belongs there, but it doesn't stick. I rummage through the nightstand drawers until I find a small roll of tape. With care, I affix the note beside an older one that says, "Your smile lights up my world."

The physical act of taping it feels significant, like I'm preserving a piece of our past. These notes aren't just pieces of paper; they're memories, fragments of the love we shared. They remind me of the simple, everyday moments, the little things that made our love so special.

Stepping back, I look at the collage of memories on the mirror. Each note a testament to our story, each word a reminder of his love. I trace my fingers over them, feeling the edges of the paper, the bumps of dried ink.

Suddenly, another memory surfaces: it was our first anniversary. We'd had a small disagreement the night before, one of those pointless arguments that couples often have. I'd woken up, still feeling a bit hurt, a bit distant. But there, on the mirror, was a note from Alex: "Even on our cloudy days, I'd choose us. Always." That simple message bringing us back together.

That's the magic of these notes; they had the power to mend. I rummage through my nightstand, searching for a sticky note pad. Nothing. The mess of old pens, paper clips, and half-used notebooks clutter my vision. My pulse quickens as I turn to Alex's drawer—I need something to write on. I yank open the drawer, and my eyes land on a crisp, untouched package of neon sticky notes. A small relief. I tear off the plastic wrapping and pull out the top pad.

I start jotting down a random note, but soon, the words come faster than I expect. My hand moves ahead of my thoughts, and I realize this isn't just a note. It's a letter. The familiar pull of our old way of communicating tugs at me, and I surrender to it. This is how we've always connected—when speaking felt too heavy, we wrote. I reach into my nightstand, pull out a piece of stationery, and begin writing to him.

Hi, My Love.

Happy New Year. I made it through the holidays. My first of many without you. New Year's Eve was different, but having Ari and her new beau, Chad, here for the holidays was a gift I'll always cherish. Chadwick Rutger is perfect for our girl. I wish you could have met him. Did you hear Ari say they are moving in together when they get to law school in the fall? They are heading out right after graduation to set up their life together. They remind me of us, my love.

I'm not gonna lie, Alex. This hit me hard. Not because they're moving in together but because Ari is officially moving out of our home. Not only am I a widow, but I'm going to be an empty nester. I thought we would be empty nesters together.

The sun greeted me this morning, just as you used to with your warm embraces. Today, after what feels like an eternity, I'll return to my desk. It's been hard, love, accepting that there's a "new normal" without you in it. I wish every day I had the option to bring you back, but some choices are beyond us.

Lately, it's been easier to choose nothing—to remain cocooned in this numbness where the pain feels a little less suffocating. But I think of the girls and our grandchildren. What legacy would I leave them if I remained stagnant in my sorrow? Would they only remember the grief-stricken mother and grandmother or the resilient woman you always believed I was?

Most of all, Alex, what would you say if you saw me like this?

Battling with the pain inside feels endless, but today, I'll try to let the walls around my heart crumble a little. Today, I'll let myself feel—whether it's the piercing pain or a glimmer of hope.

Every morning, when I look into the mirror, I search for your notes, those little messages that filled my day with love and light. I miss them, just as I miss you.

More tomorrow morning, my love. Then I will talk about today.

I fold the letter with a sense of ritual, pressing each crease into neat, careful quarters. The envelope, a perfect match to the stationery, sits patiently beside me, waiting for the words I've poured out. As I slip the letter inside, the familiar weight of the paper triggers a flood of memories. It feels like muscle memory—this action we've repeated for years.

I press my tongue to the envelope's adhesive and am immediately taken back to a hospital room bathed in the soft, dim light of early morning. I'd just given birth to Ariana—a beautiful, unexpected gift. I was exhausted but overjoyed, cradling her tiny form in my arms. Alex, sitting beside me, pulled out a letter he had written earlier that day.

"Do you want me to read it?" he asked, his eyes sparkling with unshed tears.

I nodded, too tired to speak, but eager to hear his words. He unfolded the letter carefully and began to read. I remember watching him as his voice washed over me, his words soft yet steady. He spoke of how proud he was, how grateful he felt to have me as the mother of his children, and how much he loved the family we had built together. As he read, his hand reached over and rested on Ariana's tiny belly, his thumb brushing her blanket. She slept so peacefully, unaware of the love that was filling the room.

That was our way—writing letters to each other, even when we were right there. We would read them aloud or slip them into pockets to be found later. It was the intimacy of pen and paper, of the private, intentional moments we carved out for each other amidst the chaos of life.

I press the envelope shut, knowing this letter—like all the others—holds a piece of me.

Chapter Four

January 14, 2019.

I always believed that if I stopped writing, it would be because I ran out of things to say. But now, alone in the vast silence left by Alex's absence, I have to find a way to live, to survive. I'd made a promise to my agent to return this month.

I pull the chair out from my desk and pause, letting my eyes drift around the room. It feels foreign to be here, like I'm stepping into a museum of my former life. The last time I sat here, Alex was alive, his voice echoing in my mind as I glanced up from my work to find him watching me from the doorway. Now, the silence fills the space in a way that's almost suffocating. Three years have passed, yet it feels like he was here just yesterday, telling me I should take a break, go outside, and breathe.

The walls of my studio have become a gallery of memories. Photos of our family—smiling, bright-eyed—are framed and scattered on shelves, along the walls, in between my writing awards and accolades.

The stack of books on my desk has gathered dust over the years. Ideas abandoned mid-sentence when Alex fell sick. What was once my refuge for creativity now feels like a graveyard of unfinished thoughts. My window—the one I specifically chose when Alex built my studio—offers a breathtaking view of our property. I designed this room to inspire me, to be the place where I could lose myself in words. But now, all it does is remind me of the hollow space left behind.

I've avoided this place for so long, afraid of what it would mean to sit at this desk again without him. The desk, which was once a witness to my work, our love, and our plans for the future, now stares back at me, daring me to start again.

I bring my computer to life for the first time in what feels like an eternity. The chime, once so regular, now feels foreign yet strangely comforting. Despite the hesitation, the anxiety, and the weight of memories, being back here is a victory. A statement. Life goes on, no matter the heartaches.

My gaze drifts to the digital clock: 9:27 a.m. A slight panic bubbles up as I think of the impending Zoom meeting. Trying to remember my password feels like attempting to decipher an ancient language, but I manage to log in after a few frustrating minutes.

Jaci Dyson, my agent for almost ten years, welcomes me with a warmth that damn near breaks me. "Kelsi," she begins, her voice choked, "you have no idea how much I've missed seeing you." That sense of connection, that shared history between us, fills the digital void. Her concern is obvious, but there's also a hint of practical.

"Kelsi," Jaci says, her tone soft but that familiar sharpness still there. "You know, being away for so long gives room for others to claim your spot. I'm going to ask you straight out: Are you ready to pick up where you left off on the memoir project?"

I don't even hesitate before responding. "Jaci, I can't. It's not the same book anymore. I'm not the same person anymore. Our story ended when Alex died."

Jaci doesn't miss a beat. "That's exactly why you need to revisit this, Kelsi. What you've been through. The loss, the grief, it's something so many women can relate to."

I shake my head, already feeling the weight of the conversation pulling me down. "I don't want to write about it. I can't go back and relive all that pain, not for a book or anyone. The memoir is about our life together, about building something, not about it falling apart."

"You don't have to relive the pain, Kelsi. But you can write about moving forward, about what comes after. You were writing a love story, but life doesn't stop when that love ends. You still have a story to tell."

"Why does it have to be my story, though?" I argue, frustration bubbling up. "I don't want to monetize my grief, Jaci. Alex wasn't some chapter that I can just rewrite. He's gone. I'm a widow, and I don't know the first thing about healing. What am I supposed to write, that I'm broken and there's no happy ending?"

Jaci leans back in her chair, her eyes softening as she speaks. "You don't have to have all the answers. But think about the women who are feeling what you're feeling right now...lost, grieving, trying to figure out how to move on. You've always been honest in your writing. That's what readers connect with. It's not about selling your pain. It's about showing others that they aren't alone."

I exhale slowly, feeling the sting of tears. "I can do that through my fiction. I feel like I'm betraying Alex by turning our story into something for public consumption."

"It's not betrayal, Kelsi. If anything, you're honoring him by sharing what you had and how you're surviving without him. You already wrote the first draft about your life together. Now you have the chance to show how love evolves even after loss."

I look at the unfinished manuscript on my desk, buried under a pile of papers. The first draft had been full of hope, chronicling our marriage, our family, and how we built a life together. I had written it in the middle of our story, never imagining that the last chapter would come so soon.

"I don't think I can change the manuscript," I whisper. "It was our life. It was finished before I even knew it."

"It's not finished, Kelsi. You just have to keep writing. This isn't the ending. It's the next chapter. And you're not alone in this. I'll help you. Let's restructure the manuscript. Let's take the story where it needs to go."

I swallow hard, my chest tightening. "I'll think about it."

Jaci smiles, a flicker of triumph in her eyes, but I don't share it. The idea of opening that manuscript again sends a shiver of fear through me. It's not just revisiting the words; it's resurrecting ghosts. And that terrifies me.

"Kelsi, this will reconnect you with your readership. Think about it. Call me on Monday, and we will talk about our pitching strategy. In the meantime, I'm going to send you some small op-eds to get you back in the swing of things."

We wrap up our meeting, and the moment the call ends, my inbox fills with assignments. It's overwhelming, but the pull of the familiar, the rhythm of deadlines and words, offers a strange solace.

The next few hours are a blur of typing, brainstorming, and moments of intense focus. By the time 6:00 p.m. rolls around, my back aches, and hunger gnaws at me. Stretching, I feel every joint protest. I remember the morning jogs Alex and I used to enjoy, the shared commitment to self-care that got sidelined when he got sick.

I close my laptop, but the conversation with Jaci lingers, a quiet hum at the back of my mind. My gaze drifts across my desk and lands on the wedding photo that has sat there for as long as I can remember. It's a candid shot—one where neither Alex nor I knew the photographer was capturing the moment. We're laughing, heads thrown back, eyes bright with something unspoken, something electric.

Beyond the edges of the photo, my childhood backyard stretches wide—open fields bathed in the amber glow of a setting sun. In the background, Lolly cradles our four-month-old Lexi, her presence grounding us in a secret we had yet to share: I was already three months pregnant with Lia.

I reach for the frame, brushing my fingers over the glass. The memory rushes in, vivid and untouched by time: May 28, 1988, our wedding day. I can still feel the nervous energy coursing through me as I stood at the end of the aisle, my heart pounding —not from doubt but from the sheer weight of the moment because waiting for me at the altar was Alex.

He looked so handsome that day—his curls tamed just enough to be formal but still wild in the way that made me fall in love with him. His suit fit him perfectly like it was made for him, and his blue eyes were bright against the backdrop of the green hills. I remember how he couldn't stop smiling, even when the officiant tried to start the ceremony. He kept whispering to me, "You're beautiful, Kels. You're more beautiful than I've ever seen you."

I can still hear the way his voice cracked with emotion when he read his vows. We had decided to write our own, even though I wasn't sure if I'd be able to get through mine without crying. But Alex was calm and steady, like he always was. He promised me a life full of love, laughter, and endless letters. He said, "I'll never stop writing to you, Kelsi Jo, because even when words fail me, they never fail us."

After the ceremony, we snuck away from the reception for a few minutes. I had kicked off my shoes, and we sat under the big oak tree that overlooked my childhood home. Alex pulled a folded piece of paper from his jacket pocket—a letter he'd written me the night before the wedding. He read it aloud, his voice low and full of love. He talked about how, even though we'd been together for a while, he was still in awe of me. Of us. Of our little family. Of how far we'd come.

I glance back at the photo, my heart aching with the memory. I've held on to every letter, every moment, but this photo—it's more than just a picture. It's a reminder of the promise we made to each other. A promise that, even now, I feel bound to keep.

• • •

I enter the family room; my heart skips a beat. It's Alex. His familiar face, his comforting presence, evoking a mixture of joy and heartache.

"Kelsi, my love, you did it." His voice is loving and supportive, as always.

"Alex, you're here." I desperately want to hold him.

"You didn't think I would miss your first day back to work, did you?"

I smile and walk over to where I see his image.

"I love you, Kelsi. I'm proud of you." He reaches his hand out to touch mine. I blink and trip over the edge of the couch as I try to reach him. I look up, and he's gone.

"Alex? Alex? Come back. Let's talk..." But he's gone.

I enter the kitchen and pull two wine glasses off the wine rack. My hands tremble as I fill each one up.

I sit and drink both glasses alone, knowing he's not coming back, at least for this conversation. The night stretches ahead, a blend of nostalgia and hope. The house, expansive and empty, seems too big for a single soul. But as I sip the wine, lost in memories, I realize this is my path to healing, inching forward, one step at a time.

Chapter Five

January 21, 2019.

I crave human connection, not to fill the void Alex left but to accompany it.

The invitations keep coming—dinner plans, wine tastings, weekend getaways—each one a thread linking me to the life I once knew. Every text feels like a lifeline, a gentle tug urging me back into the familiar. Yet, instead of comfort, they tighten something deep inside me, pulling the delicate threads of grief just a little tauter.

Last night, I decided to join Eve and Charlie for one of their outings with our friends—an evening that should have been light and easy. Instead, it left me feeling like an alien in my own skin. We were at this upscale outdoor bistro, the kind of place with live jazz music and conversations that flow as effortlessly as the wine.

"It'll be good for you, Kelsi Jo. Just a few hours, no pressure." Eve had insisted.

But as I sat at that round table, surrounded by couples who seemed to speak their own language of inside jokes and shared histories—the ones Alex and I used to be a part of, I couldn't help but feel like a complete outsider. At first, they welcomed me with open arms, squeezing my shoulders and offering soft condolences.

Then, the conversations shifted.

"Do you remember that trip we all took to Napa last year?" Our friend Mila nudged her husband and directed her question to the group as she glossed right over me. Her face lit up like she was there once again, lost in the golden sun and rolling hills.

"Oh God, how could I forget?" another chimed in, her eyes sparkling. She let out a laugh, a sound so carefree yet so tied to the memory.

The table erupted in shared laughter, and the story took on a life of its own, growing bigger with every detail. They were all leaning in, lost in the reminiscence of their time in wine country when everything was just right. I watched them recount the night the men, already tipsy from too many tastings, decided to race through the vineyards in the dark. Eve leaned in close, her eyes warm with the memory. "You should have been there, Kels. That was a night to remember," she whispered, her lips curved into a smile.

They talked about the rich reds, the endless laughter, the indulgent meals beneath a sky full of stars, and I sat there, a little apart from the group, feeling the space that existed between us all. I swallowed hard, nodding, but I could only think about Alex. We'd never make new memories like that. The laughter and warmth of their stories felt like needles pressing into my skin, each a reminder that my life had veered onto a different path that no one at the table could follow. The laughter didn't feel shared anymore—it was something I watched from a distance, something I couldn't reach.

Then came the comment that sealed it. One of the women, with a sincere but misplaced smile, turned to me and said, "You'll find love again, Kelsi. You're still young, and there's someone out there for you. It's just a matter of time."

My stomach turned. The words weren't meant to hurt, but

they did. I didn't want to think about "someone else." My heart was still Alex's—how could they not see that?

I excused myself soon after, citing a headache, though it was more of a heartache. As I walked away from the table, I could still hear their voices trailing behind, still lost in their world, unaware of how they'd made me feel even more adrift than before.

I pulled into the driveway and let the silence of the car settle around me. The remnants of dinner lingered in my mind—the laughter, the easy conversation, the casual cruelty of their words.

You'll find love again.

It echoed, tossed at me like it was that simple as if love were something I could replace. As if Alex had left behind an empty space just waiting to be filled. But they didn't understand—how could they? My love for Alex wasn't a placeholder. It wasn't something temporary, something I could swap out when it became inconvenient. It was a part of me, woven into my very being.

I exhaled and stepped out of the car, the cool night air brushing against my skin as I walked toward the house. Moving through the familiar spaces, I felt the weight of his absence pressing against me. The house felt bigger now, stretched by the emptiness he left behind. But it wasn't the house or even Alex that called to me. It was my writing.

I made my way outside, my fingers grazed the worn wood of the studio door before I pushed it open. Inside, the air was thick with memories. I sat at my desk, running my hand over the smooth surface, remembering the last manuscript I had worked on here—the one I abandoned when Alex got sick. The one I couldn't bring myself to revisit because it felt like a betrayal. A betrayal of him, of us, of the life we had built together.

But something shifted.

Jaci's words lingered, her gentle push to start writing again stirring something inside me. This wasn't just about picking up where I had left off. It was about telling the truth. Capturing all of it—the love, the loss, the way it all unraveled. That dinner had made one thing painfully clear: no one really knew. They remembered Alex for his laugh, for the good times, but they didn't know what it had been like. What *we* had been through. They didn't know what it was like to be left with nothing but memories and no chance to make new ones.

I opened my laptop and stared at the blank screen, the cursor blinking in quiet anticipation. My fingers hovered over the keyboard.

Just write it. Share your story. I heard Jaci's voice in my head.

A few weeks ago, I would have resisted. I wasn't ready to relive it. But now, it felt *necessary*.

This wasn't just about revisiting the pain. It was about honoring the love we had, the life we built, and the way it had changed me.

Just as I placed my hands on the keyboard, my phone lit up, vibrating across the desk. Eve's name flashed on the screen, our smiling faces in the contact photo. I hesitated. I wasn't in the mood for her tipsy ramblings, but I answered anyway.

"Hey, Eve," I said, keeping my tone neutral, bracing myself.

"Kels...Kelsi Jo," she slurred, her words thick with too much wine. "I just wanted to check on you, you know, after...dinner."

Her voice wavered, and irritation bubbled in my chest. Before I could respond, a muffled voice cut in from the background— Charlie.

"Eve, stop slurring. Just talk to her. Like a normal person."

I squeezed my eyes shut, forcing myself to stay patient. "Eve, I'm fine," I said flatly, but she barely seemed to hear me.

"You'll find someone, Kels. I mean...eventually, right? It's not like...like you're done living." She let out a loose, wine-soaked laugh, but it grated against me like sandpaper.

My grip tightened around the phone. "Eve—"

There was a shuffle on the other end, then Charlie's voice came through, clearer, apologetic. "Kelsi, I'm really sorry about this," he said, his tone heavy with regret. "She's had too much, and I didn't stop her in time."

I swallowed the lump rising in my throat. "It's okay, Charlie."

"No, it's not," he said firmly. "Tonight wasn't easy for you, and I know she said some things that weren't…thoughtful. I just wanted to apologize for both of us."

His words hung in the air between us, and something twisted in my chest—a mix of gratitude and sadness. "Thanks, Charlie. I appreciate it."

"Look, we're here for you, okay? Eve will feel terrible tomorrow. Just take care of yourself."

I nodded, though he couldn't see me. "Take care of her," I murmured.

The call ended, leaving the studio eerily quiet. I stared at the phone for a long moment, the sting of the night still settling deep. Even the people who had known me the longest didn't really understand what I was going through. It was just one more reason to write.

Slowly, my fingers moved over the keyboard, hesitant at first, then steady. I wrote about the diagnosis, the long nights spent caring for Alex, the fear that never left me—the hope I held onto until the very last moment. And then the emptiness that followed.

I paused, my eyes drifting to the wedding photo on my desk. It was strange to think that we had no idea what was coming back then. No idea how much love, how much loss, our future would hold.

I took a deep breath and turned back to the screen.

The words came faster, as if a dam had broken. Everything I had been holding back was finally spilling onto the page.

Chapter Six

I hit *send* at 5 a.m., the weight of the manuscript settling over me like the dawn light filtering through the window. Typing *The End* for the first time felt surreal—like crossing the finish line of a race I never trained for. Last night, time became irrelevant, slipping away as I plunged headfirst into the final chapters of our story, into the life Alex and I shared when I became the head of our household. The quiet hours stretched on as I recounted three years of history I never expected to write, a history I didn't think would become part of my narrative.

As the words poured out, it felt like I was piecing together the fragments of my past, tracing the edges of memories that once seemed too painful to confront. I became both the historian and the keeper of our legacy, writing with a feverish urgency, as if telling our story—my story—was the only way to make sense of it all. Once I started, I couldn't stop. It was as if Alex was right there with me, guiding my hand, reminding me that our journey didn't end with his passing—it merely shifted.

"What made you change your mind?" Jaci's voice is sharp and curious, but there's also warmth beneath it.

I take a deep breath. "Last night...last night, I had dinner with Eve and some of our old friends. It was supposed to be a nice evening. But it wasn't." I pause, letting the weight of the evening settle in. "They kept reminiscing about trips and memories, things that Alex and I will never be able to do again. They didn't mean to hurt me, but every word felt like a punch. Then one of them—she had the audacity to tell me I'd 'find love again'."

There's a pause on the other end of the line, and I can hear Jaci softly inhale as though she's bracing herself for what comes next.

"Jaci, I couldn't take it. I excused myself, went home, and something just...snapped. I realized I had unfinished business with Alex, with the book, with everything. I've been holding onto grief like it's all I have left of him, but that's not true. There's so much more, so many memories, so much love." My voice cracks a little. "So, I sat down and wrote. I added ten chapters to the manuscript."

Jaci exhales slowly, processing my words. "Ten chapters?"

"Yeah," I whisper. "Ten. About everything from Alex's diagnosis, the years of illness, his death...and what came after. The widowhood. The emptiness. All of it."

The line is quiet, and for a moment, I worry she's going to tell me it's too much, too raw. But then she speaks, her voice soft and steady. "Kelsi, I'm proud of you."

I sit back, my body still heavy with exhaustion. "I realized last night that...I don't want to just sit here in the ruins of my life with Alex. I want to honor what we had. The book is not just about our perfect marriage anymore. It's about the real story. The sickness, the loss, and everything that followed."

Jaci's voice softens. "This is exactly what your readers need. Not the perfect fairy tale. The reality. The hard stuff. They'll connect with that."

"I wasn't sure at first," I admit, my voice trembling a little. "It felt like I was betraying Alex by rewriting the ending of our story.

But, I realize now that the story never really ended with his death. It's still going. I'm still here."

"You are," Jaci agrees. "And by sharing this, you're going to help so many people feel seen. They need your voice, Kelsi."

I nod, even though she can't see me. "I just...I don't want to capitalize on my grief."

"This isn't about that," Jaci says firmly. "This is about healing, for you and for others. It's about telling your truth. The money? The sales? That's secondary."

I blink away the tears gathering in my eyes.

"Now, I'm going to read every single word. But you...you need to get some sleep."

I smile faintly, rubbing my eyes. "Maybe a nap is a good idea."

After we hang up, I sit there for a moment, staring at the screen. This is the book I never wanted to write. And yet, it's the one that feels the most real.

I've started scouting widow support groups, something I never imagined I'd do. One, a Window for Widows, particularly caught my attention—the name itself echoes the confinement I've felt since Alex passed. I need that window, something to show me the world is still out there.

It's strange, gearing up to sit with strangers and share the raw edges of my grief, but maybe it's exactly what I need. As I climb the stairs to change, the emptiness of the house presses in on me, the silent rooms standing watch like sentinels of my solitude.

Reaching the landing, I pause and look around. The stillness here is real, a quiet that's worn out its welcome. I sit on the top step, my knees pulled up, my chin resting on them. Here, in the quiet, with the dust motes floating in the slanting sunlight, I feel the weight of the silence I've been carrying. It's time to step out, to seek voices that echo my own, to find a new kind of fellowship. Maybe it's time to let go of this quiet, to let new stories in.

My voice erupts, raw and untamed, the way I used to call out to the girls, to Alex, but now it's just a cry into the void—into this hollow house, down these silent stairs, through these deserted rooms. It's a plea to the emptiness that's taken up residence in my very soul.

"Is anyone there? Please, someone, answer me!" My words ricochet off the walls, unanswered. I surrender to the rush within. My sobs are as much a part of me as my breath, as they wash over me, through me. I'm a tempest, weathering my own storm. Eventually, the tears run dry, and I rise. One by one, I shut the doors to the girls' rooms, a silent salute to the past, to memories that cling like cobwebs. I turn away, closing each door on yesterday, on the echoes of laughter and life that once filled this space.

On a whim, I decide on an early dinner alone before the meeting. A glass of wine, a quiet table, my laptop, and a chance to gather my thoughts and do some revisions to my manuscript. In the bathroom, I steady my hands to paint over the grief etched onto my face. Makeup becomes my armor, hiding the shadows beneath my eyes, giving a flush of life to cheeks still damp from crying.

Grief, that relentless beast, has no empathy.

CHAPTER SEVEN

JANUARY 22, 2019.

The door of the Lake George Community Center swings open under my hesitant touch, releasing a gust of brisk air that catches the loose strands of my hair, sending them into a brief, fluttering dance. The women gathered by the entrance pivot toward me, their collective gaze piercing through the cold, wrapping around me like a shroud.

For a heartbeat, I consider running; the urge to flee from their silent stares is as fierce as the wind outside. But my feet carry me forward, steadied by a resolve I didn't realize I possessed until this moment. I remind myself as I step through the meeting room door—I am still here, still Kelsi, a woman who's grown her roots deep into the earth, a woman who's still standing even when the world tried to bring her to her knees.

I approach the small cluster of women standing closest to the door.

"Hi," I muster the warmest smile I can. "I'm Kelsi Jo Kincaid. I called earlier today. My apologies. I can't seem to recall who I spoke with. Is this the Windows for Widows meeting?"

A woman steps forward, her presence like a beacon. A glass of red wine cradled in one hand, the other reaching out to me, nails a splash of vibrant color against the stem's clarity.

"Kelsi, yes! I remember our call," she says, her voice a comforting blend of warmth and authority. "I'm Claire Holley, the president of our Lake George chapter. Welcome, it is so nice to meet you."

Claire strides toward me, and for a moment, the room seems to pause. Her tall, elegant frame moves with a fluid confidence that immediately draws my attention. She's striking. Her cropped, pixie haircut frames her face perfectly, revealing high, sculpted cheekbones that add a certain sharpness to her features. But it's her eyes—those clear, piercing blue eyes—that catch me off guard. They radiate warmth, yet there's an unmistakable strength behind them.

She's dressed in an effortlessly chic outfit—a tailored, cream-colored blouse tucked into dark high-waisted jeans that fit her tall frame like a glove. The sleeves of her blouse are casually rolled up to her elbows, adding a relaxed air to her polished look. A simple, silver necklace gleams at her collarbone, subtle but elegant, just like her. Her shoes, a pair of tan leather ankle boots, are practical but stylish, grounding her with a kind of easy grace.

As she gets closer, I can't help but notice how she commands the space around her—not in an intimidating way, but as though she belongs wherever she chooses to be. There's something effortlessly chic about her whole demeanor, from the way she carries herself to how her clothing complements her without trying too hard. It's as if the moment she steps into a room, people can't help but notice. Yet, despite her striking appearance, she seems completely grounded, her presence putting me at ease while also making me feel a bit unsteady in comparison. Her handshake is firm, her eyes kind, a lifeline in this sea of new faces.

With a fluid motion, Claire raises her voice slightly, carrying over the soft hum of conversation, "Ladies, this is Kelsi Jo. We hope she will be joining our wisterhood soon."

As the chorus of welcomes wash over me, Claire's hand

remains on my shoulder—a lifeline, warm and assuring. Her touch seems to steady the fluttering in my chest somehow, a grounding force amidst a swarm of new faces.

Claire guides me through the room with a gentle certainty, her introductions washing over me like waves. Names escape me, slipping through my grasp like water, but there's an unspoken understanding that, in time, I'll learn who they all are. Each woman's gaze, each nod, each handshake, is a silent pact of shared experiences yet to be told.

After making the rounds, we drift toward a couch that has clearly lived through countless stories, its tweed fabric worn by the weight of years.

"Please, sit down, Kelsi," Claire says, her tone enveloping me in a warmth that defies the chill of the Lake George air that lingers in the room.

Claire remains beside me as I sink into the cushion, a sentinel of compassion. Her presence is as commanding as it is comforting; for a fleeting moment, I'm struck by her resemblance to Charlize Theron—not just in looks but in the effortless grace with which she carries herself.

I muster a small smile, grateful for the embrace of this new community. "Thanks, Claire. And thank you for making me feel so welcome," I manage, the words carrying more weight than I anticipated.

"Our goal," Claire's voice is both soft and firm, "is to serve widows in our community, to help them thrive in widowhood by creating a community of women who understand each other's journey."

Her words stir something within me, and I glance down at the patchwork of donated rugs, the faux-terrazzo peeking through, a metaphor for the fragmented path I now walk. The prickle behind my eyes warns of tears that are all too eager to fall.

"It's okay to cry, Kelsi." Claire's voice drops to a whisper. Her hand is a gentle weight on my lap, permission granted.

I tilt my face toward her, surrendering to the emotion I've

held at bay. In Claire's gaze, I find an ocean of empathy, a mirror reflecting my own loss. In her eyes, I am understood. I am not alone. The weight of my tears feels cathartic as I choke out a heartfelt thank you through sobs, "Claire, thank you. I'm a stranger to you, and here you are, holding my hand like an old friend." Claire offers me a tissue with the same gentleness she's shown since I arrived. Our eyes meet, and I see an understanding in hers that reaches beyond words.

"Kelsi, we're friends now. We've been tethered by a shared thread of loss since the moment we each said goodbye to our partners. That's the heart of A Window for Widows—it's how we find each other," she explains softly.

As she speaks, I watch the room begin to shift. Widows break away from their groups, gravitating towards seats facing the modest stage set against the far wall of the auditorium—a place of solace transformed for various community gatherings.

Claire gives my shoulder a comforting squeeze. "Come, take a seat with me at the front. I always start our meetings with a few words of hope, sometimes a prayer or a quote. I like to introduce new faces, too, but only if that's okay with you?"

The notion of being introduced sends a jolt of anxiety through me, but I'm swiftly overridden by a surge of warmth, a sense of belonging.

"Please do. I'm ready," I respond, my voice firmer than I feel.

Nodding, she guides me to two vacant chairs near the stage. "Excellent," she says as we settle in, "Let's get started. You're amongst friends here, Kelsi."

And for the first time in a long time, surrounded by the empathetic faces of my new wisterhood, I believe it.

The microphone's abrupt screech is like a cold splash of water, jolting everyone in the room to the present. Claire offers a graceful smile, her composure unshaken, as she turns a minor mishap into a moment of light-hearted connection.

"Guess that's one way to make sure I have your full atten-tion," she jokes, the warm chuckle of the group easing the last remnants of tension from my shoulders. It's a small community here, but already it feels like a sanctuary.

Claire leans into the microphone again, this time her voice clear and soothing. "Welcome, everyone. It's wonderful to see so many familiar faces and some new ones here tonight. To begin, I'd like to share a bit of wisdom from someone who has always inspired me, Oprah Winfrey," she pauses, her gaze sweeping over the crowd, making each of us feel seen. She says, 'Living in the moment means letting go of the past and not waiting for the future. It means living your life consciously, aware that each moment you breathe is a gift'."

The words settle in my chest like a gentle reminder. I'm here, living, breathing, surrounded by souls who understand the precious weight of each moment we've been given. A soft sigh escapes me, a release I didn't know I needed, as I allow myself to be in this moment, in this new chapter truly. A gift, indeed.

Claire waves at me from across the room, her dazzling smile instantly cutting through the murmur of the chapter meeting. I feel a flicker of relief to have made at least one solid connection. I straighten up a bit, waving back, feeling a little off-balance. The meeting had been heavier than I expected—raw stories of loss, heartache, and survival—and although I came here seeking connection, now that it's ending, I can't shake the nerves creeping up my spine. This is all new territory for me, meeting people in a space where the unspoken thread binding us is grief.

As she approaches, I think back to her introduction during the meeting. She had mentioned her wife, Sam, so casually, so effortlessly. It surprised me, maybe more than it should have. I'm not sure why it caught me off-guard, but I know it has something to do with my mother, Marissa. My mother, who never made space for anything that didn't fit into her narrow view of the world. A same-sex marriage would've been completely beyond her comprehension, another 'flaw' she would've judged mercilessly.

But I'm not my mother.

"Hi, Kelsi." Claire's voice pulls me from my thoughts. Her tone is light, and there's an ease in the way she says my name. "How did you like the meeting?" Her blue eyes are locked into mine, making me feel like she truly wants to know.

"I, uh, I wasn't sure what to expect, but it was…good. Emotional, but good," I stammer a little too quickly. God, I hope I don't sound like a complete mess. Suddenly, the room feels a little too warm, and I clasp my hands together to steady them.

Claire's smile never falters. "It takes some time, but you'll get used to it. Everyone's just trying to figure out their own path through this," she says, her voice filled with understanding. "We all started where you are."

I nod, feeling a little more grounded by her calmness. Something about the way she speaks makes me want to relax, but my nerves won't quite settle. Maybe it's just being around so many new people, or maybe it's the weight of everything I've been carrying since Alex died. Either way, I feel exposed, like I don't belong yet.

"How long have you been a part of the group?" I ask, hoping to keep the conversation going without fumbling over my words.

"About three years. I took over the role of chapter president about a year ago. No one else seems to want it." She giggles, casually tucking a loose strand of hair behind her ear. "It really helped me after Sam passed. It's one way I can give back." Her tone softens, but she doesn't linger in the sadness. There's something remarkable about the way she balances the weight of her grief without letting it drown her.

Before I can say anything more, Claire gestures toward the front of the room, where a few of the other women are chatting. "Did you hear about the Grand Canyon trip we're planning?" she asks. "We try to organize group trips a couple of times a year. It's a good way to get out of your own head and connect with nature and each other."

I raise my eyebrows, genuinely intrigued. The idea of getting away, of being somewhere vast and open, sounds freeing. "I did hear them mention it," I say. "It actually sounds kind of amazing."

Claire grins. "You should come. It'll be fun, and trust me, everyone's super supportive. Plus, the canyon...it does something to you. Puts everything into perspective."

I nod, considering it. Maybe it's exactly what I need—something big and raw, something that can hold the enormity of everything I've been feeling.

"I'm really glad you came today, Kelsi."

I smile, finally feeling like I'm on solid ground again. "Me too. It was...hard, but I think it's what I needed."

I glance down at my watch, "I've got to get going," I say, reaching into my bag to grab my phone. "But maybe we could exchange numbers? I'd love to hear more about the trip, and... well, it's nice to meet someone who gets it."

Claire's smile broadens. "Of course." We exchange numbers, and as she saves my contact, she adds, "Don't hesitate to reach out, okay? Even if it's just to talk."

I nod, feeling a flicker of something I haven't felt in a long time—hope, maybe. As I head toward the door, I glance back at Claire and wave one last time.

Chapter Eight

April 1, 2019.

I'm feeling a resurgence of energy with each new day. Inspiration flows into my work, and somehow, I'm finding the inspiration to write my healing. I'm knee-deep into the edits of *Until I Found Me: A Memoir of Wiving and Widowhood*.

April is when Lake George truly comes alive. After a long winter, the allure of spring unfolds. The snow has retreated, hopefully not to return until the distant months of fall. The trees burst with fresh leaves, and the blooms are a feast for the eyes, although tough on the allergies. Lake George in the spring is a fresh start—a visual promise of renewal.

A Window for Widows has been a blessing. I became an official member in March at our quarterly dinner. In the last few months, I've made many new friends, but it's my friendship with Claire that has deepened significantly. From that very first meeting, Claire and I have developed a strong, close bond.

However, the new friendships I've nurtured haven't exactly been celebrated by Eve. There's an underlying tension, a sense that I'm drifting away from old connections as I forge new ones with these women who understand the path I'm now navigating.

Over the last four decades, we've shared moments that shaped our lives—college roomies, graduation, marriages, laughing over coffee, traveling the world together—she's Lexi and Lia's Godmother. The bond between us has been irreplaceable. But lately, our paths are diverging in ways I never anticipated. While I am learning to navigate life as a widow, finding myself again, Eve and Charlie have the freedom to explore new adventures that don't include me. And I'm okay with that.

Our once-intertwined lives are slowly moving in opposite directions, growing further apart with each passing day. I've thrown myself into my work with Windows for Widows, filling my time with meetings and activities that not only help me but others like me. It's been a while since I've spent substantial time with Eve and our old group of friends. She's noticed, of course —she mentioned it with a hint of concern the last time we spoke. It's a reminder that maintaining friendships is a delicate balance, especially when your life begins to shift in unexpected ways.

Feeling that familiar gap widening between us, Eve reached out with a phone call. She sounded eager, almost insistent, wanting to pin down a time for just the two of us. She knows I've been spending more time with Claire, my new friend from the widow's group, and I can sense her discomfort. She doesn't fully understand the solace I've found in my newfound circle or why Claire seems to have taken up so much space in my life.

Today, I wake up remembering I have a coffee date with Eve. It's been a few months since we last caught up face-to-face, and I'm genuinely looking forward to it. We're meeting at The Coffee Bean, our local café, at 9:00 a.m.

As I finish getting ready, a sharp 'ding' signals a new message on my phone. A text from Eve confirming our coffee date:

Good morning. Still on for coffee at 9?

The message strikes me as formal, almost uncharacteristically so for her. I quickly reply with enthusiasm:

> Good morning! We sure are. I can't wait to see you!!!!!!! Should be there 9 a.m. sharp! Love you!

See you soon.

Outside, the weather is a perfect 68 degrees. After months bundled up, everyone is eager to break out their shorts and tank tops. I opt for my favorite Michael Kors slim-fitting jeans, a light knit peach-colored sweater, and tan-leather open-back loafers. I straighten my shoulder-length auburn hair and apply light makeup and pale pink lipstick, redefining middle-aged beauty in my own subtle way.

I pull into The Coffee Bean at exactly 9:00 a.m., scanning the parking lot for Eve's car—but she's not here yet. The moment I step inside, the rich, velvety scent of freshly brewed coffee wraps around me, warm and familiar, like an old friend. The hum of quiet conversation blends with the soft hiss of the espresso machine, creating a rhythm as comforting as the scent itself. Behind the counter, two young baristas, bright-eyed and busy, glance up with easy smiles. "Sit anywhere you'd like," one says, gesturing toward the scattered tables bathed in soft morning light. "We'll be right with you."

I spot the perfect place for us—just beyond the tables are a couple of leather couches arranged like cozy living room spaces, each featuring a small couch, loveseat, and end tables. The areas are divided by a wood-burning fireplace, always aglow with a log or two. These spots are coveted, especially in the mornings, and today, I'm lucky enough to claim one for us.

Just as I sink into the plush leather couch, the soft chime of the front door catches my attention. I glance up, and there she is—Eve, scanning the room with an air that still turns heads even after all these years. Her stride is confident and purposeful, as though the world itself would adjust to make room for her. Her hair, now streaked with silver and tied back in a loose knot, sways slightly with each step, and her earrings—oversized and jangly—catch the light, sending little prisms across the room. Eve has always had a way of commanding a space, her presence is electric, her energy almost tactile.

Her vibrant scarf drapes casually over a long, flowing jacket, the kind only she could wear without looking ridiculous. People notice Eve. They always have.

Even in her fifties, there's a youthful restlessness about her—the same free-spirited magnetism she carried through college, arms full of sketchbooks, leaving a trail of chaos and charm in her wake. But today, her movements are sharp, almost clipped, as if she's carrying a weight she doesn't want anyone to see.

When she sees me, a smile spreads across her face, but it doesn't quite reach her eyes. For a brief moment, her gaze flickers, and I can't tell if it's the overhead light or something unspoken passing between us.

I wave a little too eagerly, hoping to smooth over the awkwardness settling into my chest. She catches the gesture and starts toward me, her chin lifted just slightly higher than usual, her steps more deliberate. She looks beautiful, as always.

As she draws closer, I notice the tightness in her jaw and the way her fingers clench the strap of her oversized bag like she's holding on for dear life. Her presence fills the room, but it feels different this time. Charged. Tense. And yet, when she finally reaches me, she leans in with a dramatic flourish, her scarf sweeping the air as she kisses my cheek.

"Kelsi," she says, her voice warm but with an edge I can't place. "Always the picture of comfort, aren't you?"

Her words are light, almost playful, but there's an undercurrent there, a sharpness that catches me off guard. I laugh softly, brushing it off.

I open my arms wide, embracing her. The familiarity of her

hug floods me with a sense of home. It's been too long since we've shared this simple, comforting gesture.

"Eve, it is so good to see you. I have missed you so much," I confess, the relief and joy mingling in my voice.

Eve squeezes me tighter. "I've missed you too, Kels. More than you know. You look beautiful, and—you know what? You look happy." Her words are sincere, but I sense her probing, trying to understand the changes she sees in me.

"Let's sit," I suggest, motioning for a server. "Have you eaten, or are you just here for a strong cup of coffee?" I giggle, remembering her usual caffeine-heavy routine.

"I stopped drinking coffee right after Alex died. See, you don't know me as well anymore, do you, Kelsi?"

Eve's tone is playful yet pointed. She wants me to know she's been changing, too, exploring new interests and routines. Although, I'm not sure why Alex's death has anything to do with her timeline.

"I wouldn't say that, Eve. I think I know you pretty well," I reply, but her comment unsettles me, hinting at tensions I hadn't anticipated.

The server arrives, and we place our orders. I choose an Americano and a fruit bowl, while Eve opts for chamomile tea and a gluten-free vanilla scone—choices that underline how we've both changed in small but significant ways.

As the server departs, a thick silence settles between us, filled with unspoken questions and concerns. I can feel the weight of Eve's gaze and the shift in our dynamic. I turn to face her, hoping to bridge the gap with conversation.

"Eve, are you okay? Have I done something to upset you?" My voice trembles with emotion.

"It's what you haven't done," she begins, her voice catching. "The way you've just gone on with your life...it feels like you've abandoned our friendship." Tears start to streak down her cheeks.

I'm taken aback. I've never wanted to hurt Eve.

"I know, Eve. I'm sorry. It's not because I don't love you or cherish what we have. I'm just...in a different space now. A healing space."

"A healing space?" Eve cuts in sharply. "We've always been each other's support. But since you joined that widows' group, you've been MIA. You've replaced our coffee dates and monthly group dinners with your meetings. None of us understands. You know we've all been here for you, especially through the darkest days."

The raw honesty in her words stings. "I'm so sorry for hurting you and everyone else. That was never my intention. But as a widow, my life is different now. Being with others who understand exactly what I'm going through has been vital. It's helped me breathe again."

Eve shakes her head, unconvinced. "Honestly, your apology seems disingenuous." Her words cut deeper than she probably intended, leaving me speechless.

I search her face for the friend I know, but all I see now is resentment.

"What is going on, Eve? This isn't like you. You've never been the argumentative or jealous type." The space between us, once filled with easy laughter and shared confidences, now feels like an insurmountable divide.

"Jealous? You think I'm jealous of you and your life? Well, I'm not. Believe me, I have no desire to walk in your shoes."

Listening to Eve lob tightly wound balls of insults at me is a new and unsettling experience. I sit stunned, not knowing how to respond. Over the years, I've cherished our friendship. Through her tumultuous breakups and family dramas, I've never seen Eve like this. The waitress arrives with our drinks and breakfast at that moment, placing them down swiftly and retreating from what she can clearly sense is a heated exchange.

Eve takes a sip of her tea, her words sharp as she speaks. "Listen, we all know you've been mourning since Alex died. We've *all* been mourning him." She looks away. "We expected changes, but dropping us for some widows' group? That wasn't on anyone's radar."

I'm not looking to fight, especially not here, but I can't let her misconceptions stand. I steady my voice, trying to keep composed.

"Eve, you're not being fair. These women, my widowed friends, they're not just 'some group'. They've lost partners and soulmates. We're helping each other, empowering one another to face the world again, to live fully despite our grief."

Eve merely shrugs, biting into her scone. I push forward, heart heavy but hopeful.

"I'd love for you to meet them, Eve. Especially Claire."

"Claire. The one you've been spending so much time with?" Her tone drips with sarcasm, making it clear she's not interested.

I can't help but brighten a bit as I speak of her.

"Claire heads up a Window for Widows. She welcomed me at my first meeting, scared as I was. She's become a mentor to me."

"Your mentor?" Eve scoffs. "Why do you need a mentor? You're a grown woman and successful writer, Kelsi. What could you possibly need mentoring for?"

"Because losing Alex thrust me into a reality I was utterly unprepared for. I was lost, adrift. And these feelings of loss...Claire understands them. She guides me through them. Claire lost her wife four years ago..."

"Wait, her wife?" Eve interrupts. "You mean her husband, right?"

"No, Eve. Claire had a wife who died in a tragic accident. This group is for any woman who's lost their partner."

Eve's confusion shifts quickly to disbelief. "I thought this was a group for widows. You know, women who've lost husbands?"

I correct her gently but firmly. "It is a widows' group, Eve. It's about losing a spouse, regardless of gender."

Eve smirks, dismissing my explanation.

"Kelsi, really? And you're sure Claire isn't just...hitting on you or others? Maybe this group is just her way to meet women."

Her words slice through the tender space between us, and I'm left speechless, not just by her misunderstanding but by the venom behind it. That's all I can take. I stare at the woman next to me, feeling like I'm seeing her for the first time. Is this really Eve? Or has she always harbored these thoughts, and I've just been too enamored by our friendship to see this side of her? We've never discussed same-sex relationships before; we've never needed to.

"Are you serious right now, Eve?" My voice trembles, not with rage, but with a profound sadness. "We're fifty-three years old, behaving like petulant teenagers. This isn't us. What you're saying is not only wrong but also deeply hurtful. You're insulting me by insulting my friend." I pause, gathering my composure before I continue, "Claire's love for her wife is no different from my love for Alex, or your love for Charlie. Her loss isn't less significant because her partner was a woman. Claire and Samantha fought for the right to marry, a battle many same-sex couples have endured. They raised a son together, a family torn apart by a sudden, tragic death. Through her healing, Claire gives back to us all, helping those of us who've faced losses so profound, we never thought we'd recover."

"I think we're done here today. This isn't the reunion I envisioned when I asked you to meet." Eve looks away.

The words cut deep, reopening wounds I thought had begun to heal. Tears stream down my face as a familiar sense of loss washes over me. I want to rewind, to erase this entire conversation and start anew, but it's too late. The words hang heavy between us, and Eve seems ready to let our friendship sink into oblivion without a second thought.

I gaze across the table at the woman who was my best friend for the better part of my life. "I love you, Eve. I will always be here for you, but you have to want our friendship. And right now, it feels like you don't want anything to do with me."

As the final words escape my lips, Eve doesn't even glance up. My heart sinks as I grab my sweater and purse, lay a $20 bill next to my untouched coffee, and walk out without looking back. Eve lets me go without a second glance.

I sit in my car, gripping the steering wheel as a mix of anger and sorrow swirls inside me. We haven't had a falling out like this since I told her I was dating Alex.

For a fleeting moment, I imagine Eve might come after me, that she might see me sitting here in my car, that we might share tears, a hug, and apologies. But when Eve does walk out, she sees me and dismisses my attempt to reconcile with a firm shake of her head. She puts her hand up, signaling an end to our conversation, and swiftly drives away. The numbness sets in as I struggle to process the fracturing of a decades-long friendship.

CHAPTER NINE

May 17, 2019.

Losing a best friend after nearly four decades feels like burying a part of your own soul—an ache that echoes with every memory. It's not just the absence; it's the weight of a lifetime spent together now transformed into a haunting silence. They linger in your mind like an unfinished symphony, a phone call or text away, yet unreachable, bound by a choice that feels more like betrayal than goodbye. Those awkward run-ins around town feel like stumbling into a ghost—an uncomfortable reminder of a bond that was once unbreakable. After countless attempts to reconcile our friendship, I let Eve go.

My involvement with Windows for Widows has been a profound source of solace, offering both comfort and community in a way I never expected. The women in this group—now dear friends—have become woven into the fabric of my healing journey. Through our weekly meetings, events, and group trips, we've built a bond rooted in shared experience and unwavering support.

Now, that journey leads us to an exhilarating three-week adventure—a guided hike through the Grand Canyon, followed by a stay in Las Vegas filled with dazzling shows and a little gambling. The anticipation hums within me; every step of this trip feels like a declaration of resilience, a testament to my commitment to moving forward.

This will be my first major trip without Alex—a bittersweet milestone that stirs a whirlwind of emotions. Claire and I are rooming together for the entire trip, a shift that feels both unfamiliar and comforting. I haven't shared space with anyone outside of family since college, but through this grief journey, Claire has become my anchor, my closest friend. Her own experience with loss, combined with her years as a trained psychotherapist, gives her an insight that resonates deeply—a guiding light through the darkness we both know too well.

* * *

TWO WEEKS LATER

Everything unfolds seamlessly. Though I felt Alex's absence like a shadow beside me all day, it no longer consumed me. Instead, the breathtaking beauty surrounding me—the vast canyon, the laughter of my friends, the shared experience of something new— felt unexpectedly fulfilling. The sights of our hike, so different from the places Alex and I once explored together, stirred something deep within me—not just longing, but a quiet awakening. In the juxtaposition of grief and wonder, I found not just memories of the past, but the promise of what's still to come.

Long after the others have gone to bed, I find myself writing by the dim light of the hotel balcony; the colors of the night canyon spill across the pages of my draft. I can't help but think of Lolly. Next to my father, she was the fiercest champion of my writing. Her passion for storytelling illuminated my own path as an author.

I vividly recall the first short story I ever wrote in sixth grade. I won my first writing award for "My Secret Garden." The title reflective of the time I spent in my dad's garden with him.

My father was—and still is—a man deeply rooted in the earth. His hands were never still. By day, he was the proud owner of Barker's Boats, a family-run boat-building business on Lake George, passed down from my great-grandfather Barker. The legacy skipped a generation, in a way—Dad inherited the company by default after his own father walked out on Lolly to start a new family. He was only ten then, too young to run a business, so the workshop was dark for a few years.

But by sixteen, he was drawn to the craft, spending his afternoons learning to build boats and helping Lolly make ends meet. Over the next five decades, Barker's Boats became a fixture in the Lake George community. When retirement finally called, he offered the reins to my brother, Cory, who never shared the same passion. With no one to carry it forward, Dad sold the business about five years ago and made a permanent move to his vacation home in Boothbay, ME.

One thing he has never given up is his love of gardening. He always has to be growing something. Some of my best childhood memories were spent with my father, digging in the soil and exploring the earth.

The idea for "My Secret Garden" bloomed one warm spring afternoon. I must have been about ten, tagging along behind my father in the garden as he worked. He was on his knees, hands deep in the soil, carefully placing seedlings into neat rows, each one cradled as if it were a tiny treasure. It was the kind of spring day where the world felt like it was coming alive just for me—the air heavy with the scent of freshly turned earth and the delicate vibrancy of new green pushing up from the ground.

I was mesmerized by the transformation happening in my father's hands. To him, gardening was more than a pastime; it was a ritual, a connection to something deeper. He would murmur to his plants, offer them small reassurances. Watching him, I sensed the weight of what we were doing together—how this wasn't just a garden, but a place where life was shaped and nurtured, a place that held his devotion and, in turn, held us.

That day, as we worked side by side, my father handed me a packet of seeds and said, "Go ahead, pick a spot. This part of the garden will be yours." My very own piece of earth to tend and care for—it felt like a sacred trust. I chose a small, shaded corner where I could plant marigolds because I loved the way their bright, cheerful blooms looked like tiny suns. I began to think of it as my own secret garden, hidden away in the safe embrace of my father's larger, protective one. I never had quite the green thumb my father did, but he taught me how to tend it and keep it alive.

So, when my sixth-grade teacher announced a school-wide writing contest a few weeks later, I found myself returning to that memory. I wanted to capture that feeling—the quiet, sacred magic of the garden and the bond it represented between my father and me. In the evenings, I would sit by my window, my journal opened on my lap and write about that tiny corner of the earth, that hidden sanctuary that felt like an extension of myself.

In "My Secret Garden," I wrote about a girl who discovers a hidden, overgrown garden behind her home. She clears the weeds, nurtures the plants back to life, and, in the process, learns to believe in her own strength and resilience. Although I didn't realize it then, that girl was a reflection of me. She was discovering, just as I was, that there was a special kind of power in bringing life to something, in coaxing it to grow with patience and care.

When I entered my story in the competition, I never imagined it would win. But a few weeks later, the principal's voice echoed through the school auditorium as she announced that I'd won first place. I don't think Dad knew how much that meant to me. In that moment, the story was no longer just about a girl with a garden; it was a tribute to my father. It was a way of saying thank you and acknowledging the small sanctuary he had created in his garden and my life, giving me the space to grow and find my roots.

It was also a reflection of my Lolly. In winning that award, I discovered the power of storytelling—that a single story could capture a moment, a feeling, and preserve it like a photograph pressed between pages. The garden became more than a memory. It became the seed for something much bigger, for a future I couldn't yet see but felt certain would be shaped by the love and care of that quiet place, my own secret garden.

The first person I called when I got home from school that day was Lolly. She was ecstatic.

"You did it, Kelsi Jo," she whispered, full of emotion. "You're a writer, honey. A real writer. Don't ever let anyone steal your words. Your voice is a gift, and the world needs to hear it."

I've carried those words with me for a lifetime. I feel her words again back here in the canyon, miles and years away. They resonate in the quiet night and now I realize how much of this journey is still hers—her voice in my words, her encouragement in every sentence I write, her legacy in every story I dare to tell—especially my own.

The air is crisp and biting but feels good on my skin, keeping me grounded. I stare out at the horizon, my laptop balanced on my knees, fingers hovering over the keys but unmoving. I don't even hear the sliding glass door until it's too late.

"Trouble sleeping?" Claire's voice drifts toward me, gentle and concerned, pulling me from the fog of my thoughts.

I look over, surprised but warmed by her presence. "Oh, did I wake you? I didn't mean to—"

She shakes her head, wrapping her arms around herself for warmth. She's in her thermal long-johns, with a beanie pulled snugly over her head, looking both cozy and a little ridiculous in the best way. She sits across from me at the little round glass table, her eyes soft in the dim glow of the porch light. "I just got up to go to the bathroom and saw your silhouette out here. Thought I'd check on you."

I nod, feeling a pang of gratitude for her quiet companionship.

"Still working on the manuscript?" she asks, glancing at my laptop.

"Yeah," I say, sighing as I shut it slightly. "Just...finishing up the final edits. Hoping to send it off to my editor soon."

The silence between us settles, a comforting weight. Claire doesn't fill it with meaningless words and doesn't push me to say more than I'm ready to. That's one of the things I admire most about her—she knows when to hold space and when to lean in. And right now, that makes all the difference.

I find myself speaking before I even realize what I'm about to share. "You know, Alex was my biggest fan. Even in his last few months, he'd ask me to re-read every single page to him." A small, sad laugh escapes me. "I think he'd heard each of my books at least five times."

Claire listens, eyes never leaving mine, her focus unwavering. She doesn't interrupt; she just gives me that space, and it feels like an invitation to keep going.

"Shortly after his diagnosis, I quit writing," I say softly, the words tasting bittersweet. "I needed to be there for him. I didn't want to miss a single doctor's appointment, a single moment. I cooked every meal and made sure the house was always spotless and that he always felt comfortable in his surroundings. The last few months of his life we barely left the house." My voice shakes, a vulnerability spilling out I didn't know I'd been holding onto. "Until finally, Lexi stepped in and insisted on hospice care."

Claire reaches across the table, her hand finding mine, her palms warm from her breath. Her touch anchors me, and we sit like that for a moment, wrapped in the silence that follows, the memories hanging in the cool air between us.

"I wrote about it," I say finally, my voice barely a whisper. "I didn't think I could...or even should. But it poured out of me, every raw, unpolished moment."

There's a vulnerability in sharing this with her, an old shame lingering from my years of perfectionism, the belief that my pain should be neatly tucked away, not displayed. But Claire's eyes hold a gentle strength, a quiet understanding that somehow gives me permission.

She squeezes my hand. "Will you read it to me?"

I nod, swallowing back the tears prickling at the edges. "Yeah...I'd like that."

I open my laptop again, pull up the pages, and begin to read. The words spill out, raw and jagged, but as I read them to her, they begin to feel less like scars and more like pieces of myself I'm ready to embrace. And with each word, I feel a weight lifting.

In the final months of Alex's life, I became someone I didn't recognize. I moved in a rhythm that didn't feel like mine—a quiet dance of care. Every morning, I'd make the bed with military precision, smoothing out every wrinkle in the sheets as if a perfect bed could somehow keep him here a little longer. I measured out his medication with trembling hands, kept the house spotless, arranged fresh-cut flowers in every room, their scent a hopeful distraction from the sterile smell of illness. And I didn't stop. I couldn't stop, even as my own spirit frayed at the edges.

They say grief doesn't wait for the last breath. It begins long before, in the quiet moments when you realize that 'forever' has an expiration date, and the promises whispered in the early days of love suddenly feel like desperate pleas to time itself.

In those months, I lived for him. Every moment, every gesture, was a testament to the life we'd built together, to the vows we'd made decades earlier. But there was also something else, something I can only see now in the raw hindsight of widowhood: I was clinging to my own need to be enough. Enough to fill every void, heal every hurt, soften every blow of reality. I held onto the idea that my love, my care, and my endless acts of service could somehow anchor him to this world. In a way, I was not only fighting death— I was fighting the loss of my own identity. I was the wife, the mother, the caretaker, the perfect companion. And what was left when all that was gone?

The day hospice came to our home, I relinquished a fraction of my duties, trusting this unknown person with the one person who gave me purpose; Lexi held me as I broke, my body trembling with a release that I didn't know was possible. Letting go of him, even partially, meant letting go of the role that had defined me. And in that moment, I felt naked, stripped of every title I'd clung to. I was just Kelsi. Not Alex's wife, not his caregiver. Just a woman, shattered but alive.

That unraveling had a terrible beauty —a painful, almost sacred truth. I had given him everything, and yet, somewhere along the line, I had lost pieces of myself. But now, those pieces call to me, pulling me back to life, to my own story, waiting patiently in the quiet spaces he left behind.

As I glance at her across the table, I see her wipe a tear from her cheek. And I realize, maybe for the first time, that I don't have to carry all of this by myself. Claire and I have become the best of friends.

Chapter Ten

August 26, 2019.

Lia raises her glass, her eyes shining with pride. "To Mom, Happy Birthday!" she says, her voice brimming with emotion. "And to *Until I Found Me: A Memoir of Wiving and Widowhood*, the story that had to be told, and the one only you could write. Here's to the woman who has shown us strength, resilience, and the power of finding yourself, even when it feels impossible."

I feel my cheeks flush as the people I love most join her in lifting their glasses. Sitting to my left, Lexi beams at me, her arm resting on Wendall's shoulder, who nods with quiet admiration. Across from us sit their three children, Maddi and Finni, their faces alight with excitement as they clink their sparkling juice glasses together. Beside them, Brody, who's barely able to sit still, stares in awe at the scene, his eyes wide with wonder at the adults' toasts and the sparkle of the chandelier overhead.

Next to Lia is Doug, who sits with their two boys—now five and six years old—each eager to raise their own glasses and be part of the celebration. The boys' small hands wrap around their cups, mirroring the adults', and their eyes dart around the table, soaking in the laughter and shared glances.

At the far end of the table, Claire sits quietly, a soft smile on her face as she watches the gathering unfold. This table has been our gathering place for years, a symbol of family and togetherness, and tonight, it feels richer and fuller—a celebration not just of my birthday but of the journey that brought us all here.

I see the pride, the joy, and the quiet strength in each face, and for the first time, I feel the true weight of what I've accomplished and the love that has carried me here. Lexi leans over, clinking her glass against Lia's and then Wendall's before looking at me.

"You did it, Mom. This isn't just another book. This is *the* book—the one that lets the world get to know you a little better."

Her words hit me like a wave, the truth of them settling deep. "Thank you, Lexi," I manage, my voice barely a whisper, but she nods, understanding all the things I can't quite say.

"To Glammy's book!" chimes in Maddi, her glass of sparkling juice clinking eagerly with her sisters and cousins. They're grinning, their innocence wrapping around my heart like a warm blanket. "We're gonna read it, right, Glammy?"

I laugh, setting the champagne bottle down and gathering my composure. "Maybe in a few years, sweetheart," I say, reaching over to pat her hand. "This one's a bit...grown-up."

Claire leans forward, a mischievous twinkle in her eye. "But they'll have plenty of time to understand and be inspired by it. After all, they have a pretty amazing role model right here."

The table murmurs in agreement, and I feel the weight of the journey it took to get here—a book I started years ago, that Alex read in pieces from my early drafts, the story of our life that has now transformed, evolved, become something more. I glance at Claire, who gives me a small, encouraging nod.

"Thank you, everyone," I say, my voice trembling just a little. "I couldn't have done this without each of you. I know the book is personal. It's raw, messy, and our life, our story." My gaze drifts to the empty place where Alex would have sat, my heart giving that familiar ache. "But it's also about letting go, finding ourselves, and...moving forward. This book, *Until I Found Me*, is as much for all of you as it is for me and my readers."

The silence is filled with emotion as glasses are raised and everyone sips their champagne. Lia reaches over to squeeze my hand, her smile full of love. The kids chatter among themselves, oblivious to the depth of the moment but filling the room with the warmth of family.

Claire catches my eye again, raising her glass with a quiet smile. "To many more chapters, Kels. The best ones are still ahead."

We finish dinner, and before I can lift a dish, the girls spring into action, clearing the table with swift determination.

"Mom, it's your birthday, go relax. We've got this tonight," Lexi insists, pressing one of her familiar, affectionate kisses to my nose. There's a comforting rhythm to her words, and for once, I let myself step back, feeling the quiet joy of being cared for by my own children.

The grandkids are already halfway up the stairs, eager to disappear into their new playroom. Just a few months ago, it was Alex's office. When I completed the final draft of my memoir, I knew it was time for more than just a new chapter on paper—it was time to let this house breathe again to make space for the future. Transforming Alex's office was a bittersweet but necessary act. I kept a few of his things—small mementos, gifts I'd given him over the years, and the girls each chose keepsakes that meant something to them. The grandkids loved discovering little treasures their moms had made for their granddad, creations from long before they were born. It was like a bridge, connecting their memories to mine, giving life to Alex's legacy in a way I hadn't anticipated.

I tried to log into his old laptop, expecting the usual password we'd shared for years. But it didn't work. I tried a few variations, hoping maybe he'd just forgotten to update it, but nothing. It was a small mystery, one that seems insignificant. So, I tucked the laptop away, nestled safely in a big box of keepsakes in our closet.

The playroom itself has become something wonderful—a world for the littles to lose themselves in. I've made sure it's a paradise for each of them, with something special for everyone. And though their moms aren't exactly thrilled with the seventy-four-inch TV hanging on the wall and cartoons on loop, I just laugh and say, "That's what Glammy's house is for, right? A little spoiling, a few rules bent, and all the things they can't do at home."

As I pass through the kitchen, I glance around, noticing the faint traces of laughter and warmth still lingering from our evening together. "Where's Claire?" I ask the girls, my voice a little softer than usual.

"I think she's out on the front porch," Lia replies, flashing me a quick smile as she continues clearing plates.

I reach for the wine bottle and pour two fresh glasses, feeling a strange sense of calm settle over me. With a deep breath, I make my way to the front porch, where the air is thick with the faintest hint of autumn. I find Claire there, wrapped in the golden hues of the fading evening light, her gaze lost somewhere in the distance.

"Did I ever tell you that Alex made these chairs?" I say, handing her a glass of wine. A gentle smile tugs at my lips as I think of Alex working in the garage, painstakingly sanding and varnishing these Adirondack chairs, determined to get them just right.

Claire's eyes light up with surprise. "No, you didn't," she says, accepting the glass. "And thank you for the wine." She raises her glass toward me, her smile warm and inviting. "Here's to Alex for crafting these beautiful chairs that I probably won't be able to peel myself out of if I keep drinking this wine."

We clink glasses, laughter spilling out of us, sounding almost too carefree. For a moment, we're like two college girls sharing secrets, not middle-aged women weighed down by loss and memories.

"How do you do it, Claire?" I ask, feeling the words bubble up before I can stop them.

"How have you managed these past four anniversaries of Sam's death? With Alex's first anniversary coming up, it's all I can think about. It feels like I'm on the edge of a cliff, ready to fall back into that awful day. That's why I'm taking everyone to the Martha's Vineyard house for his one-year. I'm not sure I can face it alone."

Claire looks out over the yard, her gaze steady and thoughtful. The air is cooling, carrying whispers of the short-lived fall that will arrive soon. She takes a slow sip of her wine before speaking, her voice soft but steady.

"My dear friend, the first year is the hardest," she says, reaching out to squeeze my hand.

"But remember, it's okay to feel this. The dread, the fear, the sadness—are all reminders, but they don't define us. You're not losing him again; you're simply missing him, and that's an important distinction. Each year, I allow myself to feel the loss, but then I dedicate the day to celebrating Sam—her life, her love, our memories. I spend it with Jackson, and together, we honor her."

Her words land softly but firmly, soothing the ache inside me. "Claire, you always know what to say," I murmur, my voice thick with gratitude. "You've helped me through some of the darkest days, more than you know.

She smiles, her blue eyes crinkling at the corners. "And you've done the same for me, Kels. More than you realize."

The evening deepens, stars pricking through the dusky sky, and we find ourselves opening another bottle of red. The conversation flows easily now, loosening with the wine, and soon Lexi and Lia join us, the front porch filling with laughter and chatter. The kids dart in and out of the house, their footsteps echoing down the hall, filling every corner with life and energy. We reminisce, sharing stories of Alex and Samantha—some funny, some tender—and each memory brings a mixture of joy and bittersweet nostalgia.

As the conversation shifts, we talk about the trials of motherhood, the strange feeling of an empty nest, the paths our lives have taken. There's a warmth here, a freedom I hadn't expected, and I realize it feels good—no, it feels necessary—to speak of our spouses, to remember them with laughter rather than just sorrow.

Eventually, everyone but Claire leaves. A quiet, easy silence settles between us. I glance her way, a question rising inside me— uncertain but persistent.

"Claire," I say softly, testing the weight of my words, "have you ever thought about dating again?"

She tilts her head, studying me with a mix of curiosity and care. "No," she says after a moment. "I haven't been with anyone since Sam." Her eyes shift toward the horizon, thoughtful. "For a long time, I couldn't even imagine it. She was...everything. But I think I'm finally opening up to the idea."

I nod, letting her words sink in. There's a quiet strength in her admission, a resilience that I can't help but admire.

"I love Sam with every fiber of my being; that will never change," she continues, her voice soft but sure. "But at fifty-four, there's still a lot of life ahead. With Jackson finishing up college and heading to grad school, I've been thinking about how I don't want to spend the rest of my life alone. So, to answer your question, I'm not closing my heart to the possibility of loving someone else someday."

Her words stir something inside me—a mixture of admiration and something deeper, something I'm not quite ready to name. I wonder if I could ever reach that point where I feel ready to open my heart again. And why, I wonder, do I need to know Claire's feelings on this? Perhaps it's the shared kinship of our experiences, or maybe it's my own subconscious probing at the possibilities for my future.

Claire's openness, her willingness to see beyond the loss, fills me with hope, a glimmer that maybe, just maybe, there's more to my story, too.

Chapter Eleven

Claire's name lights up the screen. Her voice is warm and familiar, cutting through the haze of my overpacked day.

"Kelsi, don't bother with dinner tonight. Come over. I'll whip up a salad, and we can talk about the trip."

"I'll be there in an hour. Need me to bring anything?" I ask, gratitude spilling into my voice. Claire has an uncanny way of knowing when I need a lifeline, always stepping in at just the right moment.

"Just bring yourself," she says with a light laugh, her tone.

"Perfect," I reply, a faint smile tugging at my lips. As we hang up, I glance around my office, my eyes landing on the neatly stacked piles of papers and notes that represent the final threads of my work before I can shift into vacation mode. Most of my luggage is already packed, save for the inevitable last-minute essentials I always seem to forget until the eleventh hour.

I take a deep breath, mentally listing everything I still need to do. A part of me is already at Martha's Vineyard, ready to soak in the familiar comforts of the house and the family gathering ahead.

But another part lingers on the looming trip to New York the following week—the kick-off to national pre-pub promotions for *Until I Found Me.* The duality of it all presses on me: the personal and the professional, the past and the future.

I tidy my desk, organizing the stray notes and papers into neat piles. I gather the essentials I know I'll need on the Vineyard—the trusty leather crossbody briefcase Alex gifted me when my first novel hit the NYT Bestseller list. It's worn but well-loved, a reminder of his thoughtfulness and his uncanny ability to antici-pate my needs. He'd chosen it specifically for my writing trips, insisting that it was "practical, but stylish." That had been his way —thinking of me, even in the smallest details.

I slip my laptop, charger, writing notebook, pen, and high-lighter into the bag, mentally preparing myself for what lies ahead. Flying up a day early feels right. I want time alone to walk through the house, to see each room without an audience, to let myself feel everything I need to feel before the rest of the family arrives. Something about being there first feels sacred, like opening up the house not just for them but for Alex, too.

With one last glance at the neatly arranged desk, I close my office door and head out, my heart both heavy and hopeful. I'll sit with Claire tonight, laughing over dinner, and making new memories. Tomorrow, I'll return to the Vineyard, to the place that holds so much of Alex and me, ready to face whatever emotions it brings.

I'm on my way to Claire's, walking the few streets separating our homes to get some fresh air and stretch my legs. Claire's place, a cozy two-story tucked away at the edge of our subdivision, is a haven of tranquility with the Black Mountains painting a scenic backdrop. Claire and Sam built their home not long after Alex and I moved into the neighborhood. Unlike our bustling house-hold of five, they needed space for their son Jackson, making their home the perfect size for the three of them. It's crazy that we never knew we were distant neighbors all these years.

The driveway is a picturesque path, lined with towering Sugar

Maples and Yellow Birch trees, their branches heavy with an explosion of orange and yellow leaves. The crisp autumn air carries the unmistakable scent of damp earth and wood, a gentle reminder of the stark, bare winter ahead. The trees arch above, forming a canopy that filters the soft sunlight, casting dappled shadows along the winding path. It's a vibrant prelude to what's coming, yet there's a serene beauty in the transition, a moment caught between seasons.

As I approach Claire's house, the sight of her outside, tending to her garden, stops me in my tracks. Clearly, she's in her element —hands deep in the soil, a streak of dirt across her cheek, completely at peace. The rich, vibrant greens of the plants seem to come alive under her care, and there's something captivating about watching her so focused, so at ease, just like my dad.

I never knew this side of her.

"Claire," I call out, unable to hide my admiration, "I wish I had your green thumb."

Surprised by my sudden presence, she looks up, but her face breaks into a warm, radiant smile. "Believe me," she laughs, standing to wipe her brow with the back of her hand, "it took years not to kill everything I touched. It was an expensive hobby at first."

I chuckle, shaking my head as she pulls off her dirt-covered gloves and brushes the remaining soil from her fingers. I find myself captivated by the way her eyes light up when she talks about the garden, a passion that reveals a side of her I hadn't fully appreciated. Smiling, I share a memory of my father's love for the earth, too, and for a moment, it feels as though we're connecting over something quietly sacred.

We share a brief moment of laughter before Claire gestures for me to follow her inside. The front door, a solid piece of art in itself, opens into a spacious, open-plan living area that's both vast and inviting. The interior feels like an extension of Claire—warm, welcoming, yet undeniably refined. The modern-rustic decor, with its wooden beams, sleek furniture, and large windows letting in the natural light, starkly contrasts my taste, but it suits her. It feels like home—not just a house but a space filled with life, memories, and love.

As Claire walks ahead of me, I notice the way the light filters in, catching the way she carries herself with an ease that feels magnetic. There's something comforting about her presence, yet it stirs something in me that I can't quite place—a subtle, quiet awareness that lingers in the back of my mind. As we step inside, the warm and welcoming aroma of something baking fills the air. "What smells so good? I thought we were having salad," I say, surprised.

"Oh, I hope you don't mind, but I made a quiche to go with the salad. I was just in the mood to cook," Claire explains, her head tilted in that characteristic way of hers.

Dinner is as delightful as the company. Over plates of delicious fare, we discuss my upcoming trip and her plans to join me.

"Thank you for helping me see the importance of celebrating Alex's life rather than just mourning his passing," I tell her. "Everyone's excited about the trip. I haven't been to Martha's Vineyard or our house since before Alex died."

"Of course, Kels," she smiles, topping off our wine glasses. "And thank you for including me in your family's plans."

After dinner, we step out onto the deck, the sky a swirl of pastel colors over the grand mountainous vista. We share a silent, knowing look, cherishing the bond we've cultivated over the last year. As the sun sets, casting a fiery glow over the distant mountains, I feel Claire's gaze on me, but I don't ask what's on her mind.

Chapter Twelve

June, 2018.

The fire crackles softly, its glow flickering against the encroaching night as I nestle closer to Alex beneath a thick blanket. The cool summer air drifts in from the water, a stark contrast to the warmth of the flames, but it's the quiet between us that sends a deeper chill through me. It isn't awkward—just heavy, laden with all the words left unspoken, all the truths we silently acknowledge. We both know this is our last time here together. We feel it in the stillness, in the way neither of us dares to break it.

I glance up at Alex; the sight of him takes my breath away, but not in the way it used to. He's so much thinner now, his once-strong frame reduced to a shadow of what it was. His skin is pale, and his bald head is a stark reminder of what the last few years have taken from him. His blue eyes, though tired, still carry that familiar spark, but even that's starting to dim. And yet, despite everything, he's still my Alex.

"They're getting so big," he says quietly, his voice raspy but steady. His eyes are fixed on the fire, but I know he's thinking about our grandkids and how quickly time has slipped away from us.

I rest my head on his shoulder, feeling the rise and fall of his chest, knowing these moments are numbered. "Too fast," I agree, my voice barely a whisper. "I still remember the first summer we brought them here. Maddi and Finni were barely walking. Finni kept falling in the sand, determined to keep up with her sister."

Alex chuckles softly, the sound tinged with sadness. "Stubborn, just like their mother," he teases, his eyes finally meeting mine. There's love in them, a warmth that makes my heart ache.

"That was a good year," I say, remembering how all the grandkids used to run around this very yard, their laughter echoing through the air. "Every year has been good here."

Alex nods, his hand slipping under the blanket to find mine. His grip is weak, but it's there. "You've made this place a home," he says, his voice faltering. "For them, for all of us."

Tears sting my eyes as I squeeze his hand. "We did that together, Alex."

The fire crackles beside us, the only sound for a long time. The sky is turning a deep purple, the first stars beginning to twinkle in the fading light. The house is quiet, but the memories of this place, of all of us together throughout the years, linger in the air. This is our place, our sanctuary, and I don't know how I'll come back here without him.

"I don't want them to remember me like this," Alex says suddenly, his voice so quiet I almost don't hear him. There's a tremble in his words, and it breaks my heart all over again.

"They won't," I assure him, blinking back tears. "They'll remember the man who taught them to sail, who built sandcastles with them every summer. That's who they'll remember."

He turns his head slightly and presses a gentle kiss to my temple.

"You've been too good to me, Kels. I wish I hadn't taken that for granted all these years."

His words catch me off guard. "What do you mean? I never felt like you took me for granted."

He looks out over the vast ocean, where the sunset brushes the horizon with fading light. A single tear gathers in the corner of his eye before slipping down his cheek.

"I did, Kels," he whispers, his voice thick with regret. "You were so loyal, so devoted, that you didn't even see it..." His voice breaks, and he's too choked up to finish.

My own throat tightens, a weight of unspoken emotions pressing against it. I shake my head softly, reaching for his hand.

"I'm just trying to hold on to every moment we have left," Alex says.

We sit, wrapped in the memories of a life well-lived, watching the fire die down as the night deepens. The waves are soft and gentle, lapping against the shore, a steady rhythm that feels like the pulse of this place. I close my eyes and listen, committing everything to memory—the warmth of his body next to mine, the crackling fire, the scent of the ocean in the air.

"I love you," he whispers, his voice thick with emotion.

"I love you too," I say, my heart breaking as the words leave my lips, knowing that soon, I won't be able to say them to him anymore. "We should probably get you inside. Are you cold?"

"No. I don't want this moment to end."

The night stretches on, and we sit together, holding on to each other and every precious memory we've created.

Chapter Thirteen

September 17, 2019.

A pang of nostalgia tugs at my chest. It's been over a year since I set foot here, and the memories seem to hang in the air like salt from the nearby sea. Our Martha's Vineyard home and the weathered gray shingles, so distinctly New England, gleam under the midday sun, and the hydrangeas by the front porch are in full bloom, painting splashes of blue and purple across the landscape.

"Kelsi Jo!" A familiar, warm voice calls out, snapping me from my thoughts.

I turn to see Linda, my longtime friend and property manager, descending the porch steps with a clipboard in hand and a wide smile. Linda's been part of our lives for as long as we've been coming to the Vineyard. When we first bought the place, she and her husband were our neighbors. They'd lived here their entire lives, and over time, we became close. They would watch over our house whenever we were back in Lake George.

About five years in, her husband passed away suddenly from a heart attack. The big house felt empty, so she sold it, and while we never connected with the new owners, our friendship with Linda held strong. She's a tall, energetic woman in her mid-sixties, her short, silver-streaked hair giving her a practical, no-nonsense look that suits her perfectly for managing a property. Since Alex passed, she's taken care of everything, keeping the house in pristine condition and handling the rentals seamlessly.

"Linda!" I call back, a bit of my own tension easing at the sight of her. I step out of my rented minivan and smooth my dress, hoping to settle my nerves. "How's the house? I know it's been a busy season."

"Oh, busy doesn't even cover it!" she says, her voice carrying a hint of pride as she hands me the clipboard. "We've been booked solid since Memorial Day. You'll see in the ledger that it is fully occupied every week. This house has a charm people just can't resist."

I scan the pages she shows me, barely absorbing the numbers and dates. My eyes keep drifting up to the house, taking in its welcoming façade, the wide windows overlooking the ocean beyond.

Linda must notice my distraction because she clears her throat gently. "We've made a few small repairs here and there, just routine things. New faucet in the downstairs bath, replaced a few of the light fixtures that had gone out. And don't worry, the cleaning crew was in yesterday, top to bottom, including the guesthouse. She's all set for you and the family."

"Thank you. I appreciate everything," I say, my voice soft, almost lost in the sound of the waves crashing in the distance. "It feels surreal being back."

Linda gives me a sympathetic nod, her eyes kind. "I can only imagine. The last time you were here..."

"The summer before he passed," I finish for her, my voice barely a whisper. I swallow, the memory sitting heavy in my chest. "It feels strange coming back without him."

Linda places a comforting hand on my shoulder. "I know he's missed, KJ. And the Vineyard has missed you. It'll be good for you, being here with your family."

I nod, feeling the weight of her words. For a moment, the only sound is the soft rustling of leaves and the distant cry of seagulls. The place feels timeless, as though it's waited patiently for my return, as though it's held a place for Alex and me that hasn't quite faded.

"Well, if you need anything at all, I'm just a call away," Linda says, breaking the quiet. She hands me a set of keys, their weight feeling heavier than I remember.

"Thank you, Linda." I grip the keys tightly. "For everything. The house is...it's beautiful, just as I remember."

She gives a small nod and, after a quick exchange of goodbyes, heads down the drive, leaving me alone with the house that holds so many memories.

I walk up the steps, each one a little reminder of moments shared here—Alex's laughter echoing on summer evenings, the girls chasing each other on the beach, the sunsets we watched in quiet companionship, not realizing they were fleeting. I pause at the door, fingers tracing the familiar wood grain, and take a deep breath before unlocking it.

Inside, the house is pristine yet feels unfamiliar, as though it belongs to another life. The sunlight streams through the wide windows, spilling over the polished hardwood floors and casting a glow on the walls lined with family photos. My gaze catches on one of our last Fourth of Julys before Alex got sick. Everyone gathered around the fire pit, Alex's arm draped around me, both of us smiling with the ease of people who believed they had all the time in the world.

I run my fingers along the picture frame, my chest tightening. "Welcome back, Kels," I whisper to myself.

The house is just as majestic as the day we first laid eyes on it nearly twenty years ago, sprawling across the bluff like a fortress against the Atlantic. It's nearly 5,500 square feet of understated elegance, with seven bedrooms, a cozy reading nook off the family room, and windows that seem to inhale the light, pouring it into every corner.

Stepping into the all-white kitchen, I pause, taking in the panoramic view beyond the windows. The Atlantic stretches out like an endless promise, waves rolling toward our private beach. Alex and I renovated this kitchen together, down to the last cabinet pull. He always said it should be the "heart of the home" and it was. We spent countless mornings here, making breakfast with the girls, sipping coffee, sneaking kisses in between chopping vegetables or stirring sauces.

The backyard is bathed in the golden light of mid-afternoon, the swimming pool shimmering under the sun's lingering warmth. Beyond it, about 200 feet away, the familiar path winds toward the beach and our private dock. I pause by the window, watching the waves rhythmically kiss the shore—steady, soothing, unchanged.

For the first half of this visit, I decide to stay in the guesthouse —a cozy retreat tucked behind the main house with its own little porch overlooking the ocean. I jot down a long list of groceries. I want to cook most of the meals myself this week, even though I know Wendall will take over the grilling. Something is grounding about planning for a full house, about the anticipation of filling the air with the scent of home-cooked meals and the sound of laughter again. A reminder that life continues, even here, even without Alex.

* * *

Once I've stocked the kitchen and set up everything I'll need for the week, I pour myself a glass of red wine, grab my journal and a blanket, and head down to the firepit by the beach. The Adirondack chairs are exactly where we left them, arranged in a semi-circle around the fire, ready for late-night stories and warm memories. I settle into one, pulling the blanket tightly around me, the wine warming my hands as the fire crackles to life.

With the waves as my soundtrack and the firelight dancing before me, I open my journal to a fresh page. Tonight, this isn't just a journal; it's a letter to Alex, a continuation of the letters we exchanged throughout our life together. I write slowly, choosing each word carefully, feeling the weight of them as they pour onto the page.

> *My Dearest Alex,*
>
> *It's been nearly a year since you've been gone. I've missed you more than I ever thought possible, yet here I am, feeling your presence every day. You live on in the soft "I love you" that echoes as I fall asleep, and I still feel kisses on my lips in the morning. We're here in our special place, surrounded by memories and the family you loved so dearly. I am okay, my love because you are with me in everything around us.*

When I finish, I hold the letter close to my chest, breathing in the night air, letting my words become a part of it. I close my eyes, the fire's warmth wrapping around me, and as I speak the words aloud, I feel them drift into the universe—a call to Alex, wherever he may be.

As I look up, my gaze drawn through the flickering flames, I suddenly see him across the firepit. He sits in his usual chair, the one he always claimed as his own, and he's exactly as I remember him before he got sick—healthy, vibrant, dark hair curling over his forehead. Those pale blue eyes, so filled with warmth and life, are fixed on me, and he's smiling that soft, knowing smile that always felt like home.

"Alex..." I whisper, barely daring to breathe, afraid that even the slightest movement might shatter the illusion.

But he doesn't fade. Instead, he leans forward, resting his

elbows on his knees, his gaze steady and filled with love. "Kelsi, I love you."

His words settle over me, gentle yet grounding. A part of me laughs softly, wondering if maybe the wine or exhaustion is conjuring this moment. But he looks so real, so vivid.

"I miss you so much, Alex," I manage, my voice breaking. "I miss us."

His expression softens, and for a moment, it feels as if the distance between us, between life and whatever lies beyond, has dissolved. "You're stronger than you know. I'm always with you because you've kept your heart open for me," he replies, his words filled with warmth and pride.

I wipe away the tears streaming down my face, not from sorrow but from a deep, cathartic release.

As the fire dies down, he begins to fade, his form blending into the flickering embers and the cool night air. I don't reach out or try to hold on to him; instead, I watch him go, letting his presence settle within me like a light that will never truly go out.

When he's finally gone, I lift my gaze to the starlit sky, my heart full, knowing that somehow, he heard me, that he'll always hear me.

With a newfound peace, I make my way back to the guesthouse, carrying the warmth of his memory and the promise of his love. As I lie down, the familiar hum of the ocean lulls me to sleep.

Chapter Fourteen

September 18, 2019.

I smile into my coffee as Lexi updates me: they're on their way to the airport, tired but excited. The kids barely slept in shared anticipation.

"I'm hoping they pass out on the plane, or today could be cranky," she says.

"Paybacks, my dear," I say with a laugh, remembering all the sleepless nights and overtired tantrums that once made traveling with my girls an adventure of its own.

I send a quick text to make sure everyone else is airport-bound. Knowing that all my favorite people will soon be together under one roof is comforting.

Even though I had arranged for each couple to have their own rental car, I couldn't resist driving to the airport myself. The thought of waiting even a moment longer to embrace them was unbearable. The moment I spot them emerging from the arrivals gate, their surprise melts into wide grins before erupting into delighted screams—the kind that fills the air with joy and dissolves any lingering doubt about showing up. As they rush toward me, arms outstretched, I know without question—I made the right choice.

The minivan is filled with the sound of laughter, chatter, and a brief squabble over who gets the prime seat in Glammy's car. All five of my grandkids—Finni, Maddi, Brody, Simon, and Samuel—insist on riding with me despite the perfectly comfortable vehicles their parents were driving—and I wouldn't have it any other way. Their excitement is infectious.

The faint traces of airplane snacks—pretzels and fruit chews—linger in the air. Brody, the self-appointed navigator, is squished in the passenger seat beside me, ensuring we follow the GPS to the tee.

"Left turn in five minutes, Glammy," he announces, repeating the navigation voice, his serious tone making me stifle a laugh.

In the back, Finni and Maddi are whispering; heads pressed together, no doubt plotting some elaborate game. Simon and Samuel have their heads down playing their Gameboys, not the least bit concerned with their surroundings.

"Glammy, remember last time we came here, and Grandpa let us roast marshmallows by the fire?" Finni's voice is tinged with nostalgia.

"I remember," I glance at her in the rearview mirror, my heart aching a little at the memory. "And he burned three marshmallows in a row because he kept talking and forgot to pull them out of the flames."

"That's because Grandpa said burnt marshmallows are the best!" Maddi chimes in, her voice carrying a mixture of delight and longing.

I smile, blinking back the sting in my eyes. "Well, maybe this time, we'll see if we can make some perfect golden ones in his honor."

The car falls into a rhythm of shared memories and playful banter as we wind down the familiar roads lined with tall, swaying trees that seem to welcome us back like old friends. The kids' voices rise and fall in a cacophony of joy, their excitement bubbling over as we draw closer to the house.

And then, finally, we arrive. The kids press their faces to the windows, craning their necks to get a glimpse of the house.

"We're here!" Brody exclaims, his voice breaking the spell. "It looks just like it did last time!"

"You remember, Brody?"

"I think I do, Glammy!"

He was only three and a half the last time he was here, but I didn't want to dampen his excitement by discounting his memory.

I park the van, and before I even shut off the engine, the kids are tumbling out, their excitement spilling over as they race toward the front door. I take a moment, sitting in the driver's seat, to watch them. Their joy is contagious, and for the first time in a long time, I feel a sense of peace in returning to this place.

The warm summer breeze brushes against my skin as I watch the kids dart around the yard. Their parents pull up behind us, laughter and greetings filling the air as everyone reunites. As we head toward the house together, I feel the weight of memories pressing against me and the hope of making new ones with the people I love most.

Lexi breathes, "Mom, everything looks great!"

The buzz of excitement fills the air as the kids explore every nook.

Finni and Maddi immediately claim the bunk bed bedroom, determinedly banning their brother and cousins from entering. "This is our room, no boys allowed!" they declare.

Brody protests loudly, but a minor scuffle ends with parental intervention: no settling in until we sort this out peacefully.

Once peace is restored, I lead everyone to their respective rooms.

"Wait, Mom, where are you sleeping?" Ari asks, noticing all rooms are claimed.

"I'll be in the guesthouse," I say. I'll be able to escape there when I need quiet for work, especially preparing for my media tour coming up in the next few weeks.

"I'm so glad you decided to celebrate Dad here instead of back at home. He loved this place. This should be an annual tradition, Mom!" Ari wraps an arm around me, snapping a selfie.

Tonight's menu is a nod to the last days of summer: juicy grilled burgers, crispy air-fried french fries, and fresh corn on the cob—a simple spread but a family favorite that always brings a smile.

"Wendall, will you do the honors?" I ask my son-in-law, gesturing to the grill.

"You got it!" Wendall grins, holding up the plate of raw burger patties. He glances over at Doug, who's leaning against the porch railing, watching the evening settle in.

"Hey, Dougie! Grab a few beers, and let's start this grilling party."

Doug looks up, a slight smile playing at the corners of his mouth as he heads to the fridge to grab the drinks. Lia's eyes follow him, a soft, almost nostalgic expression on her face. She and Doug divorced two years ago, but they've been spending more time together recently. When Lia asked if Doug could join us for the weekend, I couldn't have said no if I tried. It's like watching an old, familiar dance unfold between them, one that's grown wiser and gentler over the years.

These two have a history that goes back to sixth grade—a lifetime of memories bound up in years of friendship, love, and heartache. They were inseparable through middle and high school, their young love as fierce as it was fragile. They got married right after graduation, almost too eager to start a life together, and within four years, they had two beautiful kids and, eventually, a divorce. Alex and I always adored Doug, but we couldn't help feeling they were just too young, thrown into the depths of adulthood before they were ready.

After the divorce, I watched them step into their new roles with remarkable grace, treating each other with a level of maturity and respect that many couples twice their age could only hope for. They co-parent seamlessly, showing up for every little moment and always putting the boys first. By setting aside their differences, they forged a new kind of love rooted in deep, unwavering friendship.

Since Alex passed, Doug has been there for Lia in ways that go beyond the usual boundaries of exes. He's been her steady presence, her sounding board, her friend, and, from the looks of it, maybe something more. I can see it in how they glance at each other, how Doug's hand rests on her shoulder a beat longer than necessary, and how Lia's laugh sounds just a little softer when he's around.

Maybe this time, they're ready to rebuild what they once had, to put their family back together, stronger and wiser than before. I've learned that life rarely gives us second chances, and if they're lucky enough to find love with each other again, who am I to stand in the way?

We settle into the rhythm of the evening, the warmth of family and good food wrapping around us like a familiar embrace, and for a moment, everything feels just right.

Dinner is a success, and everyone chips in for the clean-up. We spend the evening laughing and reminiscing about Dad, the man we're all here to celebrate. Eventually, the littles go off to bed, and I retreat to the guesthouse while the other adults pop open a bottle of champagne and settle into the hot tub.

I hear their laughter drifting through the night air from my guesthouse. Normally, the noise might keep me awake, but tonight, the sound of my girls and their partners enjoying each other's company is like a lullaby. It's comforting, almost therapeutic. Wrapped in this warmth, I drift off to sleep, feeling connected and content.

Chapter Fifteen

May 28, 2013.

The music drifts softly through the warm summer air, mingling with the sound of waves gently lapping at the shore. Our Martha's Vineyard home is alive with laughter and clinking glasses as our friends—our chosen family—celebrate twenty-five years of marriage between Alex and me. I glance around the room, catching glimpses of familiar faces bathed in the warm glow of candlelight. It's the kind of night where everything feels perfect, where I should feel nothing but joy, but there's a knot in my stomach that I can't shake.

"Where's Alex?" I murmur to myself, realizing I haven't seen him in a while.

He was by my side earlier, smiling that easy smile of his as we toasted to our love, to our life. But now, he's nowhere to be seen. He's probably just outside by the fire pit, enjoying a quiet moment or refilling his drink.

"Twenty-five years looks good on you and your groom," Charlie says, sidling up next to me with a glass of red wine in his hand. "You and Alex know how to throw a party."

I force a smile, accepting his compliment. Charlie has no idea how often I find myself searching for Alex during gatherings. But tonight is not the night for doubts. Tonight is about over two decades of wedded bliss.

"Thanks, Charlie," I say, taking a sip of my drink. "I'm so glad you and Eve could make it."

He laughs, "Wouldn't miss it for the world! And by the way, congratulations on your novel hitting the New York Times bestseller list. This makes how many now?"

Before I can answer his eyes scan the surroundings. "Have you seen Eve? I lost track of her somewhere between the champagne and dessert."

I hesitate for a moment, glancing around. "No, I haven't, actually. She must be around here somewhere." But my stomach tightens, and now I'm not just wondering where Alex is—I'm wondering where Eve is, too.

Excusing myself from Charlie, I step outside, the cool breeze from the ocean a welcome reprieve from the heat of the party. I make my way down to the fire pit by the water, and that's when I see them.

Alex and Eve, their faces illuminated by the flickering flames. It's a picture-perfect night on the island and far less chaotic outside than in. They're talking—just talking—but there's something that makes my breath catch in my throat.

That's ridiculous, Kelsi, I think to myself.

They don't see me, not at first. I stop in my tracks, half-hidden by the shadows of the trees lining the path. My heart pounds in my chest, and I can't quite explain why. It's just a conversation, right? They're friends—with the exception of Charlie, we've all been friends since college. Eve tilts her head, shyly laughing at something he's said. It's too familiar.

I watch them for a moment longer, a voice in the back of my mind telling me I should walk over, interrupt, remind them they're supposed to be celebrating with everyone else. But I don't. Instead, I watch, as a strange mix of guilt and confusion washes over me. Guilt for watching them like this, for even thinking that something could be wrong. Married people of twenty-five years have nothing to worry about. How much more solid could we be?

Then Alex notices me. His eyes meet mine across the distance, and for a split second, there's something in his expression—surprise? Guilt? But then it's gone, replaced by his usual charming smile.

"Hey, Kels!" He calls out, waving me over. "We were just talking about the years we've spent celebrating something here at this house."

I force a smile, stepping forward as if everything is fine, as if my heart isn't racing in my chest. "I was wondering where you two disappeared to."

Eve laughs, though it feels forced. "Just catching up. I couldn't help but steal your husband away for a minute," she says, her tone light, but there's something underneath it that I can't quite place.

Alex slips his arm around my waist, pulling me close. He presses a kiss to my temple, like he's trying to reassure me or maybe himself.

I let out a breath and nod, forcing myself to relax into his embrace. "We should get back to the party," I say, my voice steady. "Everyone's wondering where the guests of honor have disappeared to."

Eve nods quickly, stepping back. "Of course. I'll see you two inside." She gives us both a tight smile before heading up the path toward the house.

As we walk back together, Alex keeps his arm around me. I glance up at him, searching his face for answers, but he's as calm and collected as ever. Maybe it's just the stress of hosting or the fact that this is our twenty-fifth anniversary, and I'm feeling more emotional than usual.

As we step back into the warm glow of the party, surrounded by our friends and laughter, I can't help but glance back toward the fire pit, wondering what, exactly, I just witnessed.

Chapter Sixteen

September 19, 2019.

I wake before dawn, ten minutes before the moment that changed everything last year. At 5:47 a.m. on September 19, 2018, my beloved Alex took his last breath. I glance at my phone to confirm the time and date, then sit up, crossing my legs, wide awake in the quiet of the morning. Though I'm alone, the change of scenery is a comfort compared to the solitude of our Lake George home.

My head only touched one pillow; I slept soundly despite the undercurrent of dread for today. I remember the chatter from the girls last night, and now I'm minutes away from the anniversary of the worst day of my life.

Picking up my phone, I start scrolling through old family photos saved over the years. The digital clock reads 5:45 a.m. I walk over to the table in the small kitchen and light the special candle I brought in honor of Alex. Pulling a 5x7 framed photo of him from my suitcase, I set it next to the candle. His face smiles back at me in the photo, and my chest tightens with the ache of missing him.

A soft knock at the door startles me.

"Mom? Are you up? We saw a light on," Lia whispers as I open the door, finding all three of my girls in their pajamas, shivering in the early morning chill.

"Girls, what are you doing out here so early? Get in here. It's freezing," I urge them inside, pulling them close as they rub their hands together for warmth.

Lia looks up at me, her eyes tender. "We set our alarms so we could be with you at the exact time Daddy passed."

Their gesture touches my heart deeply, but their thoughtfulness does not surprise me. "Let's sit down," I suggest, and we gather around the whitewashed wooden table in the kitchen. Ari shares my chair, resting her head on my shoulder.

"A year ago, right at this very moment, we watched your dad take his last breath. It's been a rough year for all of us, but we made it through together as a family. I love you all so much and couldn't have gotten through the last year without all of you," I say, tears welling up. Lia hands me a tissue from nearby.

"We couldn't have done it without you either, Mom," Lexi adds, her voice thick with emotion.

The quiet weight of the moment feels both heavy and comforting, a shared understanding among us.

I have an idea.

Grabbing a couple of thick blankets from the linen closet, I hand them to the girls.

"Let's go," I direct them out the door to the fire pit area. The morning air is chilly, around 45 degrees, but the touch of humidity from the end of summer softens the bite. I gather some firewood and walk out to the private beach. By now, it's just after 6:00 a.m., and the sun is peeking over the horizon, painting the sky in hues of pink and gold. I build a fire just for us, and we sit together in silence for a while, watching the waves lap against the shore.

"Girls, I'll be right back," I tell them as I head back to the guesthouse. I grab some paper and the last wine bottle Alex and I shared on our last anniversary together. I had planned to write a letter to Alex and send it out to sea, but with the girls here, I decide on something different.

When I return, I hand each girl a sheet of my monogrammed stationery and a pen. "Each of us will write our thoughts to your dad. Then, we'll send our words out into the vast Atlantic. Who knows where our messages will end up, but your father will read them as his spirit is wherever we are," I explain.

The girls embrace the idea enthusiastically, each penning a heartfelt letter to Alex. As we write, I notice moments of quiet reflection on their faces, the soft smiles and occasional sniffles. It's not just grief—it's love and gratitude pouring out onto the pages.

By the time we seal the bottle and release it into the water, the sun has fully risen, casting a warm glow on all of us. We stand together, watching the waves carry our messages farther from shore.

Later in the day, after a leisurely breakfast and a long walk along the beach, we gather in the family room. The house feels alive again, filled with laughter and chatter. The kids spread out on the floor while we sit on the plush couches, sorting through decades of family photos. Together, we create a mosaic of memories—pictures of summers spent in this house, Alex holding the girls when they were little, our family dinners by the fire pit, and the grandkids splashing in the pool.

"Remember this one?" Lia holds up a photo of Alex teaching Ari to ride a bike in the driveway. Her face lights up, and we all laugh, the memory so vivid it feels like he's still here.

As the evening settles in, we play round after round of Uno, one of Alex's favorite family games, the kind that always brought out his competitive streak and made the grandkids laugh uncontrollably. The room is filled with joy, a reminder that even in his absence, Alex's spirit continues to bind us together.

It's a day of connection, reflection, and celebration. As I sit back and watch our family, I feel a deep sense of gratitude—not just for the memories we've shared but for the love that keeps us moving forward, one day at a time.

Chapter Seventeen

"Claire, you're here!" I pull her into a tight hug. We'd missed our daily chats these last few days, and just having her here feels like a weight lifted.

As we walk into the kitchen, I see her taking in the house with wide-eyed admiration. "Wow, Kelsi. This place is magnificent!" she says, genuinely impressed.

"Thank you. Sometimes, I think I could stay here forever," I reply, a hint of wistfulness in my voice. "But I don't need another big house all to myself. Having everyone here, though, that's been wonderful." I take her bag and set it aside in the mudroom. "We'll sort this out later. Come on, my family has been waiting for you."

Claire smiles, following me outside to the pool, where everyone gathers to welcome her with open arms. Even the grandkids run up for hugs, excited to see Glammy's friend.

Ari steps forward, her face lit with a warm smile. "Hi, Claire. It's so wonderful to finally meet you face-to-face. Mom has always spoken so highly of you." Claire extends her hand, but Ari pulls her into a hug instead, her sincerity evident in the gesture. She then introduces Chad, her partner. "Claire, this is Chad."

Chad steps forward with a polite smile. He's a steady presence beside Ari—a calming influence and a source of support for her. Chad and Ari bonded over their mutual passion for the law and a shared commitment to helping others. There's a quiet confidence about him, a maturity that has settled my own worries as a mother. It's reassuring to see Ari with someone who respects her.

Everyone welcomes Claire warmly, thanking her throughout the evening for being such a wonderful friend to me. Their appreciation for her shines in every embrace, every kind word shared over dinner.

Later, I show Claire to the guesthouse, where we'll be staying together. It's a small place with only one bedroom and a pull-out couch in the living room. I insist on taking the couch and giving Claire the bedroom.

"Kelsi, absolutely not! I'm not taking your room," Claire protests, shaking her head.

"Well, I'm on the couch until the kids leave in a few days. Then we'll move back to the main house for the rest of our stay," I say, determined to have my way. We exchange a warm, familiar hug, the kind that feels as comforting as family.

"Thank you for having me," Claire says softly, her voice filled with gratitude. I can see how humbled she is to be here, to be included in this part of my life that means so much to me.

"Of course, Claire. You've become more than just my best friend; you're a part of my family now. I don't know what I would have done without you these last seven months." I grab a couple of blankets from yesterday's message-in-the-bottle activity, and we head down to the private beach.

As we settle onto the sand, Claire looks out over the calm Atlantic Ocean, the water glistening under the moonlight. "Kelsi, this really is just lovely." She gazes at the sea that stretches endlessly before us. The surface is smooth, reflecting the night sky like a mirror as if even the ocean itself is at peace.

We sit side by side, talking for hours, sharing laughter, memories, and quiet moments of understanding. Our words blend with the gentle sound of waves lapping at the shore. Before we know it, the first light of dawn starts to edge over the horizon.

"Claire, look! The sun is starting to rise." I smile, feeling a sense of awe. "Have we really been out here all these hours? Where did the time go?"

We watch the sunrise together, feeling the warmth of a new day settling over us, grateful for the friendship that has brought us both to this moment.

Chapter Eighteen

September 21, 2019.

I quickly jump out of bed and open the door, blinking at the light, "Lia, oh my goodness, what time is it?" I feel like I just laid my head down on the pillow.

"11:00 a.m., Are you okay in here? I'm sorry I woke you up, but we figured you might need something to eat."

Lia and the boys are standing at the door, holding two trays of warmed-up leftovers from yesterday's quiche breakfast. I can't help but smile down at my grandsons and thank them.

"I am so sorry. I meant to wake up and fix breakfast for everyone," I say, glancing at the clock. "I can't believe it's so late."

Simon, six years old, hands me a tray. "It's okay, Glammy. There was plenty of food for everyone."

"You are so sweet, thank you," I take the tray from him and invite them in. "Claire must still be sleeping."

"Actually, she's been up for a bit. She came up to the main house a couple of hours ago and ate with the rest of us," Lia says.

It warms my heart to know that Claire feels comfortable enough to spend time with people she doesn't know very well.

"She's a wonderful lady, Mom. It feels like we've known her forever," Lia says.

"I'm so glad you've taken to her and vice versa. And thank you so much for bringing me breakfast." I lift Sutton onto my lap.

"I love you, Glammy. Wanna go swimming?" He wraps his arms around me.

His mother quickly intervenes, "Simon, I don't think we're swimming today. It's too cold."

Simon tries to argue, but his mother puts her foot down, ending the argument before it begins.

"Okay, well, I think it's time to go and let Glammy eat her breakfast and get ready for the day," she smiles at me and takes Sutton off my lap.

"Have you seen Claire?" I ask, wondering where she might have gone.

Lia tells me that she saw Claire head out for a run.

"Good for her! Thanks for bringing my food down here. I'm going to enjoy it and then be up to the house in just a little bit."

This is the last day the kids will be here. They're all headed home early tomorrow morning so they can get back to their lives, work, and school on Monday.

Claire and I plan to stay for a couple of extra days after everyone leaves. It's been years since I've taken the time to explore the Vineyard like a visitor, and I'm looking forward to sharing it with my best friend. We'll wander through the quaint towns, savor fresh seafood, and take in the crisp fall air—it feels like the perfect way to unwind after such an emotional week. Martha's Vineyard is stunning this time of year, with its fiery foliage and peaceful charm, and I can't wait to show Claire the places that have meant so much to me over the years. It's not just about the sights or the food; it's about reconnecting and sharing this special place with someone who's been there for me in ways I can't even begin to express.

. . .

I step out of the shower, my skin warm from the water, dry myself, and wrap the towel around my wet hair. As I catch a glimpse of my naked body in the mirror, I take in the familiar lines and curves of my reflection—the soft stretch marks tracing my belly, remnants of three pregnancies, and the lean, sculpted muscles that years of Pilates and strength training have given me. My body has been shaped by life's seasons, strong in ways that only experience can carve.

Lost in thought, I don't hear the door open. I'm humming softly, absently running my fingers through my hair, when I suddenly catch movement in the mirror. I turn, startled, to see Claire standing in the doorway, her expression frozen in surprise.

"Oh!" I jump, more out of surprise than embarrassment, unraveling the towel from my head and moving it a little closer to my body.

Claire's face turns a deep shade of red as she stammers, "I'm so sorry, Kelsi, I didn't know you were...I should have knocked. Really, I'm sorry."

Her discomfort makes me smile gently. I wrap the towel more securely around myself, giving her a reassuring nod. "It's okay, Claire. We're both women. It's nothing you haven't seen before, right?"

She shifts, looking down, clearly still flustered. "I know, it's just...I didn't mean to intrude. I'm really sorry."

"It's okay," I repeat, softening my voice, hoping to ease her embarrassment.

She finally meets my gaze, a faint smile tugging at the corner of her lips, but there's a strange, lingering tension between us—a current of something unspoken that I can't quite define. As she leaves, closing the door behind her, I feel a strange flutter in my chest, a warmth I hadn't expected.

In the quiet that follows, I realize that her reaction—the startled look, the way her cheeks flushed—has left an impression on me. It's different from how she's responded to anything else, and I find myself replaying the moment, lingering on how her eyes softened, how she seemed as taken aback as I was. A sense of awareness blooms in me, unfamiliar and unsettling, hinting at feelings I didn't realize were there.

I take a deep breath, trying to shake off the thought, but I can't ignore the subtle shift within me. Claire's presence, her kindness, her unwavering support—these things have become a steady comfort in my life. She's been a lifeline since Alex's death, but now...now I wonder if there's something more stirring beneath the surface. Something I haven't allowed myself to see until now.

I wrap myself in my towel and sit on the edge of the bed, trying to make sense of these new feelings, the unfamiliar pull of something I can't name. The memory of Alex's touch, his love, remains etched into me, but now there's a tiny spark, a curiosity toward Claire that I hadn't let myself feel before. It's unexpected, like the faintest hint of dawn after a long, dark night. And though I don't fully understand it, I can't deny the shift, the quiet yearning that lingers long after the door closes.

CHAPTER NINETEEN

The house hums with quiet energy, the way it always does before a goodbye. Our last full day here, and everything feels suspended—like the moment before a wave crashes. Golden light spills through the windows, casting long, soft shadows on the wooden floors. A salty breeze drifts in from the ocean, carrying the scent of damp sand and something else—something like nostalgia.

Claire is completely in her element at the long dining table, now commandeered as an impromptu craft station. She leans in, elbows resting on the table, helping Maddi and Finni fold delicate paper butterflies.

"Here, like this," she says gently, guiding Finni's hands with her own. "Fold this corner in, press it tight, and now, voilà! Butterfly wings."

Finni gasps in delight, eyes wide. "It looks like a *real* butterfly!"

Claire laughs, her blue eyes crinkling at the corners. "Even better. It won't fly away when you're not looking."

Maddi dusts hers with a little too much glitter, then shakes it in the air, sending a shimmer of gold across the table.

"Oh no! I made it *too* sparkly!" she cries, holding it up for inspection.

"Impossible," Claire says with a wink. "There's no such thing as too much sparkle."

I, on the other hand, have been relegated to clean-up duty. Glue sticks roll perilously close to the table's edge, stray scraps of paper stick to my arms, and I've somehow ended up wearing more glitter than the kids.

"This is why I was never an arts-and-crafts mom," I mutter, shaking glitter off my hands. "I swear, it multiplies when you're not looking."

Claire grins. "That's half the fun."

I take a step back, watching her—how natural she is with them, how easily she folds into these small moments, like she belongs here. The warmth of it settles into my chest, a feeling so familiar yet so foreign all at once.

Finni clutches her butterfly proudly. "Glammy, look! It's the prettiest one, right?"

I run my hand over her hair, now streaked with flecks of gold. "It's perfect, sweet girl."

She beams, pressing the paper creation to her heart like a treasure.

That's when I decide—we're eating out tonight. I've spent the last week in the kitchen, rolling dough, stirring sauces, feeding a house full of people. Tonight, someone else can take over.

"Alright, team," I announce. "No one's cooking tonight. We're going out."

A chorus of cheers erupts from the kids, followed by an immediate scramble for shoes and coats. The adults are slower, stretching limbs and exchanging amused glances, but no one argues.

. . .

The restaurant is warm and bustling with energy. The kids dive into their macaroni and cheese, their chatter bubbling over like champagne. The adults sip wine, trade stories, and let the conversation flow as easily as the drinks.

Claire sits across from me, her face relaxed, but there's something quiet about her tonight. She listens, nods, even laughs in all the right places, but there's a distance—a slight hesitation in her eyes, like she's here but somewhere else, too.

I catch her looking at me once for a moment before she glances away.

Is she thinking about this morning? Is that what is making her withdraw from me?

I'd laughed it off at the time, but the memory of her flustered expression lingers. The way she'd flushed when she saw me naked before she stepped back.

Embarrassment? Maybe.

I shake off the thought, reminding myself that it was nothing. Just an awkward moment between friends.

The kids are asleep before we even pull into the driveway, their heads slumped against windows and onto each other's shoulders. The house feels different when we return—quieter, heavier, like the air has shifted.

I step inside, the lingering scent of cinnamon and candle wax wrapping around me like a worn sweater. The suitcases lined up in the hallway are a reminder that tomorrow, this house won't be full anymore.

Claire stands in the kitchen, trailing her fingertips along the counter in slow, rhythmic taps. She looks down, then glances at me, forcing a small smile.

"I think I'm going to turn in."

I hesitate. The air between us feels unsettled.

"Claire," I say softly. "Are you okay?"

She looks up, just for a second, then away. "Yeah. Just tired. All those arts and crafts and a full belly, you know?"

She tries to make it sound light, but it doesn't quite land.

I nod, but something in my chest tightens. The easy warmth we always share feels...different tonight. Like something's sitting between us, unspoken.

I want to pull her back, to shake off whatever this is, but the moment feels too fragile. So, instead, I let it go.

"Good night, Kelsi," she says, her voice softer now, almost hesitant.

"Night, Claire."

I watch her walk toward the guesthouse, her steps slower than usual, her posture a little too rigid.

And just like that, she's gone—leaving me alone with the weight of something I can't quite name.

The house grows even quieter as the minutes tick by. I try to distract myself by tidying up the kitchen, wiping down already-clean counters, and rearranging the fruit bowl. But my thoughts keep circling back to Claire—her distant expression, the way she avoided my eyes. Something shifted tonight, and I don't like the awkwardness that's replaced the comfort we've always shared.

After half an hour of restless pacing and failed attempts to focus on anything else, I grab a glass of water and step outside. The night air is cool, carrying the faint scent of salt and pine. I find myself walking toward the guesthouse, the small path lit only by the dim glow of the porch light. The windows are dark except for a soft amber glow spilling from the kitchen.

I open the guesthouse door quietly, stepping into the warm, familiar space. The moonlight casts long shadows across the room, giving it an almost ethereal quality. Claire's things are neatly arranged—her book on the coffee table, a scarf draped over the back of a chair. It feels like stepping into her world, and for a moment, I just stand there, taking it all in.

I move toward her closed bedroom door, my bare feet making almost no sound on the wooden floor. My heart is racing, and I can't tell if it's from nerves or something deeper. I raise my hand to knock, hesitating just an inch from the door. The silence on the other side feels heavy, as if she's awake and waiting, or maybe it's just my own thoughts echoing back at me.

I try to steady my breathing, my mind racing with a million questions. *Should I knock? Should I just let it go? What would I even say?* Claire is my best friend—my safe place—and yet tonight, there's a wall between us I don't know how to scale. I wonder if she's thinking about this morning, the moment when she accidentally walked in on me stepping out of the shower. The memory lingers in my mind, too, not because of the embarrassment but because of the way her face flushed, the way she stammered before quickly retreating. It was such a fleeting moment, but it felt charged with something I can't quite name.

I lower my hand and lean against the doorframe, closing my eyes. I want to talk to her, to clear the air, but I also don't want to overstep. Maybe she needs space. Maybe I do, too. Whatever this is between us, it feels delicate, like a thread that could either unravel everything or weave something new.

After a few moments, I step back, leaving the door untouched. The air feels cooler now, or maybe it's just the weight of the unanswered questions pressing down on me. I turn and head back toward the main house, the sound of the waves outside grounding me as I walk.

Once inside, I settle into the oversized chair by the window. The view of the dark ocean is soothing, but my thoughts remain tangled. Maybe tomorrow will bring clarity, or maybe it won't. Either way, I know this—whatever is happening between Claire and me, it's not something I can ignore.

Chapter Twenty

For the first time in days, the house is still, the echoes of children's laughter and hurried footsteps replaced by the hum of the washer and the faint creak of floorboards beneath my feet. I stand in the living room, staring at the space where Finni's glitter-covered masterpiece once sat, now wiped clean, as though the week had been a dream.

Claire's voice breaks through the quiet. "Kels, do you want me to start the next load?" she calls from the laundry room.

"Yeah, thanks," I reply, my voice sounding thin against the hollow walls.

As we move through the house, we've fallen into a rhythm, a dance of sorts. Beds are stripped, linens folded, counters wiped down, and furniture rearranged, but it's more than just cleaning —it's erasing the vibrant chaos of the week. It feels too pristine now, like the house is trying to forget the life it had held just hours ago.

I grab a stack of throw pillows from the couch and fluff them, my hands moving on autopilot. Outside, the late morning sun filters through the windows, highlighting the faint fingerprints left on the glass by tiny hands. I leave them there for a moment, reluctant to wipe away the last trace of my grandchildren's presence.

"Let's grab our things from the guesthouse and move them here to the main house," I suggest, and Claire nods, carrying her bag across the breezeway. I settle into the primary bedroom that once belonged to Alex and me. It's a stunning room with its four-poster bed draped in soft white linens and floor-to-ceiling windows that frame the ocean like a living painting. The balcony doors are cracked open, letting in the faint scent of salt and the whisper of waves. I remember how Alex loved this room, how he'd sit on the balcony with his morning coffee, lost in the view.

The master bathroom is equally luxurious. I run my fingers along the cool edge of the sink, a lump forming in my throat. I imagine him here with me like he always was, his laughter filling the space, his hand brushing mine. The memory is sharp, but instead of the ache I expect, there's a soft warmth.

Claire settles into the room down the hall, almost as grand as mine, with its plush bedding and oversized windows. She thanks me again for including her in our time here. Her gratitude is evident, though I wave her off. "I can't imagine you not being here, Claire," I tell her, and I mean it.

* * *

Claire pulls a slice of pizza from the box, expertly catching the string of cheese before it snaps back. "You have such a beautiful family," she says, her voice soft but earnest, her eyes meeting mine briefly before returning to her plate.

"Thanks. They're pretty great." I manage a smile, swirling the wine in my glass, though my hands feel oddly unsteady.

Claire studies me with that warm, open gaze of hers.

"Want to get in the hot tub?" I ask, the suggestion spilling out before I can overthink it. It feels like a safe distraction, a way to escape the intensity of the moment without addressing the undercurrent stirring between us.

"Absolutely," Claire says, her smile easy, but her eyes seem to linger on me for a beat longer than usual.

Minutes later, we're outside, the night settling around us like a velvet curtain. The hot tub hums quietly, steam curling into the crisp air. The moon casts a warm glow, and the faint sound of waves crashing in the distance adds to the tranquil backdrop.

"I've got my suit on under this," Claire says casually, tugging at the edge of her sweatshirt.

"Me too," I reply, peeling off my oversized cardigan and stepping out of my loose lounge pants. The cool breeze brushes my exposed shoulders and stomach, and for some reason, I feel more vulnerable than I have in a long time. I catch Claire's gaze briefly before quickly glancing away, focusing on the bubbling water instead.

Claire slips off her layers with ease. Her movements are fluid and unhurried, and I can't help but notice the way the soft light highlights her toned arms and the delicate curve of her collarbone. My pulse quickens, an involuntary reaction I don't fully understand, and I busy myself lowering into the water, hoping the warmth will soothe the odd mix of nerves and anticipation that's settled in my chest.

For a while, we sit in silence, the kind that only comes with a comfortable friendship. But tonight, there's an undercurrent, an unspoken shift in the air. I feel it in the way our knees brush under the water, the way Claire's gaze seems to linger when she speaks.

The way my chest tightens when she smiles.

I glance over at her, the steam softening her features. Her navy suit clings to her, and the patio lights cast a gentle halo around her damp hair. There's a pull I can't ignore, a quiet but insistent stirring deep inside me. I chalk it up to the wine or the intimacy of the moment, but it doesn't stop my heart from beating just a little faster.

"This is exactly what I needed." Claire breaks the silence first.

I shift uncomfortably, sinking further into the water as if it could drown out the confusion swirling inside me.

"You're quiet," Claire says. "What's on your mind?"

"Nothing," I lie, but my voice betrays me. It's thin and fragile, like a thread about to snap.

She studies me for a moment, her expression unreadable. We let the warmth of the water envelop us, the bubbles rising like little eruptions of energy. I glance at Claire, her head tilted back, completely at ease, and I'm anything but. I am sitting across from her, feeling something I can't name.

I want to say something to cut through the tension, but the words stick in my throat. Whatever this is, it's uncharted territory, and I have no idea how to navigate it.

"Claire, what happened last night? You were so distant. I didn't know what to say or what I could do to make it better."

"I'm sorry. I never wanted to make you feel sad or confused. We've always been honest with each other, right?" She looks at me with desperation on her face. Something I've never seen in her before.

"Of course. That's what I love about our friendship. It's... organic and transparent..." I say.

I watch steam lift from the water's surface, creating a mist between our gaze.

"When I walked in on you in the bathroom...the other day. Something shifted in me. It scared the hell out of me, Kelsi. Because we have this beautiful friendship we've built, and then I see you...I suddenly feel these feelings for you, and I don't know how to process them." The tears are streaming down her face, leaving traces of the confusion she's been feeling the past forty-eight hours and knowing she didn't know how to talk to me. It breaks me in two.

I immediately reconcile every emotion and question I've been asking myself for the last few months. It's been right here in front of my face.

I am falling in love with Claire. I feel an unexpected sense of freedom, a liberation I haven't felt in a long time.

The mist lifts from between us.

Without thinking, I slip off the bottom of my bikini, letting it drift lazily beside me in the water. Claire's eyes widen, the moonlight reflecting off her face, but she doesn't speak. She simply watches, her expression unreadable, as though waiting for me to make sense of my own impulsive actions. I hold the damp fabric up in my trembling hand and whisper, "Skinny dip with me, Claire."

Her hesitation hangs in the air like a suspended breath. She stands slowly, her silhouette glowing under the soft silver light of the moon. Water trickles down her arms and shoulders, catching the light like stars falling to earth.

God, she's beautiful.

"Can you untie my top?" Her voice softer, quieter than I'd ever heard it.

I reach up, my fingers brushing against her neck's warm, damp skin as I fumble with the knot. My hands shake, not from the night air's chill but from the moment's intensity. The fabric loosens, slipping away and vanishing into the water. We both stand still for a beat, the air between us humming with unspoken emotion.

"Thank you," her hushed voice rough with vulnerability.

I can't look away from her. Claire stands before me with a rawness I've never seen. There is no pretense, no walls, just her. She is stunning, not just in how her body catches the light but in how she holds herself—with quiet strength and a depth that seems endless. I feel something inside me, a crack where the light suddenly pours through.

"Claire," I take a small step closer. The water ripples softly around us. "Will you kiss me?"

Her breath hitches, and she faces me fully. She searches my face for a moment, her gaze flickering with questions and unspoken fears.

"Are you sure, Kelsi?" Her voice is low, almost reverent.

I nod, my chest tightening with something that feels like clarity. My heart races, but for the first time in so long, my mind feels still, certain. "Yes," I whisper. "I'm sure."

Claire reaches out, her hands trembling as they cup my face, her touch impossibly gentle. Then, she brings her lips to mine with a softness that steals my breath. The kiss is electric, sending a current through every nerve in my body. It isn't hurried or frantic; it is deliberate, tender, and full of a passion I didn't know I'd been craving. Her lips are warm and soft, and I lean into her, letting myself feel without restraint.

In that moment, the world falls away. The weight of the past, the worries about the future—they all dissolve like fog under the warmth of the sun. There is no fear, no hesitation, only the sensation of her lips, touch, and presence.

As we pull back slightly, her forehead resting gently against mine, I open my eyes to see her looking at me with a mixture of wonder and relief. I let go of everything holding me back—expectations, grief, fear—and step fully into the moment, into her.

The night stretches long and languid, the sky deepening into ink as the last hints of dusk fade into the horizon. The brine of the ocean hangs thick in the air, mingling with the distant scent of firewood from neighboring homes. The waves crash in steady intervals—a rhythmic pulse that matches the unspoken energy between us.

I don't pull away. I don't want to.

Instead, I shift closer, my knees brushing against hers beneath the surface. The movement is small, but it feels monumental. Claire's fingers tighten around mine. The tension between us swells, thick and charged, until it becomes impossible to ignore.

She doesn't ask permission. She just moves, her hand sliding up my arm, over my shoulder, until she's cupping my cheek, her thumb brushing against my damp skin.

I tilt my head instinctively, leaning into her touch.

"Kelsi..." Her voice is barely above a whisper, but it vibrates through me, settling somewhere deep in my chest.

I answer her with movement instead of words, closing the space between us until our lips meet.

The moment she exhales against my mouth, her body melting just a little, I deepen the kiss.

A soft gasp leaves her lips.

Claire moves then, pulling me against her, our bodies pressing together beneath the water. The heat between us has nothing to do with the hot tub anymore.

I feel everything in this kiss—the grief, the longing, the quiet ache of loneliness neither of us has admitted to.

Her hands roam gently, exploring the curve of my back, the slope of my shoulder, learning me in a way no one else has before. My fingers thread through her damp hair, tugging slightly, and she groans against my lips.

The sound sends a shiver through me.

We lose ourselves there, kissing, tasting, touching. Claire finally pulls back, her forehead pressing against mine, her breath uneven.

My hands roam her body with a reverence I've never known, tracing the soft curves and hidden valleys, mapping the landscape of her in a way that feels both familiar and entirely uncharted. Each touch is electric, a spark that ignites something deep within me, something waiting to be set free. My fingertips skim over her skin, memorizing the rise and fall of each breath, the warmth of her against me. It's overwhelming—the way she feels beneath my hands, the way my own body trembles in response. I know this woman, yet this—this is discovering her anew, and it threatens to undo me.

Claire leans her head back against the edge, exposing the long line of her throat, her eyes drifting shut as she lets out a desperate moan. The moonlight catches in the droplets clinging to her breasts, making them shimmer. There's a tension humming beneath her ease, the same one I feel coiled inside of me.

"Let's go inside," I murmur.

My legs feel unsteady as I step out of the hot tub. Claire follows, grabbing the towels we left draped over the chair. She wraps one around herself and then gently drapes the other around my waist, leaving my breasts exposed. "Are you too cold? I can give you my towel to wrap around your shoulders."

Neither of us speaks as we step inside, the warmth of the house wrapping around us like a cocoon. The only sound is the distant crash of waves against the shore and the soft drip of water from our bodies onto the hardwood floors.

I lead her upstairs, my heart pounding so loudly I swear she must hear it.

The bedroom is bathed in moonlight, a soft glow spilling over the neatly made bed.

I turn to face her, taking her in—the way her eyes search mine, filled with so much emotion I can hardly breathe.

A silence settles between us, but it's not uncomfortable. It's heavy with understanding, with the unspoken truth that we are both standing at the edge of something neither of us expected but can no longer deny.

Claire reaches for me again. She releases my towel, letting it slip to the floor, her hands finding my bare skin.

I shiver—not from the cold, but from the way she touches me. Like I'm something delicate, something precious.

She guides me onto the bed, I settle underneath her, our bodies aligning. She sits up slowly, straddling me with her long, lean legs, and traces the line of my collarbone, the curve of my waist, learning me with gentle, deliberate touches.

She kisses me, this time slower, more deliberate, as though she's tasting every inch of me. My fingers tangle in her hair, pulling her closer, and she answers with a soft, lingering lick, tracing the path to ecstasy. My body reacts instinctively, hips rising and falling, craving the rhythm of her touch, lost in the delicious anticipation of what comes next.

There's no rush.

Just this.

Just us.

I reciprocate.

Fingertips grazing, lips exploring, breaths mingling in the space between words.

We make love into the early morning hours.

And for the first time since Alex died, I feel alive again.

Whole.

Wanted.

Loved.

Chapter Twenty-One

SEPTEMBER 23, 2019.

The sun is already warming the cobblestone streets of Edgartown as Claire and I step out of a small café, the aroma of freshly brewed coffee trailing behind us. I tuck a bag of pastries under my arm as Claire adjusts her sunglasses, scanning the horizon. The harbor glitters ahead, a postcard-perfect view of white sailboats bobbing in rhythm with the gentle waves. It's a scene I've witnessed countless times, yet today, it feels different—sharper, more alive, as if the island itself knows that something has shifted.

"Where to first?" Claire's voice is light but threaded with curiosity.

I pull out a small map I grabbed from the café. "Well, I thought we'd start at the lighthouse, then maybe hit the farmer's market before the crowds take over."

Claire nods, her lips curving into a soft smile and gently kisses me, "Lead the way, tour guide."

We stroll side by side along the narrow streets lined with charming white clapboard houses. I can feel the occasional brush of Claire's arm against mine, a fleeting touch that sends a ripple of warmth through me. It's a simple thing, walking together like this, but it feels monumental—an unspoken connection.

When we reach the Edgartown Lighthouse, we pause to take it in. The white tower stands proudly against the blue sky, its shadow stretching across the sand. A few families with children dart around us, laughing as they chase the tide. Claire reaches for her phone, snapping a picture of the scene before turning the camera toward me.

"Smile, Kels," she says, her voice teasing.

The camera makes me feel awkward. "I hate photos. You know this."

"Just one," she coaxes. "For me."

I relent, standing stiffly in front of the lighthouse. Claire laughs and lowers the phone. "Relax! You look like you're posing for a driver's license photo."

"Fine," I say, rolling my eyes but smiling despite myself. "Take it again."

This time, I lean into the moment, letting the breeze tousle my hair, and Claire snaps the photo, her grin widening as she checks it. "Perfect. That's the real you."

We linger by the lighthouse for a while, watching the waves roll in and out. Claire points out a few seals bobbing in the distance, their sleek heads peeking above the water like curious children. I steal a glance at her, marveling at how naturally she fits here, how effortlessly she seems to belong in my world.

Later, we head to the farmer's market in West Tisbury. The narrow lanes are lined with stalls offering everything from fresh produce to handmade jewelry. Claire buys a small bouquet of wildflowers, handing it to me with a quiet smile. "For your guesthouse," she says, her fingers grazing mine as she passes the bundle over.

"Thanks," I say, tucking the flowers into my tote bag, trying to ignore the way my heart skips at her touch.

As we wander from stall to stall, Claire picks up a jar of lavender honey, and I grab a loaf of freshly baked bread. We sample homemade jams and cheeses, nodding in approval at the vendors' proud explanations. Every so often, our hands brush as we reach for the same item or step aside to let others pass. It's subtle, unnoticed by anyone else, but it feels like a secret language between us.

Later, we find ourselves at a quiet stretch of beach near Menemsha, far from the tourist-heavy spots. Claire spreads out a blanket she brought along, and we sit side by side, watching the waves lap gently at the shore. The sun is high, its warmth soaking into my skin, and I let out a contented sigh.

"I haven't felt this relaxed in...I don't even know how long," I admit, turning to look at Claire. She's lying back on her elbows, her sunglasses perched on her nose, gazing out at the water.

"Me neither," she says softly. "This feels...easy. Like it's just us and the world doesn't matter for a little while."

I nod, the truth of her words settling deep within me. "I wasn't sure how this trip would feel, but having you here makes it...better."

Claire shifts, sitting upright to face me. "Kels, there's nowhere else I'd rather be." Her voice is steady and sincere, and it makes something inside me ache in the best way.

We sit in silence for a while; I reach for her hand, hesitating for a moment before letting my fingers intertwine with hers. She squeezes gently, her touch grounding me. Claire and I found a secluded spot away from the few other beachgoers, nestled against a cluster of weathered rocks.

We've been here for a while, watching the sailboats drift lazily in the distance, their white sails catching the sunlight like fleeting moments of clarity. My legs are stretched out in front of me, the coarse sand warm beneath my heels, while Claire sits cross-legged, her elbow casually resting on one knee. She looks effortless.

I lean back on my hands, letting my gaze wander to her profile. I can't take my eyes off her.

As the afternoon stretches on, we talk about everything and nothing—our families, our favorite places, the little things that make us laugh. When the sun begins to dip lower in the sky, painting the horizon with streaks of pink and gold, we pack up and head back to the house.

I glance at Claire, feeling a strange mix of gratitude and hope. This day, this connection, feels like the start of something I never saw coming, but now I can't imagine my life without her.

* * *

The crisp evening air greets us as we pull into the driveway, the headlights cutting through the early fall dusk. The day has been long but filled with quiet joy, the kind that lingers and settles into your bones. The leaves are just beginning to turn, flashes of gold and crimson among the green, and the unmistakable scent of autumn fills the air as we step out of the car.

"Home," I say softly, looking up at the house. Claire stands beside me, her hands tucked into the pockets of her jacket, a small smile playing on her lips.

Inside, the house feels cooler than it did this morning, and the sound of the ocean filters through the cracked windows. Without a word, we both gravitate toward the family room. I kick off my boots and toss a blanket over the couch, inviting Claire to sit with a nod.

"Just for a few minutes," I say, more to myself than her.

"Sounds perfect," she replies, slipping off her own shoes and sinking into the couch. She pulls the blanket over her legs, and I do the same. The warmth of her presence next to me is comforting, and within moments, I feel my eyes grow heavy.

I wake to the sound of waves crashing faintly in the distance. The room is dim, lit only by the soft orange glow of the hood light over the stove in the kitchen. Claire is still beside me, her breathing slow and steady. I glance at my watch—it's nearly 7 p.m.

"Claire," I whisper, reaching out to touch her arm. She stirs, blinking groggily.

"Did we fall asleep?" she asks, her voice thick with sleep.

"We did." I kiss her forehead. "I have one more surprise for us."

She sits up, brushing a hand through her hair. "Oh?"

"Dinner. I made a late reservation for us at this cozy spot in town. I figured it would be the perfect way to end our time on the island." I bury my head in the side of her neck and kiss her ear lobe.

Her face lights up with a smile, and she nods. "That sounds amazing. Do we have a few minutes to get ready?"

"We do," I reply. "I'll meet you at the top of the stairs in 30 minutes."

The house feels warmer, almost alive with energy. The rich hue of my burgundy jumpsuit complements my auburn hair, and the deep V-neckline is modest yet alluring. I pair it with elegant suede ankle boots that add just the right amount of edge, their subtle height giving me an extra boost.

Catching a glimpse of myself in the mirror, I adjust the delicate gold chain that rests against my collarbone, its simplicity adding a touch of elegance. My makeup is under-stated—a hint of mascara to highlight my eyes, a soft blush, and a swipe of rose-tinted lip gloss that catches the light. A soft spritz of my favorite perfume lingers on my wrists and neck—a warm, subtle scent that feels like an extension of me. I drape a cream-colored cashmere wrap over my shoul-ders to ward off the evening chill, the fabric soft against my skin.

My boots make a gentle rhythm against the polished hard-wood floors. There's a thrill in my step that courses through me. When I close the bedroom door behind me, Claire emerges from her room at the same time. My breath catches for a moment. She's wearing a deep navy sweater dress that hugs her tall frame perfectly, paired with knee-high brown boots. Her pixie-cut hair is neatly styled, and there's a softness to her expression that makes my heart skip a beat.

"You look beautiful," I say, my voice quieter than I intended.

Claire smiles. "And you look stunning, Kelsi. That color suits you."

Neither of us is in a hurry to move; the space between us is filled with a quiet understanding.

"Shall we?" she finally says, offering me a hand.

I take it, and together, we head down the stairs, the sound of our boots echoing softly in the quiet house.

The drive into town is peaceful, the winding roads lined with trees in the early stages of their transformation. The restaurant, tucked into a historic building with warm brick walls and a glowing sign, is as charming as I hoped it would be. Inside, the atmosphere is cozy, with flickering candles on every table and soft jazz playing in the background.

Our corner table overlooks the street, where the occasional couple strolls past, bundled in scarves and holding steaming cups of coffee. The menu is full of hearty fall dishes—roasted squash soup, braised short ribs, and apple tarts.

As we settle into the rhythm of the meal, I find myself watching Claire more than I should. The candlelight highlights the angles of her face as she talks about her favorite fall traditions. I lean in, captivated by the ease of our conversation, the natural flow of laughter and shared memories.

When dessert arrives—a warm pear crisp with cinnamon ice cream—we share it without hesitation, our spoons occasionally clinking against the dish.

"The day was perfect," Claire says, her voice soft as she looks at me.

"It really was." I smile, feeling a warmth that has nothing to do with the wine we've been sipping.

The Vineyard always feels magical, but today was something else entirely—a day of exploring, laughing, and getting lost in the beauty of this place.

Claire leans back in her chair, swirling the last bit of wine in her glass. "I think my favorite part was that little bookstore we stumbled into. You secretly signing a few copies of your books. That was really cool."

I laugh softly, the memory still fresh. "I haven't done that in forever. Honestly, I was shocked to see that bookstores and readers haven't forgotten me. And that shop. It smelled like heaven, didn't it? Coffee, old books, and leather chairs. I could've stayed there all day."

"You were definitely in your element." Claire smiles easily and warmly. "It suits you."

My thoughts start to drift, unbidden, to what's waiting for me when I leave this island. The nerves creep in, tightening my chest.

Claire seems to notice. She always notices. "You're thinking about next week, aren't you?" she asks gently.

I nod, letting out a long breath. "Yeah. The national TV promo tour—it's so much bigger than anything I've done before. I mean, I've done book signings and book tours, but this...this feels huge. Like I'm about to step onto a stage I'm not ready for."

Claire sets her glass down and leans forward. "Kelsi, you've been preparing for this for years, whether you realize it or not. Your book is incredible—raw, honest, and real. You've put your story out there. Now, you're sharing it with people who need to hear it."

I bite my lip, her words settling over me like a balm. "What if I freeze? What if they ask me something and my mind goes blank? Or worse, what if I say something stupid and make a fool of myself?"

"Then you pause, take a breath, and answer when you're ready," Claire says firmly. "No one expects you to be perfect, Kelsi. They're not tuning in to see some polished PR machine— they're tuning in because you're *you*. Honest and vulnerable and brave. That's what people will connect with."

Her confidence in me is overwhelming, and I blink back the sting of tears. "You make it sound so simple."

"It is," she says, her tone soft but unwavering. "You've already done the hard part by living it. This is just the next step. I'll be cheering you on."

I reach for her hand, giving it a grateful squeeze. "Thank you, Claire. I don't know what I'd do without you."

She squeezes back, her smile gentle. "You'd be just fine, but I'm glad you don't have to find out."

As we step outside into the cool night air, she loops her arm through mine. The stars are brighter than I've seen them in a while, and as we walk back to the car, I realize that this night—this whole trip—has been a gift. One that I never saw coming but feels like exactly what I needed.

I wake to the soft warmth of the morning light, my body stretched out in the bed. But as I blink into the light, I realize the space next to me is empty. A quiet pang hits my chest. I stretch and listen, hearing the soft hum of movement downstairs.

I glance at the clock—7:30 a.m. I swing my legs off the side of the bed, my feet landing softly on the cool floor. The remnants of sleep linger as I step into the bathroom, splashing cold water on my face. My reflection stares back at me, eyes heavy with the exhaustion of the past few days. But something about it feels different now—there's a calmness in my chest I can't quite explain.

I pull on a soft sweater and jeans, the island air still crisp this early. As I make my way downstairs, the rich aroma of brewed coffee greets me. Claire is standing by the counter, her short pixie cut damp from a shower, the delicate strands curling slightly around her ears. She's pouring coffee into two mugs, her movements relaxed and natural.

"Morning," Claire says, glancing up at me with that soft smile of hers. "I made it strong."

I laugh softly, accepting the mug from her. "Perfect. I must have been sleeping hard. I didn't even hear you get up and take a shower."

We move to the breakfast nook, the ocean stretching out before us, calm and inviting this morning. The rhythm of the waves is soothing, matching the calm that hangs between us.

"So," she says, her voice breaking the silence, "how are you feeling about everything?"

I take a sip of my coffee, staring out at the waves, trying to find the right words. "It's been...unexpected. I didn't think I'd feel this way. But waking up next to you the past two mornings feels like something real. Something new. But also a little terrifying." I pause, my hands gripping the mug a little tighter. "And today, knowing we both have to go back to everything, back to the real world—it's hard."

Claire's gaze doesn't leave mine. She's quiet for a moment, her coffee untouched. "Yeah. I get that. I didn't expect to feel so...at home with you these last few days. It's like we've created this little world for ourselves, and now we have to leave it."

My heart skips in my chest. I take in her words, trying to steady the rush of emotions.

She reaches out, her fingers gently brushing against mine, grounding me in the moment. "What we've had these past few days and nights, it's something special. And it's not going anywhere. Not even when we're back in the real world."

Her words settle over me, warm and reassuring. I meet her gaze, my chest lighter than it's been in days. "I'm glad we took the chance."

Claire's hand squeezes mine softly. "Me too, Kelsi."

Chapter Twenty-Two

"You ready?" I'd recognize my agent's Boston drawl even if her name weren't programmed into my phone—first stop, *The Today Show*, onto *Good Morning America*, and finally, *CBS This Morning*. I'm booked on the national morning shows, a first in my long career as an author. This wouldn't be happening without my fearless agent, who has more connections than God. Jaci sometimes rubs some folks the wrong way—even me, but my career wouldn't have survived the last year without her. She helped pull this book out of me when I thought I had nothing else to say.

"I think I am." Jaci doesn't like my hesitation and lets me know.

"What do you mean, 'you think'?" She pauses and releases her signature sigh of frustration. "Come on, don't let your nerves get the best of you, Kels. This is your opportunity to remind your readers you're still here."

She's right. I've been disconnected from everything when I became Alex's full-time caregiver. I didn't believe I'd be back. But here I am, with what critics claim is the best work of my career.

"Listen, I just emailed you our schedule. It's your time KJ. Get packed, sleep, and I'll see you in the City tomorrow afternoon." Behind the jagged edges of her orders, the best interest of my career is at her center.

"Sounds good," An odd feeling of strength—more like a coat of armor—washes over my entire body. Something that has been so foreign to me until now.

"A new beginning, Kels," Jaci reminds me with a surprising edge of softness to her timbre.

"I am ready."

Just as I push my phone into the pocket of my jeans, I feel its vibration against my backside. Jaci probably forgot to remind me of some superfluous detail she thinks I need to know. I swipe up; I'm surprised to see a text from Claire. We've talked a couple of times since we've been back, but nothing more than a "Hi, how are you? Let's get together soon."

> Kels…feels like forever since I've seen you. I know you're leaving for NY tomorrow. Would love to see you before you go. Up for a little company tonight?

I've used my impending media tour as a scapegoat for pushing Claire to the back of my mind, compartmentalizing the feelings swirling in my head.

Tonight, though, Claire's text feels right on time. I breathe in and exhale a cleansing breath. The kind of breath that goes way down into your belly and makes you feel like you finally have enough air to keep pushing through.

I don't think I've ever taken one of those.

> I'd love your company. Come on over. Can't wait to see you.

> Hungry?

I can always eat. Surprise me!

I give myself permission to choose what feels good. I turn the ringer on in case the girls try to call and slide my phone back into my pocket. Barefoot and with a burst of energy, I take the stairs two at a time and head up to my room to pack—I don't have to silence my steps anymore.

My unpacked suitcases litter the parameters of my room, occupying the same spot they have all week. A combination of clean and mostly dirty clothes stares back at me. I would have never done that when I was married to Alex. The idea of perfection groomed me.

"Kelsi Jo Barker, it is your job to make sure your home is comfortable for your husband," my mother would remind me when I was growing up. And she'd make sure the edges of their lives weren't fraying. Or at least no one could see the fray from the outside.

Our bedroom is always warm this time of day, no matter the season. Its west-facing window looks out over the dense autumn foliage. The leaves are rapidly changing colors, blanketing the ground; although there's a crispness to the air, as the sun sets, for a few short hours, the temperature feels more like summer than fall. I rifle through my clothes, intending to unpack and reuse the smaller suitcase.

I love using this luggage, a present from the girls six Christmases ago. They were so excited as I unwrapped the matching baby blue vintage set, embossed with my initials on the front. That was the first Christmas they'd pooled their money together to buy gifts for Alex and me.

"Girls, it's perfect. Thank you!"

"You and Dad mentioned you wanted to travel more now that we're all, well, almost all of us, out of the house," Lexi said and looked at Ari.

She was right; Alex and I always talked about traveling once the girls were on their own. And they pretty much were; they'd all started families, with the exception of Ari, who was away at college. But that plan never came to fruition. In the early days of empty nesting, Alex was always traveling for work, which made getting away for pleasure challenging. I'd only had the opportunity to use my favorite luggage when I traveled to see Dad in Maine or Ari for a long weekend before Alex got sick.

Memories stare back at me as I continue to unpack the last few weeks—dirty clothes on the left and a few untouched outfits on the right. The red string of my swimsuit peeks out of the mesh compartment hidden behind the clothes I never got a chance to wear. Flashbacks flood my mind of that night in the hot tub with Claire. I'm not sure what prompted me to ask her to untie that same string I'm staring at right now. The string that takes me right back to that very night. I tug on the tip, inching it through the small holes until it won't inch any farther. Claire will be here any minute. I've been feeling her void the last few days. I'm anxious to see her.

I decide the unpacking can wait until I get home from New York. I'll just take one of Alex's old overnight bags in the closet.

I love walking into our closet. It smells like him, like us. His business clothes are still perfectly organized and color-coded, just like I left them. I can't bring myself to pack up his side of the closet just yet.

I talk to him in here. Although moments of memories wait to be unpacked in the next room, my history lives in this space. I inhale his lingering scent; my fingers slide across his jackets like the gentle strings on a guitar. The built-in chest of drawers that line the back wall of our closet keeps the intimate parts and pieces of 'Us' safe from the outside world. From love letters to our sacred sticky note obsession, I've kept it all—the puzzle pieces of the last thirty-five years fit together seamlessly. He invades my thoughts as I pull out the cedar box my mother gave me on our wedding day.

. . .

"Something old, something new, something borrowed, something blue. This is for you, Kelsi Jo—something old. Charlotte, I mean, Lolly gave it to me when I married your father." She handed me the treasure-keeper. "It's just big enough for the little things that will come to mean so much to you one day."

I was shocked she kept, much less accepted, anything from Lolly.

I saw her reflection in the mirror and turned to face my mother eye to eye. I've spent years running from her gaze but on my wedding day, I decided to meet it. Woman to woman, seasoned wife to a new wife. Her face softened as she handed me the keepsake.

"I promised her I would give it to you one day."

"Mom, what about your things? What did you do with your memories?" I asked.

Mom smiled, and with her white-gloved hands and perfectly strung pearls, she gently pushed the tulle veil away from my face and kissed me on the cheek—a moment that was as cliche as the old 19th century "something old, something new" adage. And like a scene from *Leave It to Beaver* or maybe more like Carol Brady from *The Brady Bunch*, she turned on her heel and glided toward the french doors.

"It's your turn to make and keep your own memories. Mine have a different place now."

Chapter Twenty-Three

September 29, 2019.

I open the box, and the rich cedar odor is as pungent as the day she gifted it to me. I set it on the shelf where I can see inside. Proof of our love tucked away so it doesn't get lost: the first love letter Alex and I wrote each other, our engagement announcement, a singular wedding invitation, Alex's wedding ring.

I look down and at my left hand, and the overhead light of the closet catches the diamond solitaire, a gift for our 25th wedding anniversary. I wiggle my ring finger and watch the prisms dance.

It's just big enough for the little things that will come to mean so much to you one day.

Slowly, I slide a lifetime off my finger, place it next to Alex's wedding ring, and close the box.

I squeeze my eyes shut.

"Alex? Alex?" This time he doesn't answer.

I grab the step stool that leans against the back wall of the closet. Its unoiled hinges make a shrill squeak as I open it and place it on the unsteady carpet. I almost lose my footing as I reach up to the top shelf and feel around for the small carry-on bag Alex lugged around from country to country when he'd travel for work. My arm stretches as far as it can reach, and my hand collecting years of dust that's settled on the distressed faux leather. I finally grab ahold of it, brushing the dust off my fingers and back onto the duffle bag; it nearly hits me in the face as I drop it on the floor. Next to it lands a piece of lined legal paper folded in half. My name is written on the front in Alex's handwriting. The memories of the letters we've written over the years come rushing back.

I want to stare at his handwriting for more than a moment. It's been so long. I can see the pen in his hand, the smooth lines of the *K* and the *e*, the loop of the *l*, the curve of the *s*, and the way he used to dot the *i*—always with a tiny heart—except this time where the heart used to be there is nothing. He was probably just in a hurry and forgot. He wrote my name the same way on the other side, along with the date: September 1, 2015.

I don't want him to go away. I want to sit in this moment as long as I can, and if I don't open the letter right now, it will make him stay longer.

* * *

The doorbell sings its familiar song, and the thought of seeing Claire again prompts waves of giddy nervousness—like the rush of a roller coaster at the pinnacle of the climb.

As I hurry down the stairs, I realize I haven't bothered to put on shoes or brush out the high ponytail that's been in my hair all day. I completely lost track of time in my closet, wading through memories that I forgot about everything else.

"Claire," I exhale and open the front door as far as my arm will reach—my heart races with exhilarating uncertainty, I feel driven by a wild hope that this just might be the most unforgettable journey of my life.

I want to keep riding.

She sets the bags down on the welcome mat—a harmonious

aroma of garlic toast, olive oil, and herbs sets off an orchestrated symphony of growls, reminding me I haven't stopped to eat all day. We embrace each other like this is a reunion years in the making. The last time we were together, we started as best friends and departed as lovers. Claire's embrace tells me everything—this wasn't just a fleeting moment, not a desperate grasp between two lonely souls searching for connection. It was something deeper, something real. A bond not easily broken.

We pull away slowly, our eyes locked in a shared moment of vulnerability. Claire's eyes, deep pools of sapphire, shimmer with a familiar mischief.

"Kelsi Jo," she says with a voice that sends shivers down my spine, "You look beautiful."

"You're lying," I laugh, smoothing out my frayed ponytail, pulling at my beat-up Rolling Stones T-shirt and ripped jeans. "I look like a hot mess."

Claire smiles, her teeth flash brilliantly against her sun-kissed skin. "A beautiful hot mess."

She nudges the bags with her foot. "Brought your favorite Italian fare from Mezzaluna's."

I nod, grateful for the gesture. Lately, my kitchen has become a place of mere functionality rather than warmth and nourishment.

"You know me well. I'll open the wine." I turn on my heel and feel her soft touch pull me back around to face her. She brushes a whisp of hair from my forehead and secures it behind my ear. She softly kisses me on the mouth. I reciprocate.

We move to the kitchen, the bags rustling with every step. I set the table and open the wine while Claire takes out the dishes and plates our food. The quiet fills the room with the rich aroma of rustic delights and the subtle clinks of utensils. We are in sync, our familiarity with each other's movements is evident.

"I missed you." Claire nervously fidgets with her short, wispy bangs.

"Me too," I admit, my throat tightening. "I've thought about that night in the hot tub and the nights that followed. Us...the way everything organically unfolded every day since."

Claire looks at me, her expression tender. "Do you regret it?"

I shake my head vehemently. "No, I don't. Do you?"

She shakes her head, too. "Not the night, not the feelings."

"Thank you for feeding me." I smile and lean back in the faded wooden chair that still wobbles unevenly like it did when I was a kid. I run my hand over the table my father gave me when he moved to his house in Maine and lift the wine glass to my mouth.

"This is a special table to me. I doubt I'll ever get rid of it." I say as memories of my childhood invade the moment. Claire rests her elbows on the table and smiles.

"Tell me more," she says.

"It's kind of ironic that you've been in my house as many times as you have over the last year, and I never formally introduced you to Lolly." I point over to my grandmother's picture set between her great-grandchildren on the mantle. Claire follows my finger, squints, and puts her glasses on.

"Lolly? You've talked about her several times, but I'd love to get to know her better." She pushes her chair back and steps lightly across the great room. She picks up Lolly's picture and runs her index finger over the smooth glass that protects the old black-and-white photo of a teenage Lolly.

I grab my wine, move from the hand-me-down table, and sidle up next to Claire.

"You look just like her, Kelsi Jo." She looks at the picture one more time and places it back in its spot, straightening it so it fits exactly the way it did before she picked it up. She looks back at me curiously and, in a teasing voice, asks, "So how exactly does this connect with the table over there?" We both chuckle at my jumping around. Assuming that she would automatically know how the two intersect.

"Yeah, sorry! See, it feels like you've been a part of my life forever. Like you should just know these things." I stop talking and stare into Claire's eyes. I rub the side of her smooth cheek with the palm of my hand and guide her chin towards me. I want to kiss her. So, I do.

"The table and Lolly..." I try to catch my breath from the kiss Claire and I just shared. "So, Lolly, my dad's mother, was my favorite person growing up. Lolly split her time between her cabin in Boothbay, Maine, and South Florida. She would stay with us every year before she went to Florida for the winter. I discovered my love of writing because of my Lolly. She would sit at that table day in and day out and plunk away at her typewriter. From the time I can remember, I used to love the click of her long nails on the keys. She typed so fast, and it totally piqued my curiosity. At first, I think I was more enamored by the sounds than I was the words, but it didn't take me long to fall in love with storytelling. Lolly told the best stories." I feel like I might be boring Claire, so I stop and look at her.

"Why did you stop, Kels? I want to know everything about you." She smiles, and I continue. I tell her stories from my childhood of sitting around that old table, watching Lolly create imaginary stories off the top of her head and take them to the page.

I walk over to the old table and sit back down on the chair that Lolly sat on for years—the one that everyone knows is mine, now.

"Sometimes, when I'm struggling to write, I'll bring my laptop and sit here and channel Lolly's creativity. The way she would ask me to make up a girl's name and a boy's name, and then she'd create a story out of nowhere. Sometimes, they'd be short stories, and other visits, she'd be working on what she would call her latest masterpiece."

"What kind of stories did she write?" Claire asks from the great room couch. She's been sitting there, sipping on her wine, watching and listening intently. It's like the table has become a prop, and I'm playing out my favorite childhood memories on the stage. I lift my head and turn toward my audience of one. "Lolly loved writing romances. She was the queen of the HEA…" I smile and Claire looks confusd.

"What's an HEA?"

"Happily Ever After. That's how I learned what an orgasm was, by the way." We both laugh.

It's 10 p.m. already, and I need to finish packing. Claire follows me upstairs and keeps me company as I put the finishing touches on what I'm taking with me. Claire sits on the bed, "What's this Kels?"

I peek out of the closet and see her holding the letter in her hand, eyeing it like a specimen.

"That," I say as I walk over and sit next to her on the bed, "is a letter that I found in my closet right before you got here." I take the gallon-sized bag that perfectly fits the folded letter protecting the artifact from her and look closely at it myself. I hold it up to the light like it's something I'm not supposed to read. "It's from Alex."

Claire tilts her head with a furrowed brow, a clear look of confusion washes over her face, but she doesn't say anything.

"I was confused, too," I say with a shallow giggle. "It fell out of his suitcase when I pulled it down. Look at the date. He wrote it a week before we found out he had cancer." Claire turns the bag over and nods.

"Well, what's it say?" she asks.

"I don't know," I look into her eyes with a bit of uneasiness. I didn't realize I felt that way until just now. "I'm going to read it on my way to New York. Reading material for the plane." Another nervous laugh.

"You've got more patience than me, Kelsi Jo," Claire responds.

It's more a mixed bag of anxious than patience, if I'm being honest with myself.

I finished modeling my outfits for Claire for my interviews on Monday morning. Claire is very stylish, always up on the current trends, and always put together. I've learned quite a few fashion pointers from her. Her past mentoring shows in the clothes I've chosen. I finish packing everything in Alex's small overnight duffle bag and set it by the bedroom door.

"Done!" I flop down on the bed next to Claire. My legs dangle over the side as they've always done since the day we bought this bed; my toes barely touch the floor, yet her long limbs reach just fine. I'm used to being short, and I've always kind of liked it that way. Alex's 6'3 stature always towered over my 5'4 frame. He made me feel protected, like no one could breach his love and get to me.

Claire wraps her arm around my waist and kisses the connecting skin between my neck and collarbone. Her warm breath and open lips create an instantaneous reflex; I fall back across the bed and pull her with me. I've never laid on this bed with anyone but Alex. I feel my breath tighten. My body yearns to be touched as Claire's hands find my breasts and gently caress them. Yet my mind races and fills me with every reason why this is wrong. Insisting I have no right to betray my husband like this. He lived here; he died here, and I am disrespecting him.

My body language shifts from intimacy to withdrawal. I can't cross this boundary in the very space where Alex and I built our love story for years. I gently disengage from her embrace.

"I'm sorry, Claire, I can't do this. Not here." I feel her thoughts swirling, trying to grasp the unspoken between us. It's not a lack of desire for her; it's Alex. His presence still wrapped around every corner, every piece of furniture, every echo of laughter. The very walls whispered secrets of our past intimacy, love that had flourished like an untamed vine.

Claire, sensing the turmoil within me, gently sits up. "It's okay," she whispered, her fingers finding the strands of my hair, each stroke echoing comfort and understanding. I couldn't meet her gaze, fearing she might see the storm of emotions crashing within.

"Please understand. Please don't be upset with me," my voice quivers.

Claire's eyes hold a depth of wisdom. "Kelsi, love isn't a switch. You can't just turn it off and on. Grief needs its time." She pauses. "Remember, our last time together was different. It wasn't...here."

The weight of understanding passes between us, and for a moment, we find solace in a silent embrace.

Pulling away, Claire adjusts her clothing. "I should head out." Her voice holds a tender resignation. "I'll be cheering for you, watching you on all the shows."

A bittersweet smile forms on my lips. "I'll call when I'm back."

Her hand, warm and reassuring, trails down my face, leaving a sense of warmth on my cheek. "I'll be waiting."

She lets herself out. I sit with the memories of Alex wrapped around me like a protective shroud, a poignant reminder of a past that was both my comfort and cage.

The warm water of the shower is a reprieve, washing away both the day's weariness and the evening's reflections. As the droplets run down, so does the residual weight of emotions, leaving me with a renewed sense of calm.

I dry off and climb into bed, pulling the familiar down comforter up to my chin. Its soft, feathery embrace instantly provides a comforting warmth. My fingers find Alex's letter, carefully sealed in the plastic bag. I can feel the contours of his handwriting beneath my touch, a silent testament to the love and memories we shared. Positioning it on the nightstand feels like giving it a special spot in my nightly routine. I'll remember to pack it in the morning, just as I'll remember my keys and phone.

With a soft sigh, I whisper into the darkness, "I love you, Alex. You've always known me so well. I'll read your words tomorrow —like we've always done when we've traveled. Good night."

With thoughts of the upcoming day, I turn off the bedside light.

Chapter Twenty-Four

September 30, 2019.

Last night, sleep slipped through my fingers. I kept replaying what had happened between Claire and me—the way I pushed her away—while intrusive thoughts of oversleeping and missing my alarm were on a loop in my mind.

"Ms. Kincaid, we're waiting for you out front when you are ready." The limousine service calls at 6 a.m. sharp.

"Thank you. I'll be down in five minutes," I reply.

Outside, the early morning air is crisp and refreshing. The trees that line our street are ablaze with color—fiery reds, golden yellows, and deep, earthy oranges—casting a warm glow over the pavement. Their once-thick canopy now filters light through patchy bursts of autumn brilliance, a vivid reminder that change is in motion. From a few houses down, the faint scent of woodsmoke drifts on the breeze, comforting and familiar—a quiet promise that nothing stays the same for long.

The driver opens the back passenger door and deposits my suitcase in the back of the oversized black Escalade. I feel like I am a part of the presidential motorcade instead of being transported to the airport.

"Are you ready Ms. Kincaid?" The driver asks.

I've never been called Ms.—I've always been Mrs.

Strange how this hits differently after you've lost your person.

"Yes, thank you." I glance at my phone and write a quick text message to Jaci:

> On my way to the airport! Thanks for the fancy ride 😄

> Excellent. See you in a few hours.

"Shit," I say to myself but loud enough for the driver to know there is something wrong.

He glances in his rearview mirror.

"I'm sorry, sir, but I need you to take me back to my house, please."

"Everything okay?" the driver asks.

"I forgot something extremely important," I say in a panicked tone.

"Yes, ma'am."

As soon as he pulls into my driveway and before he comes to a complete stop, I have the door open and one foot skimming the asphalt. I grab my keys and fumble with the damn key.

"Fuck. Let's go," I demand of myself.

Finally, I put the right key in the lock and rushed up the stairs, leaving the keys hanging in the front door.

Alex's letter. Where did it go?

I freeze, panicked, tears building up, ready to break levee. I tear my neatly made bed apart, scrambling, trying to find the damn plastic bag that I was certain I wouldn't forget.

Nothing. It's not in the bed or on the nightstand where I laid it the night before. It didn't fall beside the nightstand. I don't see it anywhere. I lie on the floor and cry.

I don't give a fuck if I miss the plane or the interviews; I just want to read the last love letter Alex wrote to me. I lay flat on my stomach, defeated. Then, like a miracle, I look to the left and see the shiny tip of something underneath Alex's side of the bed. I press against the floor as flat as I can and inch my way to the other side, using the length of my arm to reach the shiny object. I grab it between my thumb and pointer finger and pull it closer to me.

The letter.

I'm finally calm enough to see months of dust bunnies clinging to my black Angora sweater that I picked up reminding me I need to clean under the bed when I get home.

I rush back down to the car.

"I'm so sorry," I say to the driver.

"Are you okay?" he asks.

"I am. Thank you." I don't care what I look like. I have all I need right here in my hand.

* * *

I want to read the letter now, but I exercise patience. The electric anticipation of New York City and my big book promotion seem to dim in the backdrop of my thoughts as my fingers nervously fumble with the letter from Alex. We had this tradition. Every time he traveled, he wrote me love letters. One on his departure and one on his return. The date scribbled on this particular letter tells me he wrote it on his way back home after being away for fourteen long days.

The overhead speaker breaks my trance, "American Airlines Flight 2662 is boarding now at gate A 27..."

I'm up in an instant, clutching the letter and my belongings. I'm hardly aware of the first-class cabin I've settled into, my thoughts racing faster than the plane ever will.

"Ma'am, can I get you something to drink? Mimosa? Coffee? Water?" a flight attendant inquires, offering a warm smile.

"Black coffee, please." A symbolic gesture, really. Lolly always drank her coffee black. The familiar, bitter scent takes me back to mornings as a child spent listening to Lolly's stories, mornings that now feel centuries away.

Tucked in my plush airline seat, the sounds of the cabin dimming, I'm torn between two worlds: one where Alex and Lolly are still alive and one where I'm on the cusp of celebrating the biggest achievement of my career. But as I hold that Ziplock baggie—the thing that's been protecting the letter since it dropped on the floor of my closet—I can't help but think that reading this final note from Alex is, in some ways, as momentous an event. This trip isn't just about my work; It's about memories, about love, and about moving forward with the strength of those who've loved and supported me fiercely: Lolly, Alex, the girls.

The hum of the engines, combined with the tranquil aura of dawn, sets a peaceful tone. I find myself cocooned in this serenity; finally, I feel my heart fluttering with excitement for my book tour. As the plane reaches cruising altitude, I take a deep breath; I open the letter, ready for whatever words Alex left for me.

I clasp the letter tightly expecting to dive into loving words, possibly one of the heartfelt messages he often wrote during our life together. But as the words unfold, the flutter of my heart becomes a hard and fast irregular palpitation, echoing the dissonance I feel with every word.

Dear Kelsi Jo,

I find myself facing the weight of many burdens, heavy with emotions, guilt, and confessions. As I've done for the last 30 years, I've put pen to paper to relay my truth, which is far from the picture-perfect reality we've crafted. There's no delicate way to communicate such revelations, so I'll be direct.

Kelsi Jo, you were the woman of my dreams when we

started dating back at NYU. Your charm and charisma felt like a warm blanket. It looked like the Christmas gift under the tree no one wanted to open because it was so carefully constructed. Perfectly folded edges secured with invisible tape—you know, the kind you pay a little extra for so it doesn't show the imperfections. So aesthetically pleasing that to rip the pretty paper and perfectly placed purple bow is to destroy the hype that's been built around it.

With each line, a looming dread replaces the initial warmth.

You were the woman of my dreams.

I *was* the woman of your dreams? My gaze hurriedly moves from sentence to sentence, the morning sunlight now piercing, too bright, too cruel.

You, the creative writer, always making up stories and bringing them to life on the page. You wrote ours, too—except our story needed more than one author. Our marriage has always been a juxtaposition of your light and my shadows. You radiated the warmth and stability of a perfect suburban upbringing while I basked in the glow of your unconditional love, despite the scars from my own fractured past. While I admired your relentless pursuit of perfection, I couldn't always keep up, and it took a toll on my spirit.

What. The. Fuck.

Kelsi Jo, over the years, I've hidden truths that gnawed at me every day. But I am forced now to stand in those truths, not for anyone else but myself. The truth is, Kelsi, I have been having an affair with Eve for the last ten years. I've been hiding behind our storybook reality, a reality that's seeped into the crevices of our life—a filler that made everything look better than the original. We never put the pen down; we've always lived our perfectly curated stories out loud.

The world is tilting—I can't tell if it's the motion of the plane or the life I've known falling off its axis. Eve? My best friend? The woman who had been my rock, especially during his sickness and subsequent loss. A crushing wave of nausea surges within me. Memories flooded back—subtle glances between them, hushed conversations, laughter a bit too intimate—nights spent at the office and long business trips.

The airplane, this capsule of metal soaring high above, feels suddenly suffocating. My surroundings become a blur. The cheerful chitter-chatter of passengers, the flight attendants moving with grace down the aisle, the scent of fresh coffee—everything seems to mock my crumbling reality.

Desperately, I reach for the airline sick bag as my stomach convulses. The contents of the light breakfast I'd had come rushing out, mirroring the abrupt upheaval of my life's narrative. The act of vomiting, though violent and jarring, is almost cathartic—as if my body is attempting to physically rid itself of betrayal's bitter taste. I wipe my mouth with a tissue and hesitate but force myself to continue reading.

But there's a deeper truth that I need to share with you. I discovered a secret from our college days—Eve and I have a child, one she never told me about, who was given up for adoption. This revelation has consumed me as I grapple with how a careless one-night stand could give rise to life. My emotions oscillated between anger and pain, and I felt I couldn't approach you, fearing your inability to forgive us—rightly so. In that whirlwind of emotions, Eve and I found understanding and comfort in each other—it was all we had left.

I met my only son a few months ago. Oh, how I wish we could have all been a family. And one day, I hope our girls will forgive me and want to meet their half-brother.

I know this revelation will cause immense pain, and for that, I'm deeply sorry. Every lie, every excuse I've given for my absence, was an attempt to prolong the inevitable confrontation of my deceit.

Your strength, which I've always admired, blinded me into thinking you could bear anything, even my betrayal. And perhaps I used this as an excuse to keep on with the affair.

It's a confession of my profound weakness.

You, my beautiful Kelsi Jo, never deserved this pain. You've consistently been the embodiment of grace, love, and resilience, even when I couldn't see it. I want to ensure that you are taken care of financially and emotionally. I've made arrangements to make certain you are secure because even in my failures, I want to offer you some semblance of stability.

Please understand that my infidelity was never about your inadequacy but rather my own imperfections and my inability to communicate my feelings and fears.

I'm sorry for tarnishing our history, our love, and, most of all, for breaking your trust. You deserved honesty, fidelity, and a partner who appreciated every nuance of the masterpiece that is you.

Alex

The enormity of this revelation leaves me breathless.

Jesus Christ.

Eve "studying abroad" for a year back in college.

Her anger when I told her I was dating Alex.

Her brokenness when I discovered I was pregnant.

How could I have been so blind?

Not just an affair, but a child—a living, breathing testament tethering their lives together, like our girls tether ours. A whirlwind of emotions swirl within anger, hurt, disbelief, and beneath it all, a profound sense of loss all over again. The pain is twofold. Not only has my husband been unfaithful, but my confidante, my best friend, has betrayed me in the most unimaginable way. How will I face the world with this newfound knowledge?

The hum of the airplane engine fades into the background as I lean back in my seat, my heart pounding in my chest. I clutch the letter tightly, the paper crinkling under the pressure of my trembling fingers. My vision blurs with unshed tears, the words I've read over and over again burned into my memory. I can't make sense of them—don't want to. The man I built my life around, the man I devoted three decades to, has unraveled before me with a single, damning revelation. Alex and Eve.

The images come unbidden, intrusive. I see Alex laughing on our wedding day, the way he looked at me like I was his entire world. I feel the warmth of his touch, the strength of his arms that carried me through so many storms. And then, like a sharp knife cutting through those cherished moments, I see him with Eve—secret glances, quiet conversations that now seem laden with meaning, stolen moments I didn't notice but should have. The betrayal slices through me, leaving an ache I've never known before. It's not just the loss of him; it's the loss of us.

"Ma'am?" A voice pulls me back, and I blink up at the flight attendant. Her face is kind, her brow furrowed with concern. "Are you feeling alright? Can I get you anything? Do you need another sick bag?"

I try to find my voice, but it feels lodged in my throat. After a moment, I manage a weak smile. "No, thank you," I whisper. "I just...I need a minute."

She hesitates before nodding and stepping away. I let out a shaky breath, the tears I've been holding back spilling over. The irony hits me like a physical blow. Hours ago, I was filled with hope, planning my book tour, excited to share my story of healing and resilience. How will I stand in front of an audience now? How will I speak about Alex, about love, about the life we built, when the very foundation of that life feels like it's been ripped away?

And Eve. God, Eve. My best friend, my confidante. The woman who knew my secrets and now, as I've come to learn, shared her own with my husband. How do I face her? How do I reconcile her betrayal with the years of friendship that feel like a cruel joke now?

I close my eyes, the sting of tears burning my already raw skin. My chest tightens as the letter's words resurface.

"I didn't know how to tell you," Alex had written. "I never wanted to hurt you."

But he did. He hurt me in ways I don't know how to recover from. My love for him is fractured now, like a mirror shattered into a thousand irreparable pieces.

I loved a man I didn't fully know.

This trip was about my future—my book, my story, my healing. Instead, it feels like I've been thrown back into the past, into a reality I didn't know existed.

I tuck the letter into my bag; its weight far heavier than paper has any right to be. The airplane begins its descent, the soft crackle of the captain's voice announcing our approach to the city. My stomach knots as the ground draws closer. I'm not ready. Not ready for the world, not ready to pretend I'm okay. I grip the armrest, my breath coming in shallow bursts as the realization crashes over me: I don't know how to move forward from this.

The plane touches down with a jolt, but it feels like I'm still falling.

Part Three

Courage starts with showing up and letting ourselves be seen.
Brené Brown

Chapter One

SEPTEMBER 30, 2019.

I begin wandering aimlessly through LaGuardia Airport.

"Jaci, cancel everything. The book, the tour. Everything," "What? Kelsi Jo, what the hell is going on with you? Do you have any idea what you're asking?"

"I...can't. I'm sorry I can't—" I mumble, feeling as if the walls are closing in on me.

"Do you realize the contracts, the money, the publicity at stake here?" Jaci shoots back. "You owe it to everyone, including yourself, to see this through. What the hell happened? Where are you? I need to know what is going on." Jaci's tone is a combination of frustration and concern.

"I'm at LaGuardia," I say, trying to bring some clarity into the whirlwind of emotions. "I can't explain it all now, but..."

"No," Jaci interrupts, "You need to. Because whatever is going on in your head, you can't just run from commitments."

I don't know how to tell her what is wrong. I have to get out of this airport. Amidst the chaos, an idea emerges, a way to find answers.

"You're running. And whatever you're running from needs to

wait until after this publicity tour." Jaci accuses, the bitterness evident.

"It has to wait. That's all I can tell you right now."

"Fine. Go. But remember, this decision has consequences."

Ignoring the sting of her words, I head towards the car rental desk.

* * *

The rhythmic hum of the car engine merges with the distant echoes of New York's urban clamor. Traffic signals become a dizzying dance of reds and greens, but my mind is miles away, caught in a kaleidoscope of betrayal and heartbreak.

On the leather seat beside me, neatly folded yet marred by my incessant handling, is the letter. Alex's once cherished handwriting, which used to evoke calm, now sends shivers down my spine. The revelation of his affair, especially with my best friend, their newfound connection, a grown son, has left my world upside down. The letter's existence is an unwanted testament to the shattering of my once fairy-tale life.

In a bid to gain some semblance of control, I pull over to the side of the highway, letting the evening's cool air wash over me. The weight of it all demands a release. I reach for my phone. Besides Lolly, there's only one voice, one presence, that has always held the power to anchor me.

After a couple of rings, his familiar voice, filled with years of experience and love, answers. "Hi, Kels."

"Daddy, I need you." A flood of emotions purge my soul.

His immediate concern is evident. "Sunshine, what happened? Are you okay?"

Trying to steady my voice, I feel the dam break. "Alex betrayed me, Dad. With my best friend. My whole life feels like a lie."

There's a weighted silence. I can imagine him processing the gravity of the situation. When he finally speaks, his voice is laced with sadness. "Where are you?"

"LaGuardia. I was supposed to…I'm on my way to Boothbay. I need you." Fresh tears stream down my face, leaving track marks of my leftover mascara.

"Oh, Sunshine. This is the publicity tour thing for the book, isn't it?" He remembers in his own way.

I shake my head yes, like he can see me through the phone, and barely get the word "Yes" to part my lips. "Everything feels so raw, Daddy. So unreal. I thought I had the perfect marriage, the perfect life."

He takes a moment before responding. "Perfection is an illusion, Kels. What's essential is how we bounce back and how we find strength in adversity. Sunsets are breathtaking. But remember, they come after the day has run its course, with all its challenges and triumphs."

I whisper, "I don't know if I'll ever find serenity again."

"You will. It'll just take some time," he assures me, his voice filled with conviction. "When you get here, we'll sit by the harbor, watch the boats, talk to Lolly."

"I miss her, Dad."

"Me too. But she always shows up in one way or another when we need her the most."

He's right.

"Thank you, Daddy. I hope to be there by dinner time."

"We'll be waiting," he says, the warmth in his voice wrapping around me like a protective blanket.

As I merge back onto the highway, the cities and towns I pass become a blur, each mile bringing me closer to the refuge I seek.

The journey is long, giving me time to reflect, to grieve, and to slowly come to terms with my new reality. The road stretches ahead, sometimes straight, sometimes winding, echoing the unpredictability of life. But one thing remains constant—the promise of my father's unwavering love.

The steering wheel feels cold beneath my fingers. Tears blur my vision momentarily as I think about the irrefutable evidence that my once beloved husband cheated on me. The fact that he's no longer here doesn't make the betrayal any less painful. I shake the thoughts away, focusing on the road. Each mile marker I pass is a reminder of the truth that was hidden from me, the years of deception—or was it more like a lifetime?

The drive through Connecticut's Gold Coast provides a temporary distraction. The sun glints off the serene waters of the Long Island Sound.

Mystic flashes by my window, its charm undeniable. The marina, filled with boats and surrounded by quaint shops, paints a picturesque scene. A family laughs on the pier, children chasing each other. Their genuine joy stings.

Newport's grandeur looms next, a stark contrast to my somber mood. Even so, the beauty of Rhode Island tugs at me as I remember the last time Alex and I visited my father. Alex planned a romantic stop for us on our way to see Dad. Immediately, I'm back in the moment, and nothing can invade the memory: a quick overnight at the romantic Cliffside Inn, wine tasting and dinner at the Newport Vineyard, bubble baths, and primitive lovemaking. We were newly empty nesters, yet we behaved more like newlyweds.

Immediately, I do the math. Alex had an affair with Eve for ten years before he was diagnosed. Ari was a senior in college when we buried her dad. I count on my hands. Clicking off each year on my thigh. They would have been in the throws of their affair—at least two years in. I was never as good at math as I am right now. Numbers don't lie like people do.

The mind plays cruel games, spewing obscene scenarios and soul-crushing assumptions. Did he make love to her like he did me? How did he know about this place? Had he brought Eve here? Had he met his son yet? Maybe their son lived here. He would be about 30 years old. Do Alex and Eve have a grandchild together?

I make my way out of this place and its memories as fast as I can, and soon Plymouth comes into view. I try to put Alex and Eve out of the way and concentrate on the road ahead.

I roll down the window, and the salty air of Cape Cod fills the car. The expansive dunes, tranquil beaches, and distant light-houses stretch out before me, a silent testament to time and resilience. The wind tugs at my hair, whispering reassurances. I ask the breeze to carry away my pain, but it's cemented down.

Boston's skyline appears ahead. The traffic is heavy, forcing me to stay present to navigate the bustling streets with their hurried pedestrians and persistent honking.

As I cross into New Hampshire, the rugged beauty of the coastline offers a brief respite. Portsmouth's charm is undeniable. The sight of the colonial-era buildings lining the streets takes me back to simpler times. Or at least, times I once thought were simple.

Maine's border sign welcomes me. It feels like a victory, having come this far despite the weight in my heart. The road ahead winds through lush forests. The scent of pine fills the car, grounding me.

Dusk sets in as I approach Boothbay's landscapes and my father's safety. Its familiar surroundings come into view, bringing with them a flood of memories. I've always admired the sprawling houses with their grand facades and perfectly manicured lawns when I've come to visit. Our girls spent many summers here with my dad, fishing and laughing. Now they bring their own children here and build new ones. The last rays of sunset paint the horizon in hues of gold and pink as the world punctuates the day. Dad's property, and I see him waiting for me by the water's edge, his silhouette illuminated by the setting sun.

With a deep breath, I step out of the car. Each step towards my father's house is both a challenge and a relief. While the journey has been long and the revelations painful, the promise of a father's embrace and the comfort of home give me strength.

I've survived the drive but haven't even come close to scratching the surface of what's ahead.

* * *

"Daddy?" I call out like a lost child in the mall.

He turns around, his flannel shirt hanging in places that used to be tight, a little more of his scalp showing through his thinning gray hair. But his eyes, those deep blue wells, remain the same — pools of love. He opens his arms wide just as he used to when I'd run to him with skinned knees or a broken toy. The universal sign that everything was going to be alright. Tears blur my vision as I bridge the gap between us, dropping the haunting letter. The world fades as I melt into his familiar arms, my face pressed against the soft fabric of his shirt, inhaling the comforting blend of soil, the sea, and that distinct cologne he's always worn.

"Oh, Sunshine."

He rests his chin atop my head, and we stand there, frozen in a moment that feels like a bridge between my past and my present. "What's happened, Kels?" His voice, deep and soothing, rumbles in his chest, vibrations I can feel against my ear.

Swallowing the lump in my throat, I pull back just enough to look up into his eyes.

"Alex and Eve. Dad...they had an affair."

"I'm sorry Kelsi—"

"But there's more."

His brow furrows in confusion. He seems to sense my hesitance. "Let's go inside, alright?" he suggests gently. "You can tell me everything when you're ready."

I allow him to guide me towards the house, his arm wrapped securely around my shoulders. The sprawling mansion, with its tall windows and ivy-covered walls, has always been impressive, a testament to the success he worked so hard for. But today, it's not the grandeur that catches my attention. It's the warmth, the memories, the promise of shelter from the storm.

We enter the living room, where large French windows offer panoramic views of the harbor. Dad gestures for me to take a seat on the plush couch while he heads to the bar cabinet, retrieving a bottle of old scotch and two glasses. He pours us each a drink, the amber liquid reflecting the soft glow of the setting sun.

Handing me a glass, he settles down next to me. "Whenever you're ready," he says softly and walks out on the wrap-around porch and lights the fire.

"Here's a blanket. You up for sitting outside?" he asks.

"I'd like that."

I take a sip, letting the warmth of the alcohol brace me for the confession ahead. But even as I prepare to speak and share the heart-wrenching truth, I take solace in this: no matter the storm, I am never truly alone with my dad by my side.

We sit on the wicker chairs facing each other, and by the glow of the fire, I hand my dad the same letter I read less than 24 hours earlier. The letter that landed me in Maine instead of on national TV promoting the book I spent the past year writing about losing my soulmate and healing from what I thought was the greatest loss and love of my life.

"Here, this will explain everything."

Chapter Two

September 30, 2019.

The silence stretches as he continues to read, each word on the paper echoing the thunderclap of revelations in my heart. The fire casts flickering shadows on his face, and I watch him intently, trying to gauge his reaction. Every furrow of his brow, every intake of breath feels amplified, and I wring my hands, the anxiety bubbling within me—it almost feels like I'm tattling on my late husband like he should be here to defend himself.

But the letter says it all—his truth, which is now mine.

Finally, Dad lowers the letter, taking a long moment to process what he's just read. The lines on his face seem deeper, carved by a mixture of pain, understanding, and something else I can't quite place.

"Kelsi Johanna. I don't know what to say. I always thought the world of Alex. I'm in shock. Sorry seems cliche and inappropriate."

He takes a deep breath. His eyes, usually vibrant, are now clouded with emotion.

The weight of the secret between Alex and Eve sits heavily

between us—a legacy of choices and actions that has shaped my life in ways I'd never fathomed.

I blink back tears. "I don't know what to do with it. It changes everything—my past, my present, my future. What am I going to tell the girls?" My voice wavers. A lone tear slips down my cheek.

Reaching out, he clasps my hand in his, the warmth reassuring. "It's a lot to take in," he says gently. "But I'm here for you."

A sob escapes me, and I lean into him, seeking the comfort I've always found in his embrace. "I'm so lost, Dad. My entire life has changed in less than 24 hours."

"I know, sweetheart. But remember, the past can't be changed. We can only choose how we move forward."

We sit like that for what feels like hours, the fire's warmth wrapping around us like a protective cocoon. The night deepens, the stars shimmering above, and the rhythmic lull of the waves in the distance offers what should feel like a semblance of peace.

Eventually, Dad breaks the silence. "What are you going to do about your media appearances?"

I sigh. "I canceled it. I need time...time to process everything. I couldn't go on national TV after this."

He nods, understanding in his eyes. "Whatever you need, Kelsi."

And in that moment, amidst the storm of emotions and revelations, one thing remains certain: with my father by my side, I'm never truly alone.

Dad clears his throat, drawing my attention back to him. "You know," he begins, choosing his words carefully, "sometimes life throws curveballs we never see coming. It's...complicated."

I chuckle bitterly. "That's one way to put it."

He takes a sip of his drink, his eyes distant. "When your mother and I were young—hell, throughout our entire marriage, we faced our fair share of challenges. Every relationship does. But I never imagined Alex would ever do anything like this—or Eve..." His voice trails off, the weight of the revelation evident in his eyes.

I squeeze his hand, needing to feel that connection. "Me either. I'm just collateral damage in a story I never asked to be part of."

He looks at me, his gaze intense. "You are not collateral damage. Kelsi, you've always had this innate ability to see the bigger picture. To find clarity amidst chaos. But remember, while the past influences us, it doesn't define us."

A lump forms in my throat. "But what if it does? What if this secret, this revelation, taints every memory?"

He leans closer, his voice soft but firm. "Then you find new moments. You build new memories. We can't let the actions of others dictate our happiness or our peace. We must take control of our narrative."

Tears stream down my face. "The book, Dad. It's my heart and soul on those pages. How can I promote it, knowing what I know now?"

"Your book is *your* truth, Kels—not Alex's and sure as hell not Eve's. It's your journey of love, loss, and healing. Yes, some of the context has changed, but the emotions and the experiences are still valid. Maybe even more so now."

"Jaci is so pissed at me right now." I look out into the darkness with my thoughts.

"Does she know what happened?" His voice, low and concerned, breaks my reverie. It's my father, looking at me with those deep-set eyes that always see through to the heart of things.

"No. When I called her from the airport, I just told her to cancel everything."

He leans forward, the lines on his face deepening with concern. "Jaci should be the first person you talk to, Sunshine." A certain gravity to his words makes my stomach twist into knots. I must face this.

We fall into a contemplative silence, the weight of our conversation settling around us like a dense fog.

"Kelsi Johanna, if there's one thing I know about you, it's that you don't like to ask for help. She's on your side. Reach out to her and let her know what is happening."

I pick at a loose thread on my sweater, buying time before voicing the question that's been haunting me. "What should I do about Alex?"

Dad sighs, running a hand through his graying hair. "I'm not sure what you mean by that. Alex is dead. What's done is done. He wrote that letter a few days before his diagnosis and then came to his senses. Listen, I'm not giving him a get-out-of-jail-free card, but he spent the last few years he was alive with you. You've always been his plus-one."

"Plus Eve makes three—there's been three of us in this marriage for years," I retort, bitterness coating my words. "I'm scared, Dad."

"I know you are," he murmurs, his arms wrapping around me, holding me close. "But remember *who* you are. You're strong, resilient, and one of the bravest people I know. Whatever decision you make, whatever path you choose, I'll be right here beside you."

He reaches out, his fingers brushing against my cheek in that comforting way only he knows. "Sunshine, you will find your way through this."

We continue to sit; the fire gradually dwindles, its embers glowing faintly, much like the hope I cling to.

After what feels like an eternity, I speak up. "Do you mind if I stay for a while?"

"Of course not." He gently places his hand over mine, just like daddies know how to do to make their baby girls feel safe.

A smile forms on my lips, the first genuine one of the evening. "Thanks, Dad."

His eyes light. "Of course. It's been years since we've spent time together like this. I'm happy to have you here."

"I need to reconnect with myself, away from the noise, the chaos. And this place, you, with its serenity and memories, feels right."

He hugs me tight, his voice thick with emotion. "I'm proud of you, Kelsi. Always remember that."

I head upstairs to my bedroom, one of five in the house my parents bought as a vacation home twenty-five years ago, back when my father's career was soaring and weekend escapes to the coast felt like a luxury.

As I climb the steps, the weight of my conversation with Dad presses down on me like a storm cloud. There's comfort in returning to familiar places during times of heartache, and this house—perched on the edge of Boothbay Harbor with its sweeping ocean views—has always been my sanctuary.

Each step on the wooden staircase creaks beneath my feet, echoing the weight of my emotions. Tonight's talk with Dad was difficult. My husband's infidelity and my best friend's betrayal, a secret burden I'd been carrying for such a short time, spills out in a torrent of tears and confusion.

My fingers brush against the doorframe of the room that was always mine and Alex's when we'd visit. Pushing it open, a wave of familiarity washes over me. The room remains unchanged, untouched by time. The walls, painted a soft blue, are adorned with family photos taken throughout the years as we've visited.

It's that window, though, that always captivated me. Stretching almost the full width of the room, it offers a view that most would consider priceless: the endless expanse of the ocean, its waves crashing relentlessly against the rocks, an eternal dance of power and grace. Tonight, those waves mirror my turbulent emotions, the ebb and flow of pain, betrayal, and loss.

I make my way to the bed, its quilt familiar beneath my fingers, warm and comforting. The room smells of the ocean, salt, and freedom intermingling, reminding me of simpler times. Dad had envisioned a haven for our family. For Mom. For me. For Cory and his family, for all of us.

He's lived alone in this big house since Mom passed away. It's too big for one person, but he wants a home big enough for his entire family to enjoy.

Honestly, I can't imagine Dad living anywhere else.

Memories flood back. Afternoons spent curled up with a book, the distant sound of the girls and their granddaddy downstairs, the soft cadence of their voices mingling with the whispers of the ocean. And my mother's funeral.

My mother's been gone for nearly sixteen years. The day of her funeral was a bright spring afternoon—an ironic contrast to the heaviness in my chest. The church was packed with people who knew her as 'Mrs. Franklin Kincaid' the poised, polished woman who hosted luncheons and never let her smile falter in public. They didn't know the Marissa I did, the woman who carried her bitterness like an invisible cloak wrapped tightly around her.

I sat in the front pew, flanked by my father and Lolly, who had flown up from Florida the moment she heard the news. Alex and the girls sat quietly beside me, their small hands folded in their laps, their wide eyes darting around the church. Lolly's presence felt like an anchor as if to say, *I've got you, darling.*

The eulogy, delivered by our family pastor, carefully curated a version of my mother's life: a loving wife, a devoted mother, and a pillar of the community. I stared at the mahogany casket adorned with white lilies, her favorite flower.

"Appearances are everything, Kelsi Jo," she used to say, and it seemed fitting that even in death, the narrative of her life was polished to perfection.

But the truth gnawed at me. The years of criticisms, the passive-aggressive remarks about my choice to pursue writing instead of a "respectable" career, her disapproval of my closeness to Lolly—all of it bubbled beneath the surface. And yet, I felt no anger, only a hollow ache for the connection we never had, for the mother she could never be.

As the service ended and we followed the casket out into the cemetery, I caught Lolly's eyes. There was an unspoken under-standing between us, a recognition of the complicated woman we were both mourning.

At the gravesite, my father stood stoic, his hand gripping mine tightly. I could feel his sorrow, deeper and more complex than my own, and I wondered if he was mourning not just the loss of his wife but the decades of unspoken resentment between them.

I hesitated when it was my turn to place a flower on her casket. The weight of our strained relationship pressed against me, but so did the flicker of something else—gratitude, maybe, for the ways she had shaped me, even in her rigidity. I placed the lily down gently, whispering, "Goodbye, Mom."

As we left the cemetery, Lolly slipped her arm through mine. "She was a tough one, wasn't she?" she said, her voice tinged with both sympathy and honesty.

I nodded, a small smile tugging at my lips. "She was."

*　*　*

This house, that fire pit—they've been a constant through the years. Countless nights, we gathered around the same fire where we sat tonight, listening to Dad recount his early days—building boats from scratch in Lake George, pouring his heart and soul into every creation. He spoke of the sacrifices, the challenges, and the quiet joy of watching a boat take shape beneath his hands.

"Life has its storms, Kelsi," he'd say, his voice steady with experience. "But how we navigate them is what defines us."

Drawing the curtains aside, I perch on the window ledge, my fingers pressing against the cool glass. The ocean stretches out before me, lit by the full moon, its intimidating and reassuring vastness. In its presence, my problems seem minuscule, yet the pain is real. The betrayal is raw.

A soft sigh escapes my lips. With its familiar nooks and comforts, this room has silently witnessed so many highs.

Tonight, it's a witness to my broken heart, the shattered dreams of a marriage gone awry.

On a whim, I dig my phone out of my purse, half-expecting it to be as silent and empty as the room around me. But the screen, as it comes to life, shocks me with its glaring brightness, one hundred two missed calls. The number blares at me, making my head spin.

And then the text messages. A cascade of texts from Jaci, Claire, the girls...and Eve.

What the fuck is she texting me for?

My heart lurches. Eve? The very mention of her name sends a ripple of emotions through me. What could she possibly want? We haven't spoken in months, not since that day at the coffee shop when she told me I wasn't a "good enough friend to her since Alex died." Thinking back on that conversation, with the truth looming over my head like a crack of lightening spitting from the sky, fills me with a rage I didn't know I was capable of feeling.

I unlock my phone, and Eve's message hits me like a wave of salt water crashing into a raw, open wound.

> Good luck tomorrow, Kelsi. I'll be watching.
> Love, Eve

Is this a cruel joke? How am I supposed to respond?
So, I don't.
Next, a group text from my daughters:

> Lexi: Love you, Mom

> Lia: We'll be watching. What time, again?

> Lexi: Lia, it's the morning shows!!!!!! Usual time. Mornings, duh!

> Lia: Okay, okay! You don't have to be so rude!

Ari: Shut up, both of you!

Ari: Sorry mom. We'll be watching. Call us in
the morning when U R getting ready!

Lexi: We love you! You're our star, our shero,
our MAMA!!!!

I start to respond to the group text, and I freeze. My girls. My God, what am I going to tell my girls...

I stop and swipe to the next message. Claire:

Hi Kelsi. I just wanted to let you know I'm
thinking of you and will be watching as you
knock the socks off of America tomorrow and
sell thousands of books. Love, Claire

I sit and stare at her text. My mind rewinds to less than 48 hours before the bottom fell out of my world.

I was so sure that fucking letter that I savored and treated like a priceless relic, not having the slightest clue that it was Alex's final tell-all, was a heartfelt love letter.

I pushed Claire away, treating our intimacy like a secret I should be keeping, like I was betraying my husband by lying with her in the bed I shared with him.

I wonder how many times he fucked Eve in our bed?

Perhaps that should be my response to her text message tonight:

Hey Eve, so great to hear from you. Question,
how many times did you fuck my husband in
my bed?

I swipe to the next message. It's Jaci:

Kelsi, where are you?

Please call me.

> I'm worried about you.

> Don't do this to your career. Nothing is worth
> ruining all you've worked for.

> CALL ME

It's after midnight, but I decide the only text I need to answer is Jaci's:

> Jax, I'm so sorry for all of this. I don't know
> where to begin, so I'll

> give you the cliff notes.

> I found a letter from Alex hidden on his side of
> the closet

> I read it on the plane.

> I thought it was his final love letter to me.

> It was a confession.

> He was going to leave me.

> He was having an affair with my best friend.

> And…

> They have a child together that Eve put up for
> adoption 30 years ago.

> > Are you fucking kidding me? We'll talk about
> > this in the morning.

Lying down, I pull the quilt around me, seeking its warmth and comfort. The rhythmic sound of the waves crashing against the cliffs provides a soothing backdrop, their eternal dance a reminder of life's ups and downs. But tonight, it feels like a cruel reminder of happier days.

In this quiet darkness, the weight of my reality threatens to crush me. It's not just the betrayal. It's the loss, the grief, the sharp sting of humiliation. I've run away to this refuge, the home that has stood strong for years, hoping to find solace. For now, though, my heart won't let me forget.

Chapter Three

I blink away sleep, the weight of yesterday's revelations pressing heavily on my chest. It feels like waking from a nightmare, only to realize that the nightmare is my reality.

I rub my temples, trying to chase away the pounding headache. Flashes of the past few days on a continuous loop—Alex, Eve, the secrets, the devastation of reality. The pain is raw and deep, and every breath feels like a struggle. A part of me wishes I could go back to the oblivion of sleep, but I know there's no escaping the truth.

The sheets are twisted around my legs, damp with the restless heat of another sleepless night. I shove them off and sit up, my body aching from too many hours of tossing and turning. The air in the room is thick, pressing down on me like a weight I can't shake. I need to move—need to do something to quiet the storm still raging inside me.

I drag myself to the bathroom, catching my reflection in the mirror. A hollowed-out version of myself stares back—eyes shadowed, their usual spark dulled to embers. I turn on the faucet and cup my hands beneath the icy stream, then splash the water over my face. The shock of it sends a shiver down my spine, but it does nothing to erase the exhaustion clinging to me.

As I step back into the room, my phone screen glows, notifications stacking up like unfinished conversations. A reminder of the life I left behind. My gaze snags on a message from Jaci. My stomach twists. The call from the airport. The rushed text late last night. I groan, rubbing a hand over my face. I owe her the full story.

Taking a deep breath, I dial her number. After a few rings, she picks up. "Kelsi Jo? My God. What happened?"

I hesitate, unsure of how to begin. I tell her everything.

Silence. Then, "I'm so sorry."

Tears prick my eyes. "I couldn't do it, Jaci. It would have been worse if I would have done the shows."

Jaci sighs. "We'll manage. I'm not sure how yet, but we will. I am doing damage control as we speak."

Gratitude washes over me. "Thank you, Jaci."

"For now, take care of yourself," she assures me. "You'll hear from me soon."

I let out a shaky breath and look at my watch. The girls and everyone else I know will have their TVs on, DVRs set, and ready to watch me talk about my book.

I need to reach out to the girls. I pick up my phone to respond with a text when it rings instead.

"Mom. Where are you? I watched *CBS This Morning*, and you're not on. What happened? Are you okay?" She's got a hysterical tone to her voice.

"Lexi, calm down. I'm at Grandaddy's." I answer, unsure of what to say.

"Why are you there? Is he okay?" Her voice still shaking on the verge of tears.

"Everyone is fine—"

"Hang on, Lia is calling." She puts me on hold, and seconds later, I hear my other daughter ask the same questions, to which I provide the same answers.

"If you and Grandaddy are okay, what's going on?" Lia speaks for both of them.

"We'll talk about it another time. All you girls need to know right now is that I'm going to spend some time with my dad."

Lia chimes in, "Mom, none of this makes sense. Why are you there when you should be on TV promoting your book? What changed?"

"Oh, my sweet girl, things can change in the blink of an eye." I found that out the hard way. It's just not time for their world to change yet.

"When will you be back?" Lexi and Lia ask in unison.

"A few weeks. I'll keep in touch," I assure them.

"We love you, Mom," Lia says.

"I'll call you soon, girls. I love you," I say and disconnect.

The weight of the unsaid words and the secrets I hold back press heavily on my chest. As I hang up, the dam holding back my emotions crumbles. The levee of tears breaks once again, and this time, the flood is relentless. Each sob rips through me, echoing the betrayal, the pain, and the unbearable burden of truths not yet shared. The room blurs, the sounds around me fade into a distant hum, and all I can feel is the raw, unfiltered agony of heartbreak and deception. For what feels like an eternity, I let the tears flow, allowing myself to grieve for the life and trust shattered.

* * *

As painful as it is, I'm determined to face it head-on and find my way through the storm. I head downstairs to make a late breakfast, but Dad beat me to it.

Dad turns to me, his eyes glinting with a mischief I hadn't seen in a long time. "Sunshine! How about a little breakfast."

I wrap my robe around me a little tighter, sit down, and watch him finish preparing a feast for just the two of us.

"You remember the stories Lolly used to tell us?" he asks.

A smile tugs at the corner of my mouth. How could I forget?

"Every summer when she'd stay with us, every night after dinner, without fail. Some of those tales seemed too wild to be true, but she told them with such conviction."

He chuckles, "Yes. Lolly always did have a flair for the dramatic."

I frown, recalling my mother's disdain every time Lolly spun a tale. She would walk out of the room, her lips pursed, muttering about how impressionable minds shouldn't be filled with such nonsense. "Mom never liked those stories."

Dad nods. "She never liked Lolly either. She felt threatened, I guess. Lolly was a free spirit, a force to be reckoned with. Your mother, as strong-willed as she was, couldn't understand that kind of freedom."

"Lolly was special," I muse. The memories of those days flood back: the scent of Lolly's rose perfume, the way she'd ruffle my hair and the warmth of her laughter. We'd sit on the porch, and she'd regale me with tales from her many adventures—always with a cigarette sometimes lit other times, not, hanging from the corner of her mouth. "What was the real reason Mom didn't like her?"

Dad's smile fades a little. "She was different, Kels. And in those days, being different wasn't just difficult; it was dangerous. Lolly sat with a lot of secrets. Secrets she hid from me until I was a grown man."

I raise an eyebrow, intrigued. "Secrets?"

He sighs, running a hand over his face. "Lolly loved to take her stories to the page. Stories too daring, too...cutting-edge, they'd said. Everyone told her to keep them locked away."

My heart aches at the thought. "That's where I got my love for storytelling. I always wondered what she did with all the things she worked on sitting at our kitchen table."

Dad walks over to the coffee table he made from leftover wooden boat hulls and pulls out several boxes from each deep drawer. Dust dances in the air as he sets it on my lap. "She left these for you. Even then, I think she knew that you'd be the one to understand and appreciate them."

I open the box with trembling hands, revealing a combination of stacks of typed-out and some handwritten manuscripts; the ink faded, but the passion is unmistakable.

"Dad. This is unbelievable. There has to be over a hundred manuscripts here." Old, rusted binder clips fasten each manuscript. "Have you read any of them?"

My dad chuckles, "I have read most of them. Quite the story-teller your Lolly was."

"Why are you just now sharing them with me? She's been gone for what, ten years now?"

He pauses and turns to face me. "Lolly had another secret, one she hid from the world." Dad's voice cracks slightly. "She loved someone, someone the world told her she shouldn't. She loved a woman and carried that love till the very end."

Tears fill my eyes as the pieces fall into place. The whispered conversations I'd accidentally overheard between Mom and Dad, the hate-filled glances from my mother, the sadness in Lolly's eyes at times.

This hits me, but not in a way that feels wrong. It's how a person feels when they are so deeply connected to someone, like I feel connected to Claire. It's like Lolly's spirit inhabited mine permanently.

Dad nods. "It was a different time, Kels. People didn't under-stand, didn't accept. My father caught her in their bed with another woman and left our family. We never heard from him again. There were family members who knew. They pushed her away and labeled her the black sheep. But I knew my mother. I knew her heart, her love, her pain."

I take a shaky breath, memories of Lolly flooding back in a new light. Her strength, her resilience, and her ability to love unconditionally. "You never judged her?"

His eyes meet mine, filled with a depth of understanding. "I never knew the truth until your mother and I married. But when

I found out, I never judged her. She was my mother. I loved her. I wanted her to be happy. She deserved it."

My heart hammers in my chest, the weight of my own secret threatening to spill over. "Dad," I begin, my voice barely above a whisper, "Do you want me to be happy, too?" I look out the floor-to-ceiling windows that overlook the cold Maine bay. "I have something I want to share with you."

He waits patiently, his steady gaze encouraging me to continue.

"I met someone," I confess, my pulse racing. "Someone who's made me question everything I thought I knew about love."

"Kels, that's wonderful—" I cut him off mid-sentence.

"Her name is Claire."

Dad's expression remains gentle. "And you're in love with her?"

"I think so. It sure feels like I am. You're the first person I've told." The tears finally spill over. "I've been so scared, and I haven't really had the capacity to think about it. I just know that every time I'm with her, it feels right. I've been scared of what it means, scared of how the world will see me...scared of how the girls will react. Scared of the full disconnect from Alex. Sometimes I felt like if I moved on, I was betraying him..."

He reaches out, wiping away my tears. "Kelsi Jo, you're my daughter. I love you, no matter what—just like I loved Lolly. My mother taught me that love has no boundaries and no labels. If Claire makes you happy, that's all I need to know."

We sit in silence; the weight of our confessions and the strength of our bond fill the room. Outside, the world continues its endless march, but in this moment, surrounded by memories and the love of family, everything feels right.

"Lolly would be so proud of you," Dad says softly.

I clutch the manuscripts to my chest, feeling the weight of Lolly's legacy. "Thank you, Dad. For everything."

He smiles, pulling me into a tight embrace. "Always, Kelsi Jo."

. . .

I leaf through the first manuscript, Lolly's handwriting stretching across each page. The weight of history, of hidden emotions, bears down on me as the day begins to unfold.

"Do you remember," I start, my voice distant as a particular memory resurfaces, "that summer, I think I was in 10th grade, and Cory was a senior?"

Dad chuckles, "The summer of the incessant rain, the leaky roof, and the tales by candlelight? Your mother would never go with us to Lolly's cabin."

I smile, "That's the one."

We both fall silent, lost in that shared memory. Lolly had spun tales of old lovers and tragic endings, of brave women and fearless pursuits. At the time, I'd thought them to be figments of her vibrant imagination. But now, understanding the layers of her hidden self, I wondered how many were fragments of her reality.

"She loved that cabin," Dad says, his eyes distant. "It was her escape, a place where she could be herself without judgment. She and...Helen used to go there."

Helen. The name rings a bell. A distant memory of a tall woman with raven-black hair and a musical laugh. I'd met her a couple of times during my childhood but never connected the dots. "Helen was her partner?"

Dad nods. "Yes. They were inseparable but kept their love affair hidden. That cabin was their sanctuary."

I imagine the two of them, in the heart of nature, away from the prying eyes of society, sharing stolen moments of genuine love. The image makes me think about Claire.

"I want to go back to the cabin," I say, a decision forming in my mind. "I want to reconnect with that part of Lolly, with that part of myself."

Dad looks thoughtful. "It's been years since anyone's stayed there. I go a couple times a year to make sure it's still standing, but I don't know what you're gonna find on the inside."

"I don't mind," I reply, determination setting in. "It feels... necessary. Especially now, when everything feels so tumultuous."

We sit there long into the evening, wrapped in our memories and thoughts. The room's only illumination comes from a single lamp and the soft glow of the fireplace. The silence, punctuated only by the ticking of the grandfather clock, feels both comforting and heavy.

Breaking the silence, I murmur, "I wonder if Claire would like to meet me at the cabin."

Dad smiles gently. "Why wouldn't she? It might be good for both of you. A place away from everything, where you can just be."

I nod slowly. "You're right. I'll ask her."

My dad reaches across the space between our chairs, his fingers wrapping around mine. His touch is warm, reassuring. "Kelsi Jo, remember, you carry the strength of generations. Lolly's resilience, her spirit, it lives on in you."

Humbled by his words, I reply, "And you, Dad, have been the bridge between those generations. You've shown me the power of acceptance, of unconditional love."

The night deepens, wrapping us in its embrace. The conversation takes a lighter turn as we reminisce about happier times, shared memories, and family jokes. Amid the laughter and stories, there's a promise—a promise of support, understanding, and an unbreakable bond.

I pick up the first of Lolly's manuscripts. The story, titled *Whispers in the Wind,* begins with a description of a young woman standing at the edge of a cliff, her hair wild, her face turned toward the sea. As I read, I'm captivated by the depth of emotion and the intricate play of words. It's a love story, but not a conventional one. It's a tale of forbidden love, of societal expectations, and the courage to defy them.

I look up from the pages, lost in thought. "Dad, did Lolly ever try to publish these?"

He shakes his head. "She wanted to but said the few agents she approached rejected her work. They said it was too avant-garde, too controversial for the times. It broke her heart, but she never stopped writing."

The injustice of it angers me. Such beautiful stories, lost to the world because of narrow-mindedness. "I want to publish them," I say decisively. "Once things settle down, I want to talk to Jaci about Lolly's manuscripts."

Dad looks taken aback. "Make sure you think this through before you make a move. It's not just Lolly's legacy; it's also her secret. Some people, even in our family, might not react kindly."

I meet his gaze, determination burning within me. "I'm tired of secrets, Dad. Lolly's stories deserve to be heard. They resonate with timeless themes of love, acceptance, and the struggle for identity. I won't let them gather dust in a forgotten corner."

The world needs to hear her voice now more than ever.

"I'm gonna turn in, Daddy. Thank you for sharing this part of Lolly with me."

Chapter Four

October 2, 2019.

I wake up a few hours later and continue to immerse myself in Lolly's stories. One tale speaks of a hidden garden, where two lovers meet under the cloak of night, their love blossoming amid fragrant roses. Another narrates the story of a woman trapped in a gilded cage, yearning for freedom, for love that isn't bound by society's chains. Each story, unique in its narrative, echoes Lolly's essence, her spirit, and her struggles.

By late afternoon, I'm emotionally exhausted. The weight of my grandmother's words, her hidden pains and joys, has taken a toll. I need a breather. I step out into Dad's garden to take in the beauty of nature. The chirping of birds, the rustle of leaves, the scent of blooming flowers—it's therapeutic.

I'm soon joined by my father. "Have you gotten much sleep?" he asks, concern evident in his voice.

"Not really, I just needed some fresh air. Lolly's stories...they're beautiful, but they're also intense."

He pats my back gently. "Take your time with them. There's no rush."

My thoughts drift to Claire.

"I'll be back in a few minutes, Daddy. I need to make a call."

"Hi," I manage to say, my voice trembling like a leaf in a storm. I won't blame her if she hangs up and never wants to talk to me again, not after the way I left things last week and my subsequent silence.

"Kelsi Jo."

"I'm so sorry," I choke out, overwhelmed by a rush of emotions and tears that blur my vision.

"I've been so worried about you. Are you okay?" Her voice is steady and comforting as always.

I realize that I've never felt more loved. We are silent—except for my tears that I can no longer harness.

I feel her reaching through the phone, wrapping me in her arms, a place where I've come to feel safe.

I am in love with her.

"Claire...so much has happened. I'm fine, but I'm not okay." My tissue rips, and I try to grab another one from the box on my nightstand, but there aren't anymore. "I...I need you."

"Where are you, Kels?"

"I'm in Boothbay, Maine." I realize right after I say that Claire has no idea why I'm in Maine. "I'm at my dad's place. I drove here from LaGuardia. Two days ago."

Instead of asking a bunch of questions to satisfy her curiosity, she says, "Send me your location. I'll be there tonight before dinner."

I think for a minute. Instead of giving her dad's address, I see Lolly's manuscript spread out across my bedroom floor. The faded typewritten address on the cover page stares back at me.

"Remember Lolly?" I ask.

"Of course. Your grandmother—"

"Yes. Meet me at her cabin." It's barely legible, but I read the address to Claire.

"I'm on my way."

I want to tell her I love her in the pause before we both hang up.

But I'll wait and tell her in person.

I can walk down the stairs without holding on—sometimes resilience reveals itself in the form of small victories. If the last forty-eight hours have taught me anything, it's that our spirit awakens when we least expect it—like a dormant seed waiting for the right condition to sprout, or walk down the stairs, or stand without our legs or our heart buckling—or simply get out of bed.

"Dad? Where are you?" I yell like an excited teenager with a newly minted license, asking for the keys to the car. The adrenaline of seeing Claire in a few hours keeps my heart in a steady state of anxious—but more so, knowing I'm going to see her for the first time surrounded by relics of Lolly.

He doesn't answer.

It's early October, and winter is trying to shove fall out of the way. I've wrapped my flannel robe around my body for a little extra warmth and continue looking for my father and find him in his beloved garden.

My father tends to his cherished garden with meticulous care, creating a sanctuary of green amidst the coastal landscape. As I approach, the earthy scent of soil and the gentle rustle of leaves greet me, inviting me into a world of tranquility and natural abundance.

In this garden, time seems to slow, and the worries of the world fade away. As my father tends to his beloved plants, he not only cultivates a bountiful harvest but also nurtures a sense of peace and belonging that resonates with me. I could spend hours here with my dad, just like I did when I was little. But today, I need to harvest something else.

"I thought I'd find you here," I say, my voice carried away by the wind as I wrap my robe tighter to shield myself from the biting chill. The gravel crunches under my feet as I approach my father, who's bent over the soil, his hands working skillfully among the rows of vegetables.

He looks up, a faint smile tugging at the corners of his lips. His hands, caked with earth, pause in their work as he brushes them against the bib of his faded overalls. This scene has a timeless quality: his movements, the earthy scent, the rustle of leaves—all blend together.

"Just out here trying to prepare for harvest. Looks like winter might be coming a bit sooner than usual." He looks at the north sky at the ominous-looking clouds rolling in over the bay.

"Dad, I'm going to Lolly's cabin. Claire's meeting me there," I inform him, my words punctuated by the crisp autumn air. There's a sense of urgency in my voice, a need to escape my reality and seek solace in the sanctuary of my grandmother.

He motions me towards him and pulls me into one of his hugs, wrapping his arms around me like he's trying to insulate me from the world.

"The keys are in the cedar box in the drawer next to Lolly's manuscript." He kisses the top of my head and releases me.

"I have one of her cedar boxes, too. Mom gave it to me on my wedding day." Pain slices through the words—Alex and me, the letter, the lies and recent secrets revealed. Even the memory of our wedding is grounded in agony.

"I love you, Dad," I say, heading back towards the house.

"I love you too, kiddo," his voice warm with affection as he continues tending to his harvest. It's a simple phrase but holds a world of meaning—a reminder that no matter how old I get, I'll always be his "kiddo."

* * *

I clean myself up, and pack a few things. I'm not sure how long I'll be there; I'm going to let Lolly guide me. She's never steered me wrong.

The wind has picked up and lets out a howl as it hits the backside of the house. I haven't turned on the TV or listened to the news since I left for New York; I have no idea what the weather is doing, but it feels like an autumn snow is headed our way. I need to leave before the weather gets any worse.

Dad's rolling crate is the perfect size to transport the majority of Lolly's manuscripts back to her cabin with me—where they belong. I carefully stack the rest of my things by the front door. The weight of her stories and secrets presses against my chest, urging me forward on this journey of discovery.

I make my way towards the family room, a familiar path, the wood discolored by countless footsteps over the years. The walls speak to me on my walk from the front door to the grandiose windows that overlook everything my father loves: his garden, his boats, and his bay. The walls whisper stories of generations past as I walk by. Black and white photos of Dad and Aunt Francie playing in the snow, Cory and Basia's Vegas wedding, their son Theo and his first T-ball photo. The wall, with its mosaic of aged frames, dust settled in the crevices that you can see when the light hits it just right. I reach the entryway of the family room, turn to the left, and come face to face with my own story, neatly boxed in by similar-looking frames and a little more dust.

Every picture is a portrait of perfection—smiles frozen in time, hair perfectly coiffed, clothes meticulously chosen. Alex's arm is always around me, a constant presence. I've been pushed so far outside the boundaries of those picture frames that I don't recognize that woman who has a slight resemblance to me. The familiar features of my face stare back, but there's a hollowness in my eyes that I never noticed before—maybe it's because I never looked close enough. And beside me stands the man I no longer recognize, his eyes betraying the lies he's told, the bond he managed to break posthumously. The pictures on the wall are not my story—they're merely fragments of a life that once was.

I tap my fingers on the cold glass and signal a goodbye. Dad blows a kiss and leaves a remnant of soil slightly smeared across his cheek.

Lolly's waiting for me at the front door. I walk back the same way I came, and this time, I don't stop to look at photos on the wall. I grab the crate with the manuscripts and carefully roll it over the gravel drive to the back hatch of my rental car. As I carefully secure the crate so the manuscripts don't spill all over the back end of the SUV, I hear the crunch of the gravel underneath the tires of an approaching car. Dad's place is off the beaten track, and getting there is intentional. The crunch of gravel inches closer, even though I'm trying to pretend I don't hear it. I don't have time for chit-chat. Hopefully, one of Dad's friends is coming to spend time with him.

The car shuts off. I take a deep breath. When I turn around, I'll simply motion a quick hello; certainly, whoever it is will see I'm on my way out.

"Mom!"

The familiar voice startles me, pulling me from the swirling whirlwind of my thoughts. Am I hearing things now? I set everything down with a sense of disbelief, turning slowly to face the unexpected interruption.

"Girls! What are you doing here?" My words come out in a rush, a mix of surprise and confusion swirling within me.

"We're worried about you. What in the hell is going on, and where are you going now?" Lia's demand for answers cuts through the chilly air. I know I owe them one, but right now is not the right time.

I sigh and wrap myself in my arms, seeking protection from having to face them. The first few snow flurries fall from the sky, and we are all shivering at this point, adding a surreal quality to the moment. "I'm sorry, girls. I know you've been worried, and there's a lot to tell you..." I trail off, unable to meet their searching gazes.

"Can we go inside, Mom? It's cold, and we can talk in there." Lexi's voice carries a note of softened concern, her words a gentle plea for warmth and understanding.

"We can, but I'm heading out soon," I reply, bracing myself

for their disappointment. They're not used to me asserting myself, to standing firm in the face of their expectations.

"What do you mean you're leaving? We drove a long way to see you." Lia is clearly annoyed.

I purposely avoid responding as I walk towards the house, hoping they follow. I understand why they are upset, but they are going to have to deal with my plans. I'm not the same woman anymore.

"Grandad!" Lia's voice rings out, startling Dad from his reverie at the kitchen sink. He turns, a smile spreading across his weathered face as he takes in the sight of us standing there.

"Am I dreaming here?" He laughs and looks at me as he simultaneously hugs both of his granddaughters. "I thought you were on your way to Mom's cabin, KJ?"

"Wait, what?" Lexi releases herself from her grandfather. "Why are you going to Lolly's cabin? Mom, what is going on here? First, you're a no-show on TV, you go missing for 24 hours, then you're your at Grandads, and now you're—"

I take a deep breath, steeling myself for the inevitable questions and the demanding need for explanations. "Sit down," I direct them to the couch, my voice firm but tinged with a note of vulnerability.

"All of you deserve answers, but I can't give them to you right now," I begin, my eyes meeting theirs with unwavering resolve. "You're going to have to trust me. I've never steered you wrong, and I won't start now. Right now, I'm asking for space. What you need to know is I'm safe, and I love you. And I will tell you everything in due time. But for now, I need to go. And yes, I'm going to Lolly's cabin. I need to spend some time alone."

I watch as they process my words, their expressions shifting from confusion to understanding. After a few seconds, Lexi takes my hand, her touch grounding me in the midst of uncertainty. "Okay, Mom. As long as we know you're okay...also, Ari is on her way," she adds, a note of reassurance in her voice.

I exhale slowly, the weight of my decisions settling around me.

There was a time when I would have put their needs above my own and canceled my plans to accommodate theirs. And part of me is tempted to do so now. But that's not what I need—not anymore.

Despite the biting cold and uncertainty that loom on the horizon, I feel a sense of purpose guiding me forward. With one last glance at the house, the glow of the lights casting long shadows in the falling snow, I steel myself against the chill and climb into the driver's seat. Lexi and Lia decide to stay and wait for Ari to arrive. I didn't bother to ask them how long they intended to be here—I just wanted to get out of there. They can figure it out on their own. And I'm sure Dad is happy to spend some time with them.

Turning the key in the ignition, the engine roars to life. With a deep breath, I shift into gear and pull away from the familiar surroundings of my father's home, the gravel mixed under the tires echoing in the quiet of the afternoon.

As I navigate the winding roads toward Lolly's cabin, the snow falls steadily, blanketing the landscape in a pristine layer of white. Each mile brings me closer to the sanctuary of the cabin; solitude mixed with my anxiousness to see Claire.

It's been years since I've been to Lolly's cabin—pre-GPS days. The days when I depended on Alex to guide my family and me. To protect us. He was my identity and my family's hero. Where did our marriage go wrong? When did I fail him? Us? It's time to confront the ghosts of the past and figure out a way to embrace the uncertainty of the future.

Traces of autumn cling stubbornly to the trees, their leaves a vibrant pallet of reds, oranges, and golds against the increasingly gray sky. The road ahead is a winding serpent of asphalt, flanked on either side by dense forests where the trees stand tall and proud, their branches interlocking to form a natural tunnel that seems to swallow the road whole. Soon, they'll be naked, exposed, vulnerable. The snowflakes grow in size and number, painting the world in a wash of white as they settle on the boughs of the ever-greens, the stark contrast between the green needles and the snow creating a scene of serene beauty.

As I navigate the twists and turns of the backroads, the tires of my car crunch over the freshly fallen snow, a constant companion in the otherwise silent world. The snow begins to blanket every-thing, smoothing out the rough edges of the landscape and casting it in a soft, ethereal glow. It's as if the world is holding its breath, caught in the magical in-between of seasons.

The further I drive, the more secluded the road becomes, the signs of human habitation growing few and far between. Here and there, a lone cabin or a rustic farmhouse appears, their smoke-stacks painting gray streaks against the snow-laden sky, but for the most part, it's just me, the road, and the wilderness. I notice these things now being in the driver's seat.

Eventually, the forest begins to thin, and the road starts its descent toward the water's edge. The lake comes into view, its surface a mirror reflecting the heavy sky above. The snowflakes continue to dance in the wind, creating a mesmerizing spectacle that seems to blur the line between water and sky.

When it finally appears, the cabin is a quaint structure of wood and stone. It sits alone on a finger of land that juts out into the water, secluded and serene, a world unto itself. The air is crisp and cold, filled with the scent of salt and pine, and as I take a deep breath, I feel a sense of peace settle over me.

Here, in this secluded cabin on the water, surrounded by the beauty of autumn snow, time seems to stand still and life's trou-bles fade into the background. I feel her.

Chapter Five

June, 1999. Mirror Lake, ME.

Lolly stretches her arms wide, and the girls launch themselves into her embrace without hesitation. Alex grabs our suitcases and I unbuckle the baby from her car seat, cradling her against me.

"GG Lolly!" The girls scream and run towards the woman who taught me how to tell stories.

"There's my girls."

"We're here, Lolly!" I say as she takes Ari out of my arms and kisses her nose and then my cheek.

"Glad you made it, darlin'. Alex, good to see you." She nods her head his way. "Come on, let's get your brood settled." The girls cling to her side, draping themselves in her sheer bohemian wrap. She handles all three girls with care and leads us inside her small two-bedroom cabin. "Helen, you remember Kelsi Jo, my favorite granddaughter, and her family. And these little people are my favorite great-grandbabies, Lexi, Lia, and baby Ari."

"I'm her only granddaughter," I say with a laugh and shake Helen's hand.

"It's nice to see you again, Kelsi Jo. I haven't seen you since you were about your oldest girl's age," Helen says. She stands up to greet me, and her chestnut eyes meet mine.

I've never heard Lolly talk about Helen before.

"Helen is in my writing group," Lolly offers before I have the chance to ask how they know each other.

"Oh! You're an author, too?" I ask.

"I wouldn't call myself an author—"

"Oh, don't listen to her. She's a brilliant writer." Lolly is quick to come to her defense.

"Thanks, Char." Helen reaches for Lolly and pats her on the arm.

I've never heard anyone call my grandmother "Char".

"I've read all your books, Kelsi," Helen says. "We can learn a thing or two from you. I'm a big fan." Helen smiles.

"Thank you. I learned everything from this woman right here." I lean into Lolly for a side hug reminiscent of my childhood. Helen's smile is steadfast as she looks at my grandmother.

"Well, that makes sense. I have, too," she says.

Lolly hands Ari back to me and quickly changes the subject directing her attention towards Alex.

"I fixed up our...my bedroom for you two and the spare room for the babies," she says.

"Lolly, I'm eleven now. I'm almost a grown-up!" Lexi announces.

"Lexi..." I reprimand.

"You're right, Lexi. You are older now, aren't you? Come here for a minute." Lolly takes Lexi aside for a private conversation.

"Do you live around here, Helen?" I ask.

"I do. I live real close." She doesn't offer any additional information, so I drop the inquiry.

"Lia!" Lexi barrels out of the guest room with Lolly in tow. "Lia, come here! I fixed up our own room. Mommy, Daddy, and Ari have to share a room, and Lolly said this is our own private space when we are here." Her excitement is palpable. Lia follows her big sister, hugging her like they just won a trip to Disney World.

"Wow, girls, what do you say to GG Lolly?" Alex chimes in.

"Thank you!" They scream in harmony.

"Lolly, that is such a sweet gesture, but where are you going to sleep?" I ask. I told her we could stay at Dad's or even a hotel, but she insisted we stay here. She wanted to spend as much time with us as possible during the day.

"I'm going to stay with Helen. She's got an extra room that she doesn't mind me using for a few nights." She and Helen smile at each other.

"Oh, okay. Do you live close, Helen?" I ask again because she didn't answer my question earlier.

"I do. Just up the street," she says.

Chapter Six

October 2, 2019.

The key won't turn. *Of course, it won't.*

I shiver—whether from the cold, nerves, or excitement, I'm not sure. Probably all three. My fingers fumble with the rusted deadbolt, the metal grinding against itself in stubborn protest, the sound scraping through me like a warning.

Then I remember Dad giving me a can of WD-40 before I left. "You'll need this for something out there,"he'd said.

The snow is coming down in sheets now. I run back to the car and grab what I need. I'm also thinking about Claire. I know she's on her way, and I hope the weather doesn't get any worse for her drive. As soon as I get inside, I'll call her.

I spray the lock and take a deep breath. This time, when I turn the key, it gives.

I push on the door handle, expecting it to swing open easily, but instead, it resists, as if reluctant to reveal what lies beyond. With a determined shove, I push with all my strength, the sound of my grunts echoing in the quiet solitude of the forest.

Finally, with one last mighty effort, I break through the

barrier and step over the threshold, feeling like I'm crossing into another world. The air inside is stale and heavy with the weight of years gone by, and for a moment, I'm enveloped in a cloud of memories.

This cabin doesn't just hold memories—it bleeds them.

As my eyes adjust to the dim light filtering through dusty windows, the scene unfolds in layers: not the worn-out furniture or the tattered recliner, but a vivid echo of my youth. I see Lolly as clearly as if she were right here, her presence so palpable I can almost reach out and touch her. I'm back on that creaking deck, a sweltering summer afternoon when I was still a wide-eyed teen with ink-stained dreams.

I remember the moment vividly. We were seated side by side, the wood under our feet warm from the sun. I leaned in, my voice small but insistent.

"Lolly, do you really believe words and stories can change the world?" I asked, my eyes searching hers for an answer.

She smiled, that enigmatic smile that always made the impossible seem within reach. "Kelsi," she said softly, "words are like seeds. They may be tiny and unassuming at first, but given time and care, they can grow into something that reshapes everything around you."

I hesitated, absorbing the weight of her words. "But what if my words are just noise—lost in the endless chatter of the world?"

Her gaze was steady and kind as she replied, "Noise becomes music when you dare to listen. Your words, your stories, are your truth. And your truth is enough—even if only you can hear it."

In that moment, the dusty old deck transformed into a sanctuary of hope and possibility. The echoes of our conversation mingled with the gentle rustle of leaves, the distant hum of life beyond the cabin walls. Even now, standing here amid the shadows of time, Lolly's voice remains a quiet guide.

· · ·

For the last few hours my focus has been on trying to get couches and chairs uncovered and warming up the place. Dad comes out here and turns on the furnace and the AC twice a year, but everything else has gone untouched—until today—I'm bringing Lolly back to life. I'm going to introduce the most important person of my past to the most important person of my future.

A soft knock at the front door releases all the butterflies in my stomach. "Claire." I fall into her; I can't hold back the tears. She holds me close with one arm and rubs her other hand down the back of my hair, consoling all the things she doesn't even know about yet. I want to tell her everything all at once. I want to forget that last time we were together—less than a week earlier—when I rejected her and she left. Damn it. I want to forget the last 72 hours.

I want to forget that fucking letter. I want to forget...Alex. But I can't. I can't just erase decades of my life. Because that would mean that I erase all that we were and everything that we created—our daughters. But he's also got a connection to Eve, a son, a secret they harbored for years. Alex always wanted a son.

Claire gently pulls away, keeping a grip on my shoulders. Making sure she doesn't let me go.

"Baby, what happened?" She asks, empathy tears streaming down her face. Her thumb gently wipes mine away. Claire doesn't skip a beat.

"Oh God, Claire—" I begin, interrupting my own thoughts that don't seem to make any sense to me. How can I make them make sense to her?

She takes my hand and leads me to Lolly's beat-up couch. We sit together on this couch that holds so many memories for me. Years of dust rise from the cushions, and she holds me like I've never been held before.

We sit in the same spot and talk for hours, only getting up to boil more hot water for our tea. Claire never loses eye contact with me and never lets go of my hand—she listens with the intensity of a good therapist and the commitment of a loyal partner. I tell her everything up to the actual details in the letter. An entire replay of the last few days—a repeat of how I discovered the letter, to making the driver turn around when we were halfway to the airport because I forgot it, to the moment at 30,000 feet in the air when my entire world stopped. When all the pressure in my atmosphere was sucked out of the air and how my body tried to purge the pain into the airline vomit bag, and how I reached for the oxygen mask because I thought we were crashing because I couldn't remember how to breathe in and out.

I stand up and walk over to Lolly's dining room table, where I lay my things in the middle of the thick dust. The old wooden table is too large for the small space she called the dining room. But she didn't care. It was the epicenter of her tiny cabin—a sacred space. Lolly always said she wanted a crowded table—her family gathered around. Family was everything to my grandmother. It was...is to me too. But now I'm left wondering what family really means.

I pull the letter from the front pocket of my backpack— folded into the tiniest square a legal-sized sheet could manage— and hand it to Claire.

The last time she saw the letter, it was folded in half and safely stored in a Ziplock bag so nothing could tarnish it. I protected that letter with my life. I considered it a relic of Alex and treated it like it was the Holy Grail—our Holy Grail—his final goodbye.

I was right about one thing—it is our final goodbye.

She carefully unfolds it. The paper is thinning out with each unfolding—appearing more and more worn as his message is read and reread. I watch Claire as she reads. I watch her body language and her facial expressions. It's like I can tell where she's at without her saying anything out loud. I know the words on the page by heart. They are forever engrained in my head—the memory of his voice attached to each syllable.

Her eyes scrunch as she pulls the letter a little farther out like she's having trouble focusing. She breathes in heavily, looks up at me, and continues silently reading. It feels like she's been reading for hours before she gets to the part that evokes another response.

"My God. Kelsi Jo. Honey. I am so..." She drops the letter. It floats to the floor.

I move the short distance from the dining room to the couch and meet her there. She holds me. But this time, her arms speak the words she can't.

"I know. I am, too," I say.

She pulls away only to look me in the eyes. She takes both of my hands in hers. I grasp them tightly, signaling that I never want to let go of them again.

"What can I do?" she asks.

"You're already doing it, Claire," I say. She picks the tattered letter off the floor and continues to read.

I take a sip of my lukewarm tea and nod at hers, and she says, " Yes, please."

She has finished the letter by the time I return from refilling our mugs. We sit with our knees touching each other, both hands grasping the warm ceramic mugs, and she speaks first.

"Who have you shared this with? Do your daughters know?" she asks.

"No. The only people who know are my agent, my dad, and you. You and Dad are the only two who have read the letter. I wouldn't have told Jaci except I kind of had to since I was a no-show in New York," I say.

"You haven't confronted Eve?"

"Not yet. And I'm not sure how I'm going to let her know I'm in on her little secret," I say with disgust. "I need to tell the girls first."

She sets her cup down and gently kisses me on my lips. A kiss that simply says, "I'm here for you, always."

Claire looks down at our hands and rubs her thumb over my knuckles. I can see the hurt in her body language. She doesn't say anything—she doesn't have to.

"I'm sorry for the way I behaved last week when—"

"Kels...It's okay." She softly kisses my hands.

"It's not okay. And I'm ashamed and so upset with myself that I treated you with such disregard," I say, full of shame.

"All the things you were feeling that night are completely normal. I should have respected your bedroom."

I try to interrupt her, but she doesn't let me speak.

"No, Kelsi. You had no idea about Alex and Eve. You're angry and hurt right now, and rightly so. But I should have never assumed that you were ready to be intimate in the bed you shared with your husband." She picks up her tea and looks away—tears streaming down her face now. We sit in silence, our warm hands clasped together for what seems like hours, saying all the things we can't speak out loud.

The urge to confess my love for her is overwhelming.

"Claire, how is it possible to feel so wounded by the man with whom I built a life, whose betrayal has fractured a lifetime of memories, yet I'm..." my voice drifts, and a feeling of fear mixed with release washes over me like a baptism of sorts. I begin again.

"...filled with such profound love for you?" She releases her breath and she looks into my soul. She lets go like she's been holding something so precious to her inside—like she no longer has to be afraid.

"You've become my anchor, more constant even than Alex ever was. But it scares me. Is this intense feeling a way to fill the void he left? Am I reaching for 'love' as a healing balm, a desperate patch over a gaping wound? To feel such revulsion and affection at once feels like a paradox. How can these emotions coexist within me? And how do I reconcile them?"

She caresses the side of my face with her soft palm and holds it there.

"Kelsi, love and pain, though opposites in emotion, intersect within the heart, especially during times of profound change. Love may feel like a beacon during this storm of betrayal because this, what we have, represents a steady presence amidst the turmoil. This doesn't necessarily mean you're overcompensating for your loss; it signifies a genuine connection.

"It's natural to seek healing and comfort, and using the word 'love' isn't just a band-aid. It's an acknowledgment of your heart's capacity to feel deeply despite the wounds inflicted by Alex's betrayal. Love doesn't negate or trivialize the pain; it exists alongside it, offering a pathway to healing. Feeling disgust and love simultaneously is the embodiment of being human."

Claire has a way of uncovering pieces of me, teaching me to see myself clearer. That's what also makes her such a sought-after therapist. I still remember our first meeting at the Windows for Widows meeting. There I was, seated in the front row, a bundle of nerves, yet feeling a sense of belonging with the other women who were grieving and healing just like me. She spoke of the loss of Sam, and her words struck me—not with judgment but with realizing that the conventions of life, love, and loss hold no true weight. Claire has helped me step in front of the screen that's been hiding who I am.

"Claire, I love you."

She pulls the neckline of her turtleneck away from her skin. I'm not sure if she's having a hot flash or simply uncomfortable— or ready to run out the door. A smile forms at the edges of her mouth, and a sense of relief washes over me before she speaks a word.

"I love you too, Kelsi."

Chapter Seven

Sunlight filters through Lolly's sheer baby blue curtains—the same ones that have hung for years in the window above the kitchen sink overlooking Mirror Lake.

"We haven't slept a wink."

"We kind of have a habit of doing that, don't we?" Claire says—a reminder of our week in Martha's Vineyard.

"We do." I smile and blush simultaneously. It's hard to believe it's been less than a month since we shared that time. A lifetime has happened inside of a few short weeks. I canceled my book tour after discovering my dead husband cheated on me with my best friend, and they have a grown 'love child' together. My dad finally told me that my grandmother had a longtime love affair with Helen—whom I thought was just her neighbor. I told my father about Claire.

And I told Claire I love her.

"Come with me." I reach for Claire's hand and guide her toward the back door; her skin is warm against the cool air of the Maine morning. Lolly's back porch is my favorite thing about this cabin—a silent witness to the ballet of daybreak over the lake.

The porch, worn by time and memories, creaks beneath our steps as the snow crunches underfoot. I can't help but remember the sunrises I shared here with Lolly, the two of us wrapped in blankets, our silhouettes entwined against the soft glow of the waking sky.

Claire's hand tightens in mine as we watch the horizon burn with the promise of a new day. The water of Mirror Lake lies still, a perfect canvas waiting for the sun's brush. I tell her about the mornings that Lolly and I would guess the palette of the sunrise, how she insisted that no two were ever the same—a life lesson wrapped in ritual.

We fall silent, letting the symphony of color and light fill the space between words. The pinks and oranges bloom across the sky, setting the lake aflame. With Claire, the past and present meld into one.

"I don't know how to start putting things back together," I say, not wanting to take my eyes off the sun's reflection rising over the lake. I look for the snow shovel Lolly used to keep in the over-sized planter on the porch. There's nothing out here anymore, not even the rocking chairs we used to sit in.

Claire still has her fingers intertwined in mine. "We've got this, Kels." Her eyes meet and hold mine. "What do you say we go in and get some sleep?"

I'd be more excited about her suggestion, but none of the beds have been touched for years. And now, just like the rest of my life, I'm unprepared to deal with any of this.

"Where do you suppose we'll sleep?" I ask Claire like she'll magically produce an answer. My voice carries a hint of playful distress. As I hear my own words, they seem so out of place in the quiet snowfall that I can't help but laugh again at the absurdity of the moment: me, not knowing where we're going to sleep or where I'm going to find bedding or blankets or heat for that matter. I've spent my life perfectly prepared for everything—until recently. It seems more and more like that was just a façade. Like I was sitting on the surface of the truth my entire life.

Claire turns to me, her eyebrows raised in mock concern. "Well, I hadn't planned on a snow bed, but there's a first time for everything," she responds with a wink. Her voice teases out more laughter from deep within me.

Soon, we're both chuckling, the sound mingling with the hush of the early season snow-draped world around us. Our knees buckle, not just from the laughter but from the relief of it all, and we find ourselves plopping down into the powdery snow. Our laughter echoes into the morning, a counterpoint to the serene hush that envelops Lolly's cabin.

I look over at Claire, snowflakes catching in her hair like tiny stars.

"This is the best therapy session I've ever had," I say.

She grins, nodding in agreement

We lay back, our bodies sinking slightly into the snow's embrace. We move our arms and legs methodically at first, then carving out angels in the snow with a carefree rhythm.

Our breath is visible in puffs of white. "Look at us," I say, "grown women making snow angels. Who would've thought this could feel so...right?"

Claire reaches out, her hand finding mine. "Sometimes, the right things are the ones that just happen," she murmurs. And I squeeze her hand, feeling the truth in her words.

Stepping back into the cabin, I can't ignore the cold wetness seeping through my clothes. Claire's shivering too, our laughter now quieted by the chill that's set in.

"We need to find some wood," I say, my teeth chattering as I speak. "Warmth first, then rest."

Claire and I cast glances at each other, our soaked clothes chilling us to the bone. "We need to get this fire started," I say, shuddering as another chill runs through me. I look around, unsure where to find firewood for the woodburning stove that sits staring at us in the small living area.

"This will help warm up this cabin fast. And we'll need it since the heating system in this old place doesn't seem to be putting out much heat."

We're feeling the weight of our spontaneous decision to roll around in the snow without the proper wardrobe. We fumble our way to the back of the cabin, where Lolly's storeroom lurks like a time capsule. It's hidden away beyond the mudroom, a tiny space behind a door that sticks with the stubbornness of age. We wrestle it open, muscles tensing against the cold that's trying to claim our bones.

The storeroom is dark, the air thick with the musk of forgotten things. Our hands search blindly until they find the coarse edges of logs, each one feeling damp and unwelcoming to the touch.

"This wood might not even catch fire," Claire murmurs, her voice echoing slightly in the tight space.

"We have to try." I grab a log from the wood pile with a determination that feels almost desperate.

We gather an armful each and lug them back to the stove.

The logs are reluctant to light, the flames from the match sputtering against the moist wood again and again. Claire finds some old newspapers and twists them into knots of promise, tucking them between the logs.

"Come on," she coaxes, striking another match.

Finally, a small flame takes hold, hungry and eager. We nurse it with breaths and hope, watching as the fire starts to grow, life blooming in the belly of the stove.

With the fire now chasing away the cold, we peel off our damp clothes, leaving them in a heap on the floor, and replace them with warm, dry pajamas. The soft fabric clings to our skin, a welcome contrast to the lingering chill.

I find a few old blankets in the hall linen closet, spread one over the couch, and drape the other over Lolly's recliner. The fabric smells faintly of lavender and mothballs, a familiar and comforting scent that speaks of Lolly's long presence in this place.

The fire crackles, wrapping the room in its glow as we settle in, exhaustion pressing against our bones.

I collapse into the chair, pulling the blanket up to my chin. Claire sits on the couch, drawing her legs up under her. The fire-light flickers, casting a dance of shadows and light around the room.

"You okay in the chair?" Claire's voice is soft, tinged with concern.

"I'm good. It's like being hugged by Lolly," I say, trying to smile. "You?"

She nods, nestling deeper into the couch. "It's not the worst bed I've ever had."

There's a silence, one that's full of all the things we're not saying, all the pain and the healing that lies ahead.

"Thank you, Claire," I whisper across the dimly lit room. "For being here, for the snow angels, for laughing with me...It feels like I haven't truly laughed in forever."

Claire's silhouette shifts, turning towards me. "Kelsi, after everything you've been through, you deserve to laugh much more."

Tears prickle at the corners of my eyes. "I hope so."

"You will," she says firmly. "We'll make sure of it."

In the fire's glow, a shift is happening inside me. It's small, like the first tentative sprout of spring, but it's there—a sense of peace.

"Goodnight, Claire," I say again, this time with a bit more certainty.

"Sweet dreams," comes her reply. "Kelsi, I love you."

"I love you too, Claire. I really, really love you."

* * *

The snow has stopped and the fall sun is already melting away the white fluff that blanketed the ground just a few hours ago. I ease out of Lolly's recliner, which groans in protest with a high-pitched squeal from its rusted joints. I freeze, but Claire remains undisturbed, cocooned in the warmth of dreams.

The wood fire stove continues to heat the room, but there's still a slight edge of chill so I keep the blanket tightly wrapped around me. My fuzzy socks, designed to keep my feet well insulated, feel more like ice skates as I lose my balance on portions of slick floor planks and make my way to the kitchen.

My cell phone, a treacherous tether to the world beyond these walls, lies in wait on the countertop—its turquoise laminate is as outdated as the concept of peace in my life. The phone holds a power I resent. Notifications are off; my naive attempt at preserving this sanctuary just a little longer.

I eye the device warily, half-expecting it to attack with bad news and the piercing buzz of obligations. The potential onslaught of messages looms in my mind—my daughters with a million questions that I'm not sure I can answer even though the answer is pretty fucking cut-and-dry: *Your father was a cheater. You have a half-brother that your dad fathered with your mother's best friend who hid that information from all of us for thirty years.* Then there's Jaci with her relentless inquiries about the tour and all those readers awaiting a tale of love and healing that has soured into fiction.

I feel the weight of Alex's deceit, of truths twisted into the cruel plot twists of a novel I never wanted to write. If life hadn't taken that grave turn, if Alex had been the man I thought he was, there'd be no shadow-child emerging from a hidden past and no letter penned by a coward.

Only cowards cheat on their spouse, devise an exit plan in letter form, and then conveniently change their mind when they discover they aren't going to live much longer. If this weren't my life, this would have been material for a sadistic, cruel plot twist.

The irony of it all churns in my stomach—widowhood was supposed to be about honoring memories, not questioning every truth I ever held dear. And now, I must weave a narrative of healing from a fabric of lies. The thought makes me nauseous.

So, what do I do with such a twisted plot? How do I pen the ending?

I let the lure of coffee pull me away. I lose myself in the ritual—the filling of the pot, the gentle scoop of the grounds, the steady pour of water.

"Good morning, or afternoon? My sense of time is a bit skewed right now."

Claire's voice cuts through the cacophony in my head, clear and warm. I didn't hear her stir and hadn't noticed the creak of the couch as she rose.

Her arms wrap around my waist, a gentle surprise that stills my spinning world. She rests her chin on my shoulder, and suddenly, the chill in the room and my bones begins to dissipate.

I lean back into her, my body instinctively responding to her closeness. The contact feels like the first stitch of healing, the beginning of mending a heart frayed by betrayal.

Claire's is a silent vow of support. And at this moment, with her arms as my sanctuary, I feel a glimmer of something potent and rare—a sense of hope.

Chapter Eight

October 3, 2019.

Y ou don't have to decide everything right now, Kelsi. But communicating with Jaci and telling the girls is a good start."

I nod, knowing she's right. "I just...I need to be honest with all of them. About everything. The tour, the book...it all feels like a lie now."

Claire squeezes my hand. "It's not a lie," she assures me. "It's just not the whole truth. Not yet."

As the morning light grows bolder, casting a golden sheen on the kitchen's worn surfaces, Claire and I sit at the small, rickety table. We're flanked by steaming mugs of coffee, the rich aroma masking the musty scent of the cabin. Claire's hand is warm over mine, grounding me as I venture into conversations I've been dreading.

We talk about timing, the right words to use, and potential reactions. The conversation about Alex and the media tour is like plotting out chapters that I'm afraid to write. Claire offers her perspective—practical and kind—helping me weave my way through the labyrinth of this new narrative.

"It'll be a shock to the girls, but they'll process everything in time." Claire says, her voice steady with a conviction I desperately want to believe. "They love you, Kelsi. They'll see your strength and draw from it."

I take a slow, measured breath, letting it settle inside me before exhaling. "And Jaci?"

Claire gives me a knowing look. "Jaci's a professional. A problem solver. She just needs to know where you stand."

A wave of gratitude washes over me. Claire's unwavering support gives me something solid to hold onto, a flicker of courage in the face of what's coming. We decide that today, I'll call Jaci and take that first step into the breach. Then, with that behind me, I'll figure out how to tell Lexi, Lia, and Ari.

Honesty, I remind myself, is the only way forward.

The conversation moves to the book, my story, and how it needs to change. Claire listens as I spill out ideas, fears, and hopes. She nods, offers suggestions, and helps me sketch a new, more authentic outline for the launch of *Until I Found Me*.

"It's not just about loss now," I muse aloud, the words tasting of a bittersweet truth. "It's about the complexities of love, about betrayal, and yes, still about healing. It's about the messy, imperfect process of picking up the pieces."

Claire gives a small, encouraging smile. "That's the story you need to tell now. And that's the story you'll share with your daughters."

Our mugs are empty, and we've barely eaten, but the conversation has filled me with a resolve I didn't have before. I will face whatever comes next. After all, isn't that what the rewrite is all about? Taking what you have and shaping it into something new, something truer.

* * *

"Jax, it's me."

"Kelsi. How are you? I'm glad you returned my call." The mix of frustration and relief in Jaci's voice threads through the line, a reminder that there's so much we need to sort out.

A pang of regret tightens in my chest. "I'm sorry. I needed some time to think. To breathe." The words catch slightly in my throat. "I know I put you in a tough spot these last few days. I'm sorry." I glance over at Claire. She's a pillar of calm, her hand gently smoothing over my back, a silent chorus of support.

Jaci exhales audibly, a release of tension. "Okay. Let's hear it," she prompts.

I feel a surprising surge of confidence. I start laying out the plan Claire and I talked about, ideas formulating into strategies. The old me would have passed the baton of responsibility to Jaci, letting her figure out the mess. But not this time. This time, I'm at the helm.

"The thing is, Jax..." I trail off for a moment, collecting my thoughts. "Since reading Alex's letter, I've been grappling with shame—like somehow all this is my fault, and I couldn't possibly let the world know that I never caught on that I was being lied to by two people I cherish—my husband and best friend."

Shame is a bitter weight on my tongue, thick with the echoes of a lifetime. I've carried it for as long as I can remember, its presence so familiar I never thought to question it. It was woven into me from childhood, stitched into my mother's warnings—*Never let them see your imperfections. Never bring shame upon yourself or this family.* A lesson taught in glances, in hushed reprimands, in the unspoken expectation that being *good* meant being small, silent, and spotless.

As I speak, a torrent of realizations wash over me. My marriage to Alex—was framed within these very boundaries of perfection, a representation I meticulously maintained to avoid any hint of disorder or failure. I remember always pulling the reins, steering our relationship to avoid any bumps that might mar the veneer we presented to the world.

"Maybe..." My voice wavers, a sign that I'm stepping into uncharted emotional territory. "Maybe I've been holding on too tightly. To Alex, to this image of perfection, to everything." I admit to Jaci, to Claire, to myself, that this obsession with control might have driven Alex away, might have created chasms too wide for either of us to see.

It's a moment of raw vulnerability, one that I would have recoiled from before, but warmth seeps into me, lending me courage.

There's a silence, a breath held between two women. In that gap, I realize just how much shame has driven me. It's been a shadow behind all my smiles, all the moments I presented a perfect facade.

"My entire life, I've been terrified of anyone seeing the imperfections," I admit. I speak the words out loud. Memories of my marriage to Alex pass before me like specters—how I interpreted every action and silence through a lens clouded by the fear of judgment and the pursuit of unattainable perfection.

I can feel Claire's presence, her hand a steady pressure. She doesn't say anything, but her silence is supportive, a quiet space for my confessions to land.

"Shame has been like a bridle," I tell Jaci, "And I've been pulling it tight, trying to keep everything on track, never allowing for a single step out of line."

I can hear Jaci's pen moving across paper, noting, planning. "We'll reframe the narrative," she says. Her voice is not just that of an agent now but of a confidante. "We'll turn this into something empowering. Your vulnerability, your honesty. It's going to resonate with many readers, Kelsi."

There's a shift in the room, almost palpable as if with this admission, I've opened the door to a new chapter—a chapter where imperfection isn't a source of shame but a facet of a more genuine story.

"Thank you," I whisper, finally allowing myself to lean into the truth. "For believing in the story, even when it changed."

"Stories evolve, Kelsi Jo."

"Jaci, before we go public, I have to tell my daughters. Can you give me a few more days?" I ask.

"Absolutely."

The call ends, and I turn to Claire. Her embrace is immediate and full of understanding. "You did it," she says.

"Now I have to tell the girls."

The hardest part of this entire mess.

Chapter Nine

October 6, 2019.

Claire and I spend the next few days breathing life back into Lolly's cabin. Each task a stitch in restoring this place that was my grandmother's sanctuary. As we scrub and polish, the scent of lemon oil and pine cleanser replaces the musty veil of years of disuse. Our shared labor is punctuated by laughter and stories, and at times, we pause to embrace or share a kiss. The cabin is starting to feel alive again, as if it's been waiting to cradle another pair of lovers.

I watch Claire's hands move methodically over the dishes, wiping away the remnants of our dry ham and cheese sandwiches and stale pretzels that I grabbed from Dad's pantry on my way out.

"I don't want to keep us a secret," I admit, the words tumbling from a place of longing within me. The thought of hiding the truth of what we are, of what we could be, feels like an unbearable weight.

"I don't either, Kels." She lays a towel on the counter and turns to face me. "First things first, you have to tell your daughters what's been going on with the situation with their dad. You want them to hear it from you, not on TV, or a book tour, or anywhere else but from you. You need to face this as a family," she says, her words wrapped in the wisdom of patience.

My heart clenches with the gravity of her advice, and I resolve then, "I'm going to tell them this weekend—right here at the cabin," like putting it out into the ether bonds me to the commitment. "I'm going to call them in the morning and invite them up next weekend."

Claire nods, her smile offering silent support for my decision. "What do you say we turn in?" Her suggestion carries the soft undertone of an invitation to unwind, to retreat to a place where words are no longer necessary.

She puts the last of the plates in the small oak cabinet. There's not much storage in the small kitchen. Lolly was much more of a minimalist than I remember her being. She had her favorite things that she held onto her entire life. These plates, for instance, I remember eating off of them as a kid.

I look around the small kitchen, my eyes searching for traces of Helen in the décor choices and careful arrangement of furniture. Maybe everything here, every chosen piece and preserved item, was a testament to their shared life—quiet, unseen, but full.

It's not lost on me that this cabin, secluded and embraced by nature, was their sanctuary from a world that wouldn't accept their love. It was a place where they could be themselves, where they could love without pretense or fear. And as I consider the courage it must have taken, a renewed determination settles within me.

I want our love to be seen, to be known. I don't want the shadows of secrecy that Lolly and Helen were forced to hide within. I decide Lolly's cabin will be the place where new beginnings are forged, where secrets end, and where a family learns to heal together. This will take time, but I feel more confident than ever that our story will have a happy ending.

. . .

We lie together in bed. Our bodies perfectly folded into each other, my head on Claire's chest. It feels good to feel her skin on mine. Claire is the only one that's sleeping. I'm learning her blueprint. Her breathing becomes heavy, a light snore passes through her lips. I've watched her the last few nights as I fall more and more in love with my best friend.

Lolly is on my mind continuously. Her life with Helen a mysterious melody that plays softly in the background of this cabin. Her stories, maybe her secrets, could lie within the pages of her manuscripts she left behind, a legacy of ink and hope I'm yet to explore.

I haven't had a chance to even glance at her work since I arrived. Claire and I have been busy trying to make this place livable—I think we've done a pretty good job. The dank, musty smell that lingered has been replaced with a cocktail of lemon furniture cleaner, ammonia, and bleach.

Earlier, Claire went to the town grocery store and filled the kitchen with all the basics and a few extras. I always considered myself a good cook, but Claire is the clear "chef" between the two of us.

Tonight, she conjured up a meal that would have seemed impossible in such a modest setting. With a single pan, Claire transformed the simplicity of chicken and potatoes into a dish that danced on the palate. The meal is hearty, the flavors rich and layered, a testament to Claire's culinary intuition. It is a humble feast but felt like a grand banquet tonight.

Lying here now, I'm profoundly grateful for this moment, for Claire, for the opportunity to rediscover the past and to build a new future from it—even knowing what got me here—truth, which is what I owe my girls and my readers. The silence around us is full of unspoken stories, the history that lingers in every nook of Lolly's retreat. It's as though the cabin itself is leaning in, eager to absorb the narrative of my truth just as it has held onto Lolly and Helen's all these years. The thought of their concealed love, blooming in secrecy, adds a gravity to our own open affection.

I wish I knew where Helen was now or if she's still alive. She'd be Lolly's age, late 90s.

With Claire's heartbeat under my ear, I think of Lolly's manuscripts again, of the stories they hold. I'm drawn to them, not just for their tales, but for the possibility of understanding, of connection with the past—the curiosity to learn from Lolly's hidden truths about love's boundless form twines through my thoughts.

I carefully wriggle free from the tangle of her arms and our warm quilt and tiptoe across the room, avoiding the creaky floorboards— I've got their locations down to a science now. The chill of the wood floor sends a little shiver up my spine as I fetch the pile of Lolly's manuscripts.

Quiet as a mouse, I slip out to the living room, the embers in the stove just waiting for a bit of encouragement. I get the fire going again, prodding it until there's a nice warm glow. There's just enough light to see by without disturbing the rest of the cabin.

I flop down on the couch, all cozied up, and reach for the bottom manuscript—Lolly's autobiography. It's been through the wringer a bit, with its scuffed cover and pages that feel like they might crumble if you're not careful.

Flipping it open, there's that old-book smell—kind of like an attic treasure. The writing is faded, but you can still make out every word. Lolly writes about her and Helen and their love, which was too big and real for the world outside to handle.

I'm reading about the day it all blew up, the day Lolly's husband caught them together. It's raw and rough—you can practically hear the rage, the disbelief. And what came after, that's even tougher—the way her own folks turned on her, like she'd committed an unspeakable crime just by loving Helen.

The flames from the stove flicker, throwing little dances of light and shadow over the page. It's just me, Lolly's words, and the crackling fire in the dead of night. It's intense, and I can't help but feel tied to her like she's passed on a torch, and it's my turn to carry it.

I keep turning pages as the night marches on. Lolly's story has its hooks in me, showing me that this kind of bravery comes from just being who you are, no matter what. It's a lesson I'm taking to heart because, pretty soon, I'll be walking my own tightrope of truth.

Sliding back into bed, I tuck into my side, feeling the cool sheets against my skin. The bed dips as Claire, half-asleep but attuned to my presence, scoots over and wraps her arm around me. Her lips find the nape of my neck, and she plants these little kisses that make my whole body buzz with a kind of warmth that blankets can't give.

"I missed you. Where'd you go?" she breathes out softly, her words tickling my ear. It's funny how just stepping out for a bit makes us miss each other like I'd been gone for hours.

"I couldn't sleep, so I thought I'd read some of Lolly's words."

Claire's fingers wander through my hair, a tender exploration that anchors me to the moment. Our kisses are conversations in themselves, speaking of the depths of our feelings, of the last year of shared smiles and tears that have brought us here.

We shift closer, the rustle of the sheets mingling with our soft laughter—a sound that seems to say we've found a secret joy that's ours alone. Her hands are gentle as they trace the contours of my face and then my entire body.

"God, I want you," I murmur against her lips, and Claire responds with a look that cradles all the tenderness of the world.

There's a grace to her movements and a reverence in her holding me as if each moment is a cherished gift. I respond in kind, my own hands conveying the depth of my affection, commitment, and awe for the woman who has become my everything.

Time slows, stretching between us like a taut wire, vibrating with tension. Claire's fingers press into my skin, tracing deliberate, knowing paths that send heat rolling through me. Her breath skims my collarbone, warm and unsteady, before her mouth follows, lips pressing, parting, tasting.

I gasp, gripping the curve of her hip, pulling her against me. The weight of her, solid and certain, grounds me even as my body arcs beneath hers. She moves with purpose—slow, precise, dragging the moment out as if savoring every reaction she pulls from me.

I tilt her face toward mine, and then I kiss her, deep and searching. She answers with a quiet moan against my lips, her hands cupping my bare breasts. The sensation is electric, a slow burn spreading outward.

We shift, tangled in sheets and limbs, the space between us vanishing. My hands skim the line of her back, nails teasing, and she shivers, her body pressing closer, breath hitching in response. The tension builds, pulses between us, sharp and aching.

"Tell me what you want," she murmurs against my jaw, her voice rough with need.

I answer with action, guiding her hand lower, gasping as she touches me exactly where I need her. The way she moves—intentional, unhurried—drives me mad. My body tightens, thighs trembling, as pleasure coils low in my stomach.

She watches me, the way I gasp. The way I arch. The way I shudder when she presses deeper. And then she shifts lower, her mouth replacing her hand, and I stop thinking altogether.

I clutch at her, back bowing, drowning in the heat of her, in the wet, open-mouthed kisses that push me higher, in the way she groans against me as if this is wrecking her just as much as it's wrecking me.

When release finally hits, it crashes over me in waves, sharp and all-consuming. I come apart beneath her, gripping her shoulders, my breath ragged, my pulse hammering against my ribs. She doesn't pull away—doesn't let me go—just kisses her way back up my body, soft, as if gathering every last piece of me in the aftermath.

And when she finally meets my gaze, her fingers brushing my

cheek, I pull her down to me, flipping us over, ready to return the favor.

As we drift, entwined, toward sleep, a profound sense of peace settles over us. In Lolly's sacred space, we've created a memory, a chapter of our story that will be whispered by the walls long after the dawn has greeted us. And in the embrace of night, in the tender care we show one another, we find a sanctuary not just in place, but in each other's arms.

We're here, in the stillness of Lolly's sanctuary, finding new ways to say 'I love you' without speaking the words. *This is us,* I think; *this is love in its most unguarded, sprawling across the canvas of night.*

CHAPTER TEN

OCTOBER 12, 2019.

I hustle down the front steps with the screen door's bang still ringing in my ears.

"Mom!" I hear Ari's voice before I even see her in the backseat of Lexi's car. I am excited to see my girls. It feels like I've been away forever, not just a handful of days. But these last few days at the cabin with Claire have changed something deep inside me. I've found a bit of the old me again, the one who thought she'd gotten lost along the way.

I pull them close into the kind of bear hug that used to fix scraped knees and broken hearts, feeling their arms, so much longer now, wrap around me, too.

"It's so good to see you, Mom," Lexi says as she pulls away to grab suitcases out of her trunk—Lia helps her. Ari continues to hug me and we all walk together to the house.

"So, do you remember any of this, Ari?" I ask, a little hopeful she's held onto those summer days we spent here when she was little. She squints at the cabin as if she can somehow squeeze the memories out of the walls.

"Kinda," she says, her voice trailing off like she's digging through a dusty old attic in her mind.

In the background, Lexi and Lia start jabbering about the adventures we had around Mirror Lake, and I can't help but get swept up in their stories, all the laughter and sunburns, the fish that got away, and the ghost stories that had us sleeping in a tangled pile on the living room floor.

It's bittersweet, watching them all try to piece together those snapshots, but I'm grateful we're doing it together, right here, right now. Because if this cabin could talk, oh, the stories it would tell—stories that I'm about to add to with a whole lot of truth.

Claire left a few hours ago so I could have this time with my girls, but offering to help anyway she could even if it is long distance.

The girls settle in, and the cabin feels full in a way it hasn't for a long time. I put together a makeshift lunch, a little spread of whatever Claire and I didn't eat over the past couple of days. It's not fancy, but it does the trick.

I'm making small talk and dancing around the big stuff. When Lexi cuts to the chase, her voice is a mix of concern and confusion.

"Mom, what is going on? I mean, this is great, but what is happening? Why are we here? Why are you here? When you left Grandaddy's, there was clearly something that you didn't want to share. We didn't question you, but we've been incredibly worried."

She's got those piercing blue eyes, so like her dad's, that always seem to know when there's something more under the surface. I sigh, putting down my fork, feeling like it's turned to lead in my hands.

"We have a lot to talk about, girls." And just like that, the idle chatter stops. It's like the air's been sucked out of the room.

I can hear the tick of the old clock on the mantle, the one I remember from those endless summer days. The forks clink softly as they're rested on the edges of plates, and three pairs of eyes turn to me.

I take a deep breath, my heart doing a drum solo in my chest. There's no easy way to do this, but it's time they knew everything. Well, nearly everything. The bit about Claire and me, that's for another day. Today's about laying it all out, about their father, about the half-truths that have kept us from seeing things as they are.

"There are some things that you don't know about your father. Things I wasn't aware of until last week."

The kitchen table has transformed into something like a makeshift confessional, a place where the truth is about to spill out. The air is tense, thick with expectation as my daughters wait.

"What are you talking about, Mom? What do you mean things we don't know about, Dad? I don't understand," Lia says with tears streaming down her face, anticipating what she doesn't know.

"Your dad," I start, finding the resolve to push through, "There was...there was someone else." The words tumble out, awkward and heavy. I glance at their faces, etched with shock and confusion.

Lexi shakes her head, strands of her hair falling forward. With a kind of frantic precision, she tucks them behind her ears and crosses her arms, like she's physically trying to ward off what I've just told her.

"No, Mom, this can't be right," she insists, her voice holding onto disbelief.

Lia and Ari are looking at me too, their eyes searching my face, holding their breath, hoping this is just a misunderstanding, some kind of dramatic pause before I reveal a different truth. But they'll realize soon enough, there's no twist coming to change the facts I'm about to reveal.

The room feels smaller somehow, as if it's shrinking with each revelation. Lexi, Lia, and Ari are still as statues, their plates of food abandoned now. Lexi's the first to recover, her brows knitting together as she leans in, bracing for impact.

"What do you mean, 'someone else'?" The directness in her voice doesn't mask the hurt that's starting to seep in.

I push my own plate away, the leftovers suddenly unappetizing.

"He was unfaithful, girls," I say, my voice steady despite the tremor I feel inside. "Your dad had an affair for years...with my... with... Eve." Saying it out loud, here in the daylight, feels surreal like the words are painting a portrait of a life I barely recognize.

Ari looks from me to Lexi and back again, her face a canvas of disbelief. Lia, ever the quiet one, has tears brimming in her eyes, but she doesn't let them fall. She's always been the stoic, the one who keeps it together.

The cabin, once a sanctuary of happy childhood memories, now holds a silence that is almost suffocating. Outside, the gentle rustle of leaves in the breeze feels like a stark contrast to the stillness within.

"It's not only that," I continue, knowing that I need to lay everything bare, "He has a child with her. A son."

The final word hangs between us, a truth that once seemed unfathomable. Lexi's hands are clenched into fists now, the knuckles white. Lia finally lets a single tear escape, and it trails down her cheek, leaving a glistening path. Ari, not fully grasping the gravity, simply reaches out, placing her hand over mine. It's a gesture so full of innocence and love that it almost breaks me.

"Mom, I've never doubted anything you've ever told me, not once. But this doesn't seem right. How did you come up with this information?" Lexi asks, her disbelief overshadowing any trust she'd ever had in me. I'm now in the one in hot seat, having to defend my position. And I'm okay with this—the entire situation is unbelievable.

I cover Ari's hand with my other one, anchoring myself with her touch. "I'm so sorry to drop this on you. I never wanted..." My voice breaks, and for a moment, I have to close my eyes against the wave of emotions. When I reopen them, I see my daughters, my world, looking back at me with a mixture of pain and love.

It's at this moment that we start to sift through the pieces of our fractured family story, trying to make sense of the chapters that were written without us knowing. It's not just about confronting the past; it's about figuring out how we come together and move forward.

The thought of showing them the letter has been gnawing at me, a persistent question that's kept me up at night these past few days. I've been back and forth on it, wrestling with whether they need to see Alex's words for themselves. Part of me—the part that's still reeling—worries they might read between the lines and find a way to pin this mess on me. But that's just fear talking, isn't it?

But then, there's the other part of me that's angry, that wants to throw the letter down on the table and say, "You want proof? Here it is." It's like this bitter urge to validate my hurt by passing it on to them; I hate that feeling. I know they're struggling to wrap their heads around all of this, and that letter…It's like a grenade. Would reading it bring them clarity, or would it just leave them scarred from the shrapnel of their father's betrayal?

The letter feels heavier than ever. It's just paper, ink, yet it's like holding a piece of dense, dark lead. I turn it over in my hands, its edges worn from the times I've unfolded and refolded it, each crease a mark of the turmoil it's caused.

"What's in your hands, Mom?" Lexi demands.

The responsibility weighs on me. Is my need for them to know everything a way to unburden myself? Or do I genuinely believe that having all the pieces of the puzzle is the only way they can start putting their worlds back together?

I look at my girls, their faces a mix of confusion and concern, waiting for me to continue.

"It's a letter your dad wrote to me just before we found out he had cancer, but I didn't find it until the night before I left for New York. It will tell you everything." My hand hovers over the folded paper. To hand it over would be to hand over the pain, the betrayal. And yet, keeping it to myself feels like holding back a piece of their story they have every right to claim.

They need to see their father for who he was, flaws and all. Maybe then we can start to understand, forgive, or simply accept and move forward. But as I sit here, the sunlight streaming in, casting long beams across the table, I know I need to be ready for the shadows that the truth might cast in its wake.

Silently, we move from the kitchen to the living room. I can't help but feel like we're in the calm before the storm. The air is still, and my palms are sweaty as I clutch the letter that's going to shatter so much of what they've known to be true.

I hand them the letter, and they sit shoulder to shoulder and begin reading. I watch their reactions closely. Lexi, the protective oldest, reads with a furrowed brow, her defenses up as if she could shield us all from the hurt. Lia, absorbs every word with a pained expression, her eyes welling up. And Ari, the youngest, looks between her sisters and me like she has something to say.

Ari's been quiet since we sat down, her usual liveliness dimmed by the weight of the room. But there's a shift, a certain resolve that comes over her as she finally lifts her eyes to meet mine.

"Mom," she starts, and there's a tremor in her voice, "I...I think I knew. Or, I suspected."

Her confession hits me harder than I expected.

"What do you mean, honey?" I ask, trying to keep my voice even, fighting the swell of concern rising in my chest.

She takes a deep breath, and it's like I can see the walls she's built around this secret start to crumble.

"Back in high school, senior year, I...I overheard Dad on the phone. It was late. I got up to get water and heard him in his study. He said her name, Eve's name."

My heart clenches, and it's all I can do to keep listening, to give her the space to get this out.

"He was talking soft, and it was...intimate."

She's picking at her nails now, a nervous habit she's had since she was a kid.

"I thought maybe they were planning a surprise for you, or it was about her work or something. I just...I didn't want to believe anything else."

The 'what ifs' start swirling in my mind like leaves in the wind. What if she had said something? Would it have changed anything? And where the hell was I when this conversation happened?

"And now," Ari's voice breaks, her young face etched with guilt, "all of this might be my fault. Because I never said anything to you."

My first instinct is to reach over and close the distance between us with the comfort that only touch can bring.

"Ari, look at me," I say gently. She raises her eyes, the green more vivid against the redness. "You are not responsible for any of this. Your dad made his choices, and you were just a kid."

"But if I had just—"

I cut her off, needing her to hear this. "No 'ifs', sweetheart. We can't live our lives on 'ifs. ' We deal with what's in front of us and do it together. This is on him and Eve, not you. Never you. Not any of you."

I look at all the girls; they wear the devastation like a mask— it's a look I've never seen on any of their faces before. Something I've tried to shield them from their entire life.

Ari bites her lip, nodding slowly, the words taking time to sink in.

"I'm so sorry, Mom."

I pull her into a hug, the kind where you try to transfer all the love and reassurance you have into another person.

"There's nothing to forgive," I whisper, but I know this wound will take time for both of us to heal. "I'm sorry you've had to carry this with you all these years. You should have never had to bear that responsibility."

Watching the girls react and process makes me hate Alex.

As they read, their emotions are laid bare. Lexi's face hardens with each sentence, the shock and hurt manifesting in the tightness of her jaw. Lia's tears start to fall freely, and Ari clings to my side, her confusion palpable.

The room is silent except for the rustling of the paper and the occasional sniffle from Lia. I watch my daughters struggle with the same pain that rocked me not too long ago—the betrayal, the hidden truths, and the sheer disbelief. It's all there in Alex's neat handwriting, a stark contrast to the messy reality it's causing.

Lexi looks up first, anger and hurt battling for dominance in her clear blue eyes. "How could he?" she whispers, the question hanging in the air.

Ari's got this lost look on her face, not quite understanding the full scope, but knowing enough that our family will never be the same.

Lia is trying to hold it together, her hand reaching out for Lexi, always trying to comfort even when she's the one falling apart.

I draw them all into a hug, this time not as a bear protecting her cubs, but as a fellow survivor bracing for the next wave.

"I know it hurts," I say, "and I'm so sorry you had to find out this way."

My heart breaks for them, for us, but I hold them tight, trying to be the strength they need even as we stand amid the wreckage of the life we thought we knew. This letter, Alex's last confession, is not the end of our story—it's a painful, ugly chapter, yes, but we're still here, still together, and that's got to count for something.

The lunch plates sit forgotten, a stark reminder that some appetites are lost to heavier things. Our shared history binds us together, and though the road ahead is uncertain, this cabin, with its resilience and whispers of old loves, seems the right place to start healing.

Chapter Eleven

I'm startled out of deep sleep and Lolly's recliner at the clinking of dishes being washed and dried by Lexi. I pick up my phone to see what time it is: 3:05 a.m. We've only been asleep for a few hours.

"Lex, honey, you don't need to clean the kitchen," I say, groggy from the semi-peaceful sleep I was in. I'm wrapped in my robe and slide my feet into my fuzzy slippers as I make my way to the kitchen. I know she's hurting.

"I'm sorry I woke you, Mom. I just...I couldn't sleep. Why don't you take the guest room. We all fell asleep in Lolly's big bed. Well, my sisters fell asleep," she says with a painful snicker.

Lexi's hair is scraped back into a ponytail that's all function, no finesse, perched high and messy on her head. The dim glow from that old kitchen lamp, the one that's always been a bit too weak, spills over her features, highlighting the tracks of tears on her cheeks and the redness rimming her eyes from the truths she learned about her Dad. It's a stark contrast to the confident, put-together image she usually projects.

She hasn't changed clothes—jeans that speak of action, a

sweatshirt that's too big, hanging off her like a question mark. The only sign she's attempted to relax is her bare feet, an incongruent vulnerability amidst the stoic facade she's holding up.

And what a facade it is, because the Lexi sitting before me now is wrestling with a new, jagged slice of reality. The hero she grew up idolizing, her dad, the man she's measured everyone else against, has stumbled off the pedestal in the most jarring way.

As for the half-brother they've just learned about, we haven't even begun to peel back the layers of that revelation. But it's there, an invisible presence among us, waiting to be acknowledged.

Lexi's posture is stiff, her arms folded like she's still trying to protect herself from the impact of the words in that letter. The look she gives me is a storm of confusion, betrayal, and the dawning of unwanted understanding.

"Mom, how do we even move forward from this?" Her voice cracks the stillness, a raw edge to her usually measured tone. "How do we start to accept...any of this?"

I reach for her hand and give it a reassuring squeeze. "Together," I tell her, my own voice firm with a resolve I hope can carry us both. "We take it one day at a time and do it together."

She meets my grip, her fingers tight around mine, and gives a small nod. It's the smallest of gestures but it speaks volumes of her willingness to face this, to try and understand the unimaginable.

Yes, the conversation is about to dive into deeper waters, with questions and answers that will test all of us. But right now, it's about steadying ourselves against the initial shockwave. I assure her that we'll navigate the complexities of this new, uncharted chapter as a unit, finding our way through the hurt and the questions that come with such a seismic shift in our family narrative.

With each passing hour that we sit and talk through the rich history of our family and her questions about mine and her father's relationship—and how Eve plays into it, her eyes become so heavy that I finally convince her to get some sleep.

"Go, take the spare bed. Let your sisters sleep, and please get some rest. I'm fine in Lolly's chair," I assure her, knowing good and well after the hard conversations I just had with my oldest daughter and the ones I've still yet to have with the other two that I'm not going back to sleep any time soon. I grab my journal from the side pocket of the recliner, my blue ballpoint pen attached to the binding on the side, and head out to the back porch. My favorite time of day—half sun peeking out over the horizon—just enough light to pen my thoughts.

Dear Alex,

It's odd, you know, writing to you just as 'Alex.' No endearing nicknames, no 'my love' or 'dearest.' Just Alex. It's a shift, a big one, but here we are.

It's hard not to think of you in fragments, pieces of the man I've loved, mourned, and now resent. You're the man whose laughter I fell in love with nearly four decades ago, whose intellect and charm were the anchors of my youth. The very same man who taught our girls to ride bikes, to brave the high dive, who could fix a leaking faucet and a broken heart with the same steady hands. And yet, here we are, surrounded by the things even you couldn't fix.

You were the most handsome man in any room, not just in my eyes but objectively, undeniably so. You were the one everyone was drawn to, the sun in our family solar system.

You're the husband I buried, laid to rest with all

the dreams and plans we still had unwritten. I buried you with a kiss, not knowing that there was so much I didn't know, so much you hadn't told me.

You were the poet, the scribe of my heart, penning love letters that I thought were as true as the ink they were written with. Letters I held close on lonely nights that now feel like strangers' words in your familiar hand.

But, you were also the cheater, the one who stepped outside the sacred circle we'd drawn around our family. The one who shared whispers and promises meant only for us, with not just anyone, my best friend.

You are the liar, the weaver of tales so convincing that I never thought to question their authenticity. You played your roles so well, perhaps too well, the lines between reality and fiction blurred to the point of nonexistence.

And you were the man who almost broke me, who brought me to my knees when I thought I could stand no longer. Yet here I am, Alex, still standing, still breathing, still putting one foot in front of the other.

In the end, you didn't break me, Alex. I am bent, undoubtedly, and I will carry the scars of this for the rest of my days. But I am not broken. The love I had for you, the life we built, it was not all a lie. It couldn't have been. And it's that sliver of truth, that kernel of the real, that keeps me from shattering completely.

I told the girls, Alex. I had to. They deserved to know why my world, and as a result, their world has suddenly shifted on its axis.

I'm not the woman I was before your letter, before your confession. That Kelsi Jo, she's been changed by this, by you. But she's also stronger. Even in your absence, the ripples of your choices are crashing over us, and we're left learning how to swim in this new reality.

You didn't just betray me, Alex; you betrayed our daughters. I've had to watch their faces as the foundation you laid for them crumbled. I've had to hold them as they sobbed, their world turned upside down by the man they adored.

And then there's your son. Our daughters' half-brother. The man who is out there, living his life, completely unaware of the hurricane he's unwittingly at the center of. How do we fit him into the narrative of our family now that you're gone? He's innocent in all of this, yet he's as much a victim of you and Eve's choices as the rest of us.

Despite this, I refuse to let this be the thing that defines us. I will not allow your actions to dictate the rest of my story. We will move forward without you, with or without your secret child. Our narrative will continue and be one of resilience and hope, not betrayal and loss.

We will survive this, Alex, but I needed you to know the cost of your choices, the real human cost. It's not just in the quiet of the night when the loneliness hits but in the everyday moments that used to be filled with laughter and love. Those moments now have a shadow cast over them, your shadow.

And still, I'm finding the grace to say that I hope you are resting peacefully. I truly do.

Kelsi Jo

I rip the letter out of my journal and step toward the gas stove, the pages trembling slightly in my hand. My fingers twist the knob, and the ignitor clicks rhythmically; a brief hesitation before the whoosh of blue flames bursts to life. The heat rises instantly, casting a soft glow on my face. I hold my words over the flame, the edges curling and darkening as the fire hungrily takes hold—the paper twists and crumbles, releasing faint wisps of smoke, carrying my words into nothingness.

Chapter Twelve

Lia's voice is soft but firm, cutting through the brisk morning air as they load the last of their bags into the car. "We love you, Mom."

It's been a weekend that's felt like a relentless wave, pulling us out into an ocean of hard truths and raw emotions. We've navigated through the storms of revelation, and now they're set to leave the cabin—a place that once harbored joyful escapes—carrying a heavy new reality back with them to Lake George.

Their faces show it all: the sleepless nights, the skipped meals, the heavy conversations we've had. My heart aches with a guilt that's hard to shake. I know it's not my doing, but I can't help feeling like I've sprung this all on them, even though it was Alex's secret to tell.

I watch them, my daughters, each one grappling with their own turmoil. Lexi, always the protector, is trying to wear a brave face, but her eyes betray her. She's always been the one to shoulder the family's burdens, and now she has another one to bear.

I can tell that Lia, my sensitive soul, is internalizing all of it, trying to find a quiet space within herself to start healing.

And Ari, she's the one who's struggling the most visibly. She's still finding her footing in adulthood, and this is a weight that none of us were prepared for.

"Drive safe, and call me when you get home," I tell them, the lump in my throat growing. I try to smile, but it's a smile that doesn't reach my eyes.

They nod, their movements a little slower, a bit more deliberate. As the car starts and they pull away from the cabin, I feel a piece of my heart going with them.

"Hey, Mom, when are you planning on coming home?" Ari asks.

"Soon. I've got a few more things I need to take care of here. I'll see you this weekend," I reply.

I'm left standing there, watching the car become a speck in the distance, the quiet of the cabin surrounding me like a shroud. They're taking more than just their luggage with them; they're carrying questions, doubts, a pain that will need time and love to heal.

I turn back to the cabin, its walls a silent witness to our family's unraveling and rebuilding.

Writing that letter to Alex was like drawing a line in the sand—my before and after. It's funny how putting words down can feel like a baptism, a cleansing. I wrote, and it was as if I was washing away a layer of pain, revealing something new underneath.

The creativity that I thought had withered is budding again, and it's all Lolly—her courage and passion that jumps off the page has sparked something in me. I remember feeling a void when Alex passed, a silence so profound I thought it might never be filled. I was convinced I'd be stuck in the echo of his absence forever, lost in his memory, unable to find my own identity again.

But life has a rhythm, a heartbeat that insists on continuing. Jaci, she wouldn't let me fade away. She nudged, she encouraged, and eventually, she convinced me that my voice still had value. That's how *Until I Found Me* came to life. It was supposed to be a testament to grief, to moving through it, and maybe, in a way, it still is.

But now, there's this new inciting incident. Not a death, not an end, but a beginning. A chance to redefine what life looks like after the rug's been pulled out from under me. It's not about living in the shadow of Alex anymore; it's about stepping out of it.

Tomorrow, I'll leave this cabin, leave the stillness behind, and head back to Lake George. But there's something I need to do first, a piece of unfinished business. A necessary closure, another step on this unexpected journey.

It feels like a chapter is closing, but the story, my story, is far from over. There's more to write, more to live, and more to learn. That's what healing is—finding your story after you thought the book had closed.

I take a deep, steadying breath as I unlock my phone, its screen lighting up with the slew of messages I've been ignoring. I swipe through the well-wishes and check-ins, all of them overshadowed by one name that seems to pulse with a life of its own. Eve Hatmaker. Nestled amongst the digital noise, her last message glares up at me.

> Good luck tomorrow, Kelsi. I'll be watching.
> Love, Eve

The "love" stings. It's a word that now feels foreign coming from her. I linger there for a moment, staring at her name, before I start typing.

> Hi Eve. It's been a long time…up for getting together?

I hit send before I can second guess myself, before I can drown in the anger that's never far beneath the surface. And just like that, the typing indicator appears. She's quick, too quick, like she's been waiting.

The message pops up with a chirp.

> Kelsi Jo! I'm so incredibly happy to hear from you. I'd love to get together. Tell me when and where, and I'll be there. Kels, I've missed you so much. I can't wait to hug you!!

Every word is a needle under my skin, her feigned innocence a salted blade. I can feel the anger coiling inside me, a serpent waking from its slumber. How dare she speak of hugs, of missing me, when all this time...

I wrestle the fury down long enough to type a response, keeping it as cool and composed as her message was warm and inviting.

> Great. How's Thursday for you?

My thumb hovers over the send button. I know this meeting is a stepping stone I need to cross, but it doesn't make the weight of what's to come any lighter.

The reply is almost instant again, as if she's sitting there with her phone in her hand, her guilt an unacknowledged shadow between us.

> Thursday's perfect. Can't wait! X

The 'X' at the end of her message feels like the final betrayal. I toss the phone down, a small part of me wishing it could shatter into as many pieces as she's shattered our lives.

Come Thursday, Eve won't find the Kelsi she's expecting. She'll find a woman tempered by pain, a woman ready to confront her face to face. And as I sit, letting the waves of anger ebb and flow, I know that this is one meeting that will change everything for both of us.

Chapter Thirteen

Claire's sleepy smile greets me, warm and inviting. "What's on your mind?" she murmurs, her hand finding my thigh beneath the sheets. She pulls me closer, our legs tangling together, grounding me in the quiet intimacy of the moment.

The room around us is a reflection of her—a space filled with art and photographs that capture life's simple beauties, each one whispering of love, loss, and the pieces of her heart still tied to Samantha and Jackson.

"I'm going to sell my house," I say, the words spilling into the stillness between us. They feel both liberating and heartbreaking, a severing of the past and a step toward something new.

I've been back in Lake George for a little over 24 hours, and I haven't been able to bring myself to stay in my own home—not with Alex's presence lingering in every corner, the weight of everything I've uncovered pressing down on me. Instead, I've been at Claire's, wrapped in her warmth and the safety of our love, trying to gather the courage to let go of the life I once knew.

We rise together, the morning unfolding lazily around us. Her bedroom now feels like a protective cocoon, the scent of morning coffee drifting in from the kitchen mingling with the lingering traces of her jasmine perfume.

As she brushes a strand of hair from my eyes, her touch is full of an unspoken strength. "Where will you go after the house sells?" she inquires, genuine curiosity lacing her words.

A moment of silence stretches between us, filled with the weight of decisions and the soft hum of the waking world outside.

"I'm thinking of moving into Lolly's cabin," I answer, my voice firmer than I feel. It's a leap into the unknown; it also means I'd be moving five hours away from my girls—and Claire.

She nods, her acceptance emanating like warmth from a fire.

The vulnerability of the moment wraps around us and it just flows off my tongue, "Claire, would you...would you consider eventually moving in with me? Into Lolly's cabin?" The question dangles between us, delicate as the morning light.

Her response doesn't come in words at first, but in the gentle press of her lips against mine, a kiss that speaks volumes, that says 'yes,' that says 'together.' When she pulls back, her eyes lock onto mine with an unspoken promise.

I watch as a myriad of emotions flit across Claire's face, her eyes reflecting the depth of our bond and the weight of my request. It's not just any question—it's a leap into a shared future, an offer of my heart and my space, where the memories of her late wife and my own new wounds lie waiting.

Her response is a soft interlude, her lips meeting mine in a kiss that feels like the beginning of an answer. It's tender and thoughtful, and as she pulls back, her gaze holds mine with a warmth that feels like sunrise.

"Kelsi Jo," she says, her voice a soothing balm. Her honesty is as beautiful as it is raw. "I've never shared a home with anyone but Samantha..."

We're on the precipice of something wonderful, but we both know that wounds of the heart take time to heal. The future is an uncharted map, with paths that could lead us anywhere—together.

"I know it's a lot to take in," I say, giving her the space she needs, the respect her past deserves. "There's no pressure for an answer now. Just know that I want you with me when the time is right. And maybe..." I trail off, letting the sentence and the hope it carries hang gently between us.

Claire nods, her smile touched with a hint of wistful understanding. "...but I would absolutely love to move in with you," she says, the notion settling around us.

We sit side by side, the world outside Claire's window slowly coming to life, as inside, we navigate the complexities of love and loss, of moving on and holding on. There's a promise in the air, in the shared silence of her room—a promise of what will be, a gentle cliffhanger in the story of us.

Chapter Fourteen

October 17, 2019.

I open the front door, my smile thin and forced, every muscle in my face taut from the effort. The weight of this moment presses down on me, but I keep my expression neutral. It's the kind of control I've perfected over the years—the ability to keep the cracks from showing.

"Eve."

"Kelsi Jo! It's so good to see you." Eve steps inside, her arms opening wide as if everything between us is fine. As if we're still the inseparable best friends we once were. She pulls me into a hug, and the scent of her expensive floral perfume fills the space between us. It's suffocating, and I barely manage to reciprocate with a one-armed pat on her back.

"I was surprised you agreed to come," I say, pulling away and closing the door behind her. "Considering how things ended between us earlier this year."

Eve hesitates, her smile faltering. "I needed time, Kels. Time to process...everything."

"Time," I repeat, my tone sharp as a blade.

"I've been worried about you, you know? I didn't see you on

the morning shows. And when I tried to call and text you, you didn't answer. And then I tried to call the girls and they…"

"The girls don't have anything to say to you."

Eve looks shocked.

"Why? We've been like family since they were born, Kels. Why wouldn't they want to talk to me?"

"What do you mean? Why do you think they wouldn't want to talk with you?"

"Well, I'm sure you told them about our spat, disagreement if you will, at the coffee shop." She answers like she's so sure of herself.

She still has no idea that I know about her and Alex.

Fucking clueless.

"No, actually, that's not why they don't want to talk to you. Let's go upstairs—I have something I want to show you."

"Upstairs?" She glances toward the staircase, her brows knitting together in confusion. "Why?"

"Because. Just follow me."

I don't wait for her response, and I hear her hesitant footsteps behind me as I climb the stairs. The silence between us is heavy, thick with unspoken words. By the time we reach the top, my pulse is pounding in my ears, and the air feels charged as if the house itself is holding its breath.

I lead her into my bedroom and motion to the bed. "Have a seat. On Alex's side."

"On Alex's side?" Her voice wavers as she glances at the pillows, perfectly fluffed and untouched.

"Mmmm hmmm," I say, my tone cold, unforgiving. I watch as she perches awkwardly on the edge, her discomfort evident in the way her hands fidget in her lap.

"This feels…strange," she says, her eyes darting around the room, avoiding mine.

"Strange?" I sit beside her, the bed dipping under our combined weight. "You know what's strange, Eve? Finding a letter from my dead husband, tucked away on his side of the closet, changes everything I thought I knew about him. About us. About you."

Her face pales, and her hands still. "What are you talking about?"

I pull the letter from my pocket, the folded paper worn and creased from the countless times I've held it, read it, and memorized its damning words.

"I found this. It's from Alex. To me. But it mentions you."

She stares at the letter as if it's a venomous snake. "Kelsi, I don't think—"

"Read it," I interrupt, shoving the letter toward her. "Go on, Eve. Read it."

Her hands tremble as she takes the paper, unfolding it slowly. Her eyes scan the words, and I watch as her expression shifts— confusion, recognition, then guilt. Her breathing becomes shallow, and tears well up in her eyes.

"Kelsi, I—" she starts, her voice breaking.

"Keep reading," I say, my voice ice-cold. "You haven't gotten to the good part yet."

She shakes her head, trying to hand the letter back to me. "I can't."

"Why not?" I snap. "Because it's too hard? Because it makes you face what you did?"

Tears spill down Eve's cheeks, her voice barely above a whisper. "I'm sorry."

A bitter laugh erupts from my throat, sharp and hollow. "Sorry?" The word tastes like acid. "Sorry doesn't even begin to cover it, Eve. You lied to me. You betrayed me. You betrayed Alex. And you had his child."

Her head snaps up, eyes wide with shock. "Kelsi—"

"It's all in the letter," I cut her off, my voice shaking with fury. "Alex tells all about the affair. About the son you had. About how you put him up for adoption and told everyone you were studying abroad. About how he was going to leave me for you after thirty years of marriage."

Eve's breath hitches, her shoulders trembling as she turns away, hiding behind a curtain of shame.

"I didn't have a choice," she whispers, her voice cracking.

"You didn't have a *choice*?" My voice rises, disbelief fueling my rage. "You had *every* choice, Eve! You could have told me. *You should have told Alex!* You could have faced the consequences of your actions like an adult. But instead, you lied. For *decades*."

Her silence is deafening.

Then, she exhales a shuddering breath, her hands clenching into fists at her sides. "He knew," she says so quietly I almost miss it.

The room tilts, my stomach twisting violently. "What?"

Eve finally meets my eyes, guilt and something else, something raw and jagged, flashing behind her tears. "He *knew*, Kelsi."

I step forward, my pulse pounding in my ears. "He knew *what*, Eve?"

She swallows hard, her lips trembling. "He knew I was pregnant. I told him, and he told me he didn't want the baby. That I needed to have an abortion."

A choked gasp claws up my throat. "I don't..." My head shakes violently as if I can shake away her words. "Why should I *fucking* believe you."

Eve flinches, but I don't stop. The betrayal is suffocating, burning me from the inside out. "You pretended to be my best friend. Standing beside me through everything. Helping me raise my daughters—all while fucking my husband behind my back!"

"I was scared, Kelsi!" she sobs, her hands gripping the edge of the bed as if it's the only thing keeping her upright.

I let out a hollow laugh. "You were *scared*? So you what, decided to blow up my life instead? You took Alex from me piece by piece until there was nothing left but more lies? You had the audacity to comfort me when he was dying, to act like you gave a damn about my grief when you, both of you, had been carrying this secret the entire time?"

Her head snaps up, and for the first time, her sorrow hardens into something sharper. Anger flashes through her tear-filled eyes. "You think I *wanted* this?" she hisses. "That I planned it?"

I glare at her, my chest rising and falling in ragged breaths. "Then tell me," I seethe. "Tell me *everything*. Tell me about how Alex *knew*."

Eve's chin quivers. Her next words slice through me.

"He *thought* I had an abortion."

The ground shifts beneath me. "What?"

Eve presses a shaking hand to her mouth, inhaling sharply before forcing herself to go on. "I told him I was pregnant. He gave me the money to take care of it. I walked into the clinic...but I *couldn't* do it." Her voice breaks. "So I left. I found a group home for pregnant women and put our son up for adoption."

Silence crashes between us, suffocating, thick with the weight of the truth.

Alex knew.

But he lived the next twenty years believing his child was never born.

Eve's voice trembles, but the words cut through the silence like a blade. "Our son found me when he was twenty years old. That's when I decided I needed to tell Alex—"

"And you didn't think to tell me, too?" My voice rises, sharp with fury. "His *wife*? The woman who shared his life, his children, his last breath?"

Eve flinches but doesn't answer.

"Why the *hell* didn't you tell me?"

"I couldn't..." Her voice is barely a whisper, a pathetic excuse that only fuels my rage.

I let out a hollow laugh, shaking my head. "Of course, you couldn't. Honesty? Integrity? That's not who you are, Eve." My chest tightens, my throat burning with the sheer weight of this moment.

Her eyes glisten with fresh tears, but she doesn't look away this time. "I loved him, Kelsi!" she cries, her voice cracking under the weight of the confession. "I loved him, and after he found out about our son...*he fell in love with me too.*"

A sharp, guttural sound tears from my throat before I even realize it's mine. My whole body tenses, fists clenching at my sides. "*Don't you dare.*" The words are low, venomous. "Don't you fucking *dare* sit here and try to justify what you did by throwing your so-called love in my face."

Eve swallows hard, shaking her head. "I..."

"No," I snap, stepping closer. "You didn't *love* him. You *wanted* what was mine. And there's a difference."

Her shoulders slump, the fire in her eyes flickering out as fast as it appeared. Guilt washes over her features, twisting her expression into something small and broken. "I didn't know what else to do," she whispers. "I thought...I thought I was doing the right thing."

She crumbles. The dam breaks, and she sobs, her whole body shaking as she wraps her arms around herself. "I couldn't raise a child," she gasps between ragged breaths. "I thought I could make it all go away...I thought if I buried it deep enough, it wouldn't matter."

"Well, it *does* matter," I say, my voice shaking but steady. "It matters to *me*. It matters to *my daughters*. And it sure as hell matters to *your son*—the son you gave away without ever telling Alex, until it was too late."

Eve lifts her tear-streaked face to mine, her eyes pleading. "Kelsi, please..."

"*Don't.*" My voice is ice, slicing through the air between us. "Don't ask for my forgiveness, Eve. Because I *don't have it to give.*"

I stare at her, the silence stretching between us like a chasm I have no interest in crossing. My mind latches on to the next question before I can stop it.

"Does Charlie know?" My voice is tight, almost brittle.

Eve's face twists with something unreadable—guilt, maybe, or resignation. Then, slowly, she nods. "I told him," she admits, voice barely above a whisper. "Right after you and I had our falling out at the coffee shop."

A fresh wave of betrayal crashes over me, sharp and searing. My hands clench at my sides as I force myself to process what she just said.

Charlie knew.

Something inside me hardens.

I inhale sharply, straightening, my spine stiffening with a finality I didn't realize I was capable of. There's no more room for tears, for anger, for second chances. There's only one way forward.

"You need to leave." My voice is cold, flat. The words are weighted with everything I can't bring myself to say. "I don't ever want to see or hear from you again."

Eve stares at me, her lips parting like she might argue, might beg—but she doesn't. She nods once, almost imperceptibly, then slowly rises to her feet. Head bowed, shoulders hunched under the weight of what she's done, she turns toward the door.

But just before she steps through, she looks back, her eyes hollow with desperation. "Kelsi," she whispers, her voice breaking. "I'm sorry. For everything."

I say nothing.

I can't.

I just watch as she walks out of the room, out of my life, leaving behind nothing but the wreckage of her betrayal.

And for the first time in *months*, I feel something close to relief.

Chapter Fifteen

The screen lights up with the familiar faces of my girls, and a wave of emotion rolls over me as I prepare to share the news. It's our Sunday ritual, this virtual gathering, but tonight there's a different kind of anticipation crackling through the digital connection.

"We got an offer on the house, girls!" The words tumble out, laced with a cocktail of relief and nostalgia. Their expressions mirror my own mix of excitement and the poignant tug of closing a significant chapter.

Lia's brows lift, her eyes brightening with a supportive enthusiasm. Lexi's smile is tinged with a hint of sadness, yet there's an unmistakable pride in her nod. And though Ari isn't with us on the call, I can almost feel her quiet strength bolstering me from afar.

"It happened so fast, didn't it?" Lia's voice is warm, her presence a steadying force even through the screen.

"Yeah, Mom, it's a big step," Lexi voice is steady, but I can hear the unspoken memories clinging to her words.

"I'll be back from the cabin tomorrow. It's time to start packing. We close right after Christmas." The sentence feels heavy, laden with the weight of decades spent within those walls now sold to strangers.

"We'll be there, Mom. We'll make it a...a celebration of sorts." Lia leans in, her image filling the screen.

"We'll pack, we'll remember, we'll laugh...and probably cry a bit too." Lexi's agreement is a soft murmur, but her determination is as clear as day.

I take a deep breath, bolstered by their support. "I love you, girls. More than you'll ever know."

Tomorrow, I'll leave the quiet reflection of Lolly's cabin and return to the home that once rang with laughter, footfalls, and whispered secrets. Together, with my daughters by my side, we'll box up the past, ready to step bravely into the future.

The screen goes dark as we say our goodnights, but the glow in my heart remains.

Chapter Sixteen

January 27, 2020.

The morning sun spills into the rustic kitchen of Lolly's cabin, casting a golden glow over the well-worn counter-tops and the fresh wildflowers sitting in a mason jar by the window. It's been nearly four months since the fabric of my life unraveled and was stitched back together into a tapestry richer and more complex than I ever imagined it could be. Sitting at the old pine table with a steaming mug of coffee, I gaze out at the serenity of Mirror Lake, reflecting on the journey that has led me here.

Claire is outside on the porch, her laughter mingling with the morning birdsong as she chats with a neighbor passing by on the woodland trail. She's brought life back to the cabin and to me, her presence a gentle but constant source of joy and comfort. I smile, watching her there, so at home in this slice of paradise we're making our own. The decision was mutual and natural, like the confluence of two rivers meeting and moving forward as one.

Claire moved in full time right after Christmas. We told our families that we were a couple right after the house sold.

"There's something important I need to share with you all."

My fingers traced the familiar grain of the old wooden coffee table in Lolly's cabin. It felt grounding, like I was borrowing a bit of its strength for what I was about to say. My daughters sat before me, their expressions varying—Lia's steady gaze a source of quiet reassurance, Ari's brows furrowed in mild confusion, and Lexi's hands fidgeting nervously in her lap.

I took a deep breath, feeling the warmth of the fire crackling behind me. "It's about Claire and me," I began, my voice steady despite the weight of my confession. "Our relationship has grown into something much more than friendship. We're in love."

A silence settled over the room, not an uncomfortable one, but one heavy with thought and processing. The kind of silence that holds a space for big truths to land. My heart hammered in my chest as I waited for their responses, the firelight flickering against the cabin walls like shadows of lives past.

"It's also about Lolly and Helen," I continued, finding a thread that felt natural to weave into this moment.

I shared their love story alongside ours.

"Just like them, Claire and I have found love in a place we didn't expect. Eventually, Claire will be moving in with me here, at the cabin."

Lia was the first to break the silence, leaning forward, her elbows on her knees. "Mom, if you're happy, that's what matters to us." Her voice was measured but warm. She smiled, a genuine one, full of understanding and calm. It reached her eyes, and I felt a small but powerful wave of relief.

Ari was next, her voice soft and a little hesitant, but no less supportive. "It's just a surprise, Mom," she said, her fingers playing absently with the hem of her sweater. "But we've seen how happy you've been these past months. If Claire is the reason, then we're glad for you."

Lexi took longer. Her gaze dropped to her hands, which were still lacing and unlacing in her lap. Finally, she looked up at me, her hazel eyes—a mirror of her father's—searching mine. "It's a lot to take in, Mom," she admitted, her voice cautious. "I just want to make sure you're sure about this. About her."

"I understand," I said, my voice softer now, as I looked at each of them. "It's a lot. But it's also something I know deep in my heart is right. It's important that you all know how much I love Claire, and that this step feels like coming home for me."

I paused, watching their faces as they absorbed my words. "But I want you to be part of this journey, too. Our family is changing, but it's still us—just a little bigger, a little braver."

The fire crackled softly in the silence that followed, its warmth a comforting counterpoint to the gravity of the moment. Slowly, the tension in the room began to ebb. Lia reached over and placed her hand on mine, giving it a reassuring squeeze. Ari offered a small smile, and even Lexi's shoulders seemed to relax.

We began to talk; the questions that flowed naturally—about Lolly and Helen, about the cabin, about how Claire and I would merge our lives under one roof. I shared stories of Lolly and Helen's quiet but fierce love, how they'd carved out a space for themselves in a world that didn't always understand them. Sitting here in their home, it felt fitting to sit by the same hearth where they'd once dreamed of their life together.

Chapter Seventeen

Today, Lia and Lexi are coming to visit Claire and me. They haven't been here since January.

Until I Found Me, the memoir that was supposed to be a homage to my late husband and the love we shared, finally launched and quickly became a best seller that stands as a testament to resilience, a narrative redefined.

Jaci, my ever-savvy agent, helped me navigate the murky waters of publicity post-scandal. "It's not just a story of overcoming death, Kelsi. It's about overcoming deceit, and that's a story that needs to be told," she had said.

And so, she pitched it—a tale not just of grief but of grappling with betrayal and finding a path to forgiveness, if not for Alex, then for myself.

The day unfolds, and the cabin becomes a hive of activity, the scent of Claire's baking fills the air, and laughter rings through the rooms. When the girls arrive, they bring with them a fresh breeze of the outside world, their energy adding to the richness of our lives.

The late afternoon sun filters through the canopy of trees surrounding Lolly's cabin, dapples of light playing on the wooden floor. I'm on the phone with Jaci, discussing dates for a book tour, when Claire slips outside. The conversation with Jaci is animated and filled with plans, but part of me is trailing Claire with my gaze, watching her graceful movements as she disappears into the blooming garden.

After I hang up, the stillness of the cabin wraps around me. Claire is standing by Lolly's old oak tree, the one that's been a steadfast sentinel to the cabin's comings and goings for decades. Her back is to me, but there's a tension in her shoulders that speaks volumes. As I approach, the scent of the earth and the hum of the lake blend into a calm symphony.

"Hey," I call out softly, not wanting to startle her. She turns, and her smile is a little nervous but radiant, like the first bloom after a long winter.

"Kelsi," she begins, her voice steady yet full of emotion, "I Facetimed the girls a few weeks ago when you were in New York City with Jaci. I wanted to ask them something important."

"You did?" My heart stumbles over a beat.

She steps closer, reaching for my hands, and holds them in her own. "They love you so much, and they see how happy we are together. They've given their blessing for me to ask you..." Her voice trails off, and the suspense sends a flutter through my core.

Claire takes a deep breath, and when she speaks again, her voice is laced with the soft gravity of the moment. "Kelsi Johanna, will you marry me?"

The question hangs in the air, a delicate possibility that sends ripples across the surface of my life, much like the pebbles we toss into Mirror Lake, watching the circles expand outward.

"Yes." The word is out before I can even think, natural and sure, a reflection of everything I feel for her. "Yes, Claire, I will marry you."

Joy dances in her eyes, and it's mirrored in my own. We stand under the protective branches of Lolly's oak, two hearts agreeing to join as one, continuing a legacy of love in this very cabin that once sheltered a love that dared not speak its name.

Our embrace is warm and firm. I lean into her, feeling the full weight of my past slipping away for the first time.

Chapter Eighteen

Claire whispers, her breath visible in the cool air. "It's perfect, Kelsi."

"It's exactly how I imagined it would be," I confess. Our wedding is just a week and a half away, and the reality of it still feels like a dream—one I'm afraid to wake up from.

Lia, Lexi, and Ari are bustling around the cabin, their voices carrying through the open windows as they debate flower arrangements and seating plans. Their excitement is infectious, and every now and then, a peal of laughter breaks through the earnestness of their planning.

"We'll need chairs here." Claire gestures towards the edge of the porch, envisioning our guests facing the lake.

I nod, visualizing the moment with the dying light painting the sky in shades of orange and pink, the perfect backdrop for our vows. "And lanterns," I add. "Lining the walkway to the deck. It'll be like walking through a starlit path to...to us."

Claire's smile widens at the thought. "That's beautiful, Kelsi. Like a fairy tale."

A knock on the screen door turns our attention back inside.

Ari's head pops out, her eyes sparkling with the same vibrancy that brightens the lake. "You two need to see this," she calls out, waving a hand at us to come in.

We follow her to the kitchen, where Lia and Lexi have laid out fabric swatches, flower petals, and a scrapbook of old family wedding photos spread across the table. It's a collage of history and future intertwined.

"This is amazing," I breathe out, touching a black and white photograph of Lolly and Helen, standing side by side on what could very well be this very porch. It's a silent testament to the journey that brought us here.

"We wanted to honor them somehow," Lexi says, following my gaze. "Incorporate their legacy into the wedding."

"It's not just our day, is it?" Claire smiles. "It's a celebration of every Barker/Kincaid woman who dared to love."

We spend the rest of the evening wrapped in wedding preparations, a flurry of creativity and shared memories. The girls share stories of their childhood, of holidays spent at their grandaddy's and here at the cabin, of Lolly's whispered tales of a love that was strong enough to defy the odds.

As night falls, we stand on the porch once more, now illuminated by strings of soft white lights that the girls have strung up in a spur of the moment of inspiration. The cabin, our home, is transforming into the venue of our dreams, a place where our family will gather to watch as Claire and I step into our future together.

The night before us is peaceful, and as Claire wraps an arm around my waist, I rest my head on her shoulder, knowing that everything, every trial, every tear, has led to this. The end of one story and the beginning of another.

Chapter Nineteen

My father stands by the window in the bedroom that was once Lolly's, his shoulders slightly hunched, his hands clasped behind his back. I pause in the doorway, taking him in—the man who has always been my quiet, unwavering strength.

"Dad?" My voice wavers, thick with emotion.

He turns, and for a moment, all I see is warmth, the depth of his love reflecting in his eyes. "You look beautiful, Kelsi Johanna." His voice is steady, but I don't miss the crack at the edges, the way emotion tightens his throat.

I step toward him, my wedding dress whispering against the floor, and reach for his hands. "Dad, what is it?"

Instead of answering right away, he reaches for a small wooden box on the windowsill. His fingers trace the worn edges before he opens it, pulling out a faded manila envelope. He holds it for a moment longer, staring at the name scrawled across it in familiar, looping handwriting—Charlotte Louise Barker.

"This," he says, his voice thick, "this belonged to Lolly. Helen gave it to me not long before she passed."

The words land like a weight in my chest. Helen. My breath catches, but I nod, urging him on.

"She told me that after Lolly passed, she held onto this," he continues. "Said she wasn't sure when the right time would be to pass it on, but that when she knew, she'd know." He swallows, emotion thick in his voice. "And when she knew her own time was coming, she gave it to me."

I press a trembling hand to my lips. "What is it?"

He carefully unfastens the rusted clasp, pulling out the aged papers inside. My breath stutters as I recognize the typewritten document beneath his fingers—a Warranty Deed.

My eyes scan the names: Charlotte Louise Barker and Ruth Helen Michaelson. The date—September 17, 1972—sits like a quiet echo of the past, a moment sealed in ink and time.

"This cabin," my father murmurs. "Lolly and Helen built a life here. A love that the world didn't always allow. And now..." He clears his throat and lifts his gaze to mine. "Now, it belongs to you."

The words steal my breath. "What?"

His hands close over mine, pressing the deed between our palms. "This is my gift to you, Kelsi Jo. On your wedding day. A home—a legacy. A place where love, true love, was nurtured and protected. It's yours now, just as it was theirs."

Tears spill freely down my cheeks. "Dad..."

He pulls me into his arms, his embrace strong, familiar, safe. "I want you to have a place where love always wins," he whispers. "Where you and Claire can build your own story, just like Lolly and Helen did."

I clutch the papers to my chest, overwhelmed by the sheer depth of what this means. Of what my father has carried for all these years. I pull away slightly, blinking back tears.

"You are the very picture of your Lolly, Kelsi Jo."

"Thank you," I whisper. "For everything."

He smiles, kissing my forehead. "It's what family does, Kelsi Jo. We carry each other forward."

And as I stand there, wrapped in my father's love, in Lolly's legacy, and in the promise of the life I'm about to begin with Claire, I know—this is the kind of love that endures. The kind that triumphs.

* * *

Stepping onto the sunlit porch, my heart dances a rhythm that echoes the soft ripple of Mirror Lake's waters. My dress, a cascade of ivory silk, hugs my form with a gentle ease, its lace trim catching the whispers of the spring breeze. I feel like a part of the season itself, blooming into a new chapter of life.

"You look incredible," Ari breathes out, standing in her pastel dress beside Lia, both my pillars today as they've always been.

Lexi, nods approvingly from where she stands ready to lead the ceremony. Her black dress is simplicity married with sophistication, a perfect fit for the role she's about to play.

Claire, standing a few feet away, steals my breath. She's traded tradition for a sky-blue gown that flows around her like a whispered promise, soft yet striking. Jackson stands by his mother like a young oak, solid and sure.

The gentle bobbing of kayaks floating just a few feet from the dock carries our nearest and dearest, a floating congregation tethered to the shores of our beginning.

The soft strum of a guitar begins to drift over the water, cueing our guests to quieten.

"Looks like it's time," Claire says, her voice steady but I can hear the quiver of emotion just beneath the surface.

I take my place beside her, our hands finding each other with a familiarity that still sends shivers up my spine.

"Shall we?" Lexi asks, her voice carrying the weight of the moment.

"We shall," I answer, my voice a blend of laughter and tears.

With a shared glance, we turn to face Lexi, who's now

opening the leather-bound book that holds the words that will bind us.

"Welcome, everyone. Let's start this beautiful chapter."

"Friends and family," Lexi's voice beckons, her eyes meeting each guest's in turn, "we are gathered here not just in the presence of this beautiful landscape but surrounded by the love that Kelsi Jo and Claire have cultivated. Today, they choose to affirm that love through marriage."

"And now, before these vows are exchanged, we take a moment to acknowledge the paths that have brought Kelsi Jo and Claire here. To the lake, this cabin, this family—they've woven a tapestry rich with experiences, joys, sorrows, and an unwavering commitment to each other."

I glance at Claire, her gaze locked on mine, a silent conversation passing between us. This is it, the precipice of forever.

Lexi pauses, allowing the weight of her words to settle like snowflakes among us. "Kelsi Jo, Claire, the vows you are about to make are a way to share your love and commitment to each other in your own words, before your family and friends."

As I face Claire, her hands in mine, I prepare to speak the words that have lived in my heart since the moment I knew she was the one. The lake, a mirror to our story, shimmers with anticipation, and our guests lean in.

"Claire, from the moment our paths crossed, you've been my unexpected blessing, the serendipitous gift I didn't know I needed. You entered my world, not as a whirlwind, but as the gentlest breeze, subtly shifting the direction of my life towards horizons I never imagined I'd explore. Standing before you now, with the mirror of this lake and the eyes of our loved ones as our witnesses, I am awash with gratitude, love, and an unwavering certainty that this, us, is where I am meant to be.

"I vow to be your partner in all things, not possessing you but working with you as a part of the whole. I vow to listen for your laughter and to look for your light on the cloudy days. I will be there to celebrate every peak and to lift you from every valley, to honor the silence just as much as the conversation, and to always strive to meet your needs, not because I have to, but because I want to.

"As we grow old together, I promise to cherish the warmth of your hand in mine and to never take our time for granted. I will stand by your side, sharing in your dreams and supporting you as you have so steadfastly supported me. I promise to laugh with you, cry with you, and be the soft place for you to land through every chapter of our story.

"Claire, you have given me a love that is deeper than the deepest lake and more vast than the night sky. My promise to you is this: I will spend every day trying to give you the same, to create a life that reflects the beauty of the love you've shown me, a love that endures, transforms, and transcends.

"So, with this ring, I give you my heart, as freely as the waters flow, as enduringly as the stars burn. I give you my spirit, my companionship, and all my tomorrows. For today, for tomorrow, for always, I am yours."

"Kelsi Jo," Claire holds my hand a little tighter. "The moment you came into my life, you brought colors I never knew existed. You painted my world with your strength, your kindness, and your boundless capacity to love. Standing here, I see not just the reflection of the trees and sky but the reflection of a love that has become my compass, my home.

"My vow to you is simple yet infinite. I promise to honor the truth in your eyes and the passion in your heart. I promise to support your dreams and to be your unwavering partner in every adventure life throws our way. I will be the harmony to your melody, the rhythm to your dance, in the music that is our life together.

"With you, I have learned that love isn't just a feeling but an action we choose every day. So I vow to choose you again and again, in a hundred lifetimes, in any version of reality. I'd find you and choose you. I promise to laugh with you in joy, grieve with you in sorrow, and grow with you in love.

"I vow to create a home with you that is filled with learning, laughter, and light, to provide a sanctuary of peace and pleasure. I will not just grow old with you but grow with you each day as we unfurl the chapters of our lives.

"Today, I give you my love, unfiltered and unreserved. I give you my tomorrows, filled with hope and the promise of more laughter, more love, and more life. From this moment on, I am wholly, joyfully yours."

Lexi begins her officiant duties, and I stop her mid-sentence.

"Hold on just one second, Lexi," I find myself interrupting, my hand raised gently.

I turn back to face Claire, her puzzled gaze resting on the document now in her hands. "What's this?" she asks, a light chuckle mingling with the ripple of laughter from our waterborne audience.

Her fingers trace the edges of the deed as she reads, her smile giving way to a small, incredulous shake of her head. From the corner of my eye, I catch Lexi's curious tilt, her mouth forming a silent, "What's going on, Mom?"

"This, my love, is more than just a piece of paper. This is Helen and Lolly's legacy; their deed to this cabin has now passed to us."

The air changes as understanding dawns, and Claire wraps her arms around me, pulling me close.

Lexi, wiping away a tear with the back of her hand, steps forward again, clearing her throat softly. "Now, where were we?" she says, her voice steadier than her hands. The crowd settles, a collective breath drawn in anticipation.

"We're here not just to celebrate the union of Kelsi Jo and Claire but to honor the foundation laid before them," Lexi continues, her gaze sweeping over the guests in their kayaks, now still and silent. "This cabin, this lake, this moment is steeped in history and love, a testament to the journey that brought us all here."

She opens the book once more, her eyes finding mine and Claire's. "Marriage is more than a legal bond. It is a promise, a vow, a choice made every day. It's choosing each other again and again, at the start and finish of every day, no matter the season, no matter the weather."

With a nod from Lexi, we turn to face each other, Claire's hand finding mine. Our fingers intertwine naturally, the touch as familiar as our own hearts beating.

"Kelsi Jo, Claire," Lexi addresses us, her voice clear and sure, "do you promise to cherish each other, to honor and respect each other, to stand together through sorrows and joys, hardships and triumphs, for all the days of your lives?"

We both answer, our voices mingling and echoing across the water, "We do."

"And so, by the power vested in me—not just by the state of Maine but by the legacy of love that surrounds us—I now pronounce you married. You may seal your vows with a kiss."

Our lips meet, a gentle collision of past and present, of memory and hope. The crowd erupts into cheers, the sound cascading across Mirror Lake, as the ripples from our kayaked guests gently lap against the porch. It's a symphony of celebration, each note carrying the weight of our shared story—a story that continues to unfold with love, laughter, and the promise of endless tomorrows.

As the sun dips lower, casting a golden sheen over Mirror Lake, I stand beside Claire, our hands linked, our futures entwined. Around us, the whispers of nature, the soft chuckles and murmurs of our family and friends, and the tranquil waters are all part of the melody that sings of new beginnings. In this place, surrounded by the echoes of a love story that spanned decades, I find a truth that feels as old as time yet as fresh as the dawn: life is an intricate tapestry of moments, choices, and serendipitous encounters. I came here seeking solace, and I found a universe waiting for me, in the eyes of the woman I love, in the history of the woman who guided me, and in the legacy of the cabin that watched me grow. I look out across the water, towards the horizon, where tomorrow waits, ripe with unseen tales and unwritten chapters.

Because, sometimes the story chooses you.

Epilogue

One year later.

One year. One year of waking up to Claire's sleepy smile. One year of unexpected stillness—of a world that shut down and forced us inward, making room for the kind of love that grows in deep, unshaken roots.

I press my forehead against the cool glass of the living room window, watching the afternoon sun spill golden light over the front yard. Claire is humming to herself as she tends to the garden we never expected to have time for.

The past twelve months weren't what we imagined. By the time I was gearing up for my book tour—the West Coast stretch I had been looking forward to—the world was already unraveling. Cancellations came in waves, each email another door closing, another certainty slipping away. And just like that, the tour was over before it truly began.

I had braced for disappointment. What I hadn't expected was the relief that came with it.

Because as much as I wanted to be out there, sharing my story, there was something deeply precious about this forced pause— about getting to live my first year as a newlywed wrapped in the quiet, in the slowness, in the simple act of learning how to exist beside Claire without the world pulling me away.

And through it all, I wrote.

My story is still unfolding, reshaping itself in ways I don't always understand. I thought I had told it all, but I now see that reinvention is never a one-time event but a lifelong unfolding. So, I keep writing, peeling back new layers, capturing the evolution as I live it.

A vibration against the coffee table pulls me from my thoughts. My phone, lighting up with a name I never thought I'd see there again.

Eve.

We've spoken. Carefully at first. Testing the waters. Acknowledging the wreckage without drowning in it. It has taken time, but the walls between us have started to crack. She has apologized in the ways that matter, in the ways that make it clear she understands what she broke. And I, in my own time, have chosen to forgive—not for her sake, but for mine.

But forgiveness is not the same as forgetting.

I hesitate before opening the message, already knowing what it will say. We've been circling this conversation for weeks now.

She wants to come to the cabin.

She wants to meet Claire.

And—perhaps the biggest shift of all—she wants me to meet him.

Her son. His son.

The grown man who doesn't know me, who doesn't know the ways our lives were tangled before he ever took his first breath. Eve wants the girls to meet him too—to start weaving something new from the frayed edges of the past.

I want to believe it's possible.

I glance back at Claire, who is gathering a handful of fresh herbs, her dress swaying in the warm breeze. She looks up, catching my gaze, and smiles—that soft, knowing smile that reminds me I am never alone in this.

I exhale slowly, my fingers hovering over the screen before I type out a response.

Let's talk. I think I'm ready.

Because maybe this is how new stories begin—not in perfect endings, but in the messy, complicated places where forgiveness meets possibility.

And maybe—just maybe—this isn't the end of our story.

It's just the beginning of hers.

And his.

Coming February 2026

The secrets she buried are no longer silent... Eve Hatmaker's story is coming to light.

Acknowledgments

Her Story So Far has gone through many iterations. What you hold in your hands is the result of a journey that began when I first started writing this book in 2020 while finishing my memoir, *Finding Fifty.* At the time, I thought this novel would be a quick project, something I'd finish within a year or two. Never, not in my wildest dreams, did I imagine it would take four long years. But just like Kelsi Jo, my heroine, I too have gone through an evolution—a reinvention filled with unimaginable ups and downs.

As I sit here writing these acknowledgments, I can't help but marvel at the life that unfolded in parallel with Kelsi's. Over these years, we lived through a global pandemic, moved across the country, opened and sold my lifelong dream of owning a book store, coffee shop and wine bar—Margin Notes Bookbar—earned an MFA, trudged through menopause, and faced one of the most challenging chapters of my life. At the end of 2024, I found myself in midlife, sitting with my own reflection, unfolding, and rebuilding.

Reinvention is not linear; it's messy, raw, and unpredictable. Perhaps that's why I identify so deeply with Kelsi Jo. Her story is, in many ways, my story too—a story of resilience, of finding one's voice amidst chaos, and of holding on to the hope of joy and love after loss.

This book would never have been completed without the incredibly strong, brilliant women in my life who carried me through my own reinvention. Dr. Madeline Smith—you inspire me beyond measure. I love you with my whole heart and cherish our friendship. Thank you for loving me through the ugly. You are the daughter, sister, and best friend I never had or knew I needed.

To my readers: thank you for taking this journey with me and Kelsi. Writing this book wasn't just about creating a fictional world; it was about navigating my own truths and finding strength in storytelling. I hope Kelsi's story resonates with you in the way it has shaped me.

To my Beta Readers, Katie, Raquel, Barbara, Madeline, and Pat, thank you for your insight and for reading Kelsi's story with your heart and soul.

A special thank you to my ARC Team. Thank you for reading *Her Story So Far* and being a part of this journey with me:

Dr. Madeline Smith
Jessicah Fontes
Katiedawn Vine
Yeiri Farias
Cari Rhone
Vanessa Buehrle
Deepika Viswanath
Nancy Burke
Lindsay Mathes
Savannah Linson
Keely Thorp
Sophia Fowler
Francisca Ochoa
Kristen Johnson
Adrienne Wilcox
Ofir Baez
Lisa Quinones
Connie Newell
Alicia Woolslayer
Lynne MacAllister
Jill Beo

Danielle Sloan
Anam Qayyum
Kamala Bocanegra
Jen Daramola
Jackie Dawes
Emma Spadoni
Shuna Morelli
Jackie Darnall
Madison Parr

Thank you to the many unnamed women who have shown me love, kindness, and strength when I needed it most. You are the quiet heroines in my story, the ones who've taught me the beauty of reinvention and the importance of holding space for others while they grow.

To every woman who has ever been told to smile through the pain, to shrink herself for the comfort of others, or to silence her voice to make space for someone else's ego—this book is for you. We are living in unprecedented times, where a war is being waged against our autonomy, our bodies, our stories, and our truth. But we are not powerless. We are not quiet. We are not done. We resist. We keep resisting. We keep fighting. And we rise—not in spite of what we've endured, but because of it. This is our rebellion. This is our roar.

All my love,
Jill

Topics & Questions for Discussion

Her Story So Far

Themes and Symbolism

1. *Resilience and Reinvention:* How does Kelsi Jo's journey reflect the themes of resilience and reinvention? In what ways does her story inspire hope and growth despite grief?
2. *Love and Betrayal:* How does Kelsi reconcile her love for Alex with the betrayal she uncovers after his death? Do you think she finds closure by the end of the book?
3. *Identity and Transformation*: What does Kelsi's transformation throughout the novel reveal about her identity? How does her relationship with Claire shape this evolution?
4. *The Role of Memory*: How do Kelsi's memories of Alex and their marriage influence her perception of the present? How reliable do you think her memories are?

5. *Mother-Daughter Dynamics:* How does Kelsi's relationship with her daughters reflect the complexities of mother-daughter dynamics? How does their bond evolve through the story?

CHARACTER ANALYSIS

1. *Kelsi Jo's Journey:* What are the key moments that define Kelsi's growth in the novel? How does her character change from the beginning to the end?
2. *Claire's Role:* How does Claire serve as a catalyst for Kelsi's healing and self-discovery? What makes their connection so meaningful?
3. *Alex's Duality:* How do Alex's secrets and virtues coexist in Kelsi's memory? How does the letter impact your perception of Alex as a character?
4. *Eve's Betrayal:* Did you sympathize with Eve at any point in the novel? Why or why not? Do you think she and Kelsi could have reconciled under different circumstances?
5. *The Girls' Perspectives:* How do Kelsi's daughters react to the revelations about their father? What does this say about their own growth and understanding?

PLOT AND STRUCTURE

1. *The Role of the Memoir:* How does Kelsi's decision to write a memoir mirror her emotional journey? What did you think of her memoir title, *Until I Found Me*?
2. *Dual Timelines:* How does the interplay of past and present timelines enhance the story? Were there any transitions that surprised or moved you?
3. *The Letter:* How did Alex's letter impact the pacing

and tone of the story? Was the reveal of the affair and the child effective, in your opinion?

4. *Ending and Resolution:* How did you feel about the book's ending? Was it satisfying? What do you imagine happens next for Kelsi and Claire?

RELATIONSHIPS AND DYNAMICS

1. *Friendship vs. Love:* How does Kelsi's relationship with Claire transition from friendship to love? Was their romantic development believable?

2. *Alex and Kelsi's Marriage:* Do you think Kelsi idealized her marriage, even before uncovering Alex's affair? How does her perception of their relationship change after his death?

3. *Kelsi's Friendship with Claire:* What makes Kelsi and Claire's bond unique? How does it compare to Kelsi's past friendships?

REFLECTION AND RELEVANCE

1. *Themes of Midlife*: How does the book portray midlife as a time for change and growth? Did this resonate with you or offer any new perspectives?

2. *Exploring Widowhood*: How does Kelsi's experience of widowhood challenge societal expectations? Did her journey feel authentic?

3. *Personal Takeaway:* What moments or themes in the novel resonated with you the most? Did it challenge or change your perspective on love, loss, or self-discovery?

EVERYONE NEEDS A LOLLY IN THEIR LIFE!

1. *Kelsi Jo and Lolly's Bond:* What role does Lolly play in shaping Kelsi's identity, both as a young girl and as an adult?

2. *Lolly as a Role Mode:* In what ways does Lolly's free-spirited nature contrast with Marissa's rigid expectations? How do these opposing influences shape Kelsi Jo's perception of herself and her choices?

3. *Lolly's Legacy:* How does Kelsi Jo honor Lolly's legacy throughout the story? What lessons or values does she carry forward from Lolly into her own life?

4. *Generational Influence:* How does the dynamic between Lolly, Marissa, and Kelsi Jo reflect the generational differences in attitudes toward love, identity, and societal expectations?

5. *Secrets and Truths:* How does learning about Lolly's sexuality and her relationship with Helen influence Kelsi's decision to be open about her relationship with Claire? How does this parallel impact Kelsi's view of her own bravery?

6. *The Importance of Lolly's Cabin*: How does the setting of Lolly's cabin serve as a physical and emotional connection between Kelsi Jo and Lolly? What does the cabin symbolize for Kelsi and her journey?

7. *Hidden Lives and Acceptance:* Lolly and Helen kept their relationship a secret for much of their lives. How does this secrecy resonate with Kelsi Jo's own journey toward embracing her relationship with Claire? How does Kelsi break free from the cycle of secrecy?

8. *Lolly as a Disrupter*: Lolly defied societal norms of her time in many ways. How does her rebellious nature serve as a quiet form of resistance, and how does this inspire Kelsi Jo to find her own voice?

9. *Lolly as a Symbol of Freedom:* How does Lolly's life and love symbolize freedom, both personal and societal? How does this theme of freedom play out in Kelsi Jo's life?

10. *And Finally:* Who is your "Lolly"?

About the Author

Jill Carlyle is the author of *Finding Fifty: A Memoir of Rising in Midlife* and a passionate storyteller dedicated to exploring themes of love, loss, resilience, and self-discovery—especially in midlife. With an MFA in Creative Writing, she draws on her own journey of reinvention and healing to create relatable, multidimensional characters that resonate with readers. The former owner of a Margin Notes Bookbar—an innovative concept combining a bookstore, coffee shop, and wine bar—Jill now story coaches and writes full-time in Florida, where she lives with her husband and three beloved furbabies.

Her Story So Far is her debut novel.

facebook.com/JillWritesaBook

instagram.com/jillcarlylewrites

tiktok.com/jillcarlylewrites

Finding Fifty: A Memoir of Rising in Midlife

9 781957 430263